Caroline Graham was born in Warwickshire in the 1930s. She was educated at Nuneaton High School for Girls and later at the Open University. She has served in the WRNS, run a marriage bureau and, during the 1960s, worked in the theatre. She was awarded an MA degree in Writing for the Theatre by Birmingham University. She has also written several radio plays, television soaps and two books for children.

Murder at
Madingley Grange

Caroline Graham

HEADLINE

First published in 1990
by Mysterious Press UK,
an imprint of Random Century Group

First published in paperback in 1991
by HEADLINE BOOK PUBLISHING

10 9

ISBN 0 7472 3596 1

Printed and bound in Great Britain by
Clays Ltd, St Ives plc

HEADLINE BOOK PUBLISHING
A division of Hodder Headline PLC
338 Euston Road
London NW1 3BH

To
Mary, Mark and Luke
Fond Memories of Sheepcote

Acknowledgements

The author would like to thank Andrew Caslin of Lay and Wheeler, Colchester, for his kind assistance.

SIMON SAYS DO THIS

1

Three greedy people were sitting around a table beneath a brilliantly striped umbrella on the terrace of a moated grange. Well, to be more precise, one was a very greedy person, one (present only in spirit) was a mildly greedy person and the last, an extremely pretty girl with dark curly hair, was hardly greedy at all. It is she who is speaking when our story opens.

'I still don't believe Hugh would agree to murder.'

'He did. I spoke to him last night.'

'You mean you got at him last night. When I rang him up at tea time he was as worried as me.'

'As I.'

'As both of us.'

Simon Hannaford tilted his chair back, rested his elegant pale grey loafers against the iron rungs of the table and looked across at his sister. Laurie was small and sturdy, her skin burnt deep apricot and freckled brown by the sun. Her eyes were blue, the irises so dark they were almost navy. She had a very direct gaze that could disconcert the devious and thick brows she felt vaguely one day might be plucked and shaped into something a bit less riotous. She wore a washed-out summer frock the colour of periwinkles and flat T-strap sandals. Her knees and nails were grubby and a gardening trowel and hand fork lay on the table next to a glass of homemade lemonade. She took a long drink and said, 'Murder makes such a mess.'

'Not necessarily.'

'Blood everywhere.'

'We could hang him. Or her.'

'Oh God, Simon . . . I don't know.'

'What about poison?'

'Aren't people sick if they're poisoned?'

'That's in real life, silly. This is just a game.'

Simon had had years of experience in meeting that navy-blue forceful gaze and met it now with calm determination. He could hardly have presented a greater contrast to Laurie. Tall and slim yet so muscular no one could have called him lanky. And, although there was a silk Paisley square at his throat and his thick fair hair was rather long, you couldn't have called him foppish either. His eyes were a peculiar greyish-green. The grey predominated when he was displeased; when confident and excited as he was now the green came into play. He picked up a sheet of foolscap closely covered with columns of figures, rolled it up and waved it under Laurie's nose as if to bring her round from a faint. She jerked her head irritably away.

'I know what it says.'

'Then perhaps you can tell me how else we could make this sort of money in just two months?' He put the paper down. 'And honestly.'

'I don't see what's honest about taking two hundred and fifty pounds off people for one weekend.'

'The murder makes it honest. And don't forget that includes their train fare. I thought that would be an added encouragement. Without denting profits too much. After all, no one's going to travel far just for two days.'

Laurie fretted her unruly brows. 'It doesn't seem right in someone else's house. Specially as this is the first time Aunt Maude's asked us to look after the place.'

'And what if it's the last time she asks us to look after the place? We'll have missed the opportunity of a lifetime. And she did say we could have friends to stay.'

'She didn't mean this sort of thing.'

'How do you know what she meant? She and Uncle were never averse to making a shekel in their time. How

4

d'you think they came by the ancestral pile in the first place?'

They fell silent. Behind them the pile, which was not all that ancestral, dating only from 1897, sheered up rosy and glowing in the sunset. Four storeys of vermilion brick luxuriously barnacled with pepper-pot turrets and gargoyles and embellished with balconies, mouldings, lintels, architraves and the thousand other ills that nineteenth-century Strawberry Hill Gothic is heir to. It was surrounded by a hundred and fifty acres of garden and woodland, the latter home to a herd of dappled deer which drove the gardeners mad. There was also a large lake.

Madingley Grange had been built by Aloysius Coker, an inventor of headache pills so innocently yet potently concocted that they had killed off thousands of Victorians and made him a millionaire. Aunt Maude's (actually she was a great aunt but that was rather a mouthful) better half, Uncle George, who had accumulated a fortune during the war (officially in ammunitions) and developed it through many an unorthodox and enterprising sideline, had purchased the house plus the contents of the cellar which he promptly attempted to absorb. Shortly afterwards, overwhelmed by the splendour of his claret and worn out by his efforts to keep one step ahead of the Inland Revenue, George passed on.

His widow bought and ran a chain of dress shops for a while, striking terror into the hearts of staff and customers alike, for Aunt Maude was a formidable woman. Once the Grange had been broken into and, alerted by crisp telephone instructions, the police had arrived to find the burglar cowering behind a suit of armour in the baronial hall. It had taken a full hour, three cups of extremely strong tea and assurances of Mrs Maberley's restraint to winkle him out. Now, having sold the business, Aunt Maude had retired and lived alone, occupying each of the twenty bedrooms in turn to keep them aired then cruising off into the sunset for several weeks before starting all over again in the Fragonard room. The cook, Mrs Posture, and elderly domestic, Ivy Tiplady, were laid off during these periods of recuperation whilst the groundsmen, full time the rest of the horticultural year, came in once a week just to put an armlock on the more aggressive forms of creeping vegetation. Fitterbee the chauffeur having delivered his employer to her appropriate point of embarkation, then moonlighted with the elderly Rolls in London.

'They'll be mad about all this – the punters,' said Simon, gesturing proprietorially towards the parkland rolling away on every side. At the shaven lawns and vaunting statuary; the crumbling dovecote and artfully tousled herbaceous border.

'Can't you see them,' he continued, 'sweeping down the great staircase in full thirties fig for dinner in the Holbein dining room. Candles flickering on the crystal and family silv – '

'Pardon?'

'Candles flickering on – '

'Before then.'

'Dinner in the Holbein – '

'Earlier. Something about figs.'

'Oh. Full thirties fig.'

'That's it,' said Laurie. 'You didn't mention dressing up.'

'It's essential. You can't have a country house murder without an adenoidal maid in starched cap and apron, a butler in full buttledress, son of the house in baggy plus fours and the daughter fetching in bugle beads.'

'That is not a country house murder, Simon. That is a country house farce.'

'They'll love it,' said her brother firmly. 'Anyway it can't be changed now. I've put it in the advertisement.'

'You've . . .!! What advertisement?'

6

'In *The Times*. "Murder at Madingley Grange".'

'Aunt Maude's only been gone five minutes.'

'No point in hanging about.'

'You had no right to do that. We've not agreed.'

'I've agreed.'

'Well you can put in another tomorrow cancelling it.'

'Laurie, we have twenty bedrooms here going to waste. With one each for you and me and Hugh – we can put the staff downstairs in those two rooms by the kitchen – '

'Staff?'

' – that still leaves seventeen. We should be able to let them all as doubles.'

'What staff?'

'Now thirty-four times two hundred and fifty – '

'Simon it is absolutely out of the question that we allow thirty-four complete strangers loose here. There are all the paintings, the ornaments, the rugs and furniture . . .'

'They're not going to come in removal vans.'

'I'm serious.'

'So am I. Everything's fixed.'

'Then unfix it.'

'Can't be done.'

'I shall stand at the front door and turn them away.'

'You wouldn't.'

'Watch me.'

Simon removed his grey loafers from the table rungs and placed his feet firmly on the flagstones. 'You always were a bossy little beast. Not to mention selfish.'

'How do you make that out?'

'Here am I offering ordinary run of the mill members of the bourgeoisie a chance to live for forty-eight hours like landed gentry plus a little bit of mayhem on the side, and you wish to deny them that supreme pleasure. You ought to be ashamed.'

'You're not getting round me like that, Simon.'

'I really am on the bottom line.'

'Or like that.'

'You wouldn't believe my debts.'

'Get a job then. You've done nothing since you left University College.'

'*Nothing*? You call seven years of plotting and planning and wheeling and dealing nothing? I've had the most brilliant ideas. None of them got off the ground. And why? Lack of cash. If I wasn't so poor I'd be a millionaire by now.'

'You talk as if you were in the gutter.'

'All of us are in the gutter, sister mine,' said Simon. 'And some of us are sliding down the drain.'

'You'll have to marry a rich widow.'

'Don't think I'm not working on it. Meanwhile my overdraft's piling up and pressure is being brought to bear. Do you want to see me knee-capped and buried up to my side parting in cement?'

'Depends when it is. I've got to be in Oxford by seven.'

'You don't give a tuppenny cuss, do you? I can starve to death as far as you're concerned. OK – what about your own future? You want to get married, I suppose?' Silence. 'You and Hugh? Dear old Hugh. Clodding and plodding and doggedly true.'

'You make him sound like a basset hound.'

'Oh he's far too tall for a basset hound,' Simon laughed. 'Well – do you or don't you?'

'Of course.'

Laurie didn't really have to think about it. She and Hugh were . . . well . . . they just were. And had always been. They had grown up together; gone to nursery and prep school and childhood parties together. Shared their holidays and Christmases and now, unless Laurie could think of any cause or just impediment, they seemed all set to be spending the rest of their lives together. And she couldn't. Not really. Because she was very fond of Hugh. In the companion along life's highway stakes he had a fair bit going for him. He was quiet and patient and even-tempered. Tolerant when she was grumpy and kind when she was sad. He never forgot her birthday, though his presents were uninspiring, and even sat with her pretending to enjoy *Gardener's World*. What more, pondered Laurie, could a girl ask?

Occasionally and feeling guilty, she believed there must be something. At her cousin's engagement party Laurie had briefly found herself side by side with Charlotte titivating in the cloakroom. (Actually Charlotte had been titivating, Laurie had been moodily trying to flatten her hair with a damp brush.) As she did so she was sharply struck by her companion's shining countenance. Her own seemed positively dull by comparison. Charlotte's cheeks had been flushed and glowing, her eyes – Laurie balked at the comparison but it could not be gainsaid – were like stars. Laurie had been wrong-headed enough to remark on this imbalance to Simon when she came upon him later in the evening, enjoying a *salmon roulade* on the stairs.

'You look a bit wistful,' he had said and she had told him why, concluding with the observation that she never saw stars when she was with Hugh, not even when he kissed her.

'You see stars,' Simon replied, 'when someone knocks you out. Not when they kiss you.'

'But something's supposed to happen, isn't it?' persisted Laurie. 'I read in a book once that the earth moved.'

'Oh, I shouldn't take any notice of Hemingway's Spanish period. The earth was always moving for him. Mainly because he was never more than five minutes away from a mass bombardment.'

So that was that. Laurie sighed and returned reluctantly to the present, aware that Simon was looking expectant. He hadn't given up. Simon never did.

'So if thirty-four is probably out – '

'No probably about it.'

'How many would be in?'

Laurie poured herself some more lemonade. She wished she knew just how far below the water level this latest 'bottom line' really was. Simon had been in a serious cash flow situation for as long as she had been able to understand what the words meant, often lurching from plenitude to penury and back again in the course of a single day. Sometimes this was due to gambling, more often to his impulsive generosity. He was always buying presents chosen, unlike Hugh's, with wit and imagination. Laurie recalled the excited disbelief with which, on her twelfth birthday, surrounded by dreary books about ponies and sensible pens and new pyjamas, she had unrolled a large poster-sized plan of a thirteenth-century monastery garden which Simon had copied from an old manuscript, blown up and painted. There was a key to all the plants and even a gardener, a bent elderly monk, raking gravel. The picture was still on her bedroom wall.

'Laurie?'

'. . . I don't know.'

'Absolute maximum?'

Laurie, knowing she was making a terrible mistake, said: 'Six.'

'*Six*. You do mean rooms?'

'No. People.'

'That's ridiculous. It's not worth doing with less than twelve.'

'Let's not do it then.' Relieved, Laurie backtracked.

'Oh don't be such a pain. House parties are terrific fun. And you know how you like people.'

'I do not "like people". I like being up to my elbows in potting compost and watering cans and flowers and seed trays.'

'Twenty then?'

'No.'

'Fifteen.'

'No.'

'Ten. A nice round figure – ' he carried on quickly as Laurie opened her mouth – 'and they're bound to be lovely upper crusters. Well behaved and stinking rich.'

'How d'you make that out?'

'Why d'you think I advertised in *The Times*? I have no intention of giving house room to the sort of people whose table manners were run up in Tesco's. Ten? *Please . . .*'

Fatally, Laurie hesitated. She seemed to hear a note of real desperation in Simon's voice. But then she often did. And he was a born actor. He had been acting his way in and out of trouble, it seemed to Laurie, for as long as she could remember. Now he leaned over and kissed her.

'You're an angel. Thanks for saying yes.'

'But I haven't,' said Laurie, knowing that by keeping silent she had. She looked across at her brother. Success had given his pallid skin a rosy glow and his eyes shone greenly. He smiled. Laurie recognized that smile. It had been present fairly regularly throughout her childhood and bathed the recipient in a rosy glow whilst at the same time giving him or her a slight frisson of alarm. A feeling that something extremely hazardous had glided closely by.

She had seen it first when she was five and her widowed mother had brought up to the nursery Victor Hannaford, whom she planned to marry, and his thirteen-year-old son. Simon had stepped forward with tremendous self-assurance, shaken Nanny's hand, kissed Laurie on the cheek and smartly removed a box of chocolate marshmallows from the top of her toy box. She had watched anxiously as they disappeared downstairs for they were her favourite sweets, and had been tremendously relieved when he returned to say goodbye and put the box back. Later it proved to be empty. Now she said: 'And there's no need to waste that smile on me.'

'What smile?'

'Your basking shark's smile.'

11

'Anyone would think you couldn't trust me.' Simon poured himself a third vodka and tonic, added lemon and ice. He swirled it round, admiring the silvery gloss on the surface before draining it in one swallow. 'Right,' he said, becoming very brisk. 'We've got ten at two fifty ... less food of course. We can raid the cellar for the wine – '

'Oh no we can't!'

'Why on earth not? All those dusty crates of plonk slowly turning to vinegar – '

'If it's plonk it'll have turned long ago. I shouldn't think anyone's been down there since Uncle George was carted up for the last time.'

'Exactly. We'd be doing Aunt Maude a favour clearing it out.'

'I doubt if she'd see it like that.'

'Anyway it'll probably all be ours sooner or later.'

'Sooner or later isn't now. And don't count your chickens. We're not the only possible heirs.'

'We're the most likely.'

'There's Hazel's son.'

'Mervyn? Aunt Maude hates him. Says he looks like a constipated squirrel.'

Laurie giggled. 'He does a bit. What about Jocelyn, then? Or that weird cousin who had nervous palpitations and used to sleep in a fish tank.'

'Hetty? She went to Australia.'

'The Handsom-Nortys?'

'After that hushed-up flotation scandal? No,' repeated Simon firmly, 'you and I are by far the best bet. Now – if we could please get back to business. How much do you think we shall have to pay the staff?'

'There you go again, harping on about staff. What staff?'

'We've got to have a butler and maid.'

'What's wrong with Mrs Posture and Ivy?'

'God – you're so dim.' Simon explained slowly and

12

clearly. 'Apart from the fact that neither of them, however cunningly disguised, could ever be mistaken for a butler there's the strong possibility that they'll tell Aunt Maude on her return what we've been up to.'

'You said she wouldn't mind.'

'Picky, picky. I shall put a help-wanted notice in the *Oxford Mail*.'

'Safer to go to an agency.'

'I've no intention of paying a huge registration fee and inflated salaries, thanks very much. Especially as our profits have now been cut to the bone thanks to all this whingeing on about numbers. The point of the weekend after all is to make a killing. I shall ask for references, of course.'

'I should hope so.'

Simon replaced his glass on the table and lifted his face to the warm, early evening sun, calmly content. He had never in a million years thought that he would be able to persuade Laurie to go along with his plan. Or, should this persuasion miraculously occur, that she would agree to more than two or, at the very most, four visitors at a time. Huckster-like he had started by suggesting over thirty, knowing this would frighten the wits out of her, and now she had actually agreed to ten. Unbelievable. Tomorrow he really would put an advert in *The Times*. He said: 'And the murder is still on?' When Laurie frowned he added quickly: 'I'll organize it all.'

'What do you know about murder weekends?'

'Done lots of research.' Simon indicated a pile of brochures sitting next to some paperbacks by the lemonade jug. He picked up a copy of *Death on the Nile* and waved it about. 'And got lots of ideas. I shall draw up a flexible plot outline, give everyone a stock character and let them get on with it.'

'It all sounds a bit vague.'

'Vagueness is vital. You've got to allow room for improvisation. Usually according to these' – patting the brochures – 'actors are involved, but I'm certainly not hiring any. They want what's called the Equity minimum. I was horrified when I discovered what it was. I thought they all did it for love. Like nuns and missionaries.'

'I shall want to vet all the replies to the advert.'

'Naturally.'

'And this butler and maid.'

'Of course. Though they'll really just be set-dressing. You can do lots of cooking before the guests arrive and tart up the house. You know – put flowers in all the rooms – '

'Thanks a lot!'

'I thought you liked flowers. Right, so that's the weekend after this. June fifteenth to seventeenth.'

'And what will you be doing whilst all this activity's going on?'

'I,' said Simon grandly, tilting his chair back again and resting his loafers once more on the rungs of the table, 'will be pressing my plus fours.'

2

Oddly enough in one respect Simon proved to be correct. Once Laurie had really thrown herself into the business of organizing the weekend her misgivings, temporarily at least, slipped away. She Hoovered and dusted and ran up and down stairs with piles of lavender-scented sheets and pillowcases making sure that each guest had fresh flowers, fluffy towels, scented soap and plenty of reading material. Plus, on their bedside tables, a handwritten menu card.

She had prepared for their delectation pigeon terrine, boeuf en croute, lemon and toffee puddings and, in case anyone was a vegetarian, some ratatouille and a Stilton and broccoli quiche. All this was in the freezer together with a hundred rolls and fifty assorted croissants and brioche. There were still pheasants to prepare and a whole salmon was in the fridge awaiting Saturday lunch. For the first time Laurie felt grateful to her aunt who, quaintly believing gardening to be no job for a lady, had refused to pay her niece's fees for the coming year at Pershore College until she had completed two full terms at the Tante Marie School of Cookery. Now, feeling crisp and capable, Laurie checked her housekeeping list over and over again, sure she had forgotten nothing. She was, of course, wrong.

Simon, as always once he had got his own way, was all sweetness, light and helpful assistance. He had driven the Mountfield Simplicity to great effect over the vast lawns, throwing up sparkling clouds of frail grass cuttings and leaving stripes of exquisite perfection. He had also obtained a mini-bus (all the guests having taken advantage of the free train offer) by trading in, temporarily, his old Karmann Ghia. The bus now stood washed and polished outside the front entrance. An amber sunstrip boldly lettered MADINGLEY GRANGE arched over the windscreen. And yesterday they had braved the cellar.

Neither of them had been down there before and they were amazed at the size of the place. It was like a small aircraft hangar dimly lit by three sixty-watt bulbs suspended from frayed old flex. A cryptish smell prevailed, the floor was gritty under their feet and the dust made Laurie sneeze. There was no echo. Rather the sneeze was immediately trapped and enfolded in an atmosphere of overpowering fustiness. As they stood, rather close together, one of the bulbs sizzled briefly and went out.

'Great,' said Simon. 'We could hardly see a thing before. I should have brought a torch.'

'I'll go and get one.'

'Don't you dare.' He caught his sister's eye. 'And there's no need to sneer.' His voice wavered theatrically. 'Who knows what horrors lurk at the bottom of the Black Lagoon?'

Laurie reached up and pushed the light. It swung backwards and forwards. Huge shapes loomed out of the dimness, receded, loomed again. Old furniture piled high, some trunks, an upturned ancient rowing boat. Tennis nets, bats and balls, a set of mallets for croquet. And crates and crates and crates of wine.

'My God . . .' breathed Simon. 'An oenophile's paradise.'

'I bet it's all off.'

'One way to find out.' Simon moved towards the nearest stack. Each set of fifty crates was enclosed in a three-sided cage made of open wire mesh over a wooden frame. He pulled out a bottle.

'Don't swing it about like that. There's bound to be sediment.'

16

'So I spoil one. There's hundreds more. What sort do we want? You're the *chef de cuisine*.'

'Some red and some white.'

'I'd have thought all that pricy training would have left you with a slightly wider grasp of chateau and vintage than "some red and some white".'

'There's no point in being precise when I don't know what we've got.'

'Well this . . .' Simon peered at a bottle. 'The label's flaked off.'

'Should tell you on the cork what it is.'

'There's obviously some serious testing to be done here. We can't give the punters stuff we haven't had a go at ourselves. You take the next three down and I'll bring these.'

'Simon . . .' Laurie had moved a few steps away. 'Here a minute.'

Simon joined her. 'Champers. Yum, yum.'

'It's Krug 1955.'

'High time we polished it off then.'

'We can't do that. It must be worth a fortune.'

'You're not going to be tiresome are you, Laurie?'

'What do the others say?'

'*Drink me*.' Simon turned Laurie firmly towards the cellar steps and gave her a little push. 'Go and find a corkscrew.' He collected three more bottles and followed his sister, nudging when she hesitated.

Back in the dining room he produced some long-stemmed tulip glasses, wiped the dirt and cobwebs from bottle number one – it still looked quite black – and eased out the cork. The wine glowed like rubies and a heavenly fragrance, massively opulent, arose from the glass. Blackcurrants, cedarwood (or was it sandalwood?), plummy and rich. Laurie emptied her glass and gazed at Simon. She looked quite stunned.

'Delicious.'

Simon pulled a further cork. 'This is a white one. I think you asked for one of each.'

The white one in its own way was equally superb. In colour a lovely buttery yellow with a greenish edge. Disbelieving the first glass, they had a second. It smelled of . . .

'Vanilla.'

'Nuts.'

'Toast.'

'*Toast?*'

'And butter.'

'I wouldn't say that,' contradicted Laurie, wagging her head. 'Seems to me – ' investigating further – 'to have a rare and subtle oakiness – '

'Spare me the wine babble.'

'Oany . . . oh . . . only . . . ocky . . .'

'One more word about rare and subtle oakiness and it all goes down the sink.'

'No!'

'Behave yourself then.'

'Yes, Simon.'

'Let's have no prating on about saucy little numbers with a quick goodbye.'

'No, Simon.' Laurie imbibed a little more. 'Gorse bushes.'

'God, you're affected.' Simon broached bottle number three.

'That's the fish and meat then.'

'What is?'

'What we've just – ' in a huge effort of concentration Laurie frowned and gripped the edge of the table – 'drunk.'

'I can see you're drunk. You're a disgrace to the family name.'

'Not true. Now . . .' Laurie laid a solemn and restraining hand on her brother's arm. 'We want something to go with the pudding.'

'Pudding, madam?' Simon wrapped a clean tea towel round bottle number three. 'Say no more.'

'I shall say what I like. Who you think you are?'

Simon poured. Hayfields newly mown under a baking sun. Mignonette crushed in the hand. Clover and wild flowers. A deep golden wine with a rim the colour of burnt sugar, rich and sweet. Fat honeybee sweetness that stayed in your mouth. And stayed. And stayed.

'Now that – ' Simon drained his glass – 'is bliss. As close, I fear, to heaven as I shall ever be in this world or the next. What are you doing down there?'

'Down where?'

'On the floor.'

'I'm not on the floor.'

'Yes you are.'

'No I'm not.'

'Well one of us is.'

'It's you.' Laurie started to laugh, rocking in her chair. 'Get up . . . *get up* . . .'

'These wines,' said Simon, struggling to his feet and nearly pulling Laurie down in the process, 'are something else.'

'I must find out what they are. An' write them on the menu cards.'

'Absolutely. Now – open up the Krug,' demanded Simon. 'And let the sunshine in.'

Hours later when Laurie felt herself capable she returned to the cellar with a torch and a little stool and rubbed the dust from the three cages. It was then revealed that Friday's guests would be drinking Mouton-Rothschild '45 with their meat, a 1962 Louis Latour Corton-Charlemagne with their fish and with their dessert a 1921 Château d'Yquem.

'And all so divine,' muttered Laurie whilst amending her menu cards, 'that I should think people would be prepared to pay two hundred and fifty pounds just for the privilege of tasting them.' And in so saying she spoke no more than the simple truth.

The next day Simon, still complaining of a faint buzzing in the ears, drove to Oxford to interview what he insisted on calling *les domestiques*. The pair were travelling down from London after apparently being alerted to Simon's advertisement in the *Mail* by a cousin in Witney.

The interview was to be conducted over tea at the Mitre, which Laurie thought a bit silly. After all, she said as her brother prepared to leave, the whole point of the operation was not to discover if they could sit nicely and be waited on but if they in their turn could wait. Simon replied that he could hardly expect the two of them to start handing round iced cakes and cucumber sandwiches in a perfectly strange hotel just to show him what they were made of.

Actually there seemed to be some discrepancy, thought Laurie, rootling through her aunt's boulle escritoire when her brother had departed, between his claim that he had been snowed under by applications and the solitary letter, wavily written on cheap lined paper, that lurked in the back of the spring clip 'Murder' file. The envelope was covered with what looked like the meanderings of a spider who had lunched too well on over-ripe flies then fallen into the nearest ink-pot. The letter itself was brief. The scrivener, one A. Bennet (Mrs) having had Simon's advertisement brought to her attention, wished to offer the services of herself and her brother for the brief period before they left to take up employment in Ireland with Lady Keele at Castle Triamory. They had previously been in service with the Hon. Mrs Hatherley. Mention was made of the highest references. Indeed the tone throughout was so high and the names dropped so grand that Laurie wondered briefly whether the references were to be offered or demanded.

She returned the letter to the file and took out the handful from Simon's punters. Here at least things seemed to be in order. Although they were one short of the ten he had hoped for all the cheques had gone through and the notepaper was, on the whole, what Simon referred to as 'respectable'.

Laurie wasn't too sure about Mr Gibbs who wrote from Peep O'Day on a showy deckle edge stamped with two vivacious bikini-clad nymphettes playing with a beach ball, especially as he seemed to be bringing two wives. But Mrs Saville (plain blue linen, raised Gothic script), Mr Lewis (unadorned good quality white), and the Gregorys (cream parchment distinguished by crossed magnifying glasses sejant and deerstalker crest over the words Grimpen Villas), were obviously made of the right stuff. Mrs Gregory, who had rung up to ask about the food and other details, sounded really charming.

They were coming from Brize Norton, not too far away. But the Gibbses came from the North and Arthur Gillette from the even norther, namely Fishwick, Berwick on Tweed. So much, commented Simon bitterly, for the notion that no one would bother to travel far for a mere weekend.

On Thursday morning the costumes arrived and Laurie asked that the skip be placed in the washing-up annexe off the kitchen. This was a vast room with a long deal table scrubbed white and much scarred in the centre and three huge stone sinks linked by old wooden draining boards and used only when the flowers were being done. Three sides of the room had floor to ceiling mahogany cupboards filled with Mason's blue and yellow Regency Ironstone crockery. A hundred of everything including egg cups. Laurie, knowing the most her aunt ever did in the entertaining line was invite the Madingley Women's Institute to tea, once asked why she kept such an elaborate service. Mrs

Maberley had explained that one must keep up appearances.

'But no one knows they're there.'

'I know they're there, Laurel,' Aunt Maude had replied. 'And that's what matters. Standards are maintained by all sorts of eccentric little practices. Like always wearing clean bloomers.'

Thinking of this formidable relative, even though she was by now safely in the middle of the Indian Ocean, made Laurie nervous. She was glad when Simon came back from the Mitre full of assurances as to the suitability of the interviewees, and they could turn their attention to the costumes. Simon had bought a long cigarette holder from Bowater's and lounged about with it whilst Laurie opened the basket.

The costumes, beautifully packed and shrouded with tissue, were beneath two boxes. Laurie lifted out the largest and passed it to Simon who started rustling through the paper. 'It's hats!'

'What do we want hats for?'

'Here's yours.' Simon handed over a lamé turban sporting white egret feathers secured by a glittering pin in the shape of a scimitar.

'I'm not wearing that!'

'Don't get acrimonious before we even start.' Simon delved again and came up with a boater and a large mustard and brown checked cap. 'And this must be for me.' He put it on. Laurie shrieked. He took it off again. 'Or possibly for Hugh. What's happened to him anyway? I thought he was coming for lunch.'

'He was. I expect he's got held up.' Laurie unpacked shoes, gloves, a sequinned evening bag. 'I must say they've done us proud.'

They turned their attention to the skip proper and Simon pulled out a canary-yellow waistcoat, a shirt patterned with winking foxes, brogues with lively questing tongues and snuff-coloured plus fours. Laurie shrieked again. Simon took the clothes and laid them on the table next to Hugh's cap with such kindly reverence you would have thought them to be newly deceased, then brought out a swallowtail coat.

'Ah,' said Simon with deep satisfaction, 'the butler's soup and fish. And this – ' he passed over a deep white piecrust frill, 'for the maid.'

Laurie placed it on her head. It fell straight down to the bridge of her nose and rested there. She bobbed. 'Ow does oi look zur?'

'Like a Neanderthal nun.' Simon slipped on a cream barathea dinner jacket and held the black braided trousers against his jeans. 'How do I look?'

He looked very dishy but Laurie had no intention of saying so. 'Like a shopsoiled gigolo. Where's the female equivalent?'

'*Voila!*' Simon waved a shimmering fall of ice-blue lamé in front of his sister in the manner of a matador with a cape. She took it cautiously.

'It's a bit slippy. Rather beautiful though. Are these the shoes? Heavens – they're like stilts.'

'The other day you were complaining because you're only five foot nothing.' Simon leaned across the skip and took his sister's hands. 'Buck up, love. Try and enter into the spirit of the thing.'

'I shall look a right pig's ear in that lot.'

'Think of the dosh then. You'll be able to buy enough potting compost to cover the county. And seed trays. And corns – '

'Corms, Simon.'

'Exactly,' said Simon with as much satisfaction as if he had just solved the Metternich–Carstairs equation. 'Now we have – ' he hoiked out a coffee and cream geometrically patterned number – 'your – ' studying the label – 'tea gown – '

'Tea gown! I don't believe it. You mean people actually changed for tea?'

'In some circles they still do.'

'Don't be so daft.'

'I suggest you wear it when welcoming them all tomorrow. You'll have to alter your make-up, though. Or rather – ' he frowned at Laurie's freckled, sunburned countenance – 'start wearing some. Ruby-red lipstick was all the crack, I believe, if those god-awful magazines in the attic are anything to go by. Plus a very thin arched brow – '

'I have no intention of plucking my eyebrows.'

'Well you can't swan around in backless lamé with the ones you've got. They're like Dennis Healey's.'

'They're fine.' Laurie smoothed the glossy dark wings with a fingertip. 'And if the success of our whole enterprise depends on – ' She was interrupted by the shrill ring of a bell, cried 'That's Hugh!' and ran into the hall.

The telephones at Madingley Grange had been installed in the forties and were great heavy Bakelite things with a receiver that put real demands on the muscles of the forearm. Laurie heaved it up to her ear. 'Hugh? Where are you?'

'Still in Gloucester, darling. I'm most awfully sorry. The thing is, halfway to the station the Land Rover blew a fuse or a gasket or whatever it is they blow . . . and we had to wait simply hours before someone came – '

'We?'

'Pacey was driving. I mean – someone had to return the thing.'

'They've got more than one car, surely?'

'Yes but by the time we'd made it back to the Hall Sir Piers had left with Frobisher in the Rolls, Nanny had gone in the Mini to visit Nanny Pargeter in Chipping Campden and Lady Kettersley-Gore had taken the Rover out shopping.'

'That's a bit quixotic, isn't it?'

'What?' A puzzled pause. 'And by the time a car did

become available it was too late to get a train that would connect to Oxford.'

'What about Betsy?'

'Toby's borrowed her pro tem. You're not miffed, are you, darling?' continued Hugh. 'You sound a bit . . . well . . . distant . . .'

'Hugh,' said Laurie, struggling to hold her voice steady and choosing her words with care. 'You know our murder weekend starts tomorrow. I shall need all the help and moral support that I can get. Now – you will be here by tea time at the very latest, won't you?' In spite of her resolve Laurie's voice broke on the last sentence and panic rushed through the gap.

'Positively. Although I'm sure you've got everything organized.'

'Well, I think I've got the food sorted. The costumes are a scream. We've laid out your plus fours.'

There was a brief hiatus; just long enough for a man who has received a non-fatal body blow to fall to the ground and pick himself up again, then Hugh said: 'There must be something wrong with this line. For a minute I thought you said you'd laid out my plus fours.'

'Ohhh no . . .' replied Laurie, sensing a possible slackening of enthusiasm in her intended. 'I said . . . um . . . It's lovely . . . outdoors . . .'

'Is it? It's raining buckets here.'

When Laurie returned to the annexe Simon said: 'You look shattered. Explain.' Laurie explained. 'What's he doing down there anyway?'

'Toby Kettersley-Gore is his best friend. They were at Greshams together. Hypaetia and Poppy are Toby's sisters. Surely you remember Pacey. She was my best friend.'

'Mmmm.'

'What do you mean, "mmm"?'

'Perhaps he's succumbed to all that propinquity.'

'Rubbish. Polly's a revolting little beast with pigtails

who used to put toads in my bed when I went to stay. And Pacey's teeth stick out and she's always rushing at people.'

'How long is it since you've seen her?'

'A year . . . eighteen months . . .'

'She might have got them fixed by now. And some men like being rushed at.'

Laurie ignored him, emptied the skip and started carrying the costumes upstairs.

3

At twelve noon on Friday Simon, having spaced the croquet hoops out on the lawns and cleaned the mallets, was preparing to drive into Oxford and collect the hired help.

'Don't forget,' he said to Laurie as he climbed into the bus, 'you're the chatelaine and you do the bossing about. Use a firm hand. And no kindly queries about his gout or suggestions that she puts her feet up – OK?' He paused, studying her frowning face. 'Now what?'

'Do you think I'll have time before you get back to pinch out the tomatoes?'

'Don't you dare go anywhere near that greenhouse! Or that filthy herbaceous border. You'll never get the upper hand if they arrive and find you standing around with straws in your hair.'

So after lunch Laurie scrubbed her nails, got out of her old dungarees and into her periwinkle-blue frock. As she waited nervously in the hall she practised an 'in charge' voice and kept telling herself that he who paid the piper called the tune. She wished she wasn't quite so hazy as to what butlers actually did. She knew for certain only that they opened doors, received visitors' outer garments and rolled around smoothly on little wheels bearing silver trays.

Her knowledge of a maid's duties was even sketchier and culled mainly from old movies in which they put up the young mistress's hair and laced her nineteen-inch waist, pushing a knee into the small of her back while crying: 'Lawdy, Miss Scarlett – y'all shoh look mighty purty.'

Feeling fairly certain none of the guests would require

this particular mix of brute strength and flattery, Laurie only hoped that A. Bennet (Mrs) could carry out whatever was the twentieth-century equivalent should she be called upon to do so.

Laurie pulled the flowers on the refectory table about unnecessarily then paced up and down a bit. Her eye caught the heavy rose velvet curtain at the far end of the hall behind which a corridor led to the kitchen and servants' quarters. Wasn't it the case that those above the salt passed through this cut-off point, 'the green baize door', at their peril? And that once the staff were firmly installed the whole area could become a no-man's-land unnegotiable except through the most ingratiating application?

Tyres crunched on the gravel. They were here! If they call me madam, thought Laurie, I shall die.

She knew at once from the slightly defiant note in Simon's 'Hullo-o-o' as he ran up the steps that *les domestiques* would leave something to be desired. Had she known then quite how comprehensive this lack would prove to be, she would have taken to her heels and not stopped running till she reached the Barbary Coast. As it was she cleared her throat nervously and stepped forward. The woman entered first. Laurie stepped back again.

Mrs Bennet was a tall streak of unrelieved gloom. Her coat and skirt were grey, her lisle stockings were grey and her limp woolly the colour of mouse droppings. Her feet were encased in the sort of shoes which expanded to accommodate barnacles and were of glacé kid. A hat, charmingly styled after the manner of a German helmet, was rammed upon her head. Her eyes, the colour of dirty grey ice, seemed huge behind pebbly glasses.

'Good afternoon, Mrs Bennet,' said Laurie, stepping bravely forward once more and holding out her hand.

'Good afternoon I'm sure madam,' said the maid, hardly opening the grim line of her mouth and just brushing Laurie's fingertips. Then, peering through the thick lenses, 'Miss, that is. And it is not necessary to use my marital designation. Bennet will suffice.'

Her tone implied that anyone who needed to be told what was surely common knowledge to a person of refinement didn't deserve a maid in the first place. The Hon. Mrs Hatherley and Lady Keele, thought Laurie peevishly, no doubt absorbed such matters with their mother's milk.

'Very well, Bennet,' she said coolly, thinking: It's only for two days and perhaps the butler might be less formidable.

He was a short man and stood preternaturally upright. But although he wore a well-pressed dark suit and a crisp white shirt and was parade-ground straight there was about this ramrod stance, Laurie felt, something slightly fishy. A disquieting impression of secret shambolism. A feeling that this was a man to crack under the slightest pressure. Such as being asked to clean a boot or make a pot of tea for one. His eyes were rheumy, his teeth stained and his cheeks almost regally purple.

Laurie did not repeat the mistake of offering a hand but simply said: 'Good afternoon . . . um. . . ?'

'Gaunt, madam.'

'Gaunt?'

'That is correct.' The butler observed Laurie's suddenly clamped lips and twitching brows and added, 'Is something wrong, madam?'

'No, no,' Laurie hastened to reply though her voice shook. 'Simon – Mr Hannaford will show you to your quarters. Perhaps, after you've washed and unpacked you would come to the library, that's the door on the far right, and I'll explain what will be happening over the weekend.'

When Simon returned Laurie immediately said: 'You might have warned me. Gaunt and Bennet!'

'There's no need to chortle.'

'I'm not chortling.'

'Well whatever it was it sounded most peculiar. I must say, though, your manner seemed just about right. Firm but dignified. I know they're not ideal – '

'That man drinks. You don't get a complexion like a baboon's bottom on Perrier and lemon squash.'

Simon rolled back his eyes. 'All butlers drink. It's par for the course. That's why the butler's pantry was invented.'

'I shall lock ours up,' said Laurie. 'They do know about wearing funny clothes?'

'Period costume. Yes. And they don't mind. Their reference from Mrs Hatherley,' he went on as Laurie continued to look disenchanted, 'was excellent.'

'Did you ring to check it?'

'I didn't see the necessity.'

'I shall then.'

But half an hour later when Gaunt and Bennet presented themselves in the library, so perfectly did they appear to embody the pre-war domestic virtues that Laurie felt her misgivings may have been a little hasty. She had pressed their outfits the previous day and could not but admire the results. Gaunt's tails were immaculate, his dickey ice-white and firmly restrained by pearl studs. Bennet's apron was a snowy exclamation point on a background of sooty black. Her starched and goffered cap was worn with unsaucy lack of compromise straight across her forehead and the basilisk gaze had become somewhat muted. Laurie was surprised to notice beneath the dark dress the swell of a quite attractive bosom and realized that Bennet, in spite of her grey hair, a few whiskery moles and a slight moustache, was hardly middle-aged. And Gaunt not that much older. As Laurie started to speak both of them looked at her respectfully.

She started by showing them the dining room and explaining the menus. Bennet seemed quite unfazed by the fact that there would be twelve for dinner in less than four hours' time, merely commenting that the Honourable Mrs Hatherley had often had twice that number at a split second's notice and them with hardly a game bird in the larder to bless themselves with.

Encouraged, Laurie led them both through the various bedrooms, giving Gaunt a list of the guests' names with their room's title alongside.

'Charmingly furbished, madam, if I might say so?' said the butler giving the *toile du Jouy* the once-over.

She showed them the vast kitchen somewhat apprehensively. It was not a cosy place (Simon called it 'Ghormanghastly') and there was no dishwasher. Aunt Maude's modest amount of dirty crockery and silver was cleaned by Ivy, Cook washed up as she went along and, when the WI came to tea, they did the same. There was a huge stainless steel unit running down the centre of the room consisting of twelve gas rings, and three ovens with a freezer at each end. The huge gaping fireplace housed an iron spit. Faggots of herbs, gathered by Mrs Maberley the previous summer during an evanescent attack of the Laura Ashleys, dangled dryly from blackened beams. The floor was stone flagged and even on a hot June day very cool. There was a Baby Belling and a little electric ring on a side table.

After opening various cupboards and showing the servants where the towels and cleaning materials were kept, and after Bennet had pointed out that stone did draw your feet something chronic and no mistake, Laurie explained that the glass and cutlery were in the armoire in the dining room.

'And the napery, miss?'

'That also.'

This professional-sounding inquiry cheered Laurie. Suddenly what had seemed impossible twenty-four hours ago – a table full of contented people chatting happily together whilst being quickly and discreetly served with delicious food and wine – began to seem not only possible but almost probable. Boldly she added: 'And there might be shoes to be cleaned.' A certain lack of response. 'Not everyone's of course. I expect some guests will prefer to do their own.' She hurried on, 'If it's too much extra work . . .' and thought: Damn – I'm sliding into subservience already.

'I thrayve on hard work, madam,' said Gaunt.

'Oh . . . terrific.'

'And now,' the butler continued, 'perhaps you would be kind enough to direct me to the pantry.'

'Ah. Well . . . the problem there is – '

'If you are serving port, madam, it should have been decanted by now.'

'We're not.'

The butler reeled delicately. 'No port, madam?'

'Or nuts. Except with the cocktails.'

'Then the waynes. . . ?'

'The what?'

'Have they been brought up from the cellar? Are they opened? Have they breathed?'

'Yes. And no. So probably not.'

Oh hell. Laurie frowned as the man stood politely expectant. They'll think I'm an absolute fool. And what, when you really came down to it, was the point of keeping him out of the pantry? If he seriously intended to start soaking up the juice he could do so anywhere. In fact you could argue that it was better that he should be doing it in a known and confined area. At least that way one could tot up the empties. And there was always the chance that she had been mistaken in her judgement of that delicate French violet complexion. The poor chap might have high blood pressure. Or heart trouble. Laurie berated herself for losing her nerve so early in the game.

'You're quite right, Gaunt,' she said. 'I just didn't get around to the drinks side of things. If you come along with me now I'll give you the keys.'

Two hours later Simon was ready to set off for the station and Hugh had still not arrived. Laurie had eventually, resentfully, taken it upon herself to ring Kettersley Hall. There had been no reply. Simon said an empty house must mean Hugh was on his way and Laurie said she hoped to heaven he wasn't bringing the entire Kettersley-Gore contingent with him.

'You could have worn the plus fours after all,' she continued, eyeing Simon's cream Oxford bags, short-sleeved shirt and sleeveless fair isle pullover.

'Don't be spiteful,' retorted Simon. 'I've no intention of inflicting such garments upon our guests. There's enough sorrow in the world as it is.'

Laurie watched him drive away and pictured his return, the vehicle disgorging hordes of avid punters all seeking mayhem, blood and gore. Nine strangers loose amongst Aunt Maude's beautiful treasured possessions. She felt her throat close in panic and flutter as if a tiny bird were trapped there. How had she allowed herself to be persuaded into this dreadful venture? A spot of discreet throat-clearing recalled her to the present. Gaunt was standing by one of the oleanders.

'I have prepared everything for drinks out here with the exception of the ace, madam. And Bennet asks if you would be kind enough to come and look at the setting for dinner.'

'Of course.' Laurie followed the stately figure into the dining room where the surface of the long Sheraton had almost vanished beneath a positive splendour of sparkling crystal, heavy silver, starched mats, napkins and fragrant flowers. 'That looks lovely. Thank you, Bennet.'

The maid tucked in her chin and made a little bob then they both stood looking expectant while Laurie realized that all three of them now had an hour and a half on their hands.

'Are things progressing in the kitchen?'

'Yes'm. Everything's in order.'

'Right. In that case I don't see why you shouldn't relax for an hour. There'll be a lot to do this evening. I don't suppose we'll finish till late. If Mr Wriothesley calls you'll find me in the – ' Laurie broke off, looking down at her silk dress. The herbaceous border was obviously out. As was her favourite retreat of all, the vegetable garden. On the other hand she urgently needed to be in close proximity to green and growing things. Her troubled spirit felt calmer at the very thought. 'You'll find me in the conservatory.'

4

'I don't like the way that owl's looking at me.'

'Shut the frigging door then.'

'You shut it. You're the one that's on your feet.'

Gaunt was lying on the bed smoking. He had removed his tail coat and rolled up his sleeves but still had his shoes on. Bennet, wearing a neon-pink shortie dressing gown and a pair of Y-fronts, paced up and down.

Their bedroom was very large and held a washbasin, one double bed (walnut veneer, circa 1950) and a narrow divan, both made up with clean cotton sheets and clean, but rather worn, cellular blankets. This opened off a sitting room which was almost impenetrable, being crammed with all the bits and pieces unwanted elsewhere. A round table, a wormy *prie-dieu*, a drop-leaf table, its bloom disfigured by many overlapping pale grey rings, six chairs with fraying petit-point seats, a broken bamboo whatnot and several cases of stuffed birds, one of which contained the observant owl.

'We shall want locking up if we don't get a result in a place like this.' Gaunt turned his back on the open door. 'Fancy leaving two kids in charge.'

'I wouldn't call him a kid. He's a cold-eyed sod. She's all right.'

'We'll walk it.' The butler stubbed out his fag. 'Dance it.'

'Where've I heard that before?'

'It's the brotherly support that keeps me going.'

'All I'm saying is – '

'We got a weekend filler here could set us up for life.'

'Don't use that word, Gordon. You know how it affects me.'

'Sorry. One up on the last job though, ain't it?' Gaunt's smile attempted to close the gap. 'Deceitful cow she was. Calling herself an honourable and wearing hooky gear. No more honourable than my left bollock.'

'No comparison.' Bennet closed the door.

'Sentimental value she said it had, that ring.'

'Fifty quid!' Bennet gave a bitter laugh. 'Last time I got sentimental about fifty quid I was thirteen and swapping car tyres while the drivers were in the knocking shop.'

'Those were the days.'

'Those were *not* the days, Gordon. Fruit machines, gas meters, minding dodgy parcels, ripping off the lead. If you think those were the days, you want your bloody head examined.'

'There was a real neighbourhood feeling.' Gaunt looked dreamily reminiscent. 'Everybody stuck together.'

'When they weren't shopping each other.'

'Dad pulled off the Ellsworthy caper.'

'Then pulled off fifteen years.'

'He trusted the wrong people.'

'And you know where the proceeds went?'

'Leave it out.' Gaunt looked deeply uncomfortable.

'On the best domestic training money can buy. Blades set him back the biggest part of ten grand. Thought it was worth it, didn't he? An ontray into the country's wealthiest establishments. And what's the return on his investment? A fish slice here, a cruet there – that wonky painting you thought was a Picasso – '

'We haven't had the luck. Till now.'

'It's not bad here.' Bennet backed off, mildly grudging. 'Not bad at all.' He flexed thin bony fingers. Twenty-twenty vision might be lacking but the touch was a hundred per cent. Those fingers were almost magnetic. Things (usually little sparkly things) were immediately attracted and stuck to them like glue. Trouble was, Ben not having the sight the stuff was frequently worthless. This was where Gordon came in. They were a team. Supposed to be. 'We could load up when they're asleep – ' a bit of enthusiasm crept into Ben's voice – 'cut the 'phone wires, take the bus . . .'

'Be back in the Smoke before you could say Bent Vernon.'

'He's Vera now.'

'Is he?' Gaunt sat up in some surprise. 'Where d'you hear that?'

'He had the operation. I shall begin to feel the need for one meself if I spend much more time in that daft schmutter.' He nodded at the black dress and white ruched frill on the bed. 'I'll swear that wig's alive. Sling the bazookas across, then. Time I got dressed.'

Gaunt unhooked the cotton-wool stuffed brassiere from the bed post and threw it. 'I'll bet they'll be a right load of wankers. Faffing about playing at being murdered.'

'Got to do something with their time. The idle rich.' Ben struggled with the hooks and eyes. 'This is a bugger.'

'You've undone enough.' Gordon chuckled coarsely then stared out of the window. 'Look at them peacocks. Dirty devils.'

'If. . . and I say *if* we decide to pull this one you won't let me down?'

'Ben!' A mixture of surprise and pained reproach. 'When have I ever let you down?'

'Never mind then – it's now I'm talking about.' Bennet put on his wig then sat by his brother on the bed. 'The past is water under the bridge as far as I'm concerned.'

At the word water Gordon looked deeply apprehensive. 'You got no faith in me.' His lip trembled. 'You've never had faith.'

'That's not fair. It just gets a bit dented sometimes.' Ben paused and looked sternly hesitant. 'You're not . . . You haven't . . .'

'No.'

'You did promise.'

'I've not touched a drop. Stand on me.'

'I bloody will if I find you near a bottle. Right – ' he got up, settling his frill – 'the coach'll be here in a minute. Get your skates on.'

In the conservatory Laurie pottered happily about. She had just finished sponging the huge leaves of a *Dieffenbachia maculata* and now pulled out a few tiny weeds, loving the feel of the peaty crumbs between her fingers. She sprayed the philodendron which was looking a bit parched and fed the abutilon before sweeping the tiles (a turquoise and white design of amaranthus with a Greek key border) and taking off her cream gardening smock. It was very grubby and had a long smear of earth across the front.

The room was so pretty with its flowering plants and chintzy bamboo furniture that people were bound to want to sit in it and there was no doubt that her smock, kept on a hook behind the door between her visits to the house, would definitely lower the tone. Laurie rolled it up and stuffed it behind one of the sofa cushions, plumping and smoothing out the others as she went along.

She paused at the door for a final check. It all looked very restful and tidy but she had the sense of something missing. Then she realized there were no books or magazines. It was the single place she had forgotten. Laurie hurried off to the library and studied the glass-fronted cases. None of the heavy volumes were what you'd call browsable. Then she spotted Simon's little stack of whodunits, unlocked the case and took them out.

Back in the conservatory she placed them on the wicker table, caught sight of her watch and gasped in horror. They would be here in minute! And even as she entertained the thought Bennet appeared in the doorway to say that the mini-bus was turning in at the main gates.

38

THE SET-UP

1

'Where on earth are all the others?'

'For heaven's sake, Mummy. We've only been on the coach a couple of minutes.'

Unmollified, Mrs Laetitia Saville glared at the innocent, sparklingly clean window a few inches from her left shoulder. It shrank in its frame. Rosemary glanced sideways at her parent's alarming profile. At the great Roman arch of a nose, the bone seemingly on the point of bursting through the skin, at the sizeable jaw and tightly clamped lips incongruously coloured petunia pink and at the fire of diamonds at her ear. Happily unconscious of the set of her own lips and the slight but definite thrust of her own jaw, Rosemary, nineteen and complacently aware that she was thought to be as pretty as a picture, settled back in her seat and imagined herself sweeping down the grand staircase – for surely all country houses had one – in her sea-green chiffon. Her mother's voice intruded sharply on this pleasing fantasy.

'Sorry, Mummy. . . ?'

'I said: "Why aren't you looking more upset?" '

'What do you mean?'

'You know very well what I mean. I don't believe you've done what you promised at all.'

'Yes I have.'

'You've finished with him entirely?'

'Entirely.'

'Then the affair can't have been very serious.'

'I loved him madly,' cried Rosemary, having already regressed to around 1935. 'I look into my heart and see only emptiness and sorrow.'

Mrs Saville sniffed. She had no time for such namby-pamby introspection. Life, according to Mrs Saville, once one's natural and domestic surroundings and any socially acceptable habitués had been licked into shape, was for living.

'But I put on a brave face,' continued Rosemary. 'And of course I am quite resilient, taking after you.'

Mother and daughter exchanged looks of mutual congratulation, rearranging their lips into tightish smiles. Mrs Saville patted Rosemary's arm. 'He wouldn't have done, you know, darling.'

'If only you'd met him – '

'I didn't need to meet him. He was in trade. And the worse sort of trade. A commercial traveller.'

'He won't always be. One day he hopes to have his own business.'

'On whose money, I wonder.'

'That's a horrid thing to say. Anyway – what's wrong with being in business? Daddy was.'

'Banking is a profession, Rosemary, like the law and the church. The Savilles have never been in business. And your grandfather, never forget, was a rear admiral.'

Fat chance, thought Rosemary, who already knew enough about her maternal grandfather to last her several lifetimes. More people started to board. Rosemary regarded them with interested distaste; Mrs Saville with horror strongly mixed with mounting indignation.

A stout man in an electric-blue pinstripe suit climbed the steps then turned and bent down. His trousers stretched over a bottom like two large fully inflated balloons. 'Come on, Mother,' he urged. 'Only two more steps and the view's enough to take your breath away.' He braced his legs like someone in a tug-of-war team and gave a huge pull accompanied by a grunt. Then he shouted: 'Shove up a bit your end, Violet. She's nearly there.'

On the second step, panting like a grampus, rested a

very short, very wide old lady. Her lack of stature was so marked that she seemed to be squatting rather than standing and this, coupled with a dark, mottled, rather warty complexion and a squinny eye gave her the look of a baffled toad. She was dressed all in black apart from her hat which was a festive Carmen Miranda number of emerald felt, topped by a mound of twinkling glass fruit.

The man in the suit and the woman pushing from behind let go for a breather and the old lady wheezed and concertinaed a little closer to the step. With a cry of 'Ay up – she's sinking' they hove to once again and, after a lot more effort, settled her opposite the Savilles where she filled two seats and overflowed into the gangway. The man turned and held out his hand.

'Howdya do. Gibbs is the name. Gibbs, Gibbs and Gibbs. Or in the vernacular, Fred, Vi and Mother.'

'Hello.' The hand was so large and so plainly under her nose that Rosemary felt compelled to reach out and quickly grace it with her own. 'I'm Rosemary Saville. And this is *my* mother.'

At this perfidious linking of herself with the appalling monstrosity adjacent Rosemary felt her parent give a great shudder as if from some traitorous blow. Or a nip from a serpent's tooth. Mrs Saville ignored the outstretched hand, treating Mr Gibbs to a glare that would have stripped the bark from a coolibah tree. He beamed back, saying, 'She don't look too grand, your mam.'

'No . . .' Rosemary was annoyed to find herself compelled to exculpate her mother's rudeness. 'It's the train. She doesn't travel well.'

'I had a schnautzer like that. The only thing that'd settle her was a saucer of navy rum.'

Violet Gibbs wriggled round in her seat and gazed at Rosemary. Violet had a foolish, doll-like face and primrose-coloured hair in lifeless curls pinned all over her head like synthetic little sausages. There was an all-

embracing ameliatory quality to her smile. She opened a
tiny wet mouth like a sea anemone and spoke.

'You been to one of these dos before, dear?'

'No. Have you?'

'Ohhh yes. Lots of times.'

'Not in a moated grange, Vi,' corrected her husband.
'Be fair.'

'That's true. Only in hotels.' Mrs Gibbs jerked her
head, indicating that Rosemary should lean forward.
Taking a deep breath and prepared to hold it for ever if
necessary, Rosemary did. Mrs Gibbs lowered her voice
as if about to impart a juicily shameful snippet of news.
'He prefers the routs.'

'I'm sorry?'

'Jousting and wassail. Whereas I,' continued Mrs
Gibbs, still in a discreet whisper, 'incline to the Wild
West more. Barbecues, shootouts and no problems with
your wimple.'

'Horns on your head,' cackled the elder Mrs Gibbs.
'Looked like an advert for Bovril.'

'D'you remember that Richard the Third lookalike
contest at Bosworth? When I got stuck in my doublet
and hose.' Fred turned to Mrs Saville with a confiding
wink. 'I were busting by the time I got me codpiece off.'

'We've come for Mother really.' Violet, who had
noticed a truly spectacular slow burn commencing in the
seat behind, rushed into deflective explanation.

Rosemary sneaked a sidelong glance at the old lady,
who had drawn open a grey silk reticule and was efficiently
stripping the transparent wrapping off a large pork pie.

'She doesn't have a lot of pleasure,' continued Violet,
'but you show her a dead body and watch her face light
up.'

'Well,' said Rosemary nervously. 'As long as it isn't
mine.'

'Oooh – she's sharp,' cried Fred. 'Who's been round
the knife box then?'

An attractive woman with smooth auburn hair climbed aboard followed by a man wearing, in spite of the warmth of the day, a long overcoat. Fred declaimed: 'This way for Castle Dracula.' Then introduced himself. 'Gibbs is the name. Gibbs, Gibbs and Gibbs. Or, in the vernacular, Fred, Vi and Mother.'

Sheila Gregory gave a chilly smile. Her husband turned and gazed piercingly at his new acquaintance. The cloth of his coat was a neat lovat check and the garment had a brief cape attached. He also wore a deerstalker, the flaps tied beneath his chin. He had a long rather pointed nose which quivered slightly when he spoke and he carried a violin case.

'You're dressed for it then, Sherlock,' continued Fred, giving the deerstalker a complicit nod. 'This your Watson? He looks a touch iffy. I wouldn't like to bend down when he's around.'

'There's always one, isn't there?' muttered Sheila to her husband, who responded by lifting a schoolmasterly finger of restraint.

'Any more for the *Skylark*, Cap'n?' queried the ship's joker.

Simon's reply was courteous but slightly distant. He had still not fully recovered from his first sight of Gibbs, Gibbs and Gibbs. How on earth people of that stamp came to be reading *The Times* was quite beyond his comprehension. Probably wrapped around their chips. 'We're waiting for Mr Gillette. And Mr Lewis – his train was due a few minutes ago.'

Two men now approached the bus, both with heavy bags. Mr Lewis staggered under the weight of his, Mr Gillette's was rolling meekly in his wake on little wheels. Like Mr Gregory he carried a musical instrument case; long, narrow and round at one end. He refused to let Simon take this and tripped over it as he climbed the steps.

Mr Lewis boarded first, ducking his head shyly at his

fellow passengers. He wore a light grey suit and had a sweet rather owlish look due largely to a lot of fluffy hair and round horn-rimmed spectacles. He settled behind the Gregorys, the back of his neck turning pink as he felt himself to be observed. Mr Gillette (pale flannels, blazer) removed his boater and sat next to Mr Lewis, who started nervously at the contact.

Fred, no doubt determined that the newcomers should not be left in ignorance of his family's appellation, either in or out of the vernacular, rose to his feet. As he did so Simon violently slammed the lid of the boot.

'Aaaahhh . . .!!!' cried Fred, slumping back in his seat. 'They got me, Vi. I'm a gonner . . .'

'Don't set me off,' said Violet with a hint of a rollick. 'You know what I'm like.'

'Mother of God –' Her husband clutched his chest. 'Is this the end of Freddo?'

'It'll certainly be the end of me,' said Mrs Saville crisply, not bothering to lower her voice, 'if I have to put up with much more of this.' She ignored Rosemary's hushings. 'If you had come to Bath as I suggested we could be in the Palm Court at the Royal Georgian by now having an aperitif.'

'They give you the runs,' the old lady informed everyone. 'Aperitifs.' She smacked her chops over the last crumb of pork pie, rolled the wrapping up into a tight ball and flicked it the length of the bus. It hit Simon on the back of the head as he was getting into the driver's seat.

'The gang's all here then?' demanded Fred.

Their cap'n forbore to reply. He drove off, making his way as quickly as the traffic would allow through Oxford then taking the B480 for Toot Balden before branching off to Madingley. Many remarks were passed about the beauty of the landscape and Simon wondered who would be the first to say: 'And so convenient for the M40.' It was Mr Gillette.

'Have you done a murder weekend before?' asked Mrs Gibbs, determinedly friendly to the couple in the front seat.

'Not precisely,' replied Derek Gregory. 'But I am by way of being an af – '

'You'll love it. Won't he, Fred?'

'He will that.'

'You're old hands then?' inquired Sheila politely.

'Old hands?' Mr Gibbs made a clucking noise at the roof of the bus as if expecting it to burst into vocal support. 'Old hands? I should think we are old hands. You'll have to get up early to beat us to the draw.'

At this remark Mr Gregory sneered. His lip lifted, his nostrils widened and his whole face assumed an expression of the most infinite superiority. Mrs Saville, sitting at an angle behind him, noticed this and, so precisely did it illustrate her own state of mind, warmed to him immediately.

'D'you remember that weekend,' Violet compounded her husband's felony, 'when the victim got murdered twice? He were garrotted at breakfast, then given the kiss of life, then stabbed to death in the Palatine Lounge.'

'That weren't a murder weekend,' replied her husband. 'That were a sunshine break. At Billericay.'

The coach sped on.

Simon had known Madingley Grange nearly all his life and was so used to its appearance that he was quite unprepared for the sudden gasps of surprise and murmurs of appreciation as the last curve in the road through the surrounding parkland was negotiated and the house suddenly swung into view. He tried to see it through his passengers' eyes and failed, merely observing to himself that hideousness on such a profoundly confident and flamboyant scale must surely be some sort of virtue in its own right. He was sorry to see, as he bumped over the drawbridge, that the swans were round the back, but one of the peacocks made up for this by elegantly sauntering into view as Simon crunched to a halt by the iron-studded main doors.

For the umpteenth time he congratulated himself on his idea of a thirties setting. The trio on the steps (where was Hugh?) could have stepped straight out of an early Christie. Reading from left to right – Gaunt, grave of feature in his swallow tails . . . Bennet, thin as the wind, lips clamped respectfully together, greying hair scraped back under her starched cap. And Laurie . . .

Good old Laurie, thought Simon. She really has gone to town. His sister was wearing the geometric patterned silk dress and high-heeled shoes. Her normally glowing complexion had quietened down to a smooth peach and her glossy wine-dark lips were parted in a determined smile.

Simon slid open the door of the bus and jumped down, suffused with satisfaction at the appropriateness of it all. And if there isn't a body in the library he thought, by this time tomorrow, it won't be due to any lack of initiative on my part. He walked round to the boot and started taking out the cases. Gaunt and Bennet flowed forward to assist.

Laurie greeted the first guest to descend: 'Hullo – I'm Laurel Hannaford, welcome to Madingley Grange,' and found herself shaking a hand like a damp flounder. It belonged to a tall man now arched into a comma of eager salutation. He had round watery green eyes and a thick dry shaggy moustache like a little straw mop.

'I'm Arthur Gillette, known as Gilly. Hard G of course.' He gave a high-pitched, neighing laugh, '*hinnire* . . . *hinnire* . . .' and Laurie imagined it ringing from the rafters for the next forty-eight hours, and flinched.

She said: 'I do hope your stay will be a happy one.' She had learnt half a dozen opening gambits whilst waiting and now realized that she had completely forgotten the other five. I'm going to sound like a parrot, she thought, by the time we've got them all safely stowed away.

A pretty, hard-faced girl alighted next followed by a tall woman of formidable aspect. She looked around, seeming especially taken with the gargoyles – no doubt in some kind of subliminal recognition.

'Delightful,' she exclaimed. 'A noble house.'

Then came an aesthetic-looking man pointing like a gundog. The sun glinted on his steel-rimmed glasses and he gazed up at the great doors and dusty ivy in a seemingly ecstatic trance. 'Marvellous . . . marvellous . . . Baskerville Hall to the life . . .'

'Derek – you're blocking everyone's way.'

Simon instructed Gaunt to show the Gregorys to the Vuillard room and they went off together, Derek still quite moony with delight. Gawping his way through the hall he bumped into a pedestal on which stood a large yellow and turquoise Chinese vase. Sheila caught it just in time.

Mother got stuck on the steps again. Laurie, alarmed, amused and repelled in equal measure by this occurrence, tried to help. Eventually the old lady came out with a forceful pop like a champagne cork and Laurie staggered back under the impact.

'Put that lady down.' Fred started as he meant to go on. 'You don't know where she's been.'

'Pleased to meet you, dear.' Violet shook hands. 'You'll be glad to get your breath back.'

'You and your husband are in the Hogarth suite,' said Laurie, once she had. 'I thought as there were three of you you might appreciate a sitting room. And the other Mrs Gibbs is just across the landing. Simon,' she added loudly, 'will help you with your luggage.'

Simon, on the point of disappearing, came back rather tight about the mouth, and picked up two cases.

'Aaahhh . . .' Violet sighed over one of the peacocks now making its stately way across the drawbridge. 'Look at his lordship. Isn't he lovely? If you ask him will he open his tail?'

'I'm afraid not.' Laurie's hard-won confidence fled. She felt an abject failure, convinced that the next two days would be full of people asking her to do and arrange things that were quite impossible.

'He's not trained then?'

'No.' She strove to justify such shameful lack of zeal. 'They're very independent.'

'Mind of his own has he?' said Fred. 'You got to be firm with animals. Show them who's boss.'

'He's always had a way with dumb creatures.'

'Can't have a happy marriage otherwise, my love.' Fred stretched out his hand to the peacock. 'Come on then . . . chuck, chuck . . .'

The bird stopped, gave Mr Gibbs a look of unspeakable disdain and made a mess on the planks. Mortified, Laurie turned her attention to the final guest and immediately a little of her confidence returned. For here was someone as shy and constrained as herself.

Mr Lewis dropped his jacket, missed shaking hands and blushed. They exchanged tentative smiles and Laurie led the way to the Watteau room where she left him standing in the middle of an expanse of aubusson with his suitcase and looking, she thought, rather endearingly lost.

2

It had been Aunt Maude's conceit to name each bedroom at the Grange after a famous artist and illustrate accordingly. But as Uncle George's reserves would not stretch to even the most modest famous original artist's canvas an Oxford painter had been hired to copy the works to be placed *in situ*. The results, though pleasant enough to an untutored eye, would not have fooled the serious gallery goer for a moment. Mrs Maberley however, quite unabashed, would describe them firmly to visitors as 'My Renoir' or 'My Degas', and woe betide the first to quibble.

Later, in the Greuze room, beneath an overly vivacious representation of *The Spoiled Child*, Mrs Saville surveyed her daughter critically.

'I don't know why it is but even when young people get the costume and cosmetics and hairstyles of another period absolutely right they still look unconvincing.' Complacently resplendant in coffee lace, Mrs Saville had replaced her diamond earrings with star sapphires. Now she crossed to the dressing table and opened a black velvet case lined with crinkle satin.

'Mummy . . .' Rosemary asked for the umpteenth time, 'are you sure you wouldn't rather sleep in that adjoining room?'

'Quite sure thank you, darling.'

'Only – this opening directly on to the corridor might be noisier. People going by and so on.'

'I must have a room with a window,' declared Mrs Saville. 'You know me and fresh air.'

'But – '

'That is an end to the matter, Rosemary.' Mrs Saville

removed a dazzling necklace from the case and returned to her original theme. 'Our family have always understood the art of the ensemble. Your grandmother's tea gowns were the talk of Fuller's.'

'I couldn't have stood the underwear. Rubber suspenders, metal hooks and eyes. And all that slithery stockinette. Ugh.'

'Fasten this please.'

Dutifully Rosemary came forward and took hold of the necklace. The clasp was two large flattish oval pearls. She linked them together then stood at her mother's side facing the cheval glass. A long moment passed while Mrs Saville admired Mrs Saville and Rosemary admired her inheritance.

It really was the most magnificent piece. One large diamond blazed, subduing the fire from eight smaller gems. These shone in a setting of seed pearls and sapphires. Mrs Saville had a superb swoop of a bosom. It started directly beneath the hollow of her neck and finished just a smidgen above what, if only a hint of indentation had been present, could have passed for her waist. As this splendid curvature rose and fell the necklace oscillated and every colour of the rainbow flashed into incandescent life. Darting and dazzling, blinding the eye, stopping the breath, filling the heart with wonder.

'I must say – ' she gave the jewels a final soothing pat as if to settle them for the night – 'I'm pleasantly surprised by the standard of hygiene.' She wrapped a lace hanky around her little finger and ran it over the bedside table. Not a speck. 'Fresh flowers too. And chocolate bath olivers. A really thoughtful touch.'

'The sheets smell of lavender.' Then, catching sight of a blue and white package next to her mother's evening bag, 'Oh Mummy . . .' Rosemary's voice filled with irritation. 'You haven't brought your cards.'

'Of course. In a civilized gathering there are bound to be enough people to make up a rubber.'

'You only played on Thursday.'

'I did not play on Thursday. The game was cancelled. Davina Bingley's mother, if you recall.'

'Mmm.' Rosemary twirled slowly – easily distracted by her own image. The sea-green dress was heaven, the slashed hem coming to eight deep points each weighted with a single pearl, but were the shoes, especially dyed, a precise match?

'I intend to put plenty of distance between myself and those dreadful tinkers from the North.' Mrs Saville made the North sound like the city of Dis. 'We shall be lucky if they don't eat with their fingers.'

'That might not be so easy, darling,' said Rosemary, pulling a wisp of chiffon through her thin jade bangle. 'I don't think there's anyone else here but the mini-bus load.'

Mrs Saville blenched. 'Surely,' she cried, aghast, 'you're mistaken.'

'I'll check, shall I?' Rosemary dashed to the door. 'Easily done. I'll count the places in the dining room.'

'Wait – '

'Shan't be a sec.'

'Have you tidied your hands?' But she spoke to the air for Rosemary had gone. Pausing to reflect briefly on how apposite was her installation in a room boasting a portrait of *The Spoilt Child*, Mrs Saville picked up her bag and checked its contents. Powder, lipstick, comb, scent bottle. She crossed to the dressing table, opened her vanity case and extracted a tiny flask of lavender smelling salts. By the end of the evening she felt she might well be needing them.

In the bedroom of the Hogarth suite, happily innocent of the opprobrium their presence was causing to seethe in a bosom not a million miles away, the family Gibbs was getting into what Fred called their carnival clobber. Violet feeling the suggested thirties to be 'a bit drab and

53

warmongery', they had opted for the roaring twenties. Fred had put on a brightly checked 'bounder' jacket then spoiled the period effect by adding a modern tie: a satin kipper displaying a pair of female legs ending in sequinned evening sandals kicking a champagne glass from which tumbled the letters OO LA LA!

'How do I look then?'

Fred turned and watched his wife, a positive delirium of cerise satin, orange feathers and swinging beads all balanced on legs like fat rosy sausages. 'Beautiful, my duck. You'll be able to dance a right fandango in that lot.' He paused. 'Give us a smile then.'

But Violet, finishing her turn, remained serious and thoughtful. 'I'm worried about the girls.'

'Don't start again. We had enough of that on the train. Consuela can cope.'

'Emerald's got that rash.'

'It's nothing – I told you.'

'She might give it to the others.'

'Course she won't. Don't talk so daft.' Fred, having crossed to the fireplace, seized on *The Countess's Morning Levee* for a snappy change of subject. 'Who's Hogarth when he's buying a round?'

'How should I know?'

'They were a comical lot.' He studied the picture more closely. 'There's a bloke here in long pink drawers and his hair in curlers.'

'That's always gone on.'

'Suppose you're right. I've often wondered . . . you know? There's money in it . . .'

'Certainly not, Fred. That sort of thing's disgusting.' Firmly Violet moved on. 'Your mother's very quiet.'

'*My* mother!' Fred staggered in simulated amazement. 'I thought she were your mother. All these years we've been putting up with her – '

'Go and see what she's up to.'

Mother was on the sofa in the adjoining sitting room.

Encased in iridescent jet, she glittered like a huge black beetle. Her mandibles moved rhythmically and she was clutching her reticule. Fred popped his head round the door.

'You're never still on the chomp. What you got now?'

The old lady opened her mouth, removed the remains of a bull's-eye, held it up between the thumb and forefinger of a knobbly mittened hand and popped it back.

'You won't want your supper.' Mrs Gibbs made a loud sucking noise. 'And you behave yourself when we get downstairs – all right?'

At this stern tone the old lady affected bewilderment and gave a timid smile. Beneath the little grey moustache her remaining teeth showed, yellow and strong like tiny tusks, giving her the air of a puzzled walrus.

'You needn't look at me like that,' Fred went on. 'You know what I'm on about. You try anything – anything at all – and home you go, toot sweet.'

'I'm as good as gold,' said the walrus.

'That'll be the day.'

'It's haunted, this place.'

'You reckon?' Fred's question was cushioned by respect. The words extrasensory perception could have been invented for his mother.

'I can smell it. Strong. Like raspberry jam on the boil.'

'Blimey.' Fred returned to the bedroom, closing the door carefully. 'She says the Grange is haunted.'

'That should add a few laughs to the weekend then.'

'She is clean, 'ent she? You did check?'

'Course I did. Both her handbag and her suitcase. Clean as a whistle.'

Violet, having discovered the biscuit barrel, was tucking in. The pretty little handwritten card said: 'Drinks on the terrace at seven thirty' but that was ages yet.

Her husband, saying: 'You're as bad as she is,' opened the window and stepped out on the balcony to give the scenery a going over. 'Gorr, Violet – ' he shaded his eyes explorer fashion – 'you could hang a fair bit of washing out here.'

'The sort of people who live in these places don't have washing.'

'They must be a right mucky lot then.'

'Turn your socks down, Fred. You look as if nobody owns you. And have a bath oliver.'

'I've had a bath,' came the reply, quick as a wink. 'And me name's not Oliver.'

Whilst Violet munched and her husband obligingly made a neat cuff on each sock, Mother was sitting very still on her sofa in front of a little papiermâché bezique table. The room was silent but for the silken slap and flutter of playing cards. The old lady halved a deck and lifted two horny thumbs. A lightning streak of white, a whirr and the pack was whole again. Then, in a flash it became a fan and, just as quickly, a tall tower.

Mrs Gibbs flung her arms wide. The cards leapt from her right hand into a perfect arc and fell, slap flutter, into her left. She halved the pack again, zipped them together and laid out in one swift movement a line of seven face down. She turned the first one over and was treating it to an intent, almost votive, scrutiny when a sound from the other room disturbed her concentration. The cards flew into the folds of her skirts like startled birds, and by the time her son and his wife came in Mother's hands were clasped innocently in her lap and her face shone with an almost saintly demureness.

Rosemary dashed along the corridor and, without waiting to knock, burst into the Watteau room.

'Darling!'

'Darling.'

The young man with the round glasses jumped up

from the window seat and came towards his visitor only to be almost knocked off his feet by the exuberance of her embrace.

'Love you.'

'Love you.'

'I've only got a sec. Ohh . . .' She eyed him up and down, her expression ecstatic. 'You look too, too divine. Gosh – ' staring at his feet. 'What are they?'

Martin looked down too. 'Spats.'

'You don't wear spats with evening dress.'

'Don't you?'

'Of course not. You must take them off at once.'

'OK.' He returned to the window seat and started unbuttoning. Rosemary joined him, saying: 'Isn't it wonderful? We're actually truly positively here.'

'So we are.'

'What did you think of Mummy?'

'Well . . .' Martin hesitated. He felt it would hardly delight his fiancé should he reveal his true opinion, which was that Mrs Saville's profile had struck him as so alarming that he would prefer in future to view only its muted reflection, perhaps on the surface of a tea tray. 'Hard to say, really. From a quick glimpse.'

'I had a terrible job getting her to come. She only agreed because I swore I'd given you up. Now you've got two whole days to make a good impression, starting tonight at dinner.'

'What if I'm not sitting next to her?'

'Use your initiative.'

'Or a loud hailer. Ha, ha.'

'This is serious, Martin.'

'Sorry.'

'Have you got your toadying list?'

'Yes.' Martin slapped his breast pocket. 'But I wish you wouldn't call it that. Makes me feel all oily.'

'Recite, please. Her favourite things. Nineteenth-century china . . .'

'Nineteenth-century China. The charm of the pekingese. Historical biography. Composers . . . um . . . Tchaikovsky . . .'

'Just *Swan Lake*.'

'Ivor Novello.'

'Just *King's Rhapsody*. And stick strictly to the music.'

'No discussion of their enigmatic variations?'

'Definitely not. And she's an admiral's daughter so keep off Jutland.'

'Where?'

'Hurry *up*, Martin.'

'Right . . . card fanatic. Loves a game of whist – '

'*Bridge*. She plays bridge.'

'Oh God.' Martin pulled out his bit of paper. 'I shall never remember all this lot.'

'You don't have to. Just one or two topics to keep you going through dinner. Then you can refer back before you talk to her again. There'll be lots of other opportunities.'

'You don't think it might be better if I was more . . . well . . . spontaneous?'

'No, Martin. This is no time to rely on natural charm. Mummy may not even notice that you have any. Oh and angel . . .' She flung herself on to his chest again. 'My room is the last but one on the other side of the corridor.'

'This end?'

'That end. I'm afraid it opens off Mother's. I tried to get the outside one but she wouldn't budge. Don't worry,' Rosemary added, for Martin had gone quite pale, 'once she's asleep a ten-gun salute wouldn't bring her round. When she's gone off I'll open my door the teensiest bit and that'll be the signal for you to come, and oh darling! we'll be together *at last*!'

'Righto,' said Martin.

When Sheila Gregory had pointed out, with a derisory snigger, the advertisement for 'A Murder Weekend:

Thirties Style', her husband's excitement had known no bounds. Ignoring her wails of protest he had booked up there and then and rushed out to post the letter – returning with a brand new deerstalker, bringing the grand total to seventeen.

Sheila had moaned and sulked and grumbled but then Derek handed her a blank cheque to hire the appropriate costumes, which cheered her up no end. For although Derek was comfortable (very comfortable indeed), prising the stuff out of him was about as easy as prising open the door to the Royal Mint.

She watched him now dressed for dinner but still wearing the Holmesian headgear. He had played a little Bercuse, very badly, on his violin, packed his pipe (the long cherrywood) with Bulwark tobacco and was now prowling happily about leaving trails of smoke on the air behind him. He halted, directing a proprietorial gaze out at the park and long avenue of pleached limes.

'Ah Sheila,' he declaimed with as much satisfaction as if he had planted them all himself, 'look at those elms. They're so . . . immemorial.'

'They are,' agreed Sheila, powdering her retroussé nose. 'At least the ones that haven't keeled over with the Dutch clap.'

She studied her complexion closely. Sheila had the pale skin and freckles that often go with red hair although the latter were invisible at the moment beneath a film of liquid ivory make-up. Her hair rippled gently into marcel waves and was restrained at two points by diamanté butterflies. She wore a cream velvet floor-length dress with a little fantail train and three scarlet poppies pinned to one shoulder. Her lips were as red as the flowers and very thin, giving the lie to the commonly held notion that all voluptuaries had mouths that were rich and full, for Sheila had a very passionate nature. A fact of which her husband was largely unaware. She hung up her day clothes in the splendid mahogany wardrobe then crossed to the bed, unzipped Derek's bloodhound pyjama case and laid out his nightshirt.

'You should let the maid do that.'

'What a pair. That butler . . . he looks as if he was built into the foundations.'

'They are marvellous,' admitted Derek. Personally he had been rather hoping for a butler with a hump but life couldn't always live up to expectations. He resumed his prowling, stopping occasionally to tap on the carved, panelled wall. He pressed his ear close to a particularly bucolic scene as if hoping to catch the sounds of distant revelry. He had the strangest ears: large and pink and so thin they seemed almost transparent. They stuck out from each side of his head like fine shavings of gammon. Sheila had often thought that if ever pigs did have wings they'd look just like Derek's ears.

'I can't understand this.' He knocked loudly on a ploughman hopefully rampant. 'There must be a hollow somewhere. They're full of secret passages, these old houses . . .'

'I wouldn't say this one's all that old.'

'It was in a room precisely like this, Sheila, that Doctor Bellini was found strangled. With an oxhide whip of singular strength and a clubbed ostrich foot for a handle.'

'The things some people collect.'

'The murderer escaped through a priest's hole.'

'A neat trick. Your jacket could do with a brush – '

'Surely you remember,' urged Derek, taking off his dinner jacket and handing it over. 'He stole a ruby from Count Markovitch. On the verge of discovery he flung it into the moat and came back for it later.'

Sheila frowned. 'Was the ruby the size of a pigeon's egg?'

'Exactly!'

'*The Case of the Constipated Moorhen.*'

'Brilliant, wasn't it?'

'Mmm.'

Sheila only half remembered. Derek always read a chapter of a whodunit aloud each night before going to sleep. His wife, who would have preferred something a bit more on the athletic side, could never tell one from another. They all joined up into a neverending stream of blunt instruments, clueless domestics, rare poisons, sinister daggers (always exquisitely wrought) and little grey cells. Often the plucky ingénue would break down at the end of some exceptionally stringent interrogation and cry: 'I can't take much more of this!' and Sheila knew exactly how she felt.

She removed a magnifying glass from the pocket, handed back the jacket and picked up her shawl. This was a beautiful fringed eau-de-nil silk painted with tiger lilies and ferns. When she had arranged it to her satisfaction she told Derek it was nearly seven thirty and why didn't he go and brush his hair. He did not reply. She turned to discover him standing stock still in the middle of the room, his nose twitching.

'Now what?'

'Sheila – we are being watched.'

'Don't be silly. Why on earth should we be watched?'

'I can feel them . . .' His voice sank sepulchrally. 'Eyes following me around the room.'

'But you're not moving round the room. You're standing still.'

Derek, who had been facing the wardrobe, wheeled about. To the left of the four poster was a sombre oil painting of a very old man in judge's robes. Derek narrowed his eyes. He picked up the dressing table stool and approached the painting by sidling sideways, dropping on his knees for the last couple of yards. Then he put the stool directly beneath the frame, climbed on to it and placed the tips of his index fingers on the judge's painted pupils. Crying: 'Now we'll see who watches who!' he poked hard. There was a soft tearing sound.

61

'Oh my God!' gasped Sheila. 'What have you done? That might be worth thousands.'

'Nonsense.' Derek climbed down, briskly dusting off his hands. 'The fabric was completely rotten, it's as old as the hills. They've probably been waiting for years for a chance to get rid of it. And we are – ' he roamed off into the en-suite bathroom – 'definitely under surveillance. I feel extremely discomposed. I wonder – ' he removed tooth mugs, paste and brushes from a shelf – 'if this mirror's two way.'

'Don't touch it!' cried Sheila with such urgency that Derek abandoned any idea of unscrewing the glass from the wall and contented himself by merely draping it with a towel.

'I think we should go now,' continued his wife, 'while there's still a stick or stone undamaged.' She crossed to the door and, as Derek prepared to follow, halted him. 'Derek, we are about to attend a formal dinner on a lovely summer evening in a beautiful country house . . .'

'So?'

'So take that ridiculous hat off.'

It was nearly seven. Bennet was turning down the sheets, leaving Gaunt briefly, magically alone. He reckoned each operation would take a good five minutes. Four to locate the bed, one to do the folding. Sometimes his brother's appalling eyesight could be a positive advantage.

Now Gaunt came into the vast kitchen, closing the door behind him with great care. The room, full of fragrant smells and the soft plop and bubble of simmering food, appeared to be empty but he still checked the walk-in broom cupboard and washing-up annexe before approaching the Baby Belling and easing open the vitreous enamel door a minim at a time, as if afraid it might creak. He peeped inside and let out a hiss of relief. Finding a hiding place had been a matter of some urgency and Gaunt had known, even as he stashed away the life-enhancing juniper juice, that the oven left a lot to be desired. It was so square and white and visible. Exactly the sort of place a certain person might suss first.

Gaunt resented deeply Ben's lack of faith. Really it gave a man no encouragement to try. And Gaunt was trying. He had been cutting down for three weeks. He was pacing himself, preparing his lights and liver and other dependent tissue for the sustained shock which a gradual change in the constituency of their amniotic fluids must inevitably bring. For gradual the procedure had to be. You could not just suddenly stop imbibing alcohol. Gaunt had done this once (one Easter Sunday morning) to please his mother and had become a trembling heap of flummoxed jelly by lunch time. No, easy was definitely the way to do it. Something the rest of the family either couldn't or wouldn't understand.

He unscrewed the cap from the gin bottle and looked around for a drinking receptacle. Nearest to hand was a cream jug. He filled this and drank the contents down, pausing to breathe halfway. Then he replaced the cap, puckered his forehead up into a frown of concentration and, Beefeaters in hand, started to wander round the room. But the more he wandered the more bereft did the kitchen seem of bottle-shaped nooks and crannies. Then he spotted a largeish stone crock which proved to be three quarters full of flour. There was a little brass scoop inside. Using this Gaunt made a space, laid the gin tenderly to rest, and covered it with the displaced flour. The cream jug had provided such a generous helping of nourishing reserves that Gaunt felt he might not need refuelling till the morrow. But just in case . . .

A savage sudden ringing in his ears made him jump and another quick nip was necessary before he was able to once more take up his duties and answer the telephone.

*

The library at Madingley Grange was rarely used. The pristine books in their diamond-paned cases seemed never to have been sullied by anything so coarse as the perusal of the human eye. They were all in sets; leather bound, gold tooled. Sets of encyclopedias and sets of Dickens. Sets of Thackeray, Trollope and Austen. Though the various authors were bound in different cloths the effect, even allowing for the thrusting scarlet Brontës, was virginal throughout.

'I think Uncle George bought them by the yard, don't you?' Laurie asked her brother. 'Six of brown, three of green and one of red to brighten the dark corners. Isn't it sad there are no children's books?'

'What's sad about not having children? Grotty little pests.'

'No shabby Nesbits with cocoa stains and trapped butter osborne crumbs. No *Wind in the Willows*. No Pooh – '

'Oh do shut up.'

'I'm nervous.'

'We're all nervous.'

'You're not nervous. You wouldn't be nervous if someone was pushing you off a cliff.' Laurie gave her damp lace handkerchief a wring, noticed the appalling state of her nails and tucked her hands out of sight. 'It's the thought of them all up there rampaging about.'

'Nobody's rampaging. It's as silent as the grave.'

'Oh God – so it is!' Laurie sprang to her feet. 'Why is it so quiet? What are they all doing?'

'Getting ready for dinner, I expect. Sit down.' Simon waved his long shagreen cigarette holder at her and Laurie, reluctantly, sat, saying: 'Then there's the cheese.'

'It's a full-time job keeping up with you. What cheese?'

'A pound of Double Gloucester for tomorrow *and* after lunch on Sunday. What if someone wants some tonight?'

'Thought you said the freezer was full.'

'You can't freeze cheese.'

'Family hold back then. I must say,' Simon smiled, hoping to jolly up the atmosphere, 'you look smashing in that shiny thing.'

'I don't feel it.' This was true. Blue lamé slithered and slipped on chestnut leather. 'I feel I'm going to start squeaking any minute.' To add to her discomfort Laurie was aware that her deep suntan stopped a good six inches from the neck of her dress. And that her recalcitrant hair, at the moment confined in a silver turban (*sans* egret), was just waiting its chance to sneak past those rigorous folds and bound about every which way.

'Hugh will be struck all of a heap,' continued Simon. 'Where is he anyway?'

'How should I know?'

'I see.' Simon lifted his lip rodent fashion and stuck out his front teeth.

'You don't "see" anything. Pacey isn't like that.'

'All girls are like that given half a chance.'

'Haven't you got anything to do?'

'All done. I've even managed to dig up some beer and a spot of Guinness for the god-awful Gibbses.'

'They're not awful. Mr Gibbs was telling me he has a large business.'

'Probably scrap metal.'

'With a staff of over two hundred.'

'Nonsense. How can an end of the pier double act and a stuffed raccoon in drag run a business? He's having you on.'

'If you're rude to them, Simon, after taking all that money, I shall be furious.'

'Rude? When am I ever rude? I shall behave impeccably as I always do.' Simon perched on the desk near a large globe, varnished deep amber from years of exposure to Uncle George's tobacco smoke. He spun it slowly, holding his finger on the very centre.

'D'you remember . . . Hey – ' Laurie looked at him. 'Do you remember what you used to call the equator?'

'No.'

'A menagerie lion running round the world.'

Laurie closed her eyes more out of irritation than with a wish to recall the past. Yet suddenly there he was. She saw him as clearly as she had when she was seven. Loping along under a brazen sun, the wind stirring his mane, looking neither to left nor right. His great paws left prints in the sand like flowers. His eyes were triangles of golden light and he was kind.

Laurie's eyes filled with quick tears and she blinked them hard away. She felt tired and cross. She didn't want to be bothered with all these people. Or with clean sheets and fresh flowers and bath olivers and cheese. Especially she didn't want to be bothered with cheese. What she really wanted more than anything else was to be a child again in the kitchen garden with Mackintosh, helping to set the shallots. The fact that this was quite impossible she laid at Simon's door. Everything was his fault. She opened her eyes, glared at him and said, unkindly: 'You're very sceptical about Hugh and me. What about your own future? When are you going to fall in love?'

'Never.' There was a sharp scraping sound. The globe stopped spinning and Simon studied his broken nail. 'It's a dead loss. So much wasted energy. Hours of heaving and sighing and mooning about and nothing to show for it at the end. Give me the clear-eyed pursuit of capitalism any day.'

'So you mean to marry money.'

'I shall certainly "fall in love", as you so soggily put it, where money is.'

'What about Rosemary Saville then? She's very pretty.'

'All heiresses are pretty. And I quote.'

'Or perhaps you've already met the unlucky girl?'

66

'That's my business.'

'You're so secretive about your personal affairs.'

'That's what personal affairs are for.'

Laurie couldn't imagine Simon, with his ironical pessimism and cool light eyes and cozening smile, in love. Not if love meant living in anguish until the phone rang then stammering at the sound of a longed-for voice. Or spending the days wire walking between cloudless skies of rapture and flinty chasms of despair. And finding the earth beneath one's feet strangely mobile. She couldn't see him going through any of that. But then, Laurie thought with a sudden bleak stab of perception, I can't see me either.

'In spite of what you say,' she continued, 'I have noticed the occasional scavenging of the herbaceous borders and the spoils disappearing in the back of your Karmann Ghia. Like the other Wednesday, for instance.'

'The detecting doesn't start till tomorrow, Marple.'

'And what about – '

The sound of the telephone made them both jump. It rang for quite a time whilst Simon made Laurie sit and wait for the butler to do his stuff. Eventually the library door opened and Gaunt glided across the parquet, bent gracefully from the waist and murmured: 'A Mr Wriothesley wishes to speak with you, madam.'

'Hugh!' Laurie lurched on unaccustomed heels across the hall. 'Darling,' she cried into the receiver, 'where are you?' Simon, following, watched his sister's grousy expression smooth out into sympathetic concern. 'Oh no – poor you. How on earth did you manage that?' She listened again then said: 'Of course we'll cope. Simon's here and we've two helpers. You mustn't worry . . . No – don't do that. You wouldn't be any use with a sprained ankle – quite the reverse . . . All right. I'll give you a call when they've all gone. On Sunday. Bye bye.' She hung up. Simon repeated his rodent leer. 'That's no funnier than it was the first time.'

'Caught his foot in a rabbit's burrow has he?'

'I believe it is now seven thirty, madam. Would you like me to summon the guests?'

'Yes please.' As she acquiesced Laurie shrank slightly from the butler's empurpled countenance and dragon's breath.

Gaunt lifted the soft hammer and swung it back with great élan, no doubt the better to make a strong connection. Unfortunately so enthusiastic was the movement that the whole of his body followed through, describing two complete circles before he succeeded in whacking the gong with great force and accuracy.

Shivers of concentric sound floated up to the gold and blue and scarlet bosses on the ceiling of the great hall, spreading along the corridors and landings, past the cloth-eared ancestors in their heavy frames and into the consciousness of the Madingley punters. Laurie gripped her brother's hand.

'Oh Simon,' she whispered. 'I'm in a terrible funk. Tell me something to cheer me up.'

'Let's see . . .' Simon tucked her arm through his and started to stroll towards the terrace. 'There is one interesting item that's just struck me.'

'What's that?'

'Now that Hugh isn't coming we shall be thirteen.'

As they stepped outside a peacock called out. A fierce harsh scream. The weekend had begun.

3

The evening was soft and warm, the coming sunset hinting at a sky of rosy gold. Birds were still up and about and a rich sweet ululation lay joyfully upon the ear. Simon, who was flourishing a silver cocktail shaker with great panache whilst admiring the stone urns foaming with white and red and lemon flowers placed all along the terrace, thought everything looked quite splendid.

Laurie thought so too. Disappointment and ill temper disappeared as she watched the distant haze of fine silver spray spouting from the dragon, twisting and twining his huge bronze coils, in the centre of the lake. Trees cast long dark shadows. The waters of the moat slapped against the stone parapet and grasshoppers rattled their dry legs. Laurie entertained the notion that Apollo might be present. That he had come, drawn by the calm formality of the landscape and the attendant welcoming stillness of the trees, to take his place amongst them all.

He had always been her favourite deity; so bright, serene and loving. Aged ten, she had argued forcefully with her classics mistress that as well as being in charge of healing, prophecy and music he was also the god of gardening. The fact that this designation had nowhere been noted in the annals of mythology bothered her young mind not a jot. Now she took a deep sustaining breath and experienced that well-known harbinger of stormy weather, a soothing calm.

Mrs Saville and Rosemary were relaxing in a pair of basket chairs. They had opted for a Gibson and a Sidecar, and Simon, having strained the drinks over ice and placed the glasses on a silver tray, handed it to

Gaunt together with a dish of freshly made caraway biscuits and some cream cheese and anchovy twists, and watched him glide off.

'Look at that,' he nudged his sister. 'Smooth as melted butter. You see how unnecessary it was – following up that reference. Wasting money on a long-distance call.'

'I don't agree.' Laurie turned away from the sighing trees. She had called the number on the Hon. Mrs Hatherley's crested paper, discreetly from the landing extension after dressing for dinner, only to find that the lady herself had flown to Biarritz. Her secretary/companion to whom Laurie connected was on the point of following and had a cab at the door as she picked up the receiver. She spoke for a flurried moment only, leaving Laurie with the disturbing information that 'poor dear Vivienne' had migrated south 'to get over the tragedy'.

But when Laurie passed this disturbing snippet of information on to her brother he laughed. 'I expect she broke a nail. You know what these *Tatler* types are like.'

Laurie looked at him now. He appeared very pleased with himself, lifting his Martini glass to toast Rosemary Saville.

Rosemary smiled her acknowledgements, leaned back and felt the flagstones warm through the thin soles of her evening shoes. She uncrossed her shiny, silk-stockinged legs, crossed them the other way and toyed with her jade bangle. She was thinking how easily and with what grace she had taken to the thirties mode. Not like the girl standing so awkwardly behind the drinks trolley. She looked quite hoydenish and wore that lovely frock in the manner of a child dressed up in its mother's clothes.

Rosemary then fell to wondering where Martin was and felt a delightful shiver of anticipation at the thought of all her secret machinations, the shiver tempered slightly with concern that her gallant might be found somewhat wanting when the moment of truth arrived.

For there had been more than a touch of wimpery, it seemed to Rosemary, in the Watteau room. She hoped she was not going to have to provide enough backbone for two. An accomplishment of which her mother had tirelessly boasted during the twenty-five years of her marriage. Rosemary's father, a shadowy figure at the best of times, had faded away entirely in 1977. A movement caught her eye.

Mr Gibbs had put his head around one of the folding terrace doors, gripped his throat with one hand, covered his mouth with the other, gargled, then struggling like mad with his invisible opponent, vanished behind a curtain. Meanwhile his wife had manoeuvred her mother-in-law to a low-backed chair. When the old lady had settled the chair completely disappeared. Her body covered the seat and back and her spreading skirts concealed the legs so that she seemed to be hovering on the air. This phenomenon struck no one present as humorous. She seemed quite at home, which surprised Simon, who was of the belief that Mrs Gibbs Senior's most natural habitat must be under a stone. Or at the bottom of a pond.

Noticing that after a suspicious sniff the caraway biscuits had been waved away, Laurie picked up a bowl of assorted nuts and braced herself to walk through the assembled company and offer this alternative form of sustenance.

Mother's eyes gleamed and her countenance creased into folds of warty anticipation. She dipped hooked fingers in the bowl and scrabbled round. Laurie was reminded of those little cranes in a glass case at the fair which claw up a pile of gimcrack and swing over to the exit chute, dropping the one thing you wanted on the way. As the old lady crammed the nuts into her mouth Fred said to Violet: 'Don't blame me if she cracks a molar.'

'Now let's get you all something to drink.' Simon bent

towards the trolley's bottom shelf where the brown ale lurked shyly behind the Punt e Mes and Oloroso. 'Mrs Gibbs?'

'Violet to you, dear. And I'll have a G and T.'

'Oh,' said Simon, coming up a layer. 'Ice and lemon?'

'Got any limes?'

'I'm afraid not.'

'Lemon it is then. And a Campari and orange for Mother. Only the juice has got to be fresh. Anything else gives her the gripes.'

'And easy on the Campari,' interrupted Fred. 'One nip and she's out the window.'

Simon beckoned the butler who put down his tray of delectables and drifted over. 'Squeeze half a dozen oranges, would you? Make sure the juice is strained.'

'Very good, sir.' Gaunt made his way towards the steps descending to the moat. Laurie hastily redirected him and Simon foolishly asked Fred what his pleasure was.

'Can't tell you that in front of the missus,' said Fred. 'I'd never hear the last of it.' He winked and gave the trolley a brief but penetrating once-over. 'Is that what I think it is?' crouching for a closer look. 'Clock this, Vi – stout.' His wife joined him and said: 'Well I never.'

'It's been a good few years since I tasted that. Remember them steak and oyster puddens in the Cock and Bull? We used to swill 'em down with that stuff.'

'Well you're not having it now. It's too rich for your blood.'

'I could have it diluted,' said Fred hopefully. 'Black Velvet. Got any champagne, Simon?'

'No,' said Simon, who had no intention of wasting his Krug on the likes of Fred.

'I'll have me usual then. Scotch. On the rocks. Talisker if you've got it.'

'Teachers?'

'That it then?' Simon gave a tight little nod. 'I suppose it'll do at a pinch.'

'He's spoiled rotten,' confided Violet. 'Won't hurt him to come down in the world for once.'

Simon picked up a chunky cut-glass tumbler and reached for the tongs. It was becoming obvious that the Gibbs's were not even going to have the decency to run true to form. Typical. He poured a generous measure of whisky, added ice, handed the glass over and made Mrs Gibbs' gin and tonic. Fred then said: 'The tide's going down from where I'm standing, John,' and returned his empty glass. Simon refilled and handed it back with a winning smile, saying: 'I'm afraid we don't have any tankards.'

Fred guffawed. 'That's what I like – a man with a sense of humour. Because without a sense of humour, Simon, where are you?'

'I assume exactly where you were before but without a smile on your face.'

'He's dry isn't he? Isn't he dry, Violet?'

Violet agreed that Simon was very dry. The Gregorys appeared closely followed by Mr Lewis. Two medium sherries and a tomato juice. First names were offered and exchanged all round with the exception of the two matriarchs. An air of gaiety began to prevail. Simon abandoned the trolley to chat and charm his way around the company at large, leaving Laurie standing next to the young man in round spectacles now known to her as Martin. She couldn't help wondering what had brought him to Madingley Grange, for he looked as ill at ease now as he had when first stumbling from the bus. She forgot her own awkwardness in trying to make him feel more at home and offered a cheese and anchovy twist.

'I made them myself.'

'Did you really?' Martin took one. The pastry was like flakes of snow and melted on the tongue; the cheese lingered longer. 'They're absolutely gorgeous.' He felt himself relax a little and was surprised because this glamorous girl, cool as iced water, was the last sort of person he usually felt comfortable with. Then he noticed her hands, very brown with short not quite clean nails. They didn't seem to go with the rest of her at all. She was asking if he was sure he didn't want something stronger in his tomato juice.

'Quite sure,' replied Martin. 'I don't want to go to sleep, you see.'

'Oh.' Laurie re-presented the tray. 'It's a bit early, isn't it? To worry about dozing off.'

'I mean – ' Martin took a twist – 'I don't want to go to sleep at all.'

'Golly. What are you going to do all night, then? Wander round the bedrooms?'

Martin's hand opened and his glass shattered on the stone flags. Tomato juice ran everywhere. 'What . . . what do you mean?'

'Oh I'm so sorry . . . Nothing . . . I was just trying to make a joke. I'm absolutely hopeless at this sort of thing. You know . . . social chit-chat . . .'

Laurie bent to pick up the pieces and, by the time Martin's glass had been tidied away and a new one refilled, some of the roses had returned to his cheeks and Laurie had become enmeshed in a frozen silence. Rigid with embarrassment she added a dash of Worcester sauce to his juice and held out the glass.

And then the most extraordinary thing happened. As Martin took the drink his fingers closed around her own and Laurie felt a warm tingling sensation as if hundreds of tiny needles were playing over her skin. The warmth continued to spread, flowing along her forearm then upwards until the whole arm felt hot, soft and malleable. Martin apologized, disentangled himself and smiled. On receipt of the smile Laurie's stomach looped the loop and flopped vigorously down again. Dazed, she was still trying to assimilate this extraordinary behaviour on the part of an organ that had always been yawningly predictable, when a voice cooed sweetly in her ear: 'If you're not *too* busy perhaps I might have a refill?'

Whilst Laurie made Rosemary a second Sidecar and, Gaunt having cracked the terrace/kitchen/terrace circuit, Mother's Campari and orange, Simon continued to mingle. He had been civil to the Savilles, gracious to the Gregorys and now braced himself for a grapple with Violet, Fred and his scrofulous old boot of a mother. Keenly aware, especially after his gaffe with the nut brown, that his knowledge of working-class life could be balanced easily on the left leg of a house mite, Simon racked his brain for a conversational opening gambit. One thing he did know from the occasional careless exposure to sordid documentaries on the fourth channel was that the majority of Fred's sort seemed to spend the larger part of their lives slumped in front of television sets, cans of lager stapled to their lower lips, a bag of crisps in one hand and an elegant sufficiency of pork scratchings in the other. He bared his teeth at Mother who squinnied malevolently back.

'I expect,' said Simon, 'whilst you're here you'll miss the . . . um . . . goggle box?'

'She never watches,' said Violet.

'Too much King Kongery,' added Mother.

'I beg your pardon?'

'Nature programmes,' obliged Fred. 'She can't abide the nature programmes.'

'Perhaps you have another hobby then, Mrs Gibbs?'

Mother nodded decisively. 'Gambling.'

'Gambling?' Probably bingo, reflected Simon. Or a whist drive at the Darby and Joan. 'What sort of gambling?'

'Poker. Blackjack.'

'Really?' Grudgingly he admitted to being surprised. 'I enjoy poker myself. We must have a game later.'

'I shouldn't, Simon,' cut in Fred. 'She'll murder you.'

Gaunt arrived with the Campari. Mother knocked it back, replaced the glass on the tray, winked and said,

'Encore, Antonio.' The butler, an expression very much like respect flitting across his features, bore the tray away.

'And you yourself, Fred. . . ?' Simon ploughed on, determined that even if his whisky wasn't up to snuff no one was going to fault him on *la politesse*. 'Do you have a favourite – '

'Me? You must be joking. What time do I have for television?'

'He's glued to his computer and telex,' explained Violet. 'Because of the markets, you see.'

'Ah. Then perhaps you. . . ?'

'Not really, dear. It's all I can do to keep an eye on the business. We employ over two hundred and they work all hours.' Violet smiled sympathetically at her host. Poor boy. Doing his best to be sociable but really quite out of his depth. That was the trouble with young people. Spent their lives glued to the telly. No wonder they had no conversation. 'Any scrap of spare time I do have – and it is scrap believe me, Simon – I like to do a bit of embroidery. Ecclesiastical mainly. I'm halfway through a lovely chasuble.'

'Chasuble,' said Simon, treading water. 'Yes.'

'And when I can I go to Mother's seances.'

Oh god, thought Simon. I wish I were in Timbuctoo. You knew where you were in Timbuctoo. All the people down on the ground, all the monkeys up in the trees. 'Seances?' he murmured. 'How interesting.'

'She's the seventh son of a seventh son,' Violet explained further. 'Or would've been if she was a boy.'

'Her grandfather on her mam's side,' chimed in Fred, 'was Trafalgar "Scamp" Gwatkin. And *his* mother was the great Gypsy Ouspenskaia. One hundred per cent pure Romany. Born in the Carpathians. Came over here horse trading. Never looked back.'

Mrs Saville, who had been listening to all this whilst apparently gazing at the horizon, was delighted to have

76

her worst hopes confirmed and gave her daughter a costive but satisfied smile.

'Very exotic,' said Simon faintly.

'People'd cover the length and breadth to have her grandad tell their stars. Very well thought of he was.'

'A better man,' said Mother, 'never wore out a balalaika. Course he was a posh rat.'

'A posh. . . ?'

'Married out. Weakened the gift in his babbies.'

'Don't you believe her,' said Fred. 'She's a wowser with the grounds.'

'I can see we won't be short of after-dinner entertainment. Now if you'll excuse – '

''Ang on.' Mother grabbed at the cream barathea and Simon jerked to a halt. She beckoned and, reluctantly, he lowered his head. She whispered and her breath blew a compelling mixture of Campari, bull's-eyes and masticated nuts into his ear.

'You got a presence, Simon. In the house. Savvy?'

'A present? What sort of present?'

'A spirit presence. Very powerful. Blackcurrants mainly.'

'Thought you said raspberry jam,' said Violet.

'It varies. Fruit though – no doubt about that. You got an ancestor was in greengrocery, Simon?'

'Certainly not. And now I really must . . .' Simon pulled himself away and almost collided with the butler winging his way back with the second Campari.

'There's something on your sleeve, Gaunt. No – underneath.' Gaunt lifted his arm and Simon made a wild grab at the glass and dish of nuts. 'Looks like flour.'

'Most mysterious, sir.' Gaunt produced a handkerchief and flicked disdainfully at the broad white streak before sashaying off. Simon returned to Laurie.

'I wonder what's happened to – ' He broke off, staring. 'What on earth's the matter?'

'I feel funny.'

'Funny peculiar? Or funny ha-ha?'

'Funny queasy.'

'You haven't been on the gin, have you?'

'Of course not.'

'Because I could swear when I set out this lot there were two bottles.'

'Simon, if I had consumed an entire bottle of gin I would not be standing here chatting to you. I'd be flat on my back under the trolley.'

Laurie moved irritatedly away and leaned on the parapet. She gazed down at the water freckled by a million pinpricks of dazzling light, then across the park. The brightness continued. Shrubs appeared, hard and brilliant, their outlines so cleanly drawn they could have been cut from paper. Leaves sparkled like green glass. Flowerbeds were gorged with unnaturally intense colour and the sky hummed with light. None of this seemed alarming. Indeed it appeared to Laurie entirely natural. As if this was the way things truly were and that she had previously been viewing the world through a grey curtain. It occurred to her that she might be slightly drunk. Simon mixed a mean Martini and she had had no time for lunch. That must be it. A mixture of alcohol and inanition. Then she recalled Mrs Tiplady, who was inclined to be otherworldly and have what she called beyond-the-veil experiences, and what Aunt Maude called one of Ivy's turns. Perhaps, thought Laurie, I am having a turn.

Disturbed by a susurration of 'ahh's' she realized the swans had drifted into view. They bobbed indifferently beneath admiring eyes, paddling vivid orange feet. Laurie hoped their appearance would go some way towards consoling Violet for the stubborn behaviour of the peacocks and was pleased when Mrs Gibbs exclaimed with pleasure, asking if that wasn't an absolute picture and it must be nice to know you'd got a mate for life.

Derek, who, magnifying glass in hand, had already disappeared and reappeared several times, now turned up again, his pilgrim's gaze directed at his host. 'What a superb setting for a murder, Hannaford. When are we going to get moving?'

'Hear, hear,' cried Mother. 'Let the dog see the rabbit.'

'Everything will be explained at dinner,' said Simon. 'It will all start to happen then.'

Derek approached the parapet, whickering in excited recognition. 'This is so like the moat where the body of the Comte de Heliot was found.' He leaned over, dislodging a small pot of myrtle which fell into the water. One of the swans hissed at him. 'He had been killed with a single thrust from an exquisitely wrought Malayan kris.'

'Good gracious.' Mrs Saville approached the parapet in her turn and peered with some trepidation over the edge.

'A strange sign was branded on his forehead and his pockets were weighted with stones.'

'Very sensible,' said Simon. 'Otherwise he'd be springing up in no time.'

'The face was hideous to behold. One of his eyes – '

'Derek.' Sheila laid a restraining hand on her husband's arm. 'The nuts are coming round again.'

'As I was about to remark – ' Simon turned once more to his sister – 'before you went into a trance, we seem to be missing Mr Gillette. Could you go and look for him?'

'Can't Bennet go?'

'She's in the kitchen. Dinner's in a sec. Gaunt's collecting the glasses. I'm keeping an eye on the trolley.' He held up the Martini jug. 'Want another stinger?'

'No thanks,' said Laurie. 'I don't think they agree with me.'

Afterward, looking back, Laurie was to see those minutes (parting from Simon, making her way across

79

the hall, ascending the great staircase) as the last truly untroubled time until the whole awful affair was over. Before then, although worried about the well-being of the visitors, the sobriety of the servants and the safety of her aunt's possessions, Laurie had not believed, not really in her heart of hearts, that anything truly dreadful would happen before Sunday tea time. When she returned from her errand to summon Mr Gillette she had changed her mind.

It seemed only fitting that, during her brief absence, the landscape had become once more transformed. Dusk had arrived not with its usual gentle grace but with what she now saw as an appropriately sinister lunge. The heavens, though still luminous, had darkened and the vivid emerald strips of grass were a heavy electric blue. The flowers in the terrace urns, so recently fleshy and exuberant, seemed now papery and bloodless. Trees massed in sombre clumps. As the gong sounded, an echo rumbled over the immense arc of the sky and a splash of rain struck Laurie's arm. People gathered their wraps about them and hurried into the house. Simon pushed the drinks trolley under cover and prepared to follow. Laurie caught his arm.

'*Simon* . . .'

'Not now, love. We're going in to dinner.'

'It's urgent!'

'It'll have to wait. Rosemary?'

Simon offered his arm. Rosemary smiled prettily. She was having some trouble with her scarf and Simon helped her adjust the folds – taking, it seemed to Laurie, far longer over the matter than seemed strictly necessary. As the couple walked past her into the house the rain, fine and grey like smoke, started to fall faster.

4

Arthur Gillette had dropped off. It was a long way from Fishwick and he was worn out. He had had a very pleasant bath, put on his maroon Marshall & Snelgrove satin dressing gown with the quilted lapels, laid down on his chaise longue and gone to sleep.

He dreamed he was in an Anderson shelter during an air raid and making a cake. Bombs thudded and went 'crump' in a muffled manner while he grated swede and weighed out rough brown flour, reconstituted dried egg, and crushed saccharines between metal teaspoons. A haybox the size of a tea chest stood by. All Mr Gillette's dreams, whether waking or sleeping, took place during or just after the thirties.

To his never-ending sorrow he had missed the actual decade, being born to middle-aged parents in 1944, but he re-created it as well as he was able, surrounding himself so thoroughly with items of furniture and artefacts from that time that not a single object in his tiny flat (apart from the electrical plugs), came from any other period. Naturally he had no television and went to his friend Phillip's house to watch the occasional series with a thirties setting.

Clothes were something else. All his underwear was spot on. At the moment he wore a Ponting's Celanese vest and some boxer shorts made from parachute silk with real linen buttons. But outer garments, culled mainly from jumble sales and Oxfam, could be worn only when the evenings were drawing in. Or during the rare but sadly short occasions when baggy trousers and collarless grandad shirts were the order of the day. If he had been very young it would have been easy. The young could wear anything. However, a middle-aged man with a slightly unusual walk was wise not to draw extra attention to himself. People could be very cruel. For this reason he had a small selection of dull outfits in current styles bought from a mail order catalogue for work at the Electricity Board where they did not encourage cross-dressing. These felt so alien to his skin they might have been doublets and slashed knickers or suits of chain mail.

He remembered vividly the precise moment when he had been shocked into an understanding of his natural place in the general scheme of things. He had always pestered his mother for stories about her childhood and when he was eight his father had what was to be the first of several heart attacks. He needed rest, and Mrs Gillette turned out the spare bedroom so that she could sleep there. A cardboard box in the back of the wardrobe had been full of copies of the *Daily Herald*, old football pools and *Woman's Weekly* magazines. Arthur had opened one of these and become immediately enthralled.

Everything was at once recognizable, almost familiar. The models with their smooth water-waved hair and drooping stockinette dresses. The cookers, elevated on to little mottled legs, even the advertisements. (Beecham's Pills! Worth A Guinea A Box!) Arthur loved the knitting patterns too: everything so thin and spare and neat, not like the great hairy things people wore today. He had been especially enamoured of a multi-coloured fair isle beret and an aunt had knitted it up for him. It used to sit on the side of his head like a confetti pancake and was his pride and joy until one evening some rough boys threw it into a pond.

That same aunt always said he was some sort of throwback and last year when there had been an evening of regression at the Corn Exchange Phillip had urged him to go, but it had not been a success. When he had 'come to' the regressors had opined that, from his meanderings, it seemed pretty clear that he had been one of that great army following Hannibal across the Alps, probably in some menial capacity. Maybe howdah maintenance.

Now, still in his dream, Arthur started to burrow into the haybox to make a hollow for the cake. But, no sooner had he put it in, than the all-clear went. A strange clanging noise instead of the usual wail. Then there were doors opening, the murmur of conversation, doors closing. He sat up, wide awake. There were sounds directly beneath his open window. Ice cubes chinked, a woman laughed and the chatter started up again. He was late at the watering hole!

Quickly Mr Gillette sprang up and got into his evening suit (the Fifty Shilling Tailor). He was a bit worried about the ribbed petersham lapels which in some lights had a faintly greenish tinge, but his panne velvet waistcoat, real silk socks and *thé-dansant* patent leather shoes looked splendid. He smoothed his hair with Bay Rum, tweezed a couple of stray whiskers from his nose and gave his mop-like moustache a quick groom. Then he pinned the long silk ribbon on his monocle to his lapel and gripped it in his left eye. The monocle was made of plain glass and was a new acquisition bought especially for the weekend with the idea of injecting a musical comedy note. Keeping it in place wasn't as easy as he'd imagined and could only be accomplished by pushing the cheekbone up really hard. This closed the lid and distorted the face, giving the effect of a mild stroke. Perhaps he should have practised more.

He hesitated about his ukelele, long stemmed, the paleish vellum brown in the centre with much strumming. Should he take it down? Surely that wouldn't look too pushy? A country house party was after all the ideal venue for his medley of songs with string accompaniment. And he couldn't help noticing that one of the other guests also had a music case. Perhaps they could get together? Gilly saw himself casually producing the uke as coffee was being cleared away.

'And now Ladies and Gentlemen, for your pleasure a little ditty entitled "She was only a colonel's daughter but she knew what Reggy meant".' Yes – it should definitely go down.

Almost ready, Gilly produced a foulard handkerchief, sprinkled it with a few drops of 4711 and tucked it into his sleeve. Then, casually humming, 'You're the cream in my coffee' he opened the top drawer of his dressing table and took out a gun.

In the candlelight the table looked very lovely. Four little posies of jasmine, pansies and stephanotis were ringed with waxy camellia leaves and linked together by prettily knotted silk ribbons. The flames of the apricot candles trembled slightly although the eight glass doors, now running with rain, were tightly closed. Everyone, with the exception of Rosemary Saville, had come to rest where their cards indicated. She demurring: 'I can sit next to Mummy any time,' had changed places with Martin.

The first course, a jellied consommé with lemon and tarragon, had been served by Bennet reasonably efficiently although it was perceived by more than one person that she touched the edge of the table in each instance with her right hand before depositing the bowls in their little beds of chipped ice more or less on the place setting with her left. Laurie, sitting in the carver's chair, did not mark Bennet's sleight of hand. She would hardly have noticed if the maid had gone around upturning the bowls on the residents' heads. For Laurie, since her visit to the Reynolds room to check on the wellbeing of Mr Gillette, had been in a positive turmoil of alarmed anticipation. Finding the door unlatched she had knocked softly and receiving no reply pushed it a little. It was then that she had seen the missing guest, reflected in the mirror, slip a gun into the breast pocket of his dinner jacket.

Quickly she withdrew to stand quaking on the landing before pussyfooting away and flying down the stairs. Imagining their next move in the seconds before what she assumed would be her divulgation, Laurie's mind created an assortment of scenarios. Simon would secretly inform the others and they would overwhelm Gilly and disarm him. At dinner Laurie (how innocently she had placed herself next to a gangster) might upset a glass of wine and insist that Gaunt take the Gillette jacket away to be cleaned and pressed.

But about this she then had second thoughts. Might not the ploy backfire? Cornered, Mr Gillette could be dangerous. Laurie saw him using the revolver impossibly, like a machine gun, mowing them all down. Or perhaps he would take a hostage (guess who?) and hold her like a shield, cold metal pressing against her temple, trigger finger jumpily vindictive. But in the event none of these alarming vignettes had been realized. Once back on the terrace she had been compelled to stand hopelessly, silently by, watching Simon make a meal of arranging Rosemary's scarf before leading her away.

Now, handing an untouched bowl of dissolving caramel-coloured jelly back to Bennet, Laurie, in spite of a constant and vigilant determination to look anywhere but at the left-hand side of Mr Gillette's dinner jacket, found her eyes being slowly dragged to that very spot. There it was. That ominous outline. That threatening bulge. She was amazed that no one else around the table had noticed it. To add to her concern he had brought down a music case now resting discreetly by the side of his chair. Laurie thought they would all be lucky if it did not contain a sawn-off shotgun.

'Did you know, Laurel, that the first helicopter was

invented in the thirties?' She pulled her gaze upwards and met those boiled gooseberry eyes. How thick and white his skin was; how pale and drained of colour his hair. He looked as if he had just been reclaimed from the sea. She shook her head. 'It really was the most topping time.' Then, after complimenting her on her costume – 'It is real lamé, isn't it?' – he lowered his voice. 'I think Rosemary's is nylon. I mean – what is the point if the fabric's not authentic?'

Laurie glued a smile to her lips then, looking up, connected directly with Simon who appeared very cross. Rightly construing this to be a comment on the fact that, although hostess, since sitting down she had not spoken a single word, Laurie added a look of bright attention to the smile and attempted to tune in to the various threads of chatter.

At her end of the table Derek was dominant, lecturing to an audience, largely engaged elsewhere, on the history of detective fiction. He had just finished assessing *The Murders in the Rue Morgue*. His wife was looking terminally bored. Martin was talking to Mrs Saville with an air of desperate vivacity.

The pheasant was served and with it the Mouton-Rothschild. Gaunt filled the glasses with exquisite precision. The napkin, carried over his arm for the purpose of catching drips, remained spotless. Fred, crying: 'Long life to the baby!' took a swig, swallowed, paused, stared at Simon and replaced his glass with tremendous care on the table.

'Bloody hell, Simon . . . Where the devil did you find this?'

'In the cellar.' Simon's tone implied, where else?

'It's marvellous, man . . .' Fred drank some more. Slowly this time, holding it in his mouth as carefully as a proud retriever with a warm game bird. 'It's . . . it's bloody marvellous.' A further swallow. 'I don't believe this . . . I simply don't believe it. Violet?'

86

'It is nice,' Violet agreed. 'Plenty of body and just enough tar. That's been down there for a good few years.'

'I suppose you realize, Simon, that what we're drinking is worth the price of the whole weekend?' Simon, who hadn't, said yes of course he did. 'Look at them all,' continued Fred. 'Chucking it down like thirsty hosses. Some folk got no idea. You behave yourself.' This last was addressed to Mother whose hooked nose, on receipt of the fumes arising from the complicated bouquet in her glass, had started to wrinkle and twitch alarmingly.

'And you shut your cakehole,' she snapped back. 'There's more in the air than meets the eye. I've niffed this pong before. Something fruity's coming through.'

'I expect the answer is a lemon, Mrs Gibbs.' Simon winked down the table at Sheila Gregory who flashed back a sultry smile.

'Don't mock, Simon,' remonstrated Fred. 'She can see things and pick things up where the rest of us are blind.'

Laurie missed all this. Although nodding at Derek's encyclopedic narrative and being exposed on her right to a positively exuberant amount of detail regarding the first Baby Austin, she still found most of her attention keenly drawn to the back of Martin Lewis's head.

She saw this whenever he spoke to Rosemary Saville, which he was doing quite a lot of the time, and could view it, she had discovered over the last twenty minutes, with only the mildest degree of discomfort. On the other hand when he turned to Rosemary's mother, presenting to Laurie a three-quarter profile, the strange nauseous feeling she had experienced on the terrace returned. Fortunately an inexplicably sharp perception where his intentions were concerned meant she was able to turn aside the moment his eye attempted to catch her own and thus avoid direct conversation. She listened though. At the moment he was addressing Mrs Saville and had just completed a dissertation on the charming habits and demeanour of the Sealyham. Then, pausing barely to draw breath, he was off on a voyage round the Orient.

'Were you aware, Mrs Saville, that in nineteenth-century China there was a concubine Yung-Kei-Fie who pretended to be drunk when she danced before the Emperor? One of her kisses was said to be worth a thousand camels.'

'No I wasn't,' replied his recipient. 'And now I am I can't say – '

'Or that the famous Samurai warrior Husan Fo was rumoured to have sired four hundred sons before he was twenty-one?' He received a look to steal the marrow from a bone but ploughed valiantly on. 'And – you won't believe this – '

'I would believe anything,' cut in Mrs Saville firmly, 'of the Chinese.'

'Oh.'

'As far as I'm concerned, Mr Lewis, East is East and West is West. Any intermingling between the two is quite against the dictates of Nature and much to be deplored.' Having thus disposed of the Yellow Peril Mrs Saville gave Martin a smile like a bunched fist and helped herself to some more carrots. 'Rather an other-ranks vegetable, I usually feel,' she boomed across at Laurie, 'but these are quite delicious. Do I detect a flavour of mint?'

'Mint and a little honey.'

Laurie, finding the suddenly disconsolate lines of Martin's profile quite unbearable, retuned into Derek's didactic which, despite gales of indifference all round, was still going with quite a swing.

'I *can't* believe none of you has heard of Wilkie Collins.' He sounded querulous. 'I mean – *The Moonstone* is where it all began.' He glared around the table. Most of the guests, engaged in murmurous discourse, ignored him. 'Everyone!' Derek pinged the side of his claret glass with his fork. 'I say – everyone?' Laurie expected him to cry: 'Hands up all those who haven't heard of Wilkie Collins.'

Conversation petered out. People gave Derek their undivided attention with the exception of Mother who was still on the consommé, mopping up the last rivulets with a piece of bread. Bennet, waiting with an expression of almost contemptuous resignation behind the old lady's chair, whipped the bowl away the moment her attention was distracted and replaced it with a helping of pheasant.

'If you're not familiar with *The Moonstone* what about *The Woman in White?*'

'Anybody's for a packet of Players,' called down Fred.

'Poe then?'

'You watch your language. We got ladies present.' Fred almost bounced in his seat with pleasure at what looked like the opening to a sparkling bit of crosstalk but Derek declined to play his interlocutor and continued to address the party at large.

'However to a real buff with his nose on the historical trail I think perhaps *Bleak House* is a bit of a pointer? No thank you.' He covered his glass with his hand and Gaunt passed to Laurie who did the same.

'Yes,' went on Derek, 'it doesn't do to discount Dickens.' He leaned forward, placed the tips of his fingers together, narrowed his eyes and hissed, in a sinister undertone: 'I'm Inspector Bucket of the Yard I am.'

There was a crash. The bottle slipped, wine flowed all over Mr Gillette's plate and trousers.

'Oh!' Laurie jumped up. 'Gaunt, how could you be so careless?'

'May hand went all numb, madam.'

'I'm so sorry, Mr Gillette. What can we do? You're soaked,' cried Laurie, thinking: If only it had been his jacket.

'No, no. Just a spot. All tickety-boo, honestly.'

Bennet removed the broken glass and plate, Gaunt mopped up the spillage, brought a clean napkin and replaced the wine glass. Gilly, still insisting that he didn't want to be any trouble and really it was quite all right and no he wouldn't care to remove his trousers and have them sponged and pressed, was in fact deeply distressed. Five years ago, when he had last had the precious suit cleaned the girl had advised him, because of its advanced age, not to risk doing it again. The little flurry of activity subsided and Fred assisted the conversation from its resting place.

'I knew you were incognito, Inspector, the minute I clapped eyes on that hat.'

'It's a character from Dickens! Surely,' continued Derek with increasing exasperation, 'even you have heard of Dickens.'

'Course I have,' replied Fred, all umbraged at this hint that his grasp of Eng. Lit. was not all it might be.

'And what do you think of him?' asked Simon, hoping to soothe Fred's feathers whilst perhaps hoiking the debate to a more rarefied level.

'Well, between you and me, squire,' came the reply, 'I think he's a bit of a Charlie.'

This sally put Fred in such good humour that he guffawed non stop. Violet said he would be the death of her, Simon thought chance would be a fine thing and Bennet removed the vegetable tureens. Derek started droning on about Maud Silver and Miss Marple, and Gilly, after admiring Mrs Saville's necklace and saying he hoped she travelled with a strong-box, asked how she had managed for fresh eggs in the thirties.

'How dare you! I wasn't even born in the thirties.' She glared at him then turned away, swinging her rigidly corseted embonpoint in Martin's direction. 'What a rude man.'

'Oh I think he's more shortsighted than rude,' said

90

Martin gallantly. 'Anyone can see that you couldn't possibly have been born in the thirties. Or even – ' he felt Rosemary's silent encouragement playing havoc with his innate truthfulness – 'in the forties.'

'Quite so,' said Mrs Saville. She gave him a gracious nod and what looked like the beginnings of a smile. A few more remarks like that, thought Martin, and she'll be eating out of my hand. Just to be on the safe side he put it in his lap and covered it with a napkin.

'I wonder,' he continued, not wishing to waste this propitious opening, 'if, after dinner, you would care for a game of whist?' The final word was hardly out of his mouth before a jade silk heel crunched down on to his delicate tarsal bones. He let out a yell of pain. 'I mean,' he gasped, 'bridge.'

'That sounds interesting,' said Mrs Saville. 'We'll try to make up a rubber. That is –' she peered almost kindly into his tear-filled eyes – 'if you have quite recovered from your fit.'

'I thought for a moment,' Derek called across the table, 'that the drama had begun. I mean – that you'd been murdered.'

'No such luck,' called back Rosemary and a rather unpleasant silence ensued, broken only by Mother gnawing on a pheasant's leg. The bone stuck out a little each side of her mouth giving her a slightly cannibalistic air. Bennet returned from the kitchen with a peach and almond torte and Gaunt removed the claret glasses, replacing them with tall, narrow-stemmed tulips. The Château d'Yquem was broached.

'So to continue on a point of similarity,' Derek droned on, 'I suggest we pick up the hobbies motif. It surely cannot have escaped anyone's notice that in times of intense deductive thought what do both Maud Silver and Miss Marple do?' Silence. 'They pick up their knitting!'

Still no one spoke so Laurie said: 'Goodness.' She

hoped the onus of keeping up the initiate's end of the symposium wasn't going to fall entirely upon her shoulders. She had never heard of Maud Silver or the Woman in White let alone Inspector Bucket of the Yard.

'Compare this activity with Holmes' violin. Less creative and intellectual naturally – they are both female after all – '

'Watch it, Derek,' said his wife.

'But if you think that coincidence is interesting,' Derek persisted, apparently blind with optimism, 'then consider this. In nearly every instance both ladies are making garments *for children.*'

Having delivered his coda, Derek sat back and raised a supercilious brow at the others, defying disagreement. There was a brief pause whilst they all took in this latest revelation and wondered how it could most usefully be woven into the fabric of their everyday lives, then Violet spoke.

'Who's Maud Silver?'

'Who's . . . Who's Maud . . .' Derek spluttered and stared, stupefied with astonishment. *'Who's Maud Silver? You know who Miss Marple is, I suppose?'* A general murmur of agreement. 'And Hercule Poirot?' Yes. Solid there as well.

'They're on television, you see,' explained Rosemary.

'But don't you read the books?' cried Derek. 'My God – I thought you'd all be aficionados.'

'We had one of them,' admitted Fred. 'But the wheel came off. Blimey, Simon – ' tasting the wine – 'you've done it again. This one's a bloody miracle. You must have a cellar down there worth thousands.'

'One does one's best.'

'I don't know what any of you are doing here . . .' Derek wrung his hands, so anguished was his disappointment. 'You might as well be at home reading Barbara Cartland.'

A deathly hush followed this intemperate remark and

the atmosphere became distinctly chilly. Mrs Saville, her tones rimed with frost, spoke for them all. 'There is no need, Mr Gregory, to be insulting.'

Sheila raised her empty glass rather pointedly and Laurie looked around for Gaunt, who arrived from the kitchen with a jug of cream. He placed this in an unnaturally poised, almost slow motion manner in the precise centre of the table before filling Mrs Gregory's glass, spilling a drop or two in the process. As people started to eat the flowery scent of the wine mingled with the lush, peachy ripeness of the pudding, producing a rich perfume. The jug went round.

'A lovely sweet, dear,' complimented Violet. 'Something in the cream too, isn't there? A twang of lemon?'

'More subtle than that, surely?' Mrs Saville's lips made pointed sippy movements around the tip of her spoon like a goldfish coming up for air. 'I would have said a suggestion of Kirsch.'

'Really?' Laurie tasted the cream. It certainly lay a little oddly on the tongue. Old Mrs Gibbs took a slurp and said: 'Mother's ruin.' Gilly declined the pudding and asked if there was any cheese.

'A little Double Gloucester, sir?' The butler was already floating across to the armoire when Laurie hissed: 'Wait!' and caught up with him. 'I don't think there's enough.'

'A slayver won't miss, madam.'

'Won't it?' Laurie watched as he lifted the green and gold Edwardian cheese dish. 'Gaunt –' she clutched at his arm, getting flour all over her fingers. 'Couldn't we just cut a little bit off and put it on a plate for him?'

'Oh, madam . . .' He gave Laurie a look of such overwhelming reproach that she hung her head, feeling as if she had been caught with her hand in the poor box. She mumbled 'Sorry' before returning to her seat where her worst fears were immediately realized.

Sheila Gregory cried: 'Oh goody – cheese!' and cut a

piece larger than Mr Gillette's. Mrs Saville showed an interest as did Martin and Violet and Fred. The single remaining square came to rest before Mother. Her talons reached out.

'Now, now,' cautioned Violet. 'You know what happens when you have cheese.' She leaned confidingly close to Simon. 'It jangles her up something terrible. First she gets nightmares, then she starts sort of warbling, then she walks in her sleep.'

'Good grief.'

'What did I say to you?' Mother had popped the cheese into her mouth and was chewing away with relish. 'She won't be told.'

'Three cheers for the gorgonzola,' croaked the old relic.

Violet shook her head sadly, tapped her forehead and said, 'See what I mean? She's very vague.'

Simon, meeting Mrs Gibbs' snapping and determined eye, was not at all happy with this definition. He thought she looked about as vague as a Bofors gun. She gulped down the cheese, emptied her glass and said, very loudly: 'What about our murder then?'

This harsh imperative sent a mild shock around the assembled company. The shock was not unpleasurable and left behind a satisfied feeling that Mother had put her finger on the nub. A murder was indeed the axle on which the wheel of their weekend was scheduled to turn and she was not the only one who felt it high time someone gave the wheel a shove. The steel frames of Derek's spectacles positively scintillated as he cried: 'Hear, hear, madam,' which appellation threw Mrs Gibbs into a state of screeching merriment.

Only Laurie was not caught up in this circle of happy expectancy. Now that the word had been spoken in this dark, suddenly still room with the faces of strangers looking ever more strange in the flickering candlelight it no longer seemed like a fit subject for a charade. Indeed

Laurie now wondered how they could ever have thought that it did. She watched Simon, his eyes deeply enshadowed, his skin golden, rise, giving a faint nod to the butler. Gaunt vanished into a dim corner of the room from where, a moment later, music flowed.

Simon had chosen well. The sinuous chords wound their claustrophobic way around the room, tendrils tightening, choking, like blanket fog. A horn called, high and beckoning. Laurie recalled her previous conviction on the sunlit terrace that Apollo had been present. Now, listening to that high, bright warning cry she struggled to re-establish in her heart those previous feelings of quiet serenity. But it was no good. The golden mask was slipping, imperceptibly. And behind it she could see another mask. Grinning, fiercely ecstatic. Dionysus, at home upon the lupercal. This is it, she thought. This is the beginning. And her heart was filled with dread.

FUN AND GAMES

1

Simon said, 'Murder,' then waited to allow any images engendered by that fearful word to develop, procreate and swarm. 'The most horrifying crime of which a human being is capable. And yet how drawn we all are into the orbit of its terrible fascination. We read of murder, we dream of murder, murder sells more newspapers and guarantees the most savage and prolific of its exponents a permanent place in the black pantheon of crime. And which of us – ' he leaned forward, hands resting lightly on the table edge and gazed at them all in turn – 'which of us has not at some time believed that the world would be a better place minus a certain personality? Or imagined ourselves to be the means of their dispatch? And now, at Madingley Grange, for someone this longing is about to be fulfilled. Because by this time tomorrow one of us will be dead – '

'Oo-er,' said Fred.

' – and one of us will be a murderer. But who will perpetrate the dreadful deed? And by what method will the victim meet his end?'

Simon got up and started to circle the table, stopping first behind Violet. 'Poison perhaps? Where one writhes and screams in unspeakable agony and the antidote is sought in vain . . .'

Derek, enraptured, murmured, *Sparkling Cyanide,* and Violet looked suspiciously at her empty pudding dish. Simon, noticing, added: 'You do well to be concerned. How easy it is to slip something into a drink. Or a plate of food. Perhaps this has already been done? Pheasant is a strong meat, after all. Who would notice the addition of some lethally subtle spice? Or we might

99

consider the cream. More than one person commented on the strangeness of the taste.'

'That's true.' Rosemary's spoon and fork clattered as she dropped them on her plate. 'And I had seconds!'

'Or there's the knife . . .' Swiftly now he moved to Sheila Gregory, pinioned her against the chair and drew the back of his thumbnail very slowly across her throat. She stifled a small cry. Simon smiled and his teeth gleamed wolf-like. 'Quick, efficient. Always a good sharp supply in the kitchen. No special skills needed. Anyone can hack away with a knife.'

'*The Orient Express*,' Derek added his gloss.

'Could it be strangulation?'

'*The Four Fifty from Paddington*.' Derek switched loyalties to British Rail.

'As a method it has the advantage of speed. Three minutes, I believe.' Simon came to rest at his sister's place. 'And of course it's so simple. You just *pounce* – ' his cool fingers tightened round her throat – 'and the murderee should not even have time to scream. Then you gently squeeze . . . and squeeze . . . producing a ringing in the ears and a red mist before the eyes – '

'Stop it!' cried Martin. 'You're hurting her.'

'Just creating a bit of ambience.' Simon lifted his hands. 'You OK?'

Laurie, sucking in a great gulp of candlesmoked air, nodded. Then, as Simon moved on, she experienced again that warm tingle, this time at her feet. It developed into a definite glow spreading up her legs and through her body until she seemed to be wrapped from head to toe in a snug blanket. She took a quick peek at the man who had been so concerned on her behalf but he was addressing a cross-looking Rosemary Saville and she couldn't see his face.

'Or perhaps our murder is the result of a robbery gone wrong.' There was a rattle of china as Bennet, collecting the dessert plates, stumbled and Mrs Saville, at whose ear Simon had pointed this suggestion, clutched her necklace protectively. 'Very easily done. The criminal is discovered, panics, seizes the nearest blunt instrument and wham! Or,' he continued quickly before Derek could identify this latest *mise en scène*, 'there's that great classic weapon of feminine retribution, the neat pearl-handled revolver. Just the right size to fit snugly into an evening bag.' He held Rosemary's glittering purse aloft, squeezing it with a suspicious frown before replacing it on the table.

'Which method – ' Simon was now back in his place – 'will our murderer use? Perhaps it will be none of these. Perhaps, by this time tomorrow, we shall have been presented with that most rare and intriguing phenomenon, a completely original method. Or – even more joyfully – the unsolvable crime.'

Derek sniggered at this and managed to look simultaneously thrilled and complacent, which remarkable accomplishment impressed everyone far more than the lecture on the history of detective fiction.

Simon looked around, more than pleased with the effect of his introduction. Every face (with the exception of his sister's) showed a mixture of alarm, excitement and enthusiasm in varying proportions. Laurie looked simply petrified. As the final chords of keening music died away a sudden disturbance in the air snuffed out the candles. At the same time there was a great crash of thunder then a sheet of razzledazzle lightning. A white flash that briefly transformed the room and table and the motionless figures into a chiaroscuro painting.

The company, stunned momentarily into silence by this apparent willingness on the part of the Almighty to create the appropriate atmosphere for their revels, burst into spontaneous applause. Mother gave a drum roll with her spoon and fork. Simon held his arms wide and took a deep, ironical bow. Gaunt switched on the lights, an air of cheerful normality returned and Derek's

101

remark, that he had felt himself just for a moment in the presence of sheer unadulterated evil, was laughed to scorn. Simon produced, apparently out of thin air, a bowler hat.

'In here – ' holding it aloft – 'are eleven folded pieces of paper. All describe two characters, one male, one female, the most appropriate of which I should like you to assume. Anyone can of course opt out and just carry on being themselves, but I do hope you will all at least make an effort. It will be so much more fun.' Whilst speaking he had sauntered down the table and was now standing behind his sister's chair. He offered her the hat.

'Just one moment!' cried Derek. 'I would like to see those papers thoroughly shuffled.' Simon obligingly shook the hat and stirred the papers thoroughly with his left hand. 'We don't want any jiggery-pokery.'

'I thought,' said Gilly, with an air of being terribly daring, 'that's just what we *do* want. Ha, ha.' Neigh, neigh.

'The person to play the victim – no, don't open it yet, Laurie – will have as well as character details on his paper, a red cross. The murderer a black.' Simon carried on around the table, dropping a square on his own plate as he passed. When Derek, as the last recipient, had been served Simon turned the hat upside down, tapped the crown in a nothing up my sleeve manner, left it on the table and returned to his seat.

'Right,' he said to the rectangle of attentive faces, 'let's see who's who, shall we?'

There was an eager rustle as people hurried to investigate their new personas, followed by a babble of amused and questioning noise. Then came a longish silence which Simon punctured by saying: 'We all expect the murderer to keep his own council but could the victim please identify himself otherwise we shall be minus a cadaver the whole weekend.'

But the silence continued until Sheila Gregory turned

to the man on her right who was busy subjecting Simon's bowler hat to the most intense scrutiny and picked up his white square. 'Oooh, Derek,' she cried, 'it's you! *You're* the victim . . .'

Laurie took one look at Derek Gregory's livid countenance, cleared her throat nervously and beckoned the maid. 'I think, Bennet, we'll take our coffee in the library.'

A comforting fire burned in the library grate. Gaunt had been round with some petits fours, Bennet with the coffee, Gaunt with the liqueurs, Bennet with the coffee again, leading Fred to remark that it were like trying to get a drink down you on the Wall of Death.

Mrs Saville's determination to put plenty of distance between herself and the dreadful tinkers from the North had been rather thwarted by Simon's cosy arrangement of armchairs and chesterfields which were grouped around the splendid Adam fireplace. And her distaste for their company was hardly ameliorated by the discovery that the plump, high-kicking legs of the chorine on Fred's tie glowed in the dark. She was at least able to turn her back on the old lady, who sat in a rocking chair a few feet away imbibing her coffee by the unusual method of mangling the rim of the cup against her withered lips and making loud slurping noises.

Laurie was just wondering if she should close the curtains against the silver rods of rain now hammering against the windows when Gilly got up, crossed to the nearest bookcase against which he had rested his music case and picked the case up.

'What about a spot of after-dinner fun? I'd be happy to give you a song.' Before anyone could reply he turned to Derek. 'Couldn't help noticing a fellow musician on the bus. Shall we make it a duet?'

'My violin,' said Derek coldly, 'is not for show in a concert party. It is the means by which I clarify my mind during periods of the most rigorous intellectual speculation.'

'Sorry. No offence I'm sure.' Gilly had grasped his instrument and was smiling with rather touching nervousness around the room.

'You have a go, lad,' said Fred. 'I like a good tune.'

So Gilly, encouraged, launched into his opening number. Alas – he could not sing. He couldn't play either. The plonks, twangs, pings and yelps were excruciating.

> 'Off to the hoe-down we would drive
> Toe steppin' high and lookin' alive
> All the guys like bees in a hive
> Clusterin' round my baby.
>
> Who do I mean why my little girl
> My little girl, my little girl
> Who do I mean why my little girl,
> The one from I-Da-Ho.
>
> After the hoe-down – '

'I wonder,' interrupted Simon, 'if we'd better not all look at the plan of the house and grounds before it gets too late. Maybe you could continue your song another time?'

Gilly, looking rather crushed, smiled over-brightly and joined the others around the coffee table between the chesterfields on which Simon had placed a long scroll weighted down with *The Rose and the Ring* at one end and *Morte d'Arthur* at the other.

'Our lad was keen on music,' Fred kindly attempted to console the Formby manqué. 'Just like you. He tried for a pop star.'

'Poor Den. He didn't get very far,' added Violet. 'Though heaven knows we spent enough on his band and all the gear.'

Gilly nodded understandingly. 'You have to have the talent.'

'Oh he had the talent – didn't he, Fred?'

'Oh yes. Bags of talent. You couldn't fault him there. He just didn't have the voice.'

Laurie watched them all as she sat uncomfortably on the edge of her chair, her thoughts a tangle of nervous apprehensions. Strand number one related to Mr Gillette (she could not bring herself to think of him as Gilly) who was now standing in front of the fire, trousers steaming, with a glass of crème de menthe. Compelled to admire the professionalism of his goofy, silly-ass disguise and alarmed at dinner to overhear his queries concerning Mrs Saville's strong-box, she had tried to question him about his job and background. He had cunningly circumvented this interrogation by dropping his monocle into the gravy.

It seemed to Laurie, here sneaking a further look, that even now he was casting a very covetous eye over the assembled *bijouterie*. She could just see him creeping about in the small hours, gun in hand, stuffing his pockets with all things precious, his face horribly distorted under a nylon stocking. (Why he should suddenly attempt this camouflage when they were all completely familiar with his features was a question far too rational to be posed in her present state of mind.)

Strand number two concerned Mr Gregory, now sitting in a red leather chair, its back pointedly to the assembled gathering. Laurie felt that Derek had a very real grievance. He had, after all, divvied up a lot of money and come eagerly along to Madingley Grange with his deerstalker, his violin and his little magnifying glass only to come a mucker at the first fence. This must be put right, and Laurie planned to do so by taking his place. She was not nervous about becoming the victim – after all it was only a game – simply about speaking up in front of everyone. She felt a suitable opportunity had not

105

yet presented itself and was bracing herself for the moment when it did.

Then, aside from these paramount concerns, smaller matters darted about, nibbling at the few remaining shreds of her tranquillity. Puzzles more than real worries but persistent nonetheless. For instance why, at dinner, had Rosemary Saville constantly been giving Martin dirty looks? Why was Mother now resting her coffee cup on her cheekbone as if it was an eye bath? And why did Gaunt, bowing ever more deeply each time he presented the petits fours, seem to find it harder and harder to raise himself up again? Laurie, quite feverish with the strain of it all, picked up once more on Simon's dissertation.

'You will see that apart from the double main doors there is one off the kitchen, one off the Gainsborough sitting room and one off the second cloakroom here . . .' He pointed at the map.

My God, thought Laurie as Mr Gillette said: 'Spiffing,' and took his steaming legs over for a closer look. A plan of the house. The successful burglar's first essential. Why not just pack all the stuff up and hand it to him in a bag marked SWAG?

'Have you marked the secret passages and hidey-holes?' Violet asked. 'And trap doors?'

'I'm afraid there aren't any. At least my aunt's never been able to find one. The place isn't as old as it looks.'

'Like my old woman,' said Fred and Violet roared with laughter and shouted she'd see him out any old day of the week, including Bank Holiday Monday.

'You can't help wondering, can you. . . ?' whispered Sheila, round-eyed, 'which one of us it is. I mean – ' her voice had become quite sepulchral – 'the murderer.'

Fred humped his shoulders and extended his arms into a threatening curve, throwing a sinister shadow on the wall. Then he made his horror noise. 'Mmwaaagghh . . .'

Rosemary screamed. Gaunt buckled a bit and lost

control of his tray. Petits fours flew everywhere. Laurie rushed forward to help pick them up and asked if he was all right.

'Quite, madam, thank you. It was just the shock, that's all. Directly behind may back as it were. Perhaps you would be so kind as to open the door?'

After the butler had trembled off Rosemary, now looking more inclined to giggle than to scream, said: 'When are we going to start playing our parts?'

'I suggest,' answered Simon, 'from tomorrow morning. It's getting a bit late now. I've left a large card on the hall table with a brief synopsis of the characters' past relationships and you can all plot and plan from that to your hearts' content.'

'Derek . . .' Sheila aimed her voice at the unyielding back of the wing chair. 'Come and have a look at the plan.' Silence. 'Derek?'

'There's not a lot of point in my coming to "have a look", is there?' came the acid response. 'As I'm the person who's going to be murdered I'm not going to be able to play.'

'Course you can play, dear.' Violet addressed the chair as if speaking to a fractious child.

'I'd have a dekko at the map anyroad,' said Fred. 'You might want to dodge about a bit. I know I would if somebody were after me wi' a chopper.'

'Actually – ' Rosemary leaned across to Sheila – 'if he gets . . . you know . . . done quite soon and we catch the person there'll be time for another before we leave and he can solve that.'

Everyone turned and stared encouragingly at the scarlet wings but they did not respond.

'If there's one thing I cannot abide,' said Mrs Saville, 'it's sulking.'

'I am *not* sulking.' Stung into action, Derek bounded to his feet. 'But I must say – ' he faced them all and glared, especially at his host – 'I think it's absolutely disgraceful that a murder weekend should be set up in such a way that one of the guests misses all the action.'

'I do think Derek has –' Laurie began but was interrupted by Mrs Saville.

'You're only saying that because the choice has fallen on you. If it had been one of us you'd have been delighted to just carry on. And after all,' she continued, 'once the body's been discovered you can join in and hunt the murderer with the rest of us.'

'Oh brilliant!' Derek's scorn was boundless. 'There's real verisimilitude. The corpse springing up and cross-questioning the suspects. Of course the fact that I'd know who the killer was might blunt the edge of the suspense a bit. What a farce!'

'Perhaps whoever it is could wear a mask?' said Mr Gillette and Laurie paled at this revelatory snippet of criminal know-how. Before he could expound further, or perhaps offer a choice from his selection, she crossed to Derek's side and laid a hand upon his arm. His face, darkened and hard done by, turned but the words 'I'd be very happy' had no sooner passed her lips than an alarming distraction occurred.

Sheila sprang to her feet, stretched out a rigid arm towards the window now black with streaming rain, and let out a loud and terrified shriek.

2

'A face . . .' Her shriek became a moan. 'Out there pressed up against the glass. It was . . . horrible . . .'

She staggered and appeared to be on the point of collapse. Derek leapt to her side, motivated, it appeared to several of those present, more by investigative lust than husbandly concern.

Simon rushed over to the window and opened it. The curtains billowed into the room like great sails and the wind and rain beat at his skin. He leaned out, gazed intently into the dark for a long moment then slammed the sash down. 'Nothing there.'

'My wife, Hannaford,' said Derek, crisp as a nut, 'is not a fanciful woman. If she says she saw a face at the window then a face at the window is what she saw.'

Pausing only to hand his trembling spouse over to the nearest comfort station (Rosemary Saville) Derek ran across the library and flung open the window. The curtains billowed into the room like great sails and the wind and rain beat at his skin. He leaned out, gazing intently into the dark. 'I think I saw him . . .' he shouted to the others over his shoulder. Then he slammed the window down. 'Running . . . a dark shape. Around the side of the house.'

'Ohhh . . .' cried Sheila, quivering anew.

'That's nonsense,' Simon argued. 'Why didn't I see him? I looked out first.'

'Elementary, my dear Hannaford. He was on his knees beneath the window waiting till the coast was clear.' Derek, only a moment ago moodily disenchanted, was now transformed. His eyes sparkled, his skin, buffeted by the elements and flushed by the thrilling knowledge that at last things were really on the move, glowed.

'All this talk of murder, I'm afraid,' soothed Simon. 'Isn't this the moment in all those old B movies – guests relaxing after dinner – when someone sees a white staring face pressed up against the glass?'

'I *didn't* imagine it!' Sheila was almost shouting. 'There was someone there. Oh Derek. . .I'm so frightened.'

'There, there.' Derek, torn between standing masterfully by his spouse and striding busily about, compromised by surging on the spot. 'We have an intruder. No doubt about it.'

'How can we have an intruder,' said Mrs Saville, who had remained phlegmatically unimpressed throughout the entire episode, 'when he's outside? Surely intruders intrude. That is their function.'

'We are all present,' said Derek with solemn lack of necessity, 'which leaves . . . the servants?' He crossed to a tapestry bell rope and raised his eyebrows at Simon. 'May I?'

'By all means,' replied Simon. 'But I'm afraid there's no bell on the other end.'

'Would you like me to call them?' Having received a reply in the affirmative Laurie was just about to leave when the door opened showing Gaunt, a silver tray under one arm, hanging on to the handle.

'Is it convenient to clear now, madam?' Laurie nodded and the butler started uncertainly stacking the cups and saucers. Derek, in ostentatious preparation for the coming interview, filled his pipe. Fred intervened when a match was produced.

'I shouldn't strike that while he's about, Sherlock –' nodding at the tottering figure – 'or we'll all go up in smoke.'

As Gaunt picked up Sheila's cup Mother called to him, a harsh croaking imperative, and beckoned him to her side. She seized the cup, rejected the saucer and waved Gaunt away. The butler, getting over by the merest inclination of his head that whilst he realized it took all sorts to make a world he had never expected to find himself actually waiting on any of them, proceeded hesitantly on his way only to find it blocked by Derek Gregory.

'Just a moment if you please.'

'Sir?' Gaunt put down his tray in readiness and drew himself up to his full height. This put rather a strain on his dickey which snapped its moorings and rolled up with a clatter like a tiny blind. When it had been safely re-anchored Derek began to speak.

'Now I'm going to ask you a question.' He thrust his face forward. 'If you answer me truthfully no harm will come to you. There is no need to be afraid.' Gaunt looked as if he wasn't at all sure about that and backed away a bit. 'Were you or were you not looking into this room through that window –' pointing histrionically – 'approximately two minutes ago?'

'Out there?'

'Precisely.'

'Two minutes ago?'

'That is what I wish to know.' Derek unbent a little. 'Take your time before answering. There is no hurry.'

Gaunt mulled it over for a brief spell then said: 'But it's pouring with rain.'

'What about your colleague?'

'She's washing up, sir. In the kitchen.'

'Very well, Gaunt. You may go – for now. But I may wish to interrogate you further. Hold yourself in readiness, please.'

The butler, having picked up his tray and balanced the last piece of crockery on top of an already teetering pile, made his way towards the door. He did not take the most direct route and at first seemed to be travelling in the opposite direction. He progressed by crossing his left

111

foot directly over his right then bringing the right alongside rather in the manner of the sidewinding snake. Coming up against the bookcase he frowned, turned and made the reverse journey in the same oblique manner, this time picking up a fair lick of speed.

Simon, nearest to the door, leapt to open it. The butler shot through and disappeared into the hall. Everyone crowded in the doorway to watch his progress. He zoomed across the black and white tiles, listing more and more to the horizontal until he reached the heavy rose velvet curtain which concealed the passage to the kitchen. Then, just as it seemed impossible that he would nʋt hit the ground entangled in its folds, the curtain was whisked aside and he was gone. The observers waited a moment for the crash which never came, then returned to their seats with a definite sense of anti-climax.

'He's a lad.' Fred wagged his head in admiration. 'Talk about on the sauce.'

'Does that white lapel,' asked Violet, 'mean he's had specialized training?'

'He must be telling the truth though,' said Sheila, 'about not being outside. His clothes and shoes were dry. He wouldn't have had time to change.' Although she had been one of the first excitedly in the doorway, Sheila now reverted to her previous expression of fearful dismay. 'So that means we've definitely got a prowler.'

'I know what it is!' Rosemary clapped her hands in a coy, pattacake gesture. 'Simon's hired someone.'

'What?'

'To lurk. In the shrubbery and . . . and places. To add to the atmosphere. I bet even now the servants are giving him a cup of tea and a plate of scraps in the kitchen.'

She beamed across at Simon, and Laurie watched in growing disbelief as her brother, far from denying his complete lack of involvement in any such domestic arrangement, allowed an expression of small-boy naughtiness to steal across his features. He shrugged disarmingly and held his hands palms upwards, in a show of surrender.

There was a collective and audible release of tensions. Several 'aahs' and 'theres'. Fred said he'd guessed as much and Sheila was almost laughing in relief, although the sound had a slightly ragged edge. Only Derek, his detecting thwarted almost before it had begun, remained frustratedly aloof.

They had all forgotten Mother. Now, alerted by the fierce creak of her chair, Laurie stared at the old lady. She was rocking backwards and forwards, more and more energetically, her little buckled slippers flying higher and higher until the impetus was enough to push her on to her feet. She was still holding the coffee cup she had demanded from Gaunt and now, wheezing slightly from the force of her corybantics, shuffled over to the fire and emptied the dregs into the flames. Then she returned to her seat, cradling the cup in her palms for a moment before squinting into it with what appeared to be malign anticipation.

'What's she doing?' Laurie asked Violet.

'Reading the grounds, dear. We're honoured – it's very rare. She only does it when she thinks there's something in the wind.'

'Really?' Laurie felt more alarmed than honoured. Earlier on the terrace she had listened to the revelations of Mrs Gibbs' Tzigane ancestry with considerable trepidation. The word Romany seemed to Laurie to smack of Ruritanian excess and one of Aunt Maude's glasses had gone already. 'She doesn't . . . hurl the cup about, does she?'

'Oh no,' Violet reassured, comfortably. 'Only if it's bad news.'

Laurie watched the old lady withdraw her attention from the blue and yellow cup and wondered how there could be any news, good or bad, when most of the grounds were securely trapped in three large cafetières back in the kitchen. Mother sucked her breath in with a bubbling hiss. Her haggish features showed no satisfaction, just a stern almost sinister prognosis.

Violet said: 'She's got something,' in a hushed voice.

Mrs Gibbs lifted her arm and pointed, straightening with difficulty an arthritic finger. Everyone followed the line which ended at Sheila Gregory. She gave a gasp, clinging to her husband's arm. Mrs Gibbs drew her lips back, revealing the tusky teeth, and spoke. One word on a long, implacable breath. 'Beware . . .'

'What do you mean?' Trembling, Sheila gazed into her husband's face. 'Darling . . . what does she mean?'

But for once Derek had no answer. He seemed as mesmerized as the rest as he stared into those glittering eyes. The old woman sat, a humped dark shape, as her ancestors must have sat in encampments and caves all over Europe, foretelling the future in the heart of a smoking fire.

'You *must* tell me,' cried Sheila. 'You can't just . . . just point at someone out of the blue and say things like that. Tell me what you mean.'

As she spoke the final sentence Sheila ran over to Mrs Gibbs and made a grab at her hand, but too late. A blue and yellow blur flashed towards the fireplace and the cup splintered into the grate. Sheila stood rooted to the spot, apparently bereft of speech. The old woman indicated that she should draw closer and Sheila, in her beautiful cream velvet gown with the scarlet poppies, knelt down.

'Death . . .' The rasping voice was scarcely audible. 'I speak of death . . . of murder . . .'

Sheila slowly rose to her feet, her face the colour of her dress, and stared blindly round. She swayed and Derek ran across the room towards her.

'Now look here,' he turned on Mrs Gibbs and although he tried to make his voice angry all present

114

noted an undertone of jubilation. The game, his shining countenance declared, was afoot and no mistake. 'I suggest you be more careful – '

'It's me, Derek.' Sheila had started to cry. 'Someone's going to murder me.'

'Not while I'm around.'

'I want to go home. Take me home, Derek – *please*.'

'No one's going to murder anyone,' said Simon calmly, 'except in fun.' He turned and smiled at Sheila. 'I'm sorry, I rather expected, as it's so late, that we would all leave the assumption of our new characters and the start of the drama till the morning, but it seems one of us couldn't wait.' He turned to the old lady. 'An absolutely splendid piece of acting, Mrs Gibbs. If everyone does as well we're in for quite a thrilling time. I assume you did draw Mad Betty stroke Black Tom? Soothsayer and gossip in our fictional melange.'

Everyone looked at Mother who remained silent and expressionless. Then the malignancy that had seemed to hover over her like a heavy cloud of dark insects dispersed. She ignored Simon's question, though. Lance-like the beam of her attention swung away from Sheila and round the room, finally coming to rest in the area that held the drinks table. Then her face, which had been enclosed and secretive, opened out showing a quite ferocious concentration. Her gnarled hands clenched and unclenched on the arms of her chair. The slow release of her breath made a little whistle. Laurie wondered if she was going to have a fit. Then Fred got up and crossed to his mother's side.

'Come on now – '

'*You!*' She turned, distraught, yelling at him. 'You cackhanded ferret! I were on the verge there . . .'

'You'll get on the verge.'

'I think it's time we climbed the wooden hill to Bedford.' Violet helped the old lady to her feet, encountering a fair bit of resistance. 'Get up, Mother.

You've done enough damage for one night. Frightening folk half to death.' On their way to the door she stopped and spoke gently to Sheila. 'You all right now, dear?'

Sheila forced a smile. 'I think so.'

'Don't let her upset you. She gets a bit carried away sometimes.'

'What . . . was it she saw? Over there?'

'Nothing, dear. Nothing at all.'

It was as if the departure of the Gibbses affirmed the evening had come to an end. People left the library and moved across the hall and up the wide staircase, talking more loudly than was strictly necessary and keeping close together. Fred, pausing only to lift the visor on a suit of armour and call, 'Beam me up, Scotty,' led the way. Goodnights echoed back and forth on the landing followed by the very firm closing of doors and the turning of more than one key in the lock.

'Well,' said Simon, popping a maraschino and almond morsel into his mouth and relaxing on the chesterfield, 'we can't complain about lack of ambience.'

'Positively not,' agreed Laurie. 'I think if I'd had one more shred of ambience I'd have run screaming up the wall. And leave those petits fours alone. I didn't make them for you.'

'I must say,' said Simon, after he had finished chewing, 'I never realized how tiring long-term insincerity could be. I shall never envy politicians again.' He stretched and yawned. 'Right. Shall we turn in then?'

'No, Simon, we will not "turn in". We need to talk.'

'What about?'

'First, what did you think you were doing telling people you've employed a paid prowler?'

'I didn't tell them.' Simon sounded quite indignant. 'They assumed.'

'You didn't disabuse them.'

'Look, Laurie.' Simon got up and took his sister's arm.

116

She shook him off. 'Be reasonable. You have to think on your feet in a situation like that. Turn the incident – in this case a silly woman thinking she saw a face at the window – to your advantage.'

'You think she didn't then?'

'Of course she didn't. There was no one out there.'

'But her husband said – '

'Oh come on – you know what he's like. He wants a corpse in every cupboard and a body in all the baths. You're surely not going to take any notice of him.'

Laurie hesitated. 'I suppose not.'

'The punters loved it all. Especially that old grampus saying her sooth.'

'You don't think . . . she really saw something. . . ?'

'Don't you start.'

'Fred said she was psychic.'

'She's no more psychic than this marzipan Brazil. I'm surprised at you giving credence to such codswallop. She certainly adds a certain spookiness to the atmosphere though. In fact it's all going swimmingly. And the food was scrumptious. Thank you.'

'Is that grisly grimace supposed to represent gratitude?'

'It's all you're going to get. Now can we go to bed?'

'I discovered something very alarming before dinner, Simon. I wanted to tell you on the terrace but you wouldn't listen.'

'Shoot, then.'

'Funny you should say that. Mr Gillette's got a gun.'

'What – old tickety-boo?'

'I saw him putting it into his jacket when I went to call him for dinner.'

'I expect it's a prop. Like Derek's magnifying glass. They've probably all brought something. I'll bet it's an absolute Black Museum up there.'

'It was a *real* gun.'

'Well, given that it was – and I'm not saying you're

117

right – people are allowed to own guns, you know. As long as they have a licence.'

'But why on earth would any respectable person bring it to a country house party?'

'Probably going on somewhere.'

'Going on somewhere? *With a gun?* Where, for heaven's sake?'

'How should I know? Poachers' Convention. Godfathers' Get-Together. Conservative Party Dinner Dance.'

'I don't believe this.' Laurie sank into an armchair. 'You're not taking it seriously at all.'

'I am, love – honestly.' Simon perched on the arm of the chesterfield. 'I just don't quite see what you expect me to do.'

'You could tackle him.'

'Oh come on. You know what I'm like on the playing field. I couldn't tackle a rubber duck.'

'I meant talk to him. Find out why he's – ' Laurie almost choked on the word – 'armed.'

'I expect he's a hit man. Got a contract out on one of the guests.'

'Please, Simon . . .'

'All right, all right. Don't get your knickers in a twist. I'll have a discreet word with him tomorrow.' He linked arms, giving Laurie's an affectionate squeeze, and they ascended the stairs in silence, stopping outside the Renoir room.

'D'you think Gaunt really is . . .' Laurie frowned, trying to recall Fred's descriptive gem. 'On the sauce?'

'I wouldn't be surprised. Night, night then. Sleep well. We've got a busy day tomorrow. Dastardly doings all round.'

'That reminds me. I'm going to offer to take Derek's place as the victim.'

Simon shrugged. 'If you like.'

'Well, you're not going to, are you?'

'What – and miss all the fun?'

'Simon – you are responsible for all this.'

'There's no mileage in altruism. Where were the five thousand when the crunch came? And after all those sardine sandwiches too.' Simon kissed her on the cheek and walked briskly away.

3

Most of the house was settling down but in the Vuillard room (*Lunch at Villeneuve-sur-Yonne*) Derek was giving his wife the third degree. Enveloped in a stinking fug of Bulwark he puffed and strode, puffed and strode. His glance was keen and he felt his gait, activated by the unspoken but powerfully potent rubric 'Hurry Watson! There is not a moment to lose' to be definitely Holmesian. And it would have been a hard heart which could have brought itself to point out that a slight flexibility around Derek's knee joints might more reasonably bring the adjective Marxian to mind.

'But what was the face *like*?'

'Derek – if you ask me that once more I shall explode! Go mad! Hit you! I've said over and over again – it was just a white blur pressed up against the glass. As soon as I screamed it vanished.'

'Would you recognize him again?'

'Of course not. I'm not even sure it was a him.'

'I see.' Derek sucked at his cherrywood, loped over to the window and stared at it punishingly. 'That fiend is out there somewhere, Sheila. Roaming the countryside. Terrorizing innocent people.' He looked across at the bed in which his wife sat, supported by a cumulus of frilly pillows. 'What I can't understand is why Hannaford didn't go after him. Bring him down.'

'Because it was just an actor. You heard what he said.'

'He didn't actually say anything. And if he did he was lying. Subterfuge doesn't fool a trained observer.' Derek turned away from his vision of a beleaguered hinterland and picked up his violin.

'Derek – it's past midnight.' A strained squealing ensued.

'I shall go out,' called Derek, his voice vying with Dvořák's *Humoresque*, 'first thing in the morning, and look for clues. The earth will be damp so there are bound to be footprints. Maybe a cigar butt . . .'

'Or even,' suggested Sheila, watching the sharp angle of her husband's elbow as it disappeared and reappeared through a dense cloud of smoke, 'a book of matches from a sleazy club in Limehouse?'

'Exactly!' Oblivious to irony Derek laid aside his instrument, knocked his pipe out on a Meissen shepherdess and started to prepare for bed. Sheila, thinking it unlikely the dramatic end to their evening would leave her an easy prey to Morpheus, unscrewed a dark brown bottle and shook out a sleeping pill.

'What's that?'

'It's a cyanide tablet, Derek. Part of my secret agent's kit.' She swallowed it with some water. 'Special offer from *Cosmo*.'

Derek gave her a stern look as he climbed into his nightshirt. He was opposed to drugs on principle and had still not come to terms with his hero's addiction. 'The capture of a person engaged in espionage is nothing to joke about, Sheila.' He got into bed, picked up the Penguin Conan Doyle and prepared to grapple with *The Red Headed League*. 'Sometimes I think you know nothing about real life at all.'

'Derek . . .'

'Mm?' Derek was annoyed at the interruption, for Jabez Wilson had just started up in his chair. An augury of better things to come.

'It's about tomorrow . . . the murder . . .'

'You already know my feelings – '

'But I've had an idea . . . Derek?' Her husband sucked his teeth with irritation. 'I don't know why you're so cross. You've already read that thing a dozen times.'

'One can never study closely enough the greatest detective that ever lived.'

Sheila could not have asked for a better lead-in. 'I absolutely agree. It's disappointing, isn't it, that the others don't seem to take things seriously.' She had got him.

'It certainly is.' Derek snapped the book to and prepared to re-air his grievance. 'I was so looking forward to a meeting of true minds. I saw us going over famous cases, comparing notes and theories. Instead of which . . .' he trailed off in disgust.

'It's just some sort of joke to them.' Derek nodded, tight-lipped. 'I think – ' Sheila slipped her arm through his – 'they need to be taught a lesson.'

Derek cheered up. 'What do you mean exactly?'

'They don't appreciate your quality, Derek. What sort of man they're up against.'

'That's true.'

'So . . . perhaps we ought to show them?'

'I think I'll give Consuela a ring.'

'You'll do nothing of the sort.' Fred was gargling and gurgling in the bathroom. 'You're on holiday.'

'We've got that party of Japanese businessmen flying in.'

'There'll be a nip in the air tonight then, Violet.'

'I'm not sure she can handle it.'

'If she could handle the Everton team when they lost seven nil on a home day she can handle anything.'

'That's different – I was there.'

'I don't want to hear no more about it. You concentrate on this weekend.' Pause. 'All right?' Longer pause. 'Who d'you think's got the murderer's ticket then?'

'Don't know.' Reluctantly Violet removed her hand from the phone. 'Not me. I was wondering about Gilly. He's that quiet. Hardly says a dicky bird.'

'Sees plenty though.' Fred appeared in the doorway, toothbrush in hand and foaming at the mouth like Father Christmas. 'I was watching him. He don't miss much.'

'He's got a funny – '

'Hang on. Got to catch up with the paper work.' Fred completed his toilet, pulled the chain and returned to the mound of emerald nylon in the four poster.

' – a funny way of talking. Like in an old film.'

'Top-hole!' Fred opened the Chinese ginger jar and started on the few remaining biscuits. 'I say, old girl – these are quate spiffing.'

'You've just cleaned your teeth – '

'It's a front. All that thirties rubbish.'

Violet stopped massaging Dew of Youth into her neck. 'A front for what?'

'He's a professional. Didn't you spot his shooter? That bulge on the left-hand side of his dinner jacket? We got a minder there.'

'A what?'

'You know what a minder is. Like Arthur's Terry.'

'But . . . what's he minding? That stuck-up woman's jewellery?'

'She is stuck up an' all. They don't impress me – folks like that. All swank and no knickers. I could buy her up tomorrow, Mrs Poncy Saville, and never feel the pinch. No . . .' Fred drew confidingly close and gave the four walls a quick shufty. Violet, infected by the apparent need for secrecy, bent her head to his. 'It's my belief he's employed by the family. There's a load of smashing stuff here just asking to be taken for a walk. Now these Hannafords – they got class. They're not going to employ some great hairy tattooed lump walking on all fours and whistling through his teeth – '

'Terry's not like that.'

'Will you listen? So they get a man who can look the part. Put people off their guard. This time he's playing silly buggers in a blazer, next he'll be something else again. He's the real detective here, take it from me.'

Violet looked impressed. 'Perhaps that song was in code?'

'It weren't in bloody tune, that's for sure.'

Violet returned to the Dew of Youth routine. 'Trust your mother to pick up a ghost.'

'I'm not surprised. I got a whiff of something meself. Just before we went out on the terrace.'

'Did you?'

'Something dry and miserable.' Fred took off his slippers. 'She's right about the fruit. I'd have said blackcurrants though, more than raspberries.'

'Perhaps he liked fruit gums. Whoever he was. Anyway – you tell her to keep it to herself. People get upset.'

'You tell her.'

'She's your mother.'

'So you keep saying.'

'And she's to stop breaking the cups. I don't think Laurel liked it.'

'She'll have to lump it then, won't she? With what we're paying they can go out and buy a china shop. Anyway – it weren't no bigger than a mouse's tit.'

'Make sure you tell her when you go in to say goodnight.'

'I've been in to say goodnight.'

'No you haven't. You've not stirred from this room since we came upstairs.' Fred gave a martyred sigh. 'Go on then. It's only across the landing.'

'You're a hard woman, Violet.' Fred put on his slippers, saying, 'And to think when I married you you were a seven-stone bundle of giggly fluff.'

Mother was sitting bolt upright in bed regarding her empty biscuit tin with some chagrin. 'You polished off all that lot?' She looked demure, innocent, outraged. 'On top of that cheese? You'll be skating about in the middle of the night like Charley's Aunt. How d'you feel?'

'Lovely.'

'You'll get lovely,' said Fred automatically. 'And you're to stop chucking the crockery about. Showing us all up.'

'It's the Romany way.'

'Well it ain't the Hannaford way and they don't like it, so pack it in. And keep quiet about roaming Harry. A low profile. You got that?'

Fred brushed his mother's leathery whiskered cheek with his lips and pictured, as he sometimes did at moments like this, an idealized replacement. A sweet old lady smelling of lavender with skin like a crumpled rose petal, kind blue eyes, snowy curls and a gentle smile. He looked down at the snarled hair on the pillow and said: 'Behave yourself. All right?'

Mother raised eyebrows like the whiskers of an elderly prawn, bruised at this undeserved chiding.

'Settle down then.'

Mother settled, pulling in an errant fold of her voluminous nightdress and, in no time at all, was snoring fit to wake the dead.

Mrs Saville stood, high wide and handsome, in duchesse satin, setting the alarm on her travelling clock. In spite of the superb dinner and apparently smooth running of the household she did not trust either of the domestics to appear on the dot of eight thirty with the Earl Grey and ginger nuts to dislodge her from slumber. She replaced the clock on the dressing table and regarded herself complacently in the long glass.

'Did I ever tell you, dear, that your grandfather once remarked on what a splendid figurehead I would make?'

'Several times, Mummy.' He was right too, thought Rosemary, casting her eye over the massive shoulders and victorious profile. The sight of these thrusting towards him through the swell would have caused the stoutest-hearted pirate to leap over the side. If her mother had been around at the time of the *Marie Celeste* there would have been no mystery worth mentioning. She further noticed about her parent a quite unpleasant liveliness. Rosemary stretched her lips wide in a simulated yawn. Usually when you did this the people yawned at yawned back. Mrs Saville's jaw remained stubbornly unoccluded. Just to underline her drift Rosemary said: 'Gosh – I'm tired.'

'Well I'm not. I doubt if I shall sleep a wink.'

'But . . .' In the doorway of her adjoining room Rosemary gaped in dismay. 'You always sleep like a log.'

'The thought of that appalling family next door will be more than enough to keep me awake, thank you. As for that disgusting old woman. You heard what she said on the terrace . . . nothing more than a gypsy.'

'I asked her when we were coming upstairs if she really had got Romany blood and she looked very mysterious and tapped her nose and said, "I got all sorts, dear – in a little cupboard under the stairs."' Rosemary giggled.

'You won't be laughing when you wake up tomorrow to find your inheritance has been stolen in the night.' Mrs Saville took her jewel box from the dressing table, locked it, put it away in a drawer and locked that.

'I'm sure they're not dishonest, Mummy. Just . . . colourful.'

'Nonsense. People of that ilk have no respect for the property of others. And did you see that disgusting thing he had around his neck?' she went on, leaping as nimbly from the theoretical to the concrete as might the Spanish ibex. 'A man who wears a tie that lights up in the dark is a man whose depravity knows no bounds.'

'It didn't actually light – '

'Don't argue, Rosemary.'

Rosemary went to bed and lay listening to her mother holding forth on the iniquitous fluidity of the present English class structure when the maid expected a day off every week as a matter of course and Jack sat down with his master. Soothed by the familiar drone, and quite against her best intentions, Rosemary drifted off to sleep.

Laurie was tired and had looked forward to going to bed yet now the evening was finally over found herself strangely unable to go through even the simplest pre-retirement rituals. Still consumed with anxiety she drifted in a directionless manner in and out of the bathroom and round and round the bedroom furniture, watched by Auguste's ultramarine *Parisian*. Eventually Laurie settled by the window seat. She slipped off her high heels, knelt on the padded tapestry cushions, opened the casement and leaned out.

The rain had stopped and the moon was radiantly bright; the sky calm and spangled with stars. She took slow deep breaths, hoping to bring her heart, still cavorting around in her breast, under some sort of control. From the terrace rose the sweet living fragrance of pinks and madonna lilies mingling with the dense smell of warm earth. Laurie, who had never seen herself as a sentimental person, stared up at the great limitless arc of the heavens and found she was on the verge of tears.

She sat on. Gradually her heart became still and images of Mr Gillette acting out his murderous caprice faded, leaving her, more or less, tranquil. She felt very strange. The evening that had just passed was gradually assuming the quality of a dream. Everything vivid and real, but in an unreal way without anchor or true focus. Had there really been a white staring face pressed up against the glass? Had Mrs Gibbs truly spoken with a savage and terrible clairvoyance while Sheila Gregory screamed back at her in fear? Had a presence been conjured up from beyond the grave?

Picturing the scene now, the participants all standing around in fancy dress, Laurie found herself regarding

them as so many waxworks. So unlike the silent trees and
shrubs and inky waters of the moat, all of which, though
unmoving, seemed to be possessed of a vibrant, guarded
energy. She heard a sound. Two doves, silver in the
moonlight and croodling tenderly to each other,
waddled across the rainwashed flagstones.

Laurie, overcome by an intense wave of emotion,
closed the window and made her way to the bathroom.
She washed her face and was disconcerted to find when
she had finished it still showed traces of rouge and
lipstick. Owning no cleansing cream or lotion she
lathered up more soap and, after two further scrubs and
rinses, all the hateful stuff seemed to have gone. She
determined not to put it on again, thirties or no thirties,
Simon or no Simon.

She cleaned her teeth and was just turning away from
the glass when she was struck by the extraordinary
vivacity of her complexion. She peered closer. Her
cheeks were blooming and her eyes, seeming very wide
apart, sparkled and shone with an almost unnatural
brilliance. Regarding this transformation with some
surprise Laurie became aware that although, as far as
she could recall, it was for her a unique phenomenon,
somewhere in the not too distant past she had observed
another in precisely this rather remarkable condition.
She stood and thought a bit, then suddenly excessively
tired, removed her slinky dress, put on her baggy striped
pyjamas, climbed into bed and fell fast asleep.

The little white square of paper from Simon's bowler
hat which, having no pocket, she had tucked into her
neck halter, fell unnoticed to the floor. Had Laurie
troubled to read it she might have slept less well. For the
paper made it plain that it was she who had been cast as
Mad Betty stroke Black Tom, village gossip and soothsayer. And that Simon's comforting explanation of Mrs
Gibbs' clairvoyance could not have been further from
the mark.

*

All was not well behind the green baize door. Whimperings, thumpings, groans and muffled cries could be heard. Ben, stripped for action, was sluicing his brother's head under a gushing stream of icy water.

'Aaarrgghh . . .' A clogged, choking gasp as Gordon struggled to come up for air. Ben tightened the muscles of his sinewy arms and forced the older man's shoulders further into the water.

'You bastard!' he shouted. 'What did you tell me? Ay? What did you promise?'

'Orrguhhaamoo . . .'

'No. Booze. This. Time.' Ben punctuated the four words by rhythmically clunking the butler's forehead against the basin's edge. Gordon's legs skidded and skated under him. 'You gin-sodden fart-arsed crapulous louse-ridden bug-eared dickhead!'

'Guggle . . . uggle . . .'

Suddenly Ben let his brother go. He watched as the dripping head and shoulders slowly rose from the basin, hesitated a moment, then slumped down, seemingly in despair.

Gordon's nose and mouth were full of water. He spouted, then snorted, then spouted again. There was a bright hard clanging in his head like the merry chatter of a tenor bell, and his eyes stung. He tested his legs and found them wanting.

'Look at you. You're so drunk you can't stand up.'

Gordon pondered this harsh conclusion. It seemed to him, accurate though it might be in some respects (he certainly could not imagine letting go of the basin's edge in anything like the near future), there was buried somewhere in its severe judgemental structure a misapprehension as to the precise disposition of cause and effect. Motivated by a gathering sense of injustice he peered through a fog of alcoholic fumes at the nearly naked figure across the room. And in a flash the truth of the matter came to him.

'I could stanup perfly for you knock me out.'

'Bullshit! If I hadn't caught the tray when you came zipping past that curtain you'd have been through the kitchen out the door and sharpening your teeth on the gravel.'

'You can't shar – '

'Shut up!'

Gordon became silent. He knew his brother in this mood. Best to say nothing. He wrung out his bow tie and drew the edges of his sodden tail coat together in a pathetic attempt to restore the status quo. Then, squaring his shoulders, he let go of his support. Quickly he grabbed it again, waited, let go much more carefully, made his way with slow deliberation to the armchair and fell in it.

'You needn't think you're dossing there.' As he spoke Ben was replacing a pair of wire clippers in a canvas work strip. He rolled it up and tied the tape in a bow. 'I've cut the wires – are you listening plank brain?' Groan. 'I've cut the wires where they run behind that big sideboard – '

'Thought you couldn't see.'

'You sarky – ' Ben launched himself ferociously across the room. Gordon cowered in his chair, hands raised protectively as Ben grabbed his bow tie. 'I followed them all the way round from the phone with my fingers, didn't I? Because where were you? Swilling your way through bottle number three . . .' Gaunt gestured. 'Two? My mistake. Excuse me.' Ben laughed a bitter laugh. 'I'd be better off with a guide dog. At least they don't drink.'

'Ben . . .' Gordon choked out the words. 'I'm . . . sorry . . .'

'You're always sorry. Sorry's your middle name.'

'Pl . . . please . . .' Gordon made feeble passes at his

throat with ice-stiff fingers. His brother let go. 'Make it up to you, Ben . . .'

'You will! No mistake.'

'Next time – '

'It's this time I'm talking about. This time! You saw the stuff that old bag was wearing. There's a pile more upstairs. We're never going to get another chance like this. I knocked her jewel box off the dressing table when I was looking for the bed.' His voice hushed in reverent recall. 'You never saw sparklers like it. And they're *real*. All you've got to do is walk in, pick up the box and walk away. We take the bus and vanish. Simple.'

Gordon let out a deep juddering breath which shook his whole frame and said: 'Hugo.'

'How can I go, you cretinous troglodyte? I can't *see*.'

'. . . going to bed . . .'

'You are not going to bed, big brother. You are going to sit there and pull as much of yourself together as you can lay your hands on while I – ' Ben put on slippers, wig and dressing gown – 'go to the kitchen and make a large pot of black coffee which I shall then get into you by whatever means proves necessary. No holds barred.'

Gordon whimpered then craned his head round, staring over Ben's shoulder in a hunted manner.

'Now what?'

'It's that owl again.'

'It's got more life in it than you, you idle sod.'

'Not idle . . . tired . . .'

'*I'm* tired, Gordon. I am very tired. I have to find enough energy for two. Enough drive and commitment and willpower for two, like I've had to all my life. I've been carrying you since the day I was born. When you took me out in my pram you used to get so pissed I had to get out and find my own way home. You've always held me down, sweating away at your crummy little fiddles. Without you I could really have been somebody.'

Gordon started to cry. 'Where's your vision, man?' Ben's voice softened. 'Where are your dreams?'

'How can I have any dreams? You won't let me go to bed.' Gordon wiped his nose with his sleeve. 'You've always been shellfish.'

'It's you who's selfish.' Ben dropped to his knees beside the morose, waterlogged heap. 'If you won't do it for me how about doing it for Mum? Ay? Imagine getting back to Whipps Cross and tipping that lot out on the kitchen table. Picture her face.'

Gordon's violet countenance broke up only to reassemble into shifting planes of unutterable sorrow. '. . . careworn . . .'

'Yes, she is careworn. Worn out with years of looking after us. And now we've got a chance to pay her back. Don't you think it's time she put her feet up? Took it a bit more easy?'

'Came off the game?'

'If that is her wish, certainly. And think how proud Dad would be.'

Gordon frowned in deep recall then said: 'Dad's inside.'

'He's inside now but he won't always be. Twelve years'll fly by. And he'll come out to a sweet little nest egg.' Ben seized his brother's hand. 'It's all within our grasp here. Just the one job and we'll have the lot. The Mercs, the Rolex Oysters, the real gold chains and handmade boots, rump steak till it comes out of your ears, Vat 29 on your cornflakes, beautiful girls, sunshine – '

'Sunshine?'

'We could be talking Marbella here, Gordon. We could be talking wall to wall fitted currency. You can do anything with money. You can re-invent your life.' Ben gazed urgently at his brother and gripped his hand more tightly, willing the sluggish blood to quicken and the heart to hope. 'You can even re-invent yourself.'

132

This was too much. Gordon, who had been looking quite chipper at the mention of Vat 29, now looked definitely alarmed. He said in a voice thick with lethargy: 'Dunno what to do . . .'

'I'll tell you what you're going to do, dozy guts. You are going to have a cold shower and then you are going to swallow several gallons of strong coffee. After which you will climb those stairs and come back down with that box. You are going to do all these things because if you don't I shall drag you into the shrubbery where no one will hear your screams and beat the living shit out of you.'

Martin got undressed again. He had already undressed once then had a long, slow bath to pass the time and got into his pyjamas. Half an hour later it struck him that to arrive in Rosemary's bedroom, even under the most pressing invitation, wearing only the light cotton garments in question looked a bit brash not to say cocksure. And if (God forbid!) his future mother-in-law woke while he was creeping through Martin felt he would be in grave need of, if not protective clothing, at least something a bit more substantial than a flimsy two-piece. That was when he had donned his light tweed suit.

Half an hour later he had taken it off. For the thought struck him whilst sitting by the radiator, an unread copy of *Home and Country* on his lap, that the most suspicious get-up imaginable to be discovered wearing while roaming the corridors of a manor house in the middle of the night (apart perhaps from a striped jersey and balaclava) was a light tweed suit. They would simply think he was scarpering with the family silver. So he climbed back into the jimjams.

Now he got out of his chair for the umpteenth time, opened his door a crack and peered out. Rosemary's remained firmly closed. His eye measured the distance.

133

It wasn't very far. He could cover it in about ten seconds although, recalling his fiancée's bouncy and promissory energy, Martin felt it might well take him more like ten minutes to make it back. He slipped on his old, shaggy camelhair dressing gown, more for the sake of something to do than because the temperature demanded it, and looked at his watch. Five to two. Very late.

Surely this meant that Rosemary, having not put their signal into effect, was by now fast asleep rather than lying with wildly beating heart longing for amorous dalliance. On the other hand what if she was lying there so entranced by dreams of said dalliance that she had simply forgotten to open the door? How would she feel then as the hours dragged by and she waited, having offered not only her heart but all the accompanying bits and pieces, to someone who did not even have the moxie to cover the few feet of axminster between himself and paradise?

Martin, for he was a kind-hearted soul, would not wish this chastening experience on anyone, least of all the girl he expected to marry. Also (and here an element of self-preservation crept in), Rosemary when thwarted was inclined to be erratic in her reactions. There might be copious tears and a quivering lower lip. On the other hand a swiftly travelling missile had been known to leave that delicate hand on the rare occasion when she failed to get her own way.

Martin took a brave deep breath, tied the cord of his dressing gown very securely around his middle and came to a decision. He would go. If she was asleep he could truthfully say on the morrow that he had at least complied with his side of the arrangements. If awake . . .

Martin was not sure what he would do in that case, for he did not feel even the slightest tweaking of desire. Cross that bridge, he thought, when we come to it. A moment later he was on his way. Below him in the hall the grandfather clock struck two.

4

Martin eased open the door of the Greuze room to be greeted by an indelicate trumpeting. He hoped it emanated from Mrs Saville and not only because this would mean that lady was drowned in slumber deep. After all no man wanted to spend the rest of his life lying next to a girl, however pretty, who sounded in her dreams like the brass section of a symphony orchestra.

The room was almost blacked out. Martin waited a moment, getting accustomed to the gloom and trying to assess the various obstacles humped in his path. What he should have done, he now realized, was to excuse himself after dinner, pop upstairs and give the place the once-over. Too late now. But there was some brightness. The curtains were not quite closed and the moon threw a shaft of cold hard light over part of the dressing table, the bed head and Rosemary's door. This was open.

Of course! That's what she had said. 'I'll leave *my* door ajar.' Although a moment's pause for reflection might have shown Martin that this optimistic insight was based on a rather dodgy premise (i.e.: that he could see through a brick wall) that pause was never made. Instead he started to move on pinched, careful tiptoe, both hands stretched out before him, clutching at the air. He groped around the outline of the dressing table then felt the foot of the bed against his knee. He took a few steps more and fell over a footstool. Flinging himself upright in an attempt to break the fall he overdid it, staggered back and stumbled, one hand resting briefly on the mattress.

He froze. The sudden unexpected obstruction had given him quite a shock. But it was as nothing to the terrible, seismic, earth-rending shock he received a moment later. For Mrs Saville, the slippery satined leviathan, broke cover, hove to on the starboard side and opened her eyes. Appalled, sweat icing his brow and his heart bucking like a maddened bronco, Martin stood rigidly still, knowing it was his only chance. Unmoving he was partly in the dark. Mrs Saville, her head bathed in moonshine, blinked. He thought: She will be irritated by the light. She will get up to close the curtains. He dared not move and dared not look away. His eyes seemed to be locked into hers. She *must* see him standing there. Martin felt his skin crawl and his muscles ache with the effort of enforced stillness while his brain was screaming: '*Run! Run!*'

He thought of all the stories he had read where people died of fear after spending the night in ghost-infested rooms or emerged the morning after with their hair snow white and their mind in tatters. Oh God . . . if you send her back to sleep I'll never . . . Never what? His life was so orderly and law abiding. Where were his peccadilloes? Sometimes he exceeded the speed limit. That would have to do. But hardly had this votive thought been offered than, with a final trumpeting arpeggio, Mrs Saville closed her eyes, turned over, subsided into the pillows and was still.

Martin forced himself to wait one whole never-ending minute before he turned and crept back to the door. It was pointless to enter Rosemary's room. Perfect fear, Martin was chastened to discover, casteth out love. No chance now of kick-starting the libido. He would be thankful just to get back to his own room in one piece.

Down below the great hall was silent but for the sluggish tock, tocking of the grandfather clock. Moonshine struck the tall leaded windows with cold impartiality and streamed over the chequered floor. Banners hung limply, drained of their daytime rallying colours and imperatives, bleached and grey as cerements. At the foot of the staircase stood a heavy suit of armour, the two halves of its visor clamped together in an aggressive swoop like the jaws of a huge, predatory fish.

There was a soft rattle of curtain rings and two figures entered this black and white enclosure. The first rather quickly as if bowled by an impetuous long arm, the second with a threatening lunge. Hissing dialogue ensued . . .

'Get up those bloody stairs.' Shuffle, snivel. 'And stop hanging around my neck. You can stand up if you want to.' A soft little cry, like a timid bird. 'When you're up there . . . *listen to me* . . .' A firm shake. 'When you're up there turn left and it's the first door on your right. The box is on her dressing table. And if you come down without it I shall have your tripes. Got that?'

Ben pushed his brother so firmly on to the first step that he all but flew up the next half dozen before coming to a tentative halt. He half turned and cast a look over his shoulder of such piteous uncertainty that the flintiest observer must have been moved to compassion. Ben made as if to climb after him. Immediately Gaunt sped up to the landing where he rested, arms stretched wide, studying first one hand then the other and attempting to work out which was which. Finally he took a couple of steps to the left, hesitated, then obviously having confidence in neither memory nor judgement, changed his mind and veered rightwards.

Ben, peering as closely into the unknown as his short sight would allow, crossed his fingers then uncrossed them in some alarm. For his ears were as sharp as his eyes were faulty and, somewhere above his head and to the left, he picked up a most peculiar noise.

A soft wobbly coo rather like that of a wood pigeon. It ran up and down the scale, little rills of trembling sound. Then it climbed high to top C and stopped. Gaunt, way off course by now and outside the Gregorys' bedroom, heard it and started to quake. Martin, closing Mrs Saville's door with exquisite care, heard it too. It seemed very close, and in normal circumstances might have caused him some perturbation. Now, so relieved was he to be going back to his room unscathed, he merely noted in passing that some people certainly chose a funny time to practise their scales and turned his attention back to the doorknob. Careful though he was, it jumped through his sweaty fingers at the last, giving a loud click.

Gaunt started, then slowly turned, frightened and guilty. Slowly Martin started to creep back to the Watteau room. And slowly, very slowly, Mother's door opened. Gaunt, alarmed by the warblings and alerted by the click, scanned the seemingly empty stretch of carpet (Martin, having hit a patch of shadow was virtually invisible), and let his tautly held breath out in a sigh of relief. But the relief was vanquished upon the instant. For suddenly, in the insubstantial darkness at the far end of the landing, he saw a figure robed all in white. It had appeared with miraculous suddenness and seemed to float in the air, glowing with a spectral incandescence.

Gaunt, hair stirring on his neck, eyes bulging with terror, teeth chattering like castanets, watched as the thing raised long white arms in the air. He saw hooked claws then heard a soft sibilance, like dry leaves in the wind, and realized that the monstrous apparition was drifting towards him.

Desperately he looked for an escape route. He tried the Gregorys' door. It was locked. And Simon's – ditto. Behind him a stained-glass window and a fifty-foot drop. Between him and the slowly approaching phantom the stairs. Gaunt did not hesitate. But then, taking flight, something even more appalling happened. Fleeing from one nightmare he encountered another doubly harrowing, more mind-bendingly dreadful. For, as he reached the top of the stairs, he collided (oh! horror upon horror!)

with something soft and swollen and hairy which cried out 'Yip!' and seized him round the middle.

Crying out in his turn, perilously balanced on the edge of both stair number one and his sanity, Gaunt, still in the clutch of his ghastly succubus, fell sideways and rolled down the stairs. Bumping and banging he went, each half turn cushioned by the bestower of the unlooked-for furry embrace until at last they reached the chequered floor with Martin on the buttered side. Gaunt, struggling to rise and run away, made a grab at what he thought was the newel post and brought the suit of armour crashing down around his head.

Bennet slipped off, and only just in time. Seconds later the landing light came on and Rosemary, tying the girdle of her dressing gown, appeared. She ran down the stairs and fell on her knees beside the recumbent form in its snug camel wraparound.

'*Martin* . . .' She supported him, slipping an arm around his shoulders and glaring at the butler. 'You!' she cried, jumping to her feet thus allowing Martin's head to reconnect with the tiles which it did with a smart crack, 'What have you been doing to him?'

Gaunt, attempting to extricate himself from vambrace, hauberk and greave, did not reply. Just lumbered resonating to his feet. No sooner had he done so than Rosemary pushed him hard in the pauldron and he clanked down again.

'What the hell's going on?' Simon appeared on the landing closely followed by his guests, all asking more or less the same question. Bennet arrived ostentatiously fastening her dressing gown and dragged the butler roughly into the vertical.

'Blimey O'Riley,' said Fred, watching the raising of the panoplied figure. 'Anybody got a tin opener? Joust a minute – I'll go and look.' He gave Gilly a nudge. 'D'you geddit? Joust a minute?'

139

'Please stay exactly where you are.' Derek was calm and authoritative. 'I'm in charge here.'

Mother appeared wide awake, draped in a tinselly shawl and wearing the hat with the mixed fruit salad. She let out a hungry cry – 'Is that the body?' – as she hobbled down the stairs.

'No it isn't,' snapped Martin's ministering angel.

'First of all I would like – '

'Rosemary – get up!'

'I won't,' retorted the spoilt child. Then, not wishing to activate suspicion in the parental bosom. 'My nursing experience may be useful.'

'You haven't got any nursing experience.'

'There's my Campfire Disasters Guiding Badge.'

'How am I supposed to investigate,' persisted Derek, 'with all this chatter? Now – ' he wheeled on the hapless butler – 'perhaps you would be good enough to explain why you are roaming around the house at – ' he flicked back the cuff of his dressing gown (dog-tooth, floor length, frog fastening) – 'at two fifteen in the morning wearing a suit of armour.'

Gaunt removed a final greave. He looked hunted and gazed around at the ring of faces as if seeking inspiration. His already excitable colouring deepened to the point where his head looked like an inflated aubergine. Bennet stepped forward.

'We thought we heard a burglar, sir.'

Gaunt, stunned by the breathtaking effrontery of this reply, hung about the newel post open mouthed.

'So you slipped on the armour for protection.' Derek nodded sagely. 'Very wise.'

'Surely,' said Simon, 'he just fell down the stairs and crashed into it.'

'I am making the deductions here.'

'Bumpus,' said Mother.

'Please – ' interrupted Laurie, 'can't all this wait? We must do something for poor Mr Lewis.'

140

'That's right.' Rosemary once more sprang to her feet, Laurie's cry of 'Mind his head' quite lost in the general hum of suggestion.

'We must get him back to his room. I'll take one arm,' offered Gilly.

'Be a lot easier if we brought him round first.'

'Yes,' Laurie agreed with Violet. 'Some water might help. Bennet – if you would, please?'

The maid went to the refectory table by the main doors, removed a bunch of peonies, larkspur and lupins from a large copper jug and returned to the circle.

'Thank you – ' Laurie stretched out her hand but Bennet, stepping past her, went up to Martin and poured the contents of the jug over his head.

'*Bennet* . . .' cried Laurie. 'I meant water from the kitchen. For him to drink. In little sips. To bring him round.'

Martin sat up and shook himself. Droplets flew everywhere. 'It's brought him round, 'm.'

Laurie glared crossly at Simon who had started to laugh then transferred her glare to the maid. Crossness became tinged with puzzlement. There seemed to be something odd about Bennet's appearance. What was it? Surely not just the fact that she was out of uniform and wearing a rather nasty peach robe plus hearty 'leather' slippers. (What big feet you have, Bennet.) Or that her hair looked impossibly immaculate for someone who had presumably just got out of bed.

But then all musings along these lines vanished, sent hurrying on their way by something as simple as a sound. But what a sound! The softest, most endearing little tremolo imaginable. Full of pathos, fraily uncomforted yet sweetly musical withal. Martin moaning. Laurie, her heart bursting with concern, fell to her knees, beating Rosemary to it by a whisker. They asked him how he was and Rosemary, very officiously Laurie thought, reintroduced the cradling routine. Derek interrupted them.

'Would you move aside, please? There's an interrogation going on here.'

'Leave him alone,' cried the vestal pair.

'I seen more blood in a plate o' winkles,' grumbled Mother.

'Simon,' said Gilly. 'Look – are you absolutely poz this isn't part of the scenario?' He waved at the supine figure on the floor. 'The murder game I mean.'

Before Simon could reply Mrs Saville snapped at him: 'If that is the case then all I can say, young man, is that you have a very warped sense of humour. Rosemary! Stop rolling about down there and go back to bed.' She stomped off, flinging huffily over her shoulder: 'And perhaps next time I suggest a weekend at the Royal Georgian you'll remember this fiasco and do as you're told.'

Rosemary, who had been tentatively patting Martin's jowls, now seeing time running out, gave them a fairly hefty slap.

'I shouldn't think that will do him much good,' said Laurie tersely.

'You always slap jowls,' replied Rosemary, equally terse. 'It's a known medical fact.'

Martin gazed at his attendants. 'Where am I?'

'There you are, you see. You've given him amnesia.'

'Nonsense.' Derek was brisk and authoritative. 'The loss of memory ploy is a very old trick.' He poked his face close to Martin. 'You'll have to do better than that, Mr Lewis.'

'Who's Mr Lewis?'

'He's well away,' said Fred.

'Is that your character, dear?' asked Violet. 'Someone with amnesia?'

'You'll not get much out of him,' opined Fred. 'Try Wilberforce here.' He approached the stately wreckage still grasping its support. 'What were you doing,' he shouted into the butler's stupefied features, 'wrestling on the floor in the middle of the night?'

'That is precisely what I am attempting to discern,' said Derek, 'if you will allow me to continue – Where do you think you're going?'

Mother, descending hand over hand on the banister, had reached the hall. She moved to the exact centre, turned round and beamed at them all. Then she stretched out her arms and started to move in circles, rhythmically and very slowly: one, two, three. One, two, three. Her white linen skirts spun palely out and the glass berries on her hat shivered. Her head was cocked in an attitude of surprised happiness as if suddenly alerted to the music of the spheres. Fred, aware of the necromantic rationale behind this dervish-like display, groaned.

Derek was furious and disconcerted at a disruption so early in what should have been a controlled and orderly interrogation. He did not know what to do. Holmes' suspects may have drawn a revolver or thrown a punch when his probing became too incisive. They *never* went into their dance. He descended to the bottom stair the better to corral his recalcitrant witness.

'Come along now, Mrs Gibbs,' he cried. 'This won't do. We must consider protocol.'

'Protocol?' Mother halted briefly, held up her hand in a gesture both beatific and benign, said: 'Stick it where the sun don't shine,' and waltzed on.

Red in the face Derek returned to his group. 'Well . . . I'm sure the rest of us understand the gravity of the situation. Now – I shall be interviewing in the library and will require you to come in one at a time.'

'Well I'm not going anywhere one at a time,' said Simon. 'I'm going back to sleep. And I suggest everyone else does the same. And the mystery – if mystery there proves to be – can be sorted out in the morning. Come along, Martin . . .' He bent down and heaved the barely sensible figure to its feet. 'No doubt the precise location of the Watteau room has escaped your memory so I'll give you a hand.'

Laurie stood torn between the longing to help Simon with his burden and the fear that should Martin's arm fall, even without his conscious volition, across her shoulders she would faint dead away. However the need to make a decision was taken quite rudely out of her hands by Rosemary Saville who pushed her aside and took Martin's arm in a manner which appeared to Laurie to be both insinuating and proprietorial.

'Just a minute . . .' spluttered the resident sleuth as his raw material started wandering off, 'I haven't . . . wait . . . if you'll just . . .'

'Derek . . .' Sheila crossed to her husband's side and held out her hand. 'You can't force people to cooperate. Come on – leave it till tomorrow.'

Derek studied the hand as if suspecting it of concealing vital evidence then, his face black with disappointment, grudgingly followed the others. Fred and Violet wrangled briefly then Fred disappeared. Violet sat down on the bottom step.

'Can we retire too, miss?'

Bennet was supporting Gaunt, who was very heavy. Laurie only half heard. She was watching with rapt attention Martin and his carriers as they disappeared along the landing. Her gaze intensified. Became almost beseeching. She chewed her lip, her fingers were screwed into the damp palms of her hands. Then a door closed. Rosemary appeared on the landing returning to her own room and Laurie's pulse and heartbeat returned to something approaching normal.

'Miss?'

'What? Oh yes – of course . . .' said Laurie. 'Do you want a hand?'

'A hand?' Bennet seemed offended, even alarmed. At the very idea her voice became quite gruff with emotion.

Laurie said: 'Goodnight then,' and watched them stagger off. She felt a sudden concern as to Gaunt's ability to cope in the morning. A butler who could not remain upright without solid support at two thirty a.m. was not a butler who was going to be zipping around with the tea and toast at eight.

Ah well, thought Laurie as she toiled upstairs, I can always give a hand. If truth be told she would much rather be doing that than going round with a strained smile making pointless conversation. Then she remembered she was planning to take Derek's place as victim. But a change of role need not alter matters. She could be murdered just as well washing up in her old frock as she could while wearing some showy rigout and playing games on the lawn.

Entering her room she noticed the square of white paper on her bedside rug, picked it up and threw it into the waste paper basket. Feeling quite pleased with herself at this symbolic casting off of whatever simperingly false persona Simon's hat had lumbered her with, Laurie climbed into bed and was just falling asleep when a sudden startling revelation presented itself. She sat up, staring into the darkness. She had recalled what it was about Bennet that had seemed so strange. It was not the awful gown or boatlike slippers. It was the fact that the maid's attractively swelling bosom had completely disappeared.

At last the squat, gyrating figure on the chequered floor came to a halt. Mother stood, cruciform, staring up at the gilded roof. Then she lowered her arms, appearing less gross; her face all-comprehending. She beckoned and Violet, knees cracking, struggled to her feet. Muttering: 'About time,' she joined the old lady and made to help her upstairs. But Mrs Gibbs resisted and shuffled off towards the back of the hall.

She wound her way between the wood and leather Cromwellian chairs and skirted the table holding the now empty copper jug before pausing by a low arched wooden door. She put both hands on this, resting her left profile, tuckered up in vigilant attention, against the centre panel.

'*Listen* . . . down there . . .'

Violet listened. At first she could hear nothing but the sluggish shifting of her heart. Then the faintest sound, hardly more than a vibration on the air. Something clammy, like a cold damp membrane, wrapped itself around her face and neck. The vibration intensified, almost thrumming, then changed character. Became a fluid gurgle, like water going down a plughole, then suddenly stopped.

After a moment's silence there was a starveling cry of great deprivation followed by much weeping. Then, just as suddenly, nothing at all.

'"E's given up,' said Mother. 'Gone orf.'

'I should think he has,' said Violet, grateful and relieved. 'This hour of the morning.' Her hands and feet were frozen.

The two ladies made for the stairs, leaving behind them a moping silence smelling richly of plums and blackcurrants with just a trace of sandalwood.

5

Next morning in the middle of breakfast, to everyone's complete astonishment, Derek announced that he was prepared to be the victim after all. The party (with the exception of Martin and Laurie) was sitting around the dining room table. The posies and smilax had given way to a pretty flowered jug holding sweet peas and gypsophila. On the armoire four silver chafing dishes rested on heated trays. The dishes held kidneys and bacon, scrambled eggs, kedgeree and sausages. There was also cold boiled ham, a wisp of croissants for the lily-livered and iced fruit juice. Everyone had helped themselves to something with the exception of Fred who had helped himself to everything. Now he polished his plate with a bit of bread, swallowed the crust and burped.

'Better out than in, eh Simon?' A cool smile. 'I must say you certainly know the quickest way to a man's heart.'

'Straight through the chest wall, I believe.'

'I said,' repeated Derek, spacing out his words, 'that I have changed my mind about being the victim.'

'How do you want to be done then, Sherlock?' asked Fred.

'Not up to him is it?' asked Mother, unrolling a croissant and tucking a kidney and a scrap of mustard inside. 'Up to Dead-Eye Dick. Whoever he is.'

'Quite so,' agreed Derek. 'But I warn him or her that I do not intend the task to be an easy one. It will be very much a case of first catchee monkey and I shall be extremely alert, I can assure you. Hide and seek's the name of the game. Also I'm setting a time limit of one o'clock. If I'm still alive then I shall regard myself as the victor rather than the vanquished and someone else must become the murderee.'

'You better watch where you're hiding,' cackled Mother, adding a dollop of quince jelly to the croissant and putting the whole contraption in her mouth. 'There's a ghost on the trot.'

'*A ghost . . .*' Derek put down his tea cup. A ghost would make things absolutely perfect. And more than make up for the butler not having a hump. Eyes shining, he urged elaboration.

'It was behind that pointy door,' said Violet. 'In the hall. Where does that lead, Simon?'

'The cellar.' Simon, who had felt briefly concerned for his guests' peace of mind following Mother's startling pronouncement, realized he need not have bothered. Intrigue and excitement were plentifully displayed but not the slightest trace of alarm. 'What did it look like?'

'Can't see through wood,' said Mother, flakes of pastry flying about. 'I'll go down for a shufty when I've finished me croyzant.'

'But,' demurred Sheila, 'you won't be able to see anything during the day, will you? I thought ghosts were nocturnal. Like bats and things.'

'Float up any time,' said Mother. 'As the spirit moves 'em.'

'Do you think – ' Gilly sounded wistful – 'we might see it too?' He blushed as he spoke, his Adam's apple bobbing.

Violet shook her head. 'You might hear it, though. I did last night. It was crying.'

'Alas poor ghost,' murmured Simon, Then, feeling the real objective of the weekend to be rather slipping out of focus, he steered the conversation back to Derek's new idea. 'Actually my sister said last night she wouldn't mind changing places with you.'

'Tell her excellent,' said Derek. 'And that one p.m. is cut-off time.'

'What is your character?' asked Rosemary, daintily forking in some scrambled egg. She was wearing very wide trousers in floaty chiffon printed with pansies, and a pale green silk blouse with a sailor collar. 'I mean – which of us would have a reason for killing you?'

'I am the local bank manager.'

'Loathed by one and all then, I shouldn't wonder,' said Simon. 'Certainly I as Kit Fanshawe, poverty-stricken tumbledown artist in love with your daughter Felicity, would be a front runner.'

'I am Felicity,' cooed Rosemary, eyes shyly on her plate.

'I shall proposition you then in the bushes.' Simon winked across the table.

'P'raps we'd all better say who we are.' Violet reached out for the Georgian coffee pot. 'So we know where we stand.'

Gilly was Herbert Pottle the village solicitor and Violet, Ada Bloggs, cleaning lady at the Vicarage. Sheila was Lorelei la Rue, a West End musical comedy star staying at a local hostelry and in hot pursuit of Kit, Mrs Saville was the rector's wife and Fred (Mrs Saville choked on her Earl Grey) was the rector. Mother would play Miss Featherstone-Gough, eccentric dog lover and hippophile.

'I thought,' said Mrs Saville, when she had quite recovered, 'that you were Mad Betty stroke Black Tom the soothsayer.'

'Well I ain't.'

'But you told us – '

'No I never. 'E did.' Mother looked sharply at Simon. 'Our proper rioter. Young Kit and caboodle there.'

Before Simon had a chance to reply – he was going to say an educated guess – Derek produced a Meerschaum and said: 'I intend to cross-question the butler after breakfast and get to the bottom of our nocturnal drama.' A leather pouch appeared. 'I fear it may prove to be a three-pipe problem.' Then, packing in the tobacco with the calm assumption of permission that so infuriates the unaddicted, 'If no one minds?'

'You go ahead, squire,' allowed Fred. 'What I always say is – where there's smoke there's salmon.'

'Well *I* mind,' said Mrs Saville. 'Most of us are still eating.'

'Ay up, Derek,' said Fred, 'you're on the tapis.' Then, waving a marmalade-coated knife at his fictional spouse, 'You behave yourself, wife, or I'll give you what for in the vestry.'

Mrs Saville rose grandly to her feet. 'The weather at least is proving clement ... I intend to walk in the grounds.' She gave her host a freezing glance. 'I will not be taking part in your childish charade, Simon, and assume you will adjust my payment for the weekend accordingly. Rosemary?'

'I'll catch you up, Mummy.'

'I would like you to come now.'

'In a sec. Just finishing my coffee. It's so delicious.' Rosemary's glance at Simon was positively burning with congratulatory approval. He felt he had not only made the coffee but climbed barefoot up a stony mountain and harvested the beans.

Mrs Saville stuck the waiting out until Violet said: 'Would you rather change with me, dear? And be the cleaning lady?' whereupon she marched off to be seen several minutes later making a hippoesque progress across the greensward.

'Daft lummock,' said Fred. 'No offence, Rosie, but she can't take a joke can she, your mam?'

Rosemary looked as though she didn't know what a lummock was but if she did and had one handy Fred would rue the day. She turned her attention once more to Simon who smiled sympathetically. How attentive and assured he was. So unlike poor Martin, getting everything wrong at dinner last night and then falling down the stairs.

'You'll have to convey my apologies,' Fred persisted. 'I haven't had your fine start in life. You see – ' he assumed an expression of grotesque melancholy – 'I come from a broken home.'

'Fancy.'

'Yes,' continued Fred, his face gathering into jovial creases of anticipation. 'Me dad were terrible at do it yourself.'

Violet yelled that were a new one on her and no mistake then asked Derek what he'd got in his pipe, moose droppings.

'Bulwark actually. Holmes got his from Bradley's in Oxford Street. Not there now of course.' He struck another match to revivify the noxious Meerschaum and dropped the match, still smouldering, on an embroidered place mat. 'All the old places have gone. It's almost impossible to get a really good black shag these days.'

'I think I can help you there, squire,' said Fred *sotto voce*, winking. 'Bombazine Jones.'

'I haven't heard of that. Is it good?'

'Unbelievable, mate.' Fred opened his wallet and passed over a small white card. 'Talk to you later.' He tapped the side of his nose. 'Mum's the word.'

'Perhaps as the victim,' said Gilly, 'it might be rather fun for you to carry this.' He reached into the inside pocket of his orange, red and cream-striped blazer and produced a gun.

Reactions varied. Gasps, hisses, and whistles (Mother). Fred ducked then pretended he'd done it as a joke and Rosemary gave an affected little hiccup and squeaked: 'Is it real?'

'Oh yes. It's a – '

'A Major Fontaine, I think you'll find.' Derek's certainty had a supercilious tinge. He took the gun with a great show of nonchalance. 'Nineteen thirty-six. Short range – about fifteen metres. Metal jacketed bullets.'

'Really? I thought it was a Baby Browning.'

'A common error. I have published a pamphlet on the small arms of this period. You'll find a copy in Brize Norton library.'

'Not published, Derek, printed,' clarified Sheila. 'And please give that gun back. You'll trip over something and set it off. No one's going to murder you. It's only a game.'

'That's right, Sherlock,' said Fred. 'You'll be OK. Just don't step out of the pentagon.'

'I think you can trust me to handle a simple firearm, Sheila,' said her husband, slipping the gun into his jacket pocket.

'Is it loaded?' asked Violet.

'Haven't the foggiest.'

'Come off it, Gil.' Fred was incredulous.

'No, honestly. It's just part of my memorabilia. The last thing I'd want to do is start poking around and opening the bally thing. Anyway as I've had it nearly twenty years, even if it is loaded I should think the mechanism's well and truly seized up by now.'

'That may be the case,' said Derek, 'but it is still preferable where weaponry is concerned that things are handled by someone who really knows what they're about.' He pushed back his chair and stood up. There was a crunching sound and a howl of distress from Gilly.

'My hat!' he cried, holding up the mangled remains of a boater with a striped band. 'That was my father's. He wore it at Henley in 1936.'

'I'm sorry.' Derek sounded more sniffy than sorry. 'If it was of value what on earth was it doing sitting on the floor waiting to be trodden on?'

'I do believe – ' Simon got up to – 'there's something similar in our skip. We hired all sorts of stuff. Let's go and look, shall we?'

'It won't be the same.' A tear-filled voice.

'No, of course not. But that's a great outfit. It does

need some sort of titfer.' Simon bit his lip as he took Gilly's arm. It was hard not to smile at the contrast between the sad eyes and droopy, sad moustache and the aggressively cheerful jacket. As they left, Gilly said: 'I was going to wear it on the punt.'

Derek followed them out, turning at the door and crying dramatically: 'Don't forget *Black Cross* – you have till one o'clock!'

'What I can't fathom,' said Violet to Sheila, 'was how you persuaded him to change his mind.'

That, it seemed, was what everyone wanted to know. Chairs were shoved closer together, elbows rested on the table edge. Only Mother stayed aloof, shaking Worcester Sauce over her cornflakes.

'What makes you think it was me?'

'A woman always knows, dear.'

'Actually you're right.' Sheila seemed hesitant. 'But I'm afraid you're going to find the reason very tame.'

'No, no,' they all cried hopefully.

'All I did was to suggest that, as he had been cast as the victim, rather than grumble and grouse he should regard it as a challenge. Throw down the gauntlet. Pit his wits against the murderer's rather than just tamely collapse at the first tap on the head. Persuasion wasn't difficult. He was upset because none of you took either him or the detective fiction genre seriously.' Fred played on an invisible violin, humming 'Hearts and Flowers'. 'He thought it would be a good thing if you were taught a lesson.'

'But won't that rather defeat the object?' said Rosemary. 'I mean without a body – '

'Of course we're both aware of our obligations to the rest of you,' continued Sheila. 'That's why I agreed that if he hadn't been murdered by lunchtime I'd take his place.'

'The one o'clock deadline,' said Fred. 'If you'll excuse the fox's paw.'

153

'But now Laurel's offered I won't have to.'

'We shall still be minus a body all morning,' said Rosemary. 'I think you're both being rather selfish.'

'I couldn't care less what you think, actually, Rosemary.'

'Now, now.' Violet, creamy and emollient. 'Birds in their little nests agree.'

Rosemary's eyes flashed and Sheila's lips tightened but before the feathers could really start to loosen up a bit something happened to distract them all. Mother started laughing. Short, strangulated barks. She was peering into her tea cup, rolling it between her palms.

'Heh, heh, heh,' she went, just like evil old ladies always have. Then she lifted her arm. Fred grabbed it just in time.

'I *told* you,' he said, wresting the cup from her hand. 'There's a spaniel in the works.'

'You'll get spaniel.'

'If you've finished, Mother,' said Violet, brightly dragging harmony back by the scruff of its neck, 'we could go and have a look at the cellar. You'd like that, wouldn't you?'

Mrs Gibbs did not reply. Cheated of her opening throw her face became hooded and peevish. She turned eyes glittering with anger on Sheila and hunched down in her chair, becoming both smaller and more powerful as if preparing to spring. Sheila stared coldly back.

'I'm not taking any notice of you, Mrs Gibbs. I don't believe in your silly ghost. And I think it was nothing short of wicked doing all that pointing and accusing last night when you weren't Mad Betty the soothsayer at all.' She got up. 'Frightening people half to death.'

Mother mumbled, almost inaudibly, 'I know what I know.'

'You don't know anything,' snapped Sheila. 'You're just a silly old woman.' And she stalked off into the sunshine.

6

Laurie was washing up in the annexe. Gaunt, wounded, sat in a wheelback chair, his leg elevated on to a wooden box. Laurie had offered earlier to telephone for a doctor but the servants had both expressed alarm at this, saying they didn't want to be any trouble and in any case were both alien to the medical profession. Laurie, rather shamedly, had not persisted. She could only have called out Lionel Murchison, Aunt Maude's doctor, knowing no other, and he was an old family friend who would certainly not keep his juicy discovery of the shenanigans at the Grange to himself. Also he might well diagnose some serious injury necessitating the removal of Gaunt in an ambulance, no doubt accompanied by an anxiously attentive sibling. Then the running of the weekend would fall entirely on Laurie's shoulders.

As it was she was having to tackle most of the chores. Admittedly Simon (after his sister had threatened to take the bus to Oxford and not come back till Sunday evening) had lent a hand preparing breakfast. He had made the coffee and grilled the sausages, glaring resentfully at his hired help the while.

'Quite honestly,' he had grumbled to Laurie, 'given a certain amount of crude scientific equipment and all that lightning we had last night I could have made something more efficient.'

He had been very blunt in the display of his feelings towards *les domestiques*, berating Gaunt soundly for wandering around in the middle of the night. Simon had declined a private view of the leg and had further explained that they would not be getting their full whack of cash for the weekend. Indeed, unless they pulled their socks up, not a penny piece would be changing hands. He concluded by suggesting that if either of them had the gall to ask him for a reference it would be couched in terms of such unforgiving clarity that any prospective employer would as soon engage two carriers of the Black Death. He had then returned to his sausages, stabbing the glossy links savagely before piling them up on a hot plate.

But the mood had not persisted and when Laurie had taken the second batch of croissants and homemade quince jelly into the dining room he had been full of smiles and pouring China tea for Sheila Gregory. Now – Laurie pulled the plug and rinsed soap from her hands – she could see him on the lawn teaching Rosemary the rudiments of croquet. This seemed to involve an awful lot of proximity. He was standing very close behind her, encircling her waist with his arms as they drew back the mallet. But there came no soft thock of wood on wood. Surprisingly, in spite of all that undivided attention, they missed and had to start all over again.

Laurie looked wistful as she dried her hands with a tea towel. Rosemary was so pretty. She was wearing a leghorn hat against the sun tied on with velvet ribbons and her lounging pyjamas rippled and floated as she moved. Her face, shadowed by the wide straw brim, looked pale and interesting.

If only I were taller, thought Laurie, suddenly anguished. Or not so brown, or so sturdy. Or had sleeker hair and elegant brows and no freckles. And nails shaped like perfect almonds and coloured strawberry pink. At least the nails were within her reach. All she had to do was stop gardening. She couldn't understand this sudden aversion to her appearance. She had never been dissatisfied before. Never been satisfied either. Just not given the matter a thought. So why this passionate yearning to be different?

Now Sheila Gregory, also curry combed to perfection,

had appeared on the lawn in a svelte white linen dress almost to her ankles, white turban and tortoiseshell sunglasses. She stood swinging her mallet helplessly and Simon, having finally coaxed Rosemary's ball through a hoop, turned his attention to the newcomer and within seconds they too were wrapt in what appeared to be an enjoyable collusion of ineptitude. Watching Sheila twist her head round laughing, her lips just inches from those of her companion, Laurie wondered what Derek would think should he observe that sensuous embrace. No sooner had the thought entered her mind than the door opened and in he came.

'Ah, there you are!' he cried accusingly. Bennet blinked at him. Gaunt struggled to rise.

'There's no need for that. You may sit. Sit,' repeated Derek and, like an obedient mastiff, the butler once more collapsed.

'Now, I am continuing my investigation into the extraordinary events that took place in the small hours of this morning. I take it I do not need to refresh your memory?'

'Hardly sir. With a broken leg to remaynd me.'

'Quite so.' Derek brushed this piffling detail briskly aside. 'First I need to know exactly why you were on the stairs at all.'

'I thought I'd left a window open.'

'He thought he heard a burglar, sir.'

Laurie was unsurprised at this lack of synchronization. Apart from their briefly united appearance on the anti-medical front the couple seemed to be fretfully living in separate worlds. Gaunt mooning over his injured limb, Bennet performing the modest tasks that faulty vision would allow in a rigidly controlled manner whilst directing a beam of anger, resentment and disapproval at the butler so powerful that, when needing to step between them, Laurie could feel it like a lance.

'An interesting and revealing reply,' quoth Derek.

'You see, Laurel, although they have had ample time to collaborate on a story they have chosen not to do so. This argues, I'm sure, either extreme cunning or complete innocence. I am inclined to favour the latter.'

'Yes,' said Laurie. 'Well . . . if you'll excuse me – '

'You do understand the seriousness of this matter?' Nods from both suspects. 'Good. Now, we'll examine the window explanation first. Gaunt?'

'I checked them all, as I thought, before I retired, sir. I'd quite dropped off when something hit me – '

'You were attacked, man!'

'No, no, sir. Just a thought. I sat up in bed. I said: "Bennet" – '

'Just a moment. You call your sister by her surname?'

'I . . . I do in my sleep, sir.'

'How very singular.' Derek put the tips of his fingers together and started loping about. 'Continue . . .'

'Bennet, I said, I don't think I checked that tall window at the end of the landing.'

There wouldn't have been a lot of point, thought Laurie. The window, an acid yellow and bright blue Burne-Jones affair of daffodils and flowing streams, was purely ornamental. Half irritated at the hold-up – there was a lot to do for lunch – and half amused she excused herself again and went next door to the kitchen to make a start.

'I cannot bear to think,' Gaunt carried on, 'that I have not carried out my duties to the best of my ability – '

'That was the cornerstone of our training at Blades, sir. Always carry – '

'Yes, yes.' Derek waved Bennet into silence. 'Get on with it man.'

'So I put a dressing gown on and went upstairs. I had been worrying unduly. The window was quite secure. But then as I turned to go back something . . . appeared . . .' The butler started to shake and covered his face with his hands.

158

'Go on . . . *go on* . . .' Derek's eyes shone.

'I can't . . . on my mother's eyes, sir . . . If you'd seen it you wouldn't ask.'

'It is your duty,' insisted the panjandrum, pressing meanly on the Achilles tendon.

'Well . . .' Gaunt drew a deep breath. 'It arose out of the floor . . . by the opposite window to mine and started sliding and . . . and slithering towards me. A phantom. It had claws and eyes like red-hot coals and it sort of . . . glowed . . .' Fear dowsed the butler's voice and he could say no more.

This didn't sound at all to Derek like Mrs Gibbs's apparition. 'Does the family have two ghosts, Laurel?' he called through the connecting doorway.

'As far as I know it doesn't have any.' Laurie, having strained the contents of her stock-pot through several folds of clear muslin, was now whisking in some egg whites. She tapped the whisk very aggressively on the side of her pan, hoping Bennet might take the hint and come to give a hand. Laurie felt herself to be in a difficult position. On the one side there was Derek, already with a large and quite justifiable grievance (Laurie, being absent from the breakfast table, was not familiar with his change of heart) at last doing what he had paid two hundred and fifty pounds to do, namely investigate a mystery. On the other in just over two hours' time ten people were expecting to sit down to walnut soup, salmon trout with new potatoes and salad of lettuce and endive, strawberries Romanof and Tuiles a l'Orange. No cheese.

'Of course!' continued Derek, still excitedly on the move, 'this second figure is, I suggest, none other than the previously spotted intruder. In other words *the man I saw running away on the terrace*. Obviously once we were all asleep he effected an entry, disguised himself with some drapery and set about his nefarious intent. That must be the solution.'

'But . . . it glowed, sir . . .'

'Phosphorescent paint, Gaunt. The oldest trick in the book. Ask Henry Baskerville. I've no doubt a thorough search will turn up this sheet or whatever it was hidden in some old trunk or chest.'

'It was a miracle how it vanished.'

'No such thing as miracles, Gaunt. The man was familiar with some secret passage. I know your employer denies the existence of such a thing but I presume there's never been a really intelligent search. An omission I intend to rectify after concluding my examination of the terrace. Now . . . let us get on to Martin Lewis – '

'Bennet!' Laurie's voice sounded cracked and shrill. Bennet left the washing-up room and hurried next door. Here Laurie asked if she would slice the cucumber. Hastily deflecting the maid's movement towards a rack of lethally sharp knives, Laurie gave her a mandoline. And, once the cucumber was done, a plateful of walnuts and a mortar and pestle.

As Bennet started to pound away Laurie noticed the bosom was gracefully back in position. How silly of her to have seen any portentous significance in its absence. Quite obviously the woman was flat chested and herself supplied the curvaceous outlines that Nature had, in some unkind humour, withheld. Nothing so strange about that. In fact – Laurie noted the huge flat feet and spinily sprouting chin – the only surprise was that Bennet felt it worth while rectifying the omission.

Reproving herself for being uncharitable Laurie got out a large wooden tray with iron handles and started to lay it with breakfast for one. She put out brioche and curls of nearly white butter and wild strawberry preserve in a dish like a scallop shell.

Laurie had been watching and listening for Martin for the past hour and a half. His early morning tea was still untouched although Bennet said she had knocked very loudly when leaving it on the landing. Now, making a fresh pot, Laurie found herself feeling resentful on

Martin's behalf. You would have thought, simply on the grounds of common humanity, that someone would have commented on his absence. Or asked how he was. Or offered to go and see. But, as far as Laurie knew, not a smidgen of interest. Even Rosemary, attentive to such a determined degree at the time of the debacle, seemed to have been quite distracted by Simon's glowing and empathetic patronage.

Not that Laurie minded that. She had not at all enjoyed the gnawing ache in her stomach when she had been forced to watch the other girl holding Martin's head in her lap. Or to experience the sharp stab of sympathetic pain each time this same poor head clunked against the hall floor. She listened now to the shrieks of gaiety from the gardens and glared mutinously out at the croquet first eleven. A fat lot they cared. Martin could be dying up there.

The tray was complete. Time to pass it to Bennet, thought Laurie. That would be best. After all if she took it up herself Martin might think it a bit odd. Her being the hostess so to speak. On the other hand . . . He was bound to wake feeling pretty fragile. That was only to be expected. And Bennet could be slightly . . . well . . . brusque. Laurie asked herself if, after a hard night, literally on the tiles, she would like the following morning to open her eyes on to a thin, unsmiling mouth and stern bewhiskered chin. Frankly she would not. She would much prefer a younger, jollier, more friendly sort of face. But, going from the ridiculous to the sublime, what if Martin had been dreaming of an exquisite lovely blonde, perhaps drifting in a cloud of flowery chiffon in that strange ethereal slow-motion way blondes have in dreams and shampoo commercials. What a come-down then to open his eyes and see a small chunky person hovering uneasily between sour Scylla and chic Charybdis and about as ethereal as a baby Charolais. No, far better for Bennet to take the breakfast.

As if to underline the seemliness of this decision the maid turned and said: 'Is that Mr Lewis's tray, 'm? I've finished the walnuts if you'd like me to take it up.'

'No – that's all right, Bennet.' Laurie was amazed as the words sprang out. 'Perhaps you could get on with scrubbing the potatoes. We usually use the sinks next door for vegetables.'

'Very good,'m.'

Crossing the hall, her calf muscles dissolving as she went, Laurie noticed a sun-bright marigold, part of the new flower arrangement in the copper jug. Feeling that the sight of it was bound to give a positive and cheerful start to anyone's day, she pulled it out and laid it tenderly across the rolls.

Martin woke slowly to the most appalling racket. After a fuddled moment or two he turned on the pillow attempting to trace the source, then wished he hadn't. The movement made him acutely conscious of the matter and construction of his head. It felt very large, quite spherical and full of extremely heavy stones. As he turned one way so they followed, first rumbling and banging then piling up in a clattering roar just above his ear. If he was unwise enough to reverse this procedure they all charged in the opposite direction. When he sat up they settled, a boulder dam, behind the eyebrows.

The noise was coming from a gang of birds. A combo on the window sill. A bit shaggy when it came to unity but bags – bags and bags – of volume. A male blackbird was especially shrill. Who would have thought, observed Martin to himself, that a tiny creature could produce such a screaming din?

He shouted: 'Go away.' They stopped for a second and peered brightly in. He waved and shouted again and they flew off, all but the blackbird who sneered and started to peck at the glass with a sound like a pneumatic drill.

Martin cowered beneath the duvet, then, ashamed of

being bested by such a minute adversary, swung his legs over the side of the bed, very wobblily stood up and promptly sat down again. He felt absolutely dreadful. Every single bone, from the fragile matchsticks in his toes to his great hulking fibulas and femurs, ached. His skin was bruised and sore and angrily red in some places as if scorched. His neck and shoulders might have been clamped overnight in a vice. His whole body felt as if it had been efficiently dismembered then inefficiently reassembled. Even his teeth throbbed. Slumped on the side of his bed Martin lowered his head very, very gradually until it rested in the palms of his hands.

Memory, piecemeal, reasserted itself. He recalled creeping along to the Greuze room. The next thing he remembered was being seized by some immensely powerful adversary that had reared up out of the gloom like a Yeti and thrown him down the stairs. After that a vague recollection of being helped back up again. And that was that.

What Martin could not conjure up was any remembrance of Rosemary in the role of devoted nurse. The cool hand on a battered brow, the tender smile, the glass of water lovingly held to a parched lip. Although water had obviously figured in the drama at some point. His hair and pyjama jacket were soaking wet.

A couple of terminals unscrambled. He saw himself standing at Mrs Saville's bedside. She had woken – or appeared to wake – and he had fled. Martin relived that moment and, in spite of the warm sun pouring in through his window, started to shiver. Perhaps this was why there had been no hint of the Florence Nightingales while he lay semi-sensible on the hall floor. Had he not (the flood gates opened) agreed with Rosemary that once her mother was completely dormant he would make his way to the Greuze room so that they could 'be together'? There was little doubt, Martin recognized sadly, that in the Don Juan stakes he was an absolute non starter.

The reel of memory wound on, projecting now the dinner party complete with sound track of sparkling repartee. Another bodge-up, with a purplish mark, like an extravagant splodge of blackberry juice, on his instep to prove it. In fact, taken all round, his attempts to convince the matriarchal head of the Saville clan that he was just the fellow to sire the next generation had been an absolute bust. This time yesterday he and Mrs Saville had never met. Now she knew him to be a young man with a sketchy knowledge of the Sealyham and early Chinese mores who wrestled with well-built men far into the night and had fits. Not what you'd call progress.

Naturally (Martin brightened a smidgen) he would not dream of marrying Rosemary without her mother's blessing. A decision that might mean shattered dreams all around – you couldn't make an omelette and so on . . . On the other hand new dreams could arise and he was sure they would both recover. Given time. And there was certainly plenty to be said against acquiring a mother-in-law built like a hippopotamus.

There was a knock at the door. Martin groaned. Then a rattle of crockery and a little girl came in. She was carrying a huge tray in the centre of which something hideously brassily frenetically orange flared, blasting its violent image on to Martin's retina. He closed his eyes. When he opened them again she had put the tray on the writing desk and was standing, blushing and looking at her sandals. She gave him a quick look, said: 'Ihopeyou'refeelingbetternow,' and stared at her shoes again.

'Yes thank you,' said Martin automatically, as one does. Then, 'No, actually.'

'Some tea might help. Shall I pour it out?'

'Please.' He watched her manipulating the heavy round-bellied pot and declined the offer of sugar. When she brought the cup over to him he realized that although only about a sniff away from five foot she was not a little girl at all but quite a big girl. Fourteen going on fifteen. She had beautiful deep blue eyes and looked vaguely familiar.

'I've brought some aspirin too. I thought you're bound to have a terrible headache. At the very least.'

'I have,' agreed Martin, touching his head and feeling an ominous gathering of the stones, prior to their migration south. 'Ohhh I have . . .'

'And there's some fresh rolls. Could I butter one for you? And homemade jam.'

'Just the aspirin. Thank you.'

'How many?' She unscrewed the bottle and he noticed that her arms were wonderfully brown, glowing and burnished by the sun.

'How many have you got?'

'I think you shouldn't have more than three.' She shook the tablets out and placed them carefully in his hand. He noticed her own was trembling and, when their fingers accidentally touched, she jumped to her feet and retreated to the door. Obviously extremely shy. She was mumbling something about having to go and look at the salmon. So she helped in the kitchen. Perhaps the daughter of that sour-faced maid.

Martin staggered over and locked the door against further interruption then staggered back to bed. He took the aspirin, throwing back his head to get them down. A grave mistake. By the time he had recovered his equilibrium the lads were back, an albatross at the glockenspiel. They launched into 'The Darktown Strutter's Ball'. Martin slid under the bedclothes and let them get on with it.

7

Derek, fingerprinting outfit to hand, was examining the terrace. He peered at the earth border between the flagstones and the wall of the house through his magnifying glass, pushing aside little clusters of heart's-ease the better to search for footprints. What he found, or rather did not find, puzzled him greatly. Was he perhaps searching beneath the wrong window?

He returned to the house and the library. Although the furniture had been rearranged he remembered quite clearly where Sheila had been sitting when she had leapt to her feet crying out in such alarm. Derek followed the direction of her pointing finger. Yes – it was the centre window all right. He crossed over and had a closer look. To clinch matters the carpet was still damp where the rain had poured in.

Back on the terrace he gave the ground a final laser-like scrutiny, breaking off several pinks in the process, before turning his attention to the window sill. This was protected by an overhanging lintel and consequently bone dry if a bit on the crumbly side. Derek shook out his sand-fine aluminium granules and blew at them delicately. A certain amount went up his nose, the rest disappeared into the moss and assorted crevices. Undaunted he gave his glass plenty of play zooming in then drawing dramatically back. It wasn't easy to discern the impression of a human hand but impression there must be for the lack of footprints in the border meant that to press his face to the window the intruder *must* have had his hands upon the sill. More powder was shaken out. Ideally of course one dusted for evidence on a highly polished surface innocent of exposure to the elements. But no detective worth his salt expects to have it easy all the time.

Derek naturally did not entertain for a second the idea that the face that had so distressed his wife belonged to an actor. He believed that Simon had simply fallen in with Rosemary's suggestion to reassure the other guests, and also to accept credit for what would have been, had he really had the wit to think of it, an excellently inventive piece of stage management.

Now, having hunkered down to give the border a final scrutiny just in case, tucked in amongst the crumpled heart's-ease and newly truncated Mrs Sinkins, there should be a button or wisp of hair or Bolivian cigar stub, Derek had to admit defeat. Flowers and earth. That was it.

He got up and ruminated for, in the absence of physical clues, the intelligence must be brought into play. As always when stymied Derek imagined himself in the shoes of the master. What would Holmes do? No sooner had the question been posed than the answer was vouchsafed and in a trice Derek was back in the Vuillard room and strangling the life out of Offenbach's 'Barcarolle'. But clarification did not come easy. 'Pale Hands I Loved' and 'O! Silver Moon' had also given up the ghost before the direction of his next step was disclosed. 'I must,' said Derek aloud, returning the tormented instrument to its case, 'question Martin Lewis.'

He pulled out his half hunter. Eleven thirty. High time all decent folk were up and about. Of course there was nothing, he mused as he crossed the landing, to actually link the face at the window with the fracas on the stairs. Yet connection there must surely be. Two such remarkable occurrences in one evening could not be mere coincidence. He arrived at the door of the Watteau room and knocked firmly.

There was no response. Derek waited a moment then

167

tried the handle. Locked. He rapped again then put his lips to the jamb. 'Lewis?' Even less response. Derek pursed his lips. If people thought they could escape interrogation by cowering behind locked doors they had better think again.

He raised both fists and thundered on the panels. From behind them came a faint cry. But Martin did not appear. Eventually Derek decided to desist – the man was bound to emerge at lunch time – and turned his attention to the landing and the mystery of the butler's 'phantom'.

Derek discounted, as any perceptive investigator was bound to do, the glaring red eyes and hooked claws. When questioned the butler had still been in a highly nervous state and probably anxious to curry sympathy from his employers, perhaps hoping that allowance might then be made for his bizarre nocturnal behaviour. So . . . eliminate what must surely be impossible (a second ghost levitating through the floorboards) and whatever remained, *however improbable*, must be the truth.

Gaunt had been standing in front of the Burne-Jones stained glass and staring down the length of the landing at its companion piece when the apparition had materialized. Now Derek approached the second window and studied it closely. It featured a woman with a large loose knot of gamboge hair, a full jaw and heavy-lidded, rather vacant eyes. Her skin was milky, almost pale blue, and she carried a sheaf of arum lilies. Like most of the Pre-Raphaelite females she looked half asleep.

But Derek had no time to waste on the appreciation of aesthetic nuance. Pausing merely to ascertain that the window was no more and no less than it purported to be, he turned his attention to the walls and floor. Here difficulties immediately became apparent.

The skirting board ran, on one side, the complete length of the landing and on the other side as far as the stairs without any crack or join, making the existence of a secret panel very unlikely. Also between the two doors on Derek's left hand (Mr and Mrs Gibbs and the Savilles) and those on his right (Mrs Gibbs Senior and Laurel) were half moon tables rimmed with gilt filigree holding miniatures and other bibelots. Neither of these, Derek knew, being so quickly on the scene in question, had been at all disturbed. Nevertheless he determined to leave no square inch unexamined and, starting by the window, began to push and peer at the faded terracotta wallpaper.

He moved the tables out and back again but was forced, after ten minutes' scrupulous examination, to concede defeat. There was no secret panel in either of the walls. On to the carpet, squinting through his magnifying glass, pressing the thick pile hoping to discover a furrow, maybe around four feet square, indicating a cunningly concealed trap door. But no such luck.

Derek stood up, rubbing his aching knees and facing, head on, a rather alarming conclusion. Given the impermeability of walls and floor the interloper could only have emerged from one or the other of the Gibbs' bedrooms. And, appreciating that creeping through a room with two sleepers would be twice as hazardous as creeping through a room with one, Derek was inclined to plump for the old lady's.

He was about to effect an entry when Martin's door opened and the suspect himself peered out. With a bay of satisfaction Derek galloped along the landing. The door slammed shut. Thwarted, he sniffed round the keyhole till the sound of running water convinced him he was wasting his time then, not wishing to let the grass grow, pounded back the way he had come and into the Degas room.

The first thing that struck him as he entered was the smell. Or rather smells. There seemed to be several all struggling for supremacy. The most attractive came from a shallow turquoise bowl full of pot pourri. This was underscored by a pungent warm stabley odour which could have been horse liniment, in its turn nuzzling up to the powerful scent of aniseed balls.

Derek inhaled deductively and began to look around. The place must be teeming with clues. And, almost certainly, harboured somewhere the phosphorescent sheet, for chummy would hardly hamper his escape by carrying it with him. In an armchair Derek found a long roll of bright pink linen-like material stuck with bones at regular intervals and flaunting vivid pink laces. He examined it closely, then, unable to see how it was in any way germane to the proceedings, re-rolled it and put it back. On the bedside table was an empty biscuit tin, an up-to-date copy of *Old Moore's Almanac* and *That's The Spirit! Necromancy for Beginners* by Iris Wendover.

The bathroom held a no-nonsense bristle toothbrush with a bone handle, a cake of Dentifrice, a punitive wire hairbrush and a small unlabelled glass jar containing a thick, yellowish substance that could well have been bear grease.

Derek returned to the bedroom, sat down and thought hard. There was a real problem here and no mistake. A two-pipe problem if truth be told, but he was loathe to light up in that confined space fearing that, even if he opened all the windows, revealing traces of Bulwark would still remain, fighting it out with the pot pourri and horse liniment and aniseed balls.

It seemed there were two places where the phantom could have hidden. Behind the floor-length curtains or in the wardrobe. The curtains were a bit on the skimpy side and certainly when drawn would not have concealed a largeish male figure. There was also the chance that the old lady might have decided to re-open them, thus making discovery and subsequent capture (for Derek could not see Mrs Gibbs chirruping nervously and fainting away) fairly certain. No – the wardrobe was the place.

This was a large rosewood affair without legs, nearly seven feet tall. It had double doors decorated with ebony and silver. Derek opened one and stepped inside. More liniment overlaid by mothballs. Lots of clothes suitable for a short squat elderly lady, some of which he had seen already, more rolled-up pink things with day-glo laces and several pairs of knickers the length and circumference of airport windsocks draped over a bar hanger. But of chummy's spoor no sign.

Derek slid the hangers back and forth and tapped hard on the unyielding wood but had to emerge frustrated, still minus his sheet and still without a clue. He checked under the bed and on the bed and searched the tallboy before coming, reluctantly, to the decision that he may have been mistaken in his previous assumption and that it was the Hogarth suite that he should be investigating. He prepared to leave, stopping at the door for a final reconnaissance. And then he saw it. On top of the wardrobe, dead centre. A flat white folded thing.

Trembling with excitement he placed the only chair in the room, a lyre-backed Hepplewhite with cream and lemon satin upholstery, by the side of the wardrobe, put his muddy shoes firmly on the seat and climbed up.

He gripped the rim of the wardrobe with his right hand and stretched out his left arm as far as it would go. Not quite far enough. He went round the other side and repeated the procedure. Same result. Snookered at both ends, Derek gnashed his teeth. He was determined to get hold of the thing and, even as he gave a little jump to lengthen his reach, imagined himself stepping on to the terrace when everyone was gathered for lunch and suddenly, dramatically, flinging his sheet before them with a cry of: 'What price your phantom now?'

He jumped again, a little higher. His fingers brushed the cloth. One more elevation should do it. Derek crouched to get plenty of spring. Then, in mid-air, the thought struck him that what he should have done was to place his chair at the front of the wardrobe where it would have been simplicity itself to reach the sheet (a pristine, unillumined flannelette).

Even as he took aboard this apprehension his fingers grasped the folds of fabric and he dropped back, pulling it all with him, hitting the chair with one foot, his other going through the delicate centre strut of the lyre and snapping it in half. Swathed now in folds of white, Derek staggered and fell backwards, hitting his head hard against the wall. To his alarm, far from providing the support one might reasonably expect it gave way and he felt himself falling. Unable to see he flailed around on his back, pulling at the sheet and kicking away the chair. Finally he unravelled himself, got to his feet and stood staring at what was before him. A couple of feet from the wardrobe, directly beneath a silver and opal wall sconce, a door had swung open.

Eyes bulging, mouth agape, almost choking in excited disbelief, Derek stood looking at it. He dropped his sheet – how trivial its discovery seemed now – and stayed very still for a long moment, holding his breath and glowing with self-esteem. He had done it! *He had found the secret passage*.

A plane climbed into the blue unfurling a stream of sudsy curd. Sheila Gregory and Simon paused in their combined efforts to coax a croquet ball through the nearest hoop and tilted back their heads to watch. The silver plane drifted higher and higher. And further and further away.

How uncomplicated, Simon thought, how orderly and clear everything must seem from that celestial view-point. Now that the weekend was upon him, now that everyone was well and truly here and all the machinations were afoot and there was no turning back, Simon suddenly felt monstrously encumbered and experienced a stab of envy for the unshackled man with his head in the clouds.

'Ohhh . . . I've hit it the wrong way.'

'So you have.' He brought his attention back to Sheila and left his arm around her waist as they walked over the warm velvety grass to retrieve the ball. Rosemary, two shots ahead, gave a little cry of chagrin and came tittuping back to join them.

'You'll never guess what I've done, Simon.'

'So tell us,' said Sheila.

'I gave such a swing with my mallet I've knocked my hoop clean out of the ground.'

'Oh dear,' said Simon.

'You're supposed to be hitting the ball,' said Sheila. 'Not the hoop.'

'You've been playing for nearly half an hour, Mrs Gregory,' responded Rosemary. 'Won't your husband be feeling neglected?'

'I shouldn't think so. He's probably off hunting the prowler. Won't your mother be feeling neglected?'

'I shouldn't think so. She's very independent. And we spend so much time together she welcomes a break from my company.'

'She must do. I would myself.'

'And I'm quite old enough to venture out without her. I was nineteen last month.'

'Only nineteen?' Sheila removed her tortoiseshell sunglasses the better to study the infant phenomenon. 'But surely . . .' She tailed off with the implication that only an excess of good manners halted a more formal declaration of disbelief.

'Perhaps you need stronger glasses, Mrs Gregory? I understand in middle age . . .' Rosemary's laugh tinkled frostily.

'Let's go and sort out the problem, shall we?' Simon strode off, fluttering prettiness and svelte seduction in steamy pursuit. He picked up the hoop and rammed it back into the turf. 'There we are.'

'Ohhh . . .' said Rosemary, rosy-tipped fingers brushing his sleeve. 'I simply *adore* practical men.'

Hardly anyone was present on the terrace for midmorning coffee which was served rather late. As Laurie hurried out with the tray she found only Mrs Saville and Mrs Gibbs sitting bolt upright in the morning sunshine. They were about fifteen feet apart and silence stretched between them, thick as mud and getting thicker. Both ladies had abandoned their brief flirtation with the fashions of a bygone age. Mrs Saville wore a greige linen dress with a tan belt, Mrs Gibbs a hideous yellow-ochre cardigan scrunched up at the neck by a rabbit's-foot brooch, a skirt the colour of spinach with a dippy hem, black net mittens and the hat. Laurie took the old lady some coffee and offered a blue majolica dish of *langues de chats*.

'I understand from my brother, Mrs Gibbs, that you've seen a family ghost.'

'Can't say seen. 'E weren't there arter breakfast,' said the old lady. 'Not a whiff. You can't count on 'em. Come and go like jack rabbits. I'll have another look-see afore me dinner. These'll give me some gyp,' she added, puckering at the biscuits and scooping up all but three.

Mrs Saville accepted one, pointedly holding it aloft like an auctioneer before placing it in her saucer. 'This is so delightful, Laurel.' She waved at the tubs of oleander and bay and waddling doves. 'I quite wish the weekend could last for ever.'

Laurie, who thought it already had, murmured something suitably grateful. One of the peacocks, scenting a patisserie free-fall, approached dragging his magnificent train of bright-eyed feathers.

'Good boy,' instructed Mrs Saville, releasing a vanilla-scented crumb. 'What a charming sight. Is it really the case that their tails are so powerful that they can break a man's leg?'

'Ummm . . . I think that's swans.'

'Oh surely not. Swans have hardly any tail at all. I can see you're not a bird person, Laurel.'

Laurie cheerfully admitted that was indeed the case and she couldn't tell storks from bitterns. Mrs Gibbs then hooked her little fingers in the corners of her mouth, let out a piercing whistle and called for more snake oil. Laurie took over the coffee pot.

'How's that butler, young 'un? Still incognito?'

'He's injured his leg, I'm afraid.'

'Serve him right. Taking to armour at his time of life. You have to work up to that sort of thing. Start with something small. Like a meat safe. Pass it on.'

Laurie smiled. 'I will.'

Mrs Saville closed her ears against this squalid drivel and concentrated on a gold-fringed filament of sky overhead. The doves warbled a roundelay, underscoring the sound of girlish laughter. By craning her head Mrs Saville could see her daughter, strolling with Simon across the grass. His arm rested across Rosemary's shoulder and their heads were close. Mrs Saville sat back again, nodding with satisfaction. She had been quite sure that Rosemary had not loved her latest acquisition madly in spite of all fervent protestations to the contrary. Rosemary had loved several young men 'more than anything else in the entire world, Mummy' over the last three or four years, some more unsuitable than others. None as wildly unsuitable as the last, who seemed, if Rosemary's disjointed burblings were anything to go by, to be some sort of traveller in double glazing. One of those 'cowboys' no doubt who went round knocking on doors persuading the elderly to part with their savings, then disappearing with nary a splinter installed, only to turn up months later on some consumer protection programme running hell for leather down the high street pursued by a fat man with a microphone.

Now Simon – Mrs Saville took another peep only to find that Sheila Gregory had muscled in on the happy couple – Simon was of a different stripe altogether. If not wealthy himself he obviously had extremely satisfactory connections. Of course his attentions to Rosemary might merely be those of an assiduous host but Mrs Saville did not think so. She had seen the signs too often in the past. And if Rosemary liked him the young man would really have very little to say in the matter. Not many things or people that Rosemary itched to get her pretty hands on remained unsubjugated for long.

Yes – Mrs Saville finished nibbling her *langue du chat* – things here were turning out far better than she had expected. There were really only two flies in the ointment of her content. One minor (the irritating presence of the rag and bone contingent), the second of far greater significance. Until now Mrs Saville had found hardly anyone with the time or inclination to play contract bridge. They all seemed preoccupied either with this childish murder or with croquet, and some people were simply doing nothing at all, as if there was no harm in squandering time, that most precious and finite of possessions.

The only person who had shown the slightest interest in the game was young Mr Lewis, and Mrs Saville could not help feeling that his odd nocturnal behaviour, coupled with paroxysms of apparently uncontrollable yelping, made him, as a partner, far from ideal. Yet, if no other devotee of the tables showed their hand, approach him she must. For, as far as cards were concerned, Mrs Saville was an obsessive. A day without play to her was a day so without savour as to be hardly worth the living. She never went anywhere without at least two packs in her possession and, when not actually engaged in the cut and thrust of battle, would sometimes hold one of the pasteboard rectangles talismanically in her hand and experience a tremor of excited anticipation. Nothing of course like the excitement that arose when they were turned surface upwards and the rejuvenating heiroglyphs were revealed.

The one great disappointment of Mrs Saville's life was that Rosemary remained impervious to the thrills and alarms such happenstance could wreak in the human breast. She had even once referred to card games as pointless. True she had been twelve at the time but the wound had been deep and slow to heal. Mrs Saville's thoughts returned to Martin. If enough people could not be found for a rubber he would know other games. Card players always did. The tips of Mrs Saville's fingers tingled at the very thought.

She was feeling especially deprived at the moment for her usual bridge group, a cowed compliant bunch, had failed to meet the previous Thursday due to the fact that Davina Bingley's mother had thoughtlessly died. Miss Bingley, Mrs Saville's regular partner, had rung up timorously with the news at five thirty, 'Far too late,' as Mrs Saville had crisply informed her, 'to find a substitute.' The rest of the group had been glad of a breather, for Mrs Saville was an alarming opponent. Nerveless, forceful and almost invincible. On the rare occasions that she was defeated her rival had hardly drawn a victorious breath before being pounded by waves of silent fury as cards for a return bout were hurled down.

Now she folded her copy of the *Telegraph* (all the posh papers had been delivered in time for breakfast), drained her coffee and prepared to move. Not that she wasn't perfectly comfortable in her present position but she had no intention of being forced into conversation with her companion. Mrs Saville felt she had imbibed enough homely maxims of unlettered wisdom already. But then something happened to put any idea of a move right out of her mind. She heard a sound. A contracted whirring.

Brief and ending with a tight snap; then a heavyish tap. All this immediately repeated. Mrs Saville did not need to turn her head. To an *exalté* of the tables the sound of a deck being split, shuffled and reassembled is unmistakable.

What dreadful luck! How absolutely and utterly galling that of all the visitors to Madingley Grange the one person with whom any sort of social discourse was absolutely out of the question should be another gamester. Violet, or even at a pinch the unspeakable Fred, might just have been permitted to wear the mantle of opponent. After all, once the game had commenced the sheer amount of energy and attention needed would help to water down the more obnoxious aspects of their personalities. But this foul old gypsy ... Mrs Saville clenched her fists in sheer frustration. And the old woman was keen, too. She also needed to play, otherwise why travel with a pack?

Here Mrs Saville made her first mistake. The word 'need' implying as it did a certain vulnerability in the player, a dependence upon the game, was quite inappropriate when applied to Mrs Gibbs. Cards were not for her the means of passing a pleasant hour or weapons with which to best a quailing adversary. Rather were they the tangible manifestation of life's dark undertow. She did not *play* cards but regarded them as the divine instrument of sibylline revelation. Momentarily their display would halt the celestial flux of rushing meteors and shifting incandescent stars and act on these marvels like isinglass in a pan of soup, clarifying and making bright, exposing to the eye of the seer runic patterns of dynamic precision and power. True on occasion Mrs Gibbs gambled but she did so supremely, like an Olympian, with a stylish impassivity that bordered on disdain.

Mrs Saville knew nothing of theurgy and was irritated to find her attention being tugged sideways, again and again, to encompass the humped form of the old lady. Mrs Gibbs had hitched her chair closer to the table. She placed her right arm across the front of her body, the hand, slightly arched, resting on the metal rim. Then swiftly she flung her hand across the table, describing a semi-circle. There was a multi-coloured blur as the cards fluttered and fell, immaculately edge to edge. Then the old lady covered the final card with her left hand, reversed the procedure and the cards, turning on their backs were, with thrilling, almost magical speed and precision once more in the palm of her hand.

Mrs Saville, her mouth dry, stared. The old lady then took ten cards and set them out, face upwards, in the form of a five-pointed star. She leaned over them, her face ferocious and enclosed, her lips pushed forward judiciously. She was mumbling. The same syllables over and over again. It sounded to Mrs Saville like 'nearly nearly nearly'. Then Mrs Gibbs made another catch-all movement and the cards were gone. An involuntary 'Oh!' escaped Mrs Saville. Immediately she turned her head away.

Several minutes passed, then, as the old lady showed no signs of having even heard, let alone being about to respond to, Mrs Saville's exclamation, she sneaked another look. It appeared that Mrs Gibbs was about to start a run of patience. Cards were laid down, each appearing to flower suddenly at the tips of her fingers when required. Mrs Saville, gazing at the silent figure in the vile cardigan, had never seen anything like it. Suddenly, although her glance had not once lifted from the table, Mrs Gibbs said: 'You'll know me next time, missus.'

Mortified to find herself in the discomfiting position of *voyeur*, Mrs Saville made an embarrassed gobbly clucking sound. This attracted the attention of one of the doves which flew up and tried to sit on her lap. There was a brief tussle during which she attempted to remove the bird and think of an appropriate reply. To apologize was naturally out of the question. On the other hand something must be said, if only to make it plain that she was not the sort of person to be left with the penultimate word.

Her mind formed various rejoinders, all quite squashing. She selected the most pointed and was consequently horrified when her lips parted and the words 'Perhaps you might care to play' emerged. She leaned back, palpitating in her wicker chair, regarding the old woman with trepidation and dismay. How had this rash utterance come about? Surely not because of some obscure and sinister 'fluence? No. That was nonsense. She was simply the victim of nothing more alarming than her own overwhelming compulsion to play a game, any game, of cards.

As Mrs Saville mulled over her strange predicament her attention was caught by the extraordinarily long lobes of Mrs Gibbs' ears. Wrinkled leathery flaps pierced by black pearls, they really looked quite mummified. Mrs Saville had a book at home on famous murder trials which had left her with the definite impression that long earlobes were a sure sign of the killer temperament. Any move therefore that might put her in a confrontational position vis-à-vis the old lady was to be resisted at all costs. She picked up her chair and closed the gap between them.

'No one seemed very interested in bridge last night, did they?' No reply. 'Hard to settle down, perhaps, after Mrs Gregory's little drama.' Ditto. 'Of course there are games that only two can play. If you'd care. . . ?'

'Games.' Mrs Gibbs hawked and spat the word like a gob of phlegm.

Mrs Saville had offended. Obviously all that necromantic feinting and carrying on was meant to impress. And playing cards quite beneath Mrs Gibbs' dignity.

'Just to pass the time till lunch.' Mrs Saville's voice,

attempting airiness, failed miserably. 'D'you play gin?' A violent head shake. 'I'll teach you.' She reached out for the cards. The old lady barked 'Oy!' and gathered up the pack. A scroop of silk, the reticule gaped and the cards vanished.

'No matter. I have some.' Mrs Saville opened her handbag. 'You must teach me that trick. Where you made them open out and jump back so quickly.' That would put them in their place at the bridge club. Especially Major Withers.

Mrs Gibbs shrugged. Her dark eyes glimmered with a complicated mixture of emotions: irony, malice, amusement, anger. But she spoke softly. 'I don't do tricks.'

'I didn't mean to be patronizing,' said Mrs Saville, as near to making amends as she had been in her entire life. She waited a moment, then, as no revelations seemed to be forthcoming, continued. 'Right. Gin is it?' She dealt two hands of ten cards. 'Now this is a very easy game. As the non-dealer you take what we call the "up" card. You see. . . ?' A smile of encouragement. 'Oh. I will then . . .'

'Load of rubbidge.'

'At least try,' coaxed Mrs Saville, anguished at seeing the chance of her first game in three days slipping away. 'Next step – I'll explain about the deadwood – '

'Deadwood,' snorted the old lady. 'Some folks got that between the ears.'

'Aces are low,' persisted Mrs Saville, biting back her natural response and willing her body to remain seated. She continued her explanations and the ladies played four games; Mrs Gibbs, in casually audacious style, winning three.

'That was rather naughty,' said Mrs Saville, fizzing with exhilaration. 'Pretending you hadn't played before.'

'I ain't played it afore. And I ain't playing it again neither.'

'Very well.' Although the old lady was obviously lying

181

Mrs Saville had no intention of being forced into a quarrelsome position. She could see the thread of Mrs Gibbs' attention was a grudging and slender one, ready to snap at the slightest hint of adverse criticism. 'Perhaps there is something *you* would like to play?'

'Blackjack.'

'I'm not sure. . . ?' Mrs Saville tailed off, hoping she was not about to be exposed to the lurid history of some swarthy ancestor.

'Vanty Oon.'

'Ah yes – I've played Vingt-et-Un. But it is usual,' she continued with a nice hesitancy (after all the old lady looked as if she didn't have two pennies to rub together), 'to play for a modest stake. Nothing too high of course. At home we usually – '

'Yeh,' said Mrs Gibbs. 'I'll hack that.' And reopened her bag.

Mrs Saville brought out a soft chamois drawstring purse full of fifty pence pieces without which she never travelled and put it on the table. Mrs Gibbs produced a roll of grubby notes held together by an elasticated band and as thick as a till roll.

The outside note was a twenty pounder and when she removed the band and bent the wad backwards to make it lie flat it became plain that the rest were as well.

Mrs Saville's heart stopped, gathered speed and thundered on. How common, she thought, feeling quite dizzy at the sight of such purse-proud insolence. How incredibly vulgar. Confident though she was of her ability to trounce all comers, Mrs Saville had no intention of contending with such lubricous display. She said nothing but tugged open her leather sac and tipped out a little heap of coins. She was stacking them in a tidy pile when, fatefully, she glanced up and caught Mrs Gibbs' eye. What cold contempt. What sovereign disdain. And more, and worse. For surely there lurked also in that glance a trace of disappointment. As if she,

Laetitia Saville, had been tried against who knew what arcane piquantly crackpot ideal and been found wanting. How dare she? An old gypsy woman. *How dare she?* Pallid with anger Mrs Saville removed the coins and put a cheque book in their place.

'Woss that?'

'It is a cheque book,' said Mrs Saville, speaking very distinctly and thinking to forge ahead in the 'who's looking down on who' stakes. She then brought out her Mappin and Webb gold propelling pencil with the jewelled initials. The old lady picked it up, held it to her ear and rolled it between her fingers as if it were a cigar. She nudged the cheque book with it.

'Lav paper.'

'I bank,' said Mrs Saville icily, 'at Coutts. They are the nonpareils of the financial fraternity. Their cheques are honoured throughout the world by all right-thinking people.'

Mrs Gibbs laughed then, a corvine squawk. 'Crazy as coots,' she cried, livery wattles flapping. '*Caw, caw, caw.*'

'And I am not so familiar with vingt-et-un that I am prepared to play for stakes like that.' She pointed at the greasy wad of notes.

'And I ain't playing that daft gin.'

'We could have a nice game of casino.' Seeing that the cawing and wattle-shaking were about to start again she added quickly: 'What do you suggest then?'

'Poker.'

'*Poker?*'

'You can tickle that, can'cha?'

'Naturally.' Mrs Saville sounded defensive. It was true she had played the game in her time and with considerable success, having by nature the precise expression – impassivity lightly laced with disbelief – that the successful poker face must necessarily command. But although she found the suggestion exciting

183

(already her palms felt slightly damp) she had far rather Mrs Gibbs had chosen a more salubrious option. Poker to Mrs Saville's mind had a definitely sleazy image, conjuring up a ring of stout perspiring men, shirt sleeves high and gartered, wreathed in smoke and surrounded by beer bottles. A nice game of casino would be much more to the mark. She said so.

'Draw poker. Jokers wild.'

'I don't care to be railroaded, Mrs Gibbs.'

The old lady picked up the cards, halved and quartered them, then, with a crisp snap and flutter, made the pack whole and pushed it back. 'Cut. Aces high.'

Mrs Saville took the pack and pointedly shuffled once more. Although she had seen no evidence of chicanery she found the very speed at which Mrs Gibbs moved highly suspect. She shuffled again, tapped the cards neatly into shape and placed the pack in the centre of the table. The old lady curled her lip back, exposing a yellow snaggle tooth, and nodded a directive.

Mrs Saville cut. The king of hearts! Advantage Laetitia, she thought triumphantly. Mrs Gibbs reached out and turned over the top card. It was the ace of spades. There was a long silence whilst Mrs Saville took in this flukey quirk of fate. Because, of course, that's all it was. These things happened sometimes. Foolish to regard them as omens. And after all she was not committed to any definite number of games. She could stop playing any time she chose. It was not likely that the old lady, who had, after all, been dragooned into participation, would object.

'Very well, Mrs Gibbs,' she said, making her second mistake. 'Draw poker, jokers wild, it is.'

8

Derek produced his pencil torch and shone it into the cavity. The door opened on to a cemented area about five feet square from which steps went steeply down. The wall, originally whitewashed, was now grey with cobwebs. Derek hesitated. Didn't some spiders bite? He cleared his throat warningly before stepping into the passage.

No sooner was he there than a further and much more alarming supposition came to mind. This was the getaway route. Chummy's retreat. What if he had not got clear of the house last night? What if he planned to make a further robbery attempt? *What if he was still in there?*

Derek stepped back again. Naturally he must explore this new discovery. He had no intention of being cheated of the boost to his pride that telling of such an exploration would bring. But it was the height of folly to do so unprotected. Holmes armed himself as a matter of course when embarking on a hazardous mission ('the Eley's Number Two I think Watson!') and was an excellent shot, as the state of Mrs Hudson's walls could testify. Even the faithful doctor had been known to carry an old army revolver. Derek looked around for a weapon.

The fireplace first. A pretty affair of primrose and leaf-green William de Morgan tiles with a tiny little basket of a grate filled with dried flowers. But no poker. He scouted further afield. The heaviest item that was anything like portable was the old lady's hairbrush. Derek seized it and, facing the bathroom mirror, narrowed his eyes and made a couple of savage swings and chops. Not good enough, especially as he could not count on the element of surprise. It was his opponent, already *in situ*, who would have that advantage. Derek put the brush down and returned to the bedroom.

And then he remembered. 'Fool that I am!' he cried aloud, pulling from his pocket Gilly's gun. Here was protection indeed. His imagination waxed fat, exchanging his previous modest fantasy for one vastly more grandiose. Far from just announcing his discovery of the secret passage, Derek now saw himself emerging at the other end, chivvying before him a cringing hoodlum. That would show them all, and no mistake.

Derek moved boldly forward, the gun warm and heavy in his hand. He pictured the miscreant cowering, hands aloft, on seeing his approach. 'See this, you villain!' he would cry, waving the pistol. 'This is a Major Fontaine Thirty-Four. Short range, detachable box and radial lever. One blast from this and you won't know what hit you.'

Fortunately there was a wooden handle on the inside of the door so that Derek was able to close it behind him. He did not wish to leave it ajar, possibly alerting Mrs Gibbs should she return. This was his tunnel and he would spring it on the startled and admiring assembly when he was good and ready.

Once the door was closed darkness was complete. Derek directed the thin beam of his torch to the edge of the first step and began, very carefully, to descend. High above his head were the beginnings of the final roof support beams. He thought he heard a bit of scuffling up there and pointed his torch, hoping it wasn't bats. Bats bit you. And drove you mad if they got in your hair. He couldn't actually see any but that might be because his light wasn't too strong.

Derek stood very still and listened, gammony ears alert. He had definitely not imagined the scuffling but now it seemed to be coming from a much lower level and some distance ahead. He redirected his torch. Rats. More biters. But at least they would not (unless he had chanced on an astonishing new strain of *Rattus decumanus*) be flying into his hair.

Derek kept a firm grip on his gun and crept on, hugging the dusty wall for there was no handrail on his right-hand side. Just a sheer drop into darkness. The air was cold and clammy and malodorous. Derek wrinkled his nostrils. Most unpleasant. Musty, like mildewed paper or rotting fabric. Perhaps – for it seemed to be taking him for ever to get anywhere – the steps went down, not just to the ground floor but beyond. Right under the house to the cellar. Maybe that's where the smell was coming from. They probably stored unwanted furniture and other rubbish down there. Or – Derek suddenly stood quite still – it might be a crypt! He wished now he'd paid attention when Simon was talking about the layout of the Grange last night. Did the late Victorians have marble effigy-type tombs beneath their manor houses? Perhaps this was where Mrs Gibbs' ghost hung out. Consoling himself with the thought that, if this proved to be the case, at least it would be way beyond the stage where biting strangers might appeal, Derek, the huge hump of his shadow behind him, began once more to descend.

But then something awful happened. A horrible clinging moist thing stretched suddenly across his face. Derek cried out and, flinging his arm up to brush it away, dropped his torch. It rolled and clattered to the bottom of the steps where it lay, glowing up at him out of the humble dark, like a tiny Cyclops. Pulling off the threads of cobweb, Derek gave himself a moment to recuperate then, feeling the way with his now trembling left hand, rapidly covered the remainder of the steps.

He picked up his torch which had rolled against a wall fitting almost flush to the last stair, and quickly discovered a handle, twin to the one he had left behind. He put his ear against the outline of the door but could hear nothing. Derek felt cheated. He had been hoping for voices. A gathering of the clans. Never mind. He would not let a shortage of spectators detract from his satisfaction. Even if he had not successfully apprehended the intruder he had still successfully traversed the unknown and was about to emerge victorious. Nothing could take that triumph away. He turned the handle and pushed.

Something was in the way. He pushed harder and whatever it was shifted slightly. He put his gun down on the bottom step then, gritting his teeth with fervid determination, almost threw himself at the door. It opened about a foot and immediately masses of shiny green fleshy leaves thrust themselves into the gap. He was outside. Something quite unexpected. Derek pushed a little harder and heard a dragging bumping sound as of a heavy object being propelled over a hard surface. One more big heave should do it. And so it proved. The heave was followed by a tremendous crash. The door flew open with such force it nearly came off its hinges and Derek stepped out into the conservatory.

It was very quiet, flooded with the most extraordinary light. The roof was seagreen, curved into ribs, and through this the sunshine poured, subdued and distorted by the thick glass, becoming soft, luminous and wavery. The air was very hot and damp. Hoses snaked about the floor and water trickled and hissed. Just behind his exit door an enormous terracotta jar lay on its side in several pieces. Its occupant, the plant with the shiny leaves, reclined in loose mounds of earth. The exposed roots were most unpleasant, hairy and with great rosy carbuncles that looked like lumps of raw flesh.

Derek closed his secret door, leaving a barely visible gap, and was just about to rush off and impart his thrilling news when he was halted by a sudden recollection. In the excitement of his discovery he had quite forgotten his arrangements with Sheila. He had certainly been successful at keeping out of everyone's way. In fact so engrossed had he become in his investigations that he was now left with – a quick glance at the half hunter – less than ten minutes to get himself murdered in.

Martin and Sheila met head on crossing a tiny conceit of a bridge in the shrubbery. Nothing more than six arched planks and handrails of peeling bark. A willow-pattern bridge beneath which ran a trickle of crystalline water bobbing over spotted stones.

Martin said: 'Sorry,' and stepped back. Sheila without smiling or thanking him crossed over. She appeared very cross.

'Have you seen Simon?'

'No,' replied Martin. 'I haven't seen anyone. I've only just got up. Have you seen Rosemary?'

'Rosemary?' Sheila looked at him sharply and Martin blushed.

'Just thought she might like a game of tennis.'

'I'm sure she will. If you can find her,' said Sheila tartly. 'Games of all sorts seem to be her speciality.'

'Here, I say . . .' began Martin but Sheila had flounced off. Not an easy accomplishment in a severely tailored outfit with not a furbelow in sight, but flounce she did. Martin wondered what had upset her.

He went over the bridge to find his path immediately diverged, both trails disappearing into a wild-looking tangle of small trees, flowering shrubs and brambles. Martin tossed a coin and turned left.

He passed an early purple buddleia, blossoms so pulsating with butterflies that the whole tree seemed about to take off and a tangle of summer jasmine, a column of pale stars, twining around an old blenheim orange. Many of the shrubs had T-shaped iron markers giving their Latin names, and clematis clambered everywhere.

Tranced with delight at the scents and sounds Martin continued along the path. It was by a gigantic Kiftsgate, a landscape in its own right, that he heard, intermingling with the warbling of birds and the zizz and drone of insects, human voices. Rising and falling; one deep, the other much lighter. Then a girl laughed.

Martin looked around. Although the voices sounded very near he could see no one. He strolled on a bit trying to follow the sound to its source and came to a little arbour partially concealed by a swag of honeysuckle. He pushed the fragrant curtain aside. There was a stone statue of Cupid and Psyche in the bower and a love seat. On the seat, plainly determined not to let all this romantic ambience go to waste, were Simon and Rosemary. They jumped up when they saw Martin. Simon waved away his blurting apology and Rosemary patted her hair. Then Simon lifted his companion's hand rather formally to his lips, saying, 'I shall be in real trouble if I don't give a hand with lunch. See you both in half an hour?'

After he had gone there was a brief silence sticky with accusation. Martin looked severely at Rosemary who twirled her leghorn hat by the ribbons and stuck out her smeary lower lip. At last he said: 'What on earth do you think you were doing?'

'*Me?* You've got a cheek. I might ask you the same question.'

'What have I done?' asked Martin, genuinely puzzled.

'I'm not blind. I saw you gazing into Laurel Hannaford's eyes on the terrace yesterday. If I hadn't come over and asked for another drink you'd still be standing there.'

'What absolute rubbish,' said Martin, aware, even as he spoke, that the conviction in his voice was muted. For it was true that he had felt strangely content as the recipient of that deep blue gaze from the girl in the shimmering dress. But an easy friendliness was all it

190

was. What Rosemary suggested was nonsense. As Martin recalled those few moments of closeness and listened to his fiancée cheapening them by the name of flirtation he became angry.

'At least whatever I was doing I was doing it where you could see me. Not skulking in some mangy grotto.'

'How dare you! I've never skulked in my life. And anyway, after your ridiculous performance in the middle of the night, I didn't think you'd care what I did.'

'It wasn't my fault the butler threw me down the stairs.'

'I despise people who blame others for their incompetence.'

'Gave my head a terrible crack.' Silence. 'Hurts like hell.' More of the same. 'I wouldn't be surprised if it needs stitches.'

'Oh don't be such a wimp.'

'I see. As I obviously failed on the field of battle, Rosemary, perhaps you would have preferred it if I'd been brought down to breakfast on my shield?'

'A little bump on the head.'

'Thank you very much. This is a wound honourably received, I'll have you know. I was making my way back from your room when it happened.'

'Well you can't be very good at it. I didn't even wake up.'

'There's no need to be coarse.'

'And what on earth induced you to babble on to Mother at dinner time about Sealyhams and the Chinese?'

'I misread your list – all right? Am I not allowed one single error?'

'Two actually.'

'Couldn't you give me a dispensation? One and a half minutes' kindness perhaps, instead of the regulation hearty breakfast?'

'How could anyone mistake the word Sealyham for

the word pekingese? They are not even remotely similar. SEE LEE HAM. PEEK ING EESE.'

'Oh shut up!' Rosemary drew in her breath. A huge gasp of amazement. Her eyes bulged. 'I'm sorry, darling . . . No, I'm not . . . Well, yes I am but only for being rude. Things had to . . . have to be said.' Martin drew in his breath. 'The fact is – '

'The fact is, Martin, that coming away on this weekend is the most sensible thing I ever did. It has enabled me to see you in your true colours. Mummy was quite right when she said you weren't good enough for me. I'm only grateful that I found out in time. You must regard our engagement as at an end.'

'What – null and void?'

'Precisely.'

'Righto.'

'Is . . . is that all you've got to say?' Rosemary produced a wisp of apricot chiffon and dabbed daintily at the corner of a dry eye.

'Er . . .' Martin ruminated. 'Your lipstick's all smudged.'

'Beast!' Rosemary stamped her sandalled foot and flounced off, making a much better job of it than Sheila due to the wide trousers.

Martin sat down in the lovers' bower and took a deep lungful of the perfect air. It wasn't long till lunch and he wished to spend the time quietly sorting out his emotions. It was not easy to get comfortable on the hard bench. His shoulders still felt bruised and his knees and ankles a bit on the mangled side. His head too, although the stones seemed to have permanently rolled away, remained spongily tender. So why, Martin wondered, given this extreme discomfort, plus the fact that he was now unmistakably one fiancée short, was his heart as light as a feather?

Laurie was hiding in the vegetable garden. Ostensibly

she had gone there to pick lettuces for lunch. Now, gathered, they lay already wilting in the hot sun at her feet. She sat on an old zinc bucket hugging her knees and drowning in a turmoil of emotion. She felt miserable, elated, panicky, nauseous and alarmed. There was a persistent lump in her throat no sooner swallowed than back again.

She had hoped that the orderliness of the enclosed garden, the neat vegetable parterres, low box hedging and formal herringbone paths would have a calming effect upon the disorderly tumult in her mind. Often during childhood visits, if her aunt or uncle had been grumpy, she would come out here, fill her small watering can from the rain butt and sprinkle the herbs, radiating out like the spokes of a wheel from a sundial centre. But today the garden had lost the power to heal.

Suddenly, unbearably irritated by sitting still, Laurie got up and started wandering about. Her arms and legs were heavy and she felt stupid and unnaturally detached as if she were in some sort of limbo; marking time waiting for she knew not what. She longed to go to sleep, a miraculous healing sleep where, when she woke, the mysterious disturbance would have flown away and she would be her old, undistressed self again.

She broke off a sprig of myrtle and was inhaling the sweet prickly scent when the old iron gate creaked and her brother came in.

'Bennet's waiting for the lettuce. Lunch is in ten minutes.'

'Oh.'

'Are these them?' Simon picked up four hot, dry, wilting plants.

'Yes. Webb's Wonder.'

'They don't look very wonderful to me. They look pathetic.'

'I picked them half an hour ago.'

'I think you should pick some more.'

'*You* pick some more,' flared Laurie. 'You've done nothing all morning but swan around on the croquet lawn.'

'No need to snap.' Simon hitched up his cream Oxford bags and crouched down. 'Got a knife?'

'They just pull.'

'So they do.' He tugged out four lettuces and stood up again. 'Everything set for one o'clock?'

'How should I know?'

'Aren't you in charge?'

'Oh yes – it's always me isn't it? Everything falls on me.'

'I know the help's not ideal – '

'Help? A butler as drunk as a newt and a maid as blind as a bat? All we need is a frog and a brace of fenny snakes. We could open on Friday in *Macbeth*.'

'You are in a tizz, Lol – '

'Don't call me that! You know I hate it.'

'I really am terribly grateful for everything you've done. Honestly. I can't think of anyone else, given this bloody disaster, who could have resisted saying I told you so.'

'I told you so.'

'That's not like you.'

'Yes it is. It's exactly like me. I'm fed up to the teeth.'

'I'll make it up to you.'

'No you won't. You never do.'

Simon sat down on the edge of a cucumber frame, feeling the metal warm against his legs, and regarded his sister with genuine concern. 'Spit it out then.'

'Nothing to say. Anyway I have to go and look after the salmon.'

'You're too late.' Simon stamped his face with woe. 'It's dead.'

'That's about as funny as Gilly's "Girl from Idaho".'

'Please!' Simon put his hands over his ears. 'One more rendering will send me out of what is left of my mind.

Three choruses after breakfast and he's serenading the Gibbses in a punt on the lake now. I'm hoping they'll jump over the side in despair and drown.' Simon reached for the bucket, pulled it close and patted it. 'What's up?'

'Don't know.' Laurie regarded the scuffed, dusty toes of her sandals. 'Actually . . . to tell you the truth . . . I feel really unhappy.'

'Well, we can't all be happy at once. There's just not enough to go round. It'll be your turn tomorrow.'

'Mmn.' Laurie sounded most unsure. 'Are they . . . all down now?'

'Think so. Would you believe Mrs Saville and Gypsy Rose Gibbs are playing cards on the terrace?'

'That's . . . everyone, is it?'

'Yes. Martin has finally showed his face. And I must say it's looking rather the worse for wear.'

'Oh him.' Laurie's voice tightened. 'He makes me sick.'

'I'm sorry to hear that. He seems quite pleasant.'

'No – I mean actually. Every time I look at him I feel sick. Or else I want to cry. And then I get dizzy.'

'I see. Anything else?'

'The flowers and trees seemed to vibrate and shine and become all . . .'

'Rose coloured?'

'Bright and glittery and yes, since you mention it, a bit on the pinkish side. Then, when I gave him his drink, he smiled and said "thank you".'

'Knocks you sideways. That sort of repartee.'

Laurie's eyes filled with tears. 'I don't know what's the matter with me.'

'That's easy. You're in love.'

'*In love?*' Laurie stared, banjaxed. 'Is that it then? Seeing him even when he's not there, feeling sick when he is and the scenery jumping about?'

'More or less.'

'Why do people keep going in for it then if it's so awful?'

'The first time's the worst.' Simon rose, pulling her up with him. 'And the best, of course. Don't worry – he'll be gone tomorrow and you'll never have to see him again.'

'Ahhh . . .' Laurie swung out over a chasm on a rope of sand. 'Simon!'

'Oh dear, you have got it bad. What about Hugh?'

'Who?'

'Never mind.'

'I shall die.'

'No you won't. You'll miss dinner and tomorrow's cornflakes and be as right as a trivet by lunch time. Come on – ' he picked up the lettuce – 'you take two and I'll take two. They'll be baying for their victuals any minute. I never knew such a ravenous bunch. I'm sure they've all consumed at least two hundred and fifty pounds' worth of nosh already.'

They reached the gate and, as Simon held it open and Laurie walked through, she said: 'Don't you think Rosemary Saville's absolutely awful?'

'Of course not,' replied Simon, fastening the latch. 'The family's in banking.'

9

On the terrace a long trestle had been set out with a
brightly checked cloth and napkins and greenish chunky
Italian tumblers with bubbles in the glass. Simon
thought it looked just right. Informal and quite festive.
He pictured everyone sitting around in the sunshine
quaffing away, voices raised in laughter and friendly
exchange. It would be just like one of those marvellous *en
famille* lunches the French and Italians were so good at
but without ghastly bambinos hurling the pasta about.

He had manoeuvred Mother and Mrs Saville to the
far end of the terrace simply by picking up their table
and walking off with it. They had followed as if attached
by invisible reins before immediately sinking into the
chairs he had repositioned and going on with their game.

Gaunt, having struck the gong at his third attempt,
limped and hunch-hobbled over to his employer. Simon
braced himself for a lengthy gripe about the winter of his
minion's discontent.

'Miss Laurel asks should she send the soup out, sir.'

'Give it five, Gaunt. Get the bibs tied on.'

'Very good, sir.'

Rosemary appeared, her lips freshly painted shiny
geranium red, and the boating party made their way
towards the house, brief midday shadows preceding
them. They had enjoyed a pleasant morning once the
musical accompaniment had ground to a halt. Gilly had
wielded the punt pole with great élan whilst his
companions reclined plumply, trailing their hands in the
water. Violet admired the waving fronds of willow, the
immense bronze dragon and the ducks and moorhens
skimming about and Fred questioned their boatman as

197

to his reasons, 'your *real* reasons, mind' for being present at the Grange. He then offered his own theory and Gilly argued in vain that he was neither hitman nor minder, simply a clerk for the Electricity Board seizing the chance to live and breathe thirties-style for a short spell.

He was still protesting as they crossed the drawbridge and Fred stopped, almost in mid-stride, and stared. Violet bumped into him and Gilly said: 'What is it? What's the matter?'

Fred turned and looked at his wife, his nostrils pinched with anger. 'I thought you said she was clean.'

Violet followed his gaze. 'She was. I looked through all her luggage, her clothes, everything.'

'She must have had them in that bloody bag. You could get the crown jewels in there. It's the size of an elephant's scrotum.'

'She didn't. I checked.' Violet stumbled after Fred as his step quickened. Gilly, still in the dark but scenting drama, scuttled along behind.

On the terrace the ladies played on, Sheila standing behind Mrs Saville's chair. Mother, aware of her son's approach, ignored it. Mrs Saville, in the grip of the game, her eyes glued to the cards in her fist, did not hear Fred even when he spoke.

She was in a state of feverish excitement, having just examined her new hand and discovered that she was only one card short of a royal flush. This delightful revelation was all of a piece with the story so far. Things were going supremely well. Six games had been played; five had been won. On fortune's cap Mrs Saville was the very button. The dark forces on the other hand, having won the toss and the first round, were definitely on the skids.

Not that the five games had been easy. On the contrary. In spite of her experience Mrs Saville had felt herself to be occasionally on dizzyingly unfamiliar ground. Sometimes almost on the verge of losing control as if a tugging dancing spirit were abroad and leading her astray. Yet still she was winning; subjugating that humped toad-like shape opposite that had hardly raised its eyes since play began.

'I shouldn't have any truck with her, missus.' Fred's voice finally penetrated this flood of self-congratulation. He leaned over the table and picked up the deck.

'What do you think you're doing?' cried Mrs Saville. Then, when he showed signs of stowing the pack away: 'They belong to me.'

'Beg your pardon.' Fred put them back. 'Only you're out of your class, Mrs S.'

'She's doing very well,' said Sheila.

'He doesn't mean to be rude, dear,' said Violet. 'But there's no point in playing against someone who's got the gift.'

'I might be more impressed by that sort of superstitious mumbo-jumbo if I wasn't winning. And five games to her one.'

'You're on the seventh now?'

'Yes. And don't waste your time exchanging significant glances.' Mrs Saville reached out, briefly touching the five twenty-pound notes tucked under her aperitif glass. 'I have no intention of giving up at this stage, I assure you.'

'You don't understand – '

'I understand perfectly,' retorted Mrs Saville. 'You bring her down here, you neglect her dreadfully, going off boating or whatever, and then, when I take pity on the poor old thing and try to give her a little pleasure, you feel guilty. Never mind, Mrs Gibbs.' Mrs Saville forced herself to reach out and pat the gnarled old fist, all knobs and bones. She didn't want the old lady to think her family's aspersions had fallen on receptive soil. 'I'm discarding.' She pushed out the rogue card. 'If you would be so kind?'

Mrs Gibbs, with a token and patently insincere cringe

away from her son, dealt a replacement from the top of the pack. Her whiskery chin rested on her breast and her lip quivered. 'Never have any fun . . .'

'Aren't you ashamed?' said Mrs Saville, turning over her card. 'Your own moth – ' Her eyes widened. Sheila Gregory gave a low whistle and Mrs Saville turned and glared. 'You must *never* do that. The whole point of poker . . .' But she spoke to empty air. Sheila had spotted the drinks trolley and wafted off.

Everyone started to sit around the long table and a moment later Simon joined the gamesters. 'We're having lunch now, ladies.'

'Ohhh . . .' A fan of cards pressed against her bosom, Mrs Saville turned an expression of exquisite suffering upon her host. 'Not *now*. We're in the middle of a game. And I have – ' She struggled to modify the strength of feeling in her voice, '. . . quite a good hand.'

'I got to check on the cellar. See if Flash Harry's back.' Mother started to struggle up from her seat. 'Gizza lift, daughter.'

'Wait! Simon – couldn't you be a sort of referee. . . ?' Mrs Saville thrust her five cards at him. 'Keep them in your pocket and then bring them back when we're sitting down after lunch. So we can continue the game with the same hand.'

'Happy to.' Simon stored the cards away. 'I'd better keep yours as well then, Mrs Gibbs.'

'Shouldn't we get someone else?' said Mrs Saville quickly. 'You might just forget which hand is in which pocket.'

So Gilly was asked and put Mother's cards away carefully inside his blazer. Assisted by Violet she disappeared into the house, Fred and Simon joined the others and Mrs Saville was left briefly alone at the far end of the terrace.

She sat, her back to the rest of the company, restively alert, her stomach churning. Little point in trying to tackle food; she would not be able to swallow a single mouthful. She closed her eyes, seeing again the three stylized royals with their ginger scrolls of hair and pinched, weak mouths. And the nine and ten pips attending. A straight flush! When she discarded the three of clubs she knew, even with her present run of amazing luck, what her chances were of picking up the nine of hearts in return. Yet pick it up she did.

The only hand that could beat her now was a royal flush. Ace high. And whilst Mrs Saville appreciated that the odds against her partner holding such a prize were phenomenal, such prodigious coincidence could occasionally occur. There was, of course, one way of finding out.

Mrs Saville hesitated. She had never cheated at cards in her life and regarded anyone who did as disgracefully dissolute. Never, ever, not under any circumstances, could she have imagined herself belonging to that number. Yet could the step she now realized she was seriously considering be called cheating? Not really. Technically it was more sort of . . . checking. It would not tell her what cards Mrs Gibbs held. (That really would be cheating.) Simply the ones that she did not.

And after all, Mrs Saville argued with herself, had she not experienced something very strange, something alien and disturbing emanating from her partner during their half dozen games together? Nothing so ridiculous naturally as superhuman power, but was there not a talent there (Mrs Saville thought of Mother's tricks) that was altogether out of the ordinary? And consequently a need – one might almost argue a duty – to redress the balance somewhat? To make things a little more fair.

Mrs Saville's hands stole out towards the cards. She watched the fingers, encouraged and dismayed. Watched them pick up the deck and flip quickly and quietly through. All four aces were there. The hands crept back into Mrs Saville's lap.

She expected to feel triumph. Or shame. Or pleasure and excitement. Instead she felt an instant deep abiding calm. When Rosemary called 'Mumm*ee*', she calmly left the table and calmly joined the others and in no time at all was calmly enjoying an aperitif.

The first course had been served and was being zestfully dispatched before Violet and Mother rejoined the company. Violet slipped quietly into her seat. Her face was pale, stained with Dutch-doll circles the colour of foxgloves. She caught Fred's eye and, as he made to speak, frowned, shaking her head. A bare movement.

Mother came to rest more noisily, wheezing and puffing. She looked fierce: suffused with energy and satisfaction. The salmon arrived reposing on a sea of jelly chippings the colour of butterscotch and surrounded by rosettes of mayonnaise and transparent slices of cucumber. Bennet brought out the sauce, new potatoes and salad and everyone helped themselves to wine. Today there were no place cards so people sat where they liked, Mrs Saville, in spite of her virtuous concern for Mrs Gibbs' wellbeing, coming to rest as far from the family as she possibly could.

Simon at the head of the table inquired courteously after the ghost hunters' results (Mrs Gibbs looked waggish, Violet shrugged) then turned to his younger companions. Rosemary, petulant at losing his attention even for a moment, paused in the act of lifting a silver fork weighted with *saumon à la sauce verte* to her lips and spoke.

'Don't you just *adore* rusticity, Simon?'

'In moderation,' replied Simon, pleasurably aware of the pressure of Sheila Gregory's calf against his own.

'You can't adore anything moderately, silly,' giggled Rosemary. Her tongue, prettily pink like a cat's, slipped out, catching a tiny rivulet of straying sauce.

'Oh I don't know,' said Sheila. 'I adore some things, and some people, very moderately indeed.'

Gaunt, still sluggish but fairly frisking along in comparison with his earlier revs per minute, grabbed at the occasional shoulder for support as he attempted to top up the guests' glasses.

'I think,' said Simon, 'that people can continue to help themselves, Gaunt. Less chance of flooding.'

'If you say so, sir.'

As the butler staggered off Fred called down the table: 'You get him from Battersea Dogs' Home, Simon?'

'I beg your pardon?'

'Him being a lurcher, like?' Delighted with his wit, especially when Martin as well as Violet laughed, Fred cracked his knuckles and helped himself to more potatoes. 'Nothing like dining ay la fresco is there, Martin?'

'No.' Martin smiled, but absently. He had gradually become aware that, ever since he woke, overshadowed by all his aches and pains and the upset with his ex-fiancée there had been at the back of his mind a quiet but persistent desire to see Laurie again. He was disappointingly conscious of the empty chair facing Simon at the other end of the table but had no intention of asking his host where his sister might be. Apart from a natural disinclination to draw attention to himself such a query might well invoke some sarcastic response from Rosemary. He watched her now, her hand on Simon's arm, prating on about the landscape.

'You must need absolutely oodles of staff.' She dragged out the 'oo' through a scarlet rosebud.

'Just a couple full time. And there's a boy.'

'I can't be doing with gardening,' said Violet, looking slightly more like her old self. 'Too much like outdoor housework. And talk about language. All that pricking out and hardening off. There's a time and place for remarks like that. I wonder that man in the muddy wellies at Pebble Mill can look his neighbours in the face.'

When Bennet came to remove the plates Martin caught her attention and, keeping his voice low, asked about the whereabouts of Miss Hannaford.

'She's up to her eyes at the moment, sir. What with Gaunt being one leg short of the pair so to speak. She's eating on the wing. That's why I didn't lay her place.'

'Then who – ?' Martin watched the wreckage of the salmon being borne away. He glanced around the table. The al fresco lunch was plainly a success. Flushed from smiling mouths by copious draughts of wine, streams of easy chatter flowed. Even Mrs Saville, no doubt recalling her stunning collection of cards in Simon's pocket, parted with a modicum of steely bonhomie. It was getting quite bacchanalian. But where in this merry throng, thought Martin (having comprehended the reason for the empty chair), was Derek?

There was Mrs Derek, giddily throwing back her head and laughing at one of Simon's sallies. And there was everyone else apparently having the time of their lives. But of the great detective, no sign. Martin wondered if the other guests knew something he didn't. If some plan encompassing Derek's disappearance had been made earlier when he (Martin) was still asleep. Surely it was not possible that no one had noticed the man's absence? Much more likely, assumed Martin, feeling a pang of sympathy for the ridiculous sleuth, that it had not been considered of sufficient interest to spend time discussing. He waited for a bit of conversational slack then said very clearly: 'Sheila? What on earth's happened to your husband?'

'You're the third person to ask me that.' Sheila looked down the table, bored and a little vexed. 'I expect he's hot on some trail or other.'

'You missed breakfast, Martin, so you wouldn't know,' explained Fred. 'But the idea was that he'd give us till one o'clock to murder him and if we hadn't managed it by then he'd won on points.'

'You'd think,' said Mrs Saville, 'that someone would have done it by now. There are nine of us after all.'

'But only one would be looking,' Gilly pointed out.

'The murderer . . .' Fred's voice throbbed. He rose, hunched his shoulders, spread his arms and made his horror noise. Violet said: 'Stop acting so daft,' and pulled him back into his seat.

'It's now half past . . .' Gilly's Adam's apple bobbed excitedly. 'You'd think, given his temperament – no offence, Sheila – he'd have been here on the stroke, thrilled to bits because he'd beaten us.'

'All congratulatious,' said Mother.

'Unless he's been . . . well . . .' Martin tailed off delicately.

'Done,' said Mother with great relish, and her eyes shone.

Mrs Saville didn't like the way things were going. The last thing she wanted, with the state of play extant, was her partner gallivanting (well, paltering) all over the place hunting a murderer. Money was around to be won – the currency till roll came vividly to mind – and Mrs Saville had no intention of letting it permanently disappear into that *poult de soie* duffle bag.

But the slight eddy of concern whipped up by Martin's question was vanquished by the arrival of a huge white china dish of Strawberries Romanof.

'Don't you just adore *fraises du bois?*' cried Rosemary, clapping her hands.

'I do,' said Sheila. 'Not that these are they. Far too large. Cream?' She passed the jug, watching, brows raised, as Rosemary lathered the fruit. 'Goodness. Right over the million cal mark.'

'Oh I can eat what I like.' Rosemary touched her waistline and smirked.

'Mm. It's either the figure or the complexion that goes, isn't it? Of course make-up can work wonders.' The ladies exchanged golden syrup smiles.

'I think,' said Simon, 'that I should go and look for your husband. He may not have heard the gong. Of course there'll be plenty of food left but I do feel guilty that he's not enjoying lunch with the rest of us.'

'I'll go.' Sheila got up. 'He may be in the kitchen, grilling the staff about last night.'

'Grilling the staff,' called Fred. 'That's a good 'un.'

'I expect she'll be glad of the exercise,' said Rosemary loudly as Sheila walked away. 'After all those potatoes.'

When Gaunt had staggered around with narrow-stemmed glasses and the guests had helped themselves to Château d'Yquem a haze of contentment spread around. Everyone savoured the berries lying in an exquisite minglement of strawberry and orange juices and curaçao, and Fred raved about the wine.

The silence became heavy and still, owing something to the enervating sun and more than a little to the alcohol already consumed. Second helpings of pudding were offered and devoured. The dishes were being scraped clean for the second time and Fred had just said: 'Mind out, Violet – you'll have the pattern off that plate,' when Mother dropped her spoon with a loud clatter. She turned her hag-like profile, frozen into a strained compressed gravity, towards the house. A second later, ripping through the still warm air, came a terrible piercing scream.

MURDER

1

Everyone leapt out of their seats, shocked into instant sobriety. Startled stares were exchanged, genuinely fearful until Violet cried: 'It's the body! She's found the body . . .'

'He's copped it after all then, old clever dick,' said Fred. '*Come on* . . .'

An unnecessary directive. Already Simon and Rosemary were halfway across the terrace, the rest streaming behind. Even Mother managed, with a crab-like scuttle, to almost keep up. Mrs Saville was last, looking down her nose and concealing her concern at this unexpected turn of events.

Uncertain of the precise location from which the fear-filled scream had emanated, the guests came to a halt in the hall. Simon had just said: 'We must spread out,' when Laurie, almost lost behind a vast blue and white striped apron, and the vestibular Gaunt appeared, both looking extremely alarmed. Simon had just started to reassure Laurie when Bennet ran into the hall, crying: 'Oh sir! You must come. It's in the conservatory . . . Oh sir! It's Mr Gregory – he's dead . . .'

'*Avanti!*' cried Simon and they all charged off. Laurie, having observed the pale and dreadful stamp of Bennet's countenance, followed more slowly. By the time she reached the conservatory the others were bunched together just inside the door staring in an impressed and exhilarated manner at a gorily dramatic tableau.

Derek Gregory was lying on his back, eyes wide open, mouth agape. The front of his shirt was splashed with red. There was also a long streak of red, glaringly vivid, down the front of Sheila's dress. And terrible sticky stains the same colour all over the long knife she held in her hand. Just behind Derek a huge pot had fallen over and earth and chunks of terracotta were spread about. Sheila stood staring at them all, an expression of absolute horror on her face, then she dropped the knife and covered her face with her hands. Her shoulders twitched and shook and she started to cry.

'That's a bit of all right, ay Violet?' asked Fred. 'You can't fault that. She's as good as some of them on the telly.'

'Better,' improved Violet, starting to applaud. All but Laurie and the servants joined in and the place fairly rocked. Someone whistled and Gilly called 'encore' only to be told by Fred not to be gormless, they hadn't solved this one yet.

Throughout her warmly enthusiastic reception Sheila had continued to evince signs of the most acute distress. Now, as the last smattering of applause died away, she looked at them in turn with blank incomprehension.

'What's the matter with you all?' she shouted. 'Are you mad? I've told you my husband's dead and you're . . . you're . . . Oh God – won't someone please do something . . . Help me . . . *please* . . .'

'She's getting a bit carried away,' said Fred. One or two people started to look rather uncomfortable. The group drew a bit closer together. Glances were exchanged along 'now what?' lines. Simon left the audience and crossed over to the actors. He studied Sheila's trembling lips and wild eyes then knelt down by Derek, felt his pulse and leaned his head against the splotched shirt. He ran his hands over the body then, to Laurie's horror, closed Derek's eyelids before standing up, face deathly pale.

'I'm afraid Sheila's right. He is dead.'

Still uncertain, half convinced yet unable to really believe, the guests murmured to each other. Fred spoke.

'Look, Simon, a joke's a joke – '

'No joke,' said Simon. He was silent for a long moment before once more stumbling into speech. 'When . . . When I was at University College . . . I worked at Guy's in the long vac. As a hospital porter. Believe me . . . I know a corpse when I see one.'

At the word corpse Sheila gave a cry and pitched forward. Simon moved just in time and stood, looking nonplussed and deeply unhappy, with her in his arms. Violet came forward to help.

'You'd better get her some tea . . . or brandy,' said Simon, handing over the half-swooning woman. 'Whatever you think best. Fred, bring that cloth thing – over there.'

Fred crossed to the sofa. There was an Indian printed bedspread draped across the back. He pulled it off and took it to Simon who placed it carefully over Derek. It was a few inches short and his feet peeped out. As Simon bent to pick up the knife Fred said quickly: 'I shouldn't do that, squire.'

'Why not?' But Simon let it lie and straightened up, frowning. 'Ohh . . . I see. I suppose no one should touch anything. But then I don't think anyone has . . . Except Sheila of course.'

'You're right there, Simon. Shurshy la famm. Know what I mean?'

'For heaven's sake.' Simon lowered his voice almost to a whisper. But Sheila and the rest of the company had departed. Mother, who had showed signs of desiring closer acquaintance with the remains, leaving only under pressure. Fred and Simon moved towards the door.

'Better lock him up.'

'I suppose so.' Simon turned the heavy iron key, tested the door then put the key in his pocket. 'God – what a mess.'

They found the others in the second sitting room. Bennet, having made tea for the servants not long before,

211

had already produced a strong sweet cupful for Sheila who was sipping at it when she wasn't sipping at an extremely generous measure of brandy. Violet gently mopped the younger woman's tear-stained face. Simon crossed to Laurie, who looked pale and drawn. She said: 'I've asked Bennet to make us all tea.'

'Good.'

'You look like death.'

'Don't.'

'Sorry. What on earth are we going to do?'

It was the butler who returned with the tray. Lurching less but still far from functioning on that perfectly even keel that Blades would consider *de rigueur*.

'My sister is rather incommoded, madam.'

'I'm not surprised,' said Laurie, who felt pretty incommoded herself. 'Put everything down on the coffee table, Gaunt. People can help themselves.'

After everyone had, with more than one guest gussying up the beverage with a splicing of Courvoisier, they all sat around, Mrs Saville choosing a position near the window where she could keep an eye on the card table. Looks were exchanged. Apprehension, suspicion, uneasy excitement. Fear.

Sheila, head resting awkwardly on Violet's shoulder, had stopped sobbing but had become alcoholically loquacious. 'Poor Derek . . .' she was now wailing whilst wringing her hands. 'Lying there all alone . . . in a pool of his own blood . . . with a knife in his heart . . .'

People murmured consolingly. Laurie murmured too, but, desperately sick and worried as she was, could still rustle up enough irritation to wonder who else's blood Derek could possibly have been lying in a pool of with a knife in his heart.

At last Sheila became quiet and they all sat very still. Intensely aware of each other and holding themselves rather carefully, perhaps afraid that the slightest movement might reactivate that animus of rioting disorder

212

which had wreaked such havoc in the conservatory. Eventually Fred spoke.

'Well,' he said, for once understating the case, 'here's a turn-up for the book.'

The phrase hit the spot. Most of those present had experienced by proxy precisely such a scene. The suspects gathered together after the crime waiting to be cross-questioned by the detective. Except, of course, in this instance there was no detective.

'A right shame ain't it?' Fred voiced the thought. 'He'd have loved this – old Derek. A real murder.'

This set Sheila boo-hooing again and crying, for the umpteenth time: 'I can't understand it . . . Who would want to kill him . . . poor darling . . .'

That of course was the nub. In books it was frequently the widow especially if, as was the case here, she then came into a generous helping of the readies. But no one, not even Rosemary who was far from pleased at Sheila's sudden re-entry into the eligibility stakes, was quite crass enough to put this perception into words.

'Well,' said Mrs Saville, sitting bolt upright and musing once more on the curious discrepancy between the daily routine at Madingley Grange and that of the Royal Georgian Hotel, Bath, 'none of this bizarre behaviour has anything to do with me. I haven't moved from the terrace all morning. As Mrs Gibbs will, I'm sure, confirm.'

'Clears you both, then,' said Fred. 'Point of fact our whole family's out the bog if we're talking alibis.'

Alibis! Suddenly people looked more lively although still carefully holding in place their masks of sympathetic concern. Something wildly out of order might have just occurred but matters were now being eased back on to the correct procedural rails. Once the correct questions had been rigorously asked, and honestly answered, the dense clouds of suspicion would lift and the bright truth shine forth.

'Vi and me,' continued Fred, 'was on the lake. With Gillygillyossenfeffer. Right, Gil?'

'Absolutely.' Gilly looked sulky. He had been rehearsing what he thought of as his testimony for the defence – length of time in punt, previous experience in negotiating same, brief description of water wildlife and skill in embarkation – only to have the opportunity of presenting it snatched from under him.

'So that's five of us sorted – '

'Hold on,' Simon interrupted. 'Didn't Violet and your mother go into the house just before one? We were halfway through the soup, I seem to remember, before they turned up.'

'We were together all the time.' The foxglove bloom had reappeared. Violet looked across at Mother in what seemed to some of those present a slightly threatening manner.

'Except when I went to the doings,' said Mrs Gibbs.

'They don't want to know every sordid detail,' chided Fred. Mrs Gibbs immediately put on a vague, far-away look suggesting spiritual uplift.

'We weren't in the cellar five minutes,' said Violet. 'It was getting her up and down all them steps that took the time.'

'And while Mrs Gibbs was. . . ?'

'I waited in the hall. The butler and maid went by a couple of times with stuff for the table, but no one else.'

'I wonder,' said Fred, back in the director's chair, 'if Simon with his bit of medical know-how could tell us how long Derek had . . . well . . . been lying there.'

'Not long,' said Simon, staring at his feet. 'He was still warm.' Then, as Sheila gave a litle cry: 'I'm sorry.'

'He couldn't have been killed before eleven, say, when we had our coffee?'

'I doubt it.'

'I may be able to help here.' Martin spoke for the first time. 'Someone knocked on my door mid-morning. It took me a few minutes to open it – I was feeling rather groggy – when I did I saw Derek at the far end of the landing.' An interested murmur. 'I'm afraid I didn't feel up to conversation so I didn't actually speak to him. Now I wish I had.'

'Even so, Martin, that's important,' said Fred. 'It's narrowed things down. When did you come out of your room for good?'

'About twelve.'

'And you didn't see him again?' Martin shook his head. 'What did you do after that?'

Martin frowned. Recollection, even of such recent events, was far from automatic. The realization that the small girl now sitting, eyes tightly shut, features frozen into a mask of miserable anxiety was that same soignée creature with whom he had felt so oddly comfortable the previous evening had pushed everything else aside. They were all looking at him expectantly.

'I wandered round the gardens.'

'Meet anyone?'

'Rosemary and Simon.' Martin reddened then, as the air of expectancy intensified. 'I . . . er . . . talked to Rosemary for a few minutes. Simon returned to the house – then Rosemary did the same. I sat on a bench till I heard the gong for lunch.'

'You'd confirm that, Simon?' Simon nodded. 'And can you tell us what you were doing before then?'

'Teaching Rosemary and Sheila to play croquet. Not very successfully, I'm afraid.'

'Does that mean you were in sight of each other all the time?'

'More or less. I came back around twelve thirty, to see how things were going, and saw Bennet on the terrace. She'd just finished laying the table for lunch. She said Laurie had gone to pick some lettuces ages ago so I went off to the vegetable garden – '

'Just a minute, Simon. Are you saying you didn't go into the house at all?'

'That's right. When we came back I sat down for lunch with the others. And Laurie went straight to the kitchen. Isn't that right?'

Laurie nodded. She could not speak. She felt herself to be locked in a bubble of the most appalling unhappiness and despair. How laughable now, how puerile, seemed her previous concern that one of the guests might run off with the family silver. If only that were all they would have to confess to Aunt Maude on her return. Anguished, Laurie relived the scene, so long ago now it seemed, under the large umbrella on the terrace when Simon had put forward the whole disastrous plan. Why had she let herself be persuaded? She had known in her heart that it was wrong. She had even (she thought now with the advantage of hindsight) felt a definite premonition of disaster. If only she had stood firm. It was the story of her life. Simon says, do this, and she did. Never again, Laurie vowed bitterly. Never ever again.

'And I can vouch for Sheila's return,' said Mrs Saville in a sharp voice. 'She came and stood behind my chair. Most irritating.' Then, remembering, 'If you'll forgive me saying so, my dear.'

Everyone looked at Sheila, who said: 'Straight after that I had an aperitif. Then sat down at the lunch table.'

'I did go into the house,' admitted Rosemary, 'for urgent running repairs,' adding coyly, 'to my lipstick. But just to the downstairs cloakroom. I was no more than a couple of minutes.'

Bennet arrived with fresh tea and Fred got his second wind. 'Just a sec, love,' he began as the maid was leaving, 'and you'll have to forgive me for this, Sheila, but somebody's got to put this question – ' He turned back to Bennet: 'I understand you saw Mrs Gregory cross the hall looking for her husband.'

'That's right, sir.'

'How soon would you say after she left the hall did she scream?'

'Within a second or two. She wandered down that little corridor that leads to the conservatory, then she screamed. I ran to see what had happened and found her bending down and picking up the knife.'

'You mean . . . pulling it out of his chest?'

'Stop it! Stop it!' Laurie sprang to her feet. 'You're treating this as if it's still a game. Someone has *died*. It's not up to us to play at finding motives or check alibis. We have to get the police.'

'Whoops!' Fred leapt across the room and grabbed at Bennet's tea pot. 'You'll have that all over the floor.'

'I beg your pardon, sir.' The maid turned to Laurie. 'And miss.'

'Oh what the hell does a spot of tea on the carpet matter?' said Laurie. 'We shouldn't take something as dreadful as this, Fred, and enjoy it. It's too terrible.'

'Hang on.' Fred sounded miffed. 'Nobody can say any of us are enjoying this. But the murder's happened and when the police do turn up they're going to be asking lots of questions. It does no harm to get things clear in our minds. What difference does half an hour make? Rushing around like blue-arsed flies won't bring Derek back. What do you think, Simon?'

'Well . . . I agree . . . I suppose . . .'

Laurie looked across at her brother and hardened her heart against his tentative smile. This proved surprisingly easy to do. Still she did not persist in her argument. For if there was such a thing as post-murder protocol she was quite unfamiliar with the finer details. And certainly Fred was right in stating that they had missed the boat as far as calling the police straight away was concerned. And if half an hour had already passed a few more minutes would hardly signify. She noticed the maid, still drooping whey-faced against the door frame, and said: 'I should go and sit down for half an hour,

217

Bennet. I'll see to the tea.' Bennet, after rubbing vaguely at the spilt drops on the carpet with her shoe, disappeared.

'So now we know,' said Fred, before the door had barely closed, 'that Sheila could not possibly have struck the blow that killed her husband. Not – ' he added hastily as Sheila showed fresh signs of turning on the waterworks – 'that any of us thought for a moment that she had.'

'D'you think, Sheila – ' Violet sounded very gentle – 'he might have done it himself?'

'No.' The widow was quite vehement. 'Derek was the last person ... Especially today. He was so looking forward to outsmarting you all.'

'So if suicide is out,' said Gilly, 'and none of us is the bad hat, who on earth – '

'The prowler!' cried Rosemary. The others looked startled then sighed, almost en masse, with relief. 'Derek must have disturbed him in the conservatory. I expect that's how the pot came to be broken.'

Laurie didn't believe a word of it. She understood the relief, the grasping at any straw. Who would not be delighted at the idea that a malign outsider had been responsible for leaving Derek spatchcocked on the Amtico? But to Laurie this glib conclusion seemed ill reasoned. For a start it did not seem to her, in spite of the broken pot, that there had been a fight. The earth had not been scuffed about, as surely it must have been during a struggle? And Derek himself was so calmly and neatly disposed, lying flat on his back, arms by his sides. No one fell just so. The body had been placed in that position after death.

'Or perhaps,' suggested Mrs Saville, 'the butler was lying last night and the prowler actually is one of the servants. They're bizarre enough, heaven knows.'

'It wouldn't be the domestic staff,' quavered Sheila. 'Derek was very hot on that. The butler never does it.'

218

'But that's in books, dear,' replied Mrs Saville in a 'give me strength' voice. 'We have to forget our murder game. We have a real crime now.'

'D'you think I don't know that?' Out came the by now sodden handkerchief. 'That's my husband lying there . . .'

'Alternatively,' Mrs Saville swept on, 'perhaps the prowler was someone Derek actually recognized. A person from his past determined to settle an old score.'

'Now,' murmured Simon, 'I think we really are entering the realms of fiction.'

Martin shifted uneasily in his chair. He was becoming more and more aware of Laurie's distress. He found himself wanting to offer comfort and wished he had the nerve to cross the room, sit next to her and take her hand.

'I think – ' Fred was back in charge – 'we should look for clues. P'raps starting with an examination of the body – '

'That's it!' Laurie got up and made for the door. 'I shouldn't have agreed with you,' she called over her shoulder to Simon, 'we should have rung the police the second we discovered this. What are they going to think? How are we going to explain the delay?'

She was in the hall now, almost running, Simon close behind calling: 'Laurie – wait. Listen.'

'I've done listening, Simon.' She picked up the phone. 'It was listening to you that got us into this terrible mess.' Laurie dialled a nine. 'Anyway, I know what you're going to say. Everyone's got to have their money's worth, haven't they?' And another. 'Have a bit of fun solving things while that poor man . . .' A third. 'Lies there – leave that phone *alone*, Simon . . . Hullo? . . . Hullo?' She paused, staring at her brother, half angry, half alarmed. 'What have you done?'

'How do you mean?'

'It's dead.'

'Are you sure?' Simon took the receiver, wiggled the rest and listened. 'My God – so it is.'

'Don't look so surprised.'

'It's nothing to do with me.'

The others, who had followed, now started asking questions. Simon's denials got quite heated. Gilly wondered if someone had simply pulled the plug.

'It's not that sort of phone,' said Laurie. 'It was put in years ago.'

'It wouldn't surprise me,' said Violet, 'if the line wasn't down after that storm last night.'

'Oh.' Laurie's face lightened a little. 'I'd forgotten that.'

'You see,' said Simon, defiant and vindicated. 'A perfectly natural explanation.'

'Don't let's jump to conclusions.' Gilly plainly thought this element of tameness undesirable. 'I think we should follow the cord back . . .' He proceeded to do just that '. . . and see what we can find . . . For all we know it may have been deliberately cut.'

Watched by the others he set off tracing the flex which ran, neatly stapled to the skirting board, through the hall and into the dining room before going up, via the ceiling, to the outside. More than one of those present watching him happily running off were uncomfortably reminded of their previous bloodhound in residence. A triumphant cry reached their ears and Gilly was running back.

'I was right! Cut clean through. Underneath that big sideboard. Indicating, of course, premeditation. What a sell.'

Laurie's accusatory look returned and Simon's expression of bewilderment deepened.

'Right,' said Fred. 'Now we know where we stand. Whoever killed Derek was obviously determined to delay the arrival of the police for as long as possible. And the only reason for that must be so he can get clean away. Which means it definitely wasn't one of us.'

'Surely,' said Mrs Saville, her voice crackling with disdain, 'no one believed for a moment that it was? After all, apart from the fact that *most* of us patently do not hail from the substrata of society, there is also the fact that we had never met before this weekend. No one but a madman runs around killing people to whom he has not even been introduced.'

None of the Gibbses was prepared to overlook that qualifying adjective. 'There's been more than one criminal amongst the upper crust.' Violet was quite shrill. 'Trouble is – you got the right connections you can get away with the crown jewels.'

'I reckon,' said Fred, sans-culotte, squaring up to Mrs Saville, 'if every man got his just deserts the gaols'd be stuffed with aristos and politicians. Not to mention rear admirals.'

'Think with their bum,' said Mother. 'Rear admirals.'

Laurie slipped away. She could not bear it. More time squandered in trivial disputation. Once she reached the outside of the house she raced to the garage and climbed into the mini-bus. Luckily Simon had left the keys in the ignition for she had no intention of asking his permission. There would simply be more harangues of the 'let's not be hasty' variety. More perfectly logical-sounding reasons why although of course the police must be notified, was there really any call for them to be notified right away? This very instant? Laurie was sick of such casuistry. She knew, as they must all know, what the right thing to do was. And, before anyone realized where she had gone and why, she intended to do it.

She felt a bit nervous. The bus was an unknown quantity and she had only driven a couple of times since passing her test. On the other hand Oxford was not far, the road was straight and there would be plenty of parking space at the police station. She turned the key and pressed the accelerator. Nothing. Once more. Same result. Not even the exhausted wheeze you got when the battery was flat. She tried once more, knowing she was wasting her time. Then she heard footsteps approaching, running, covering the ground as quickly as had her own. Simon, his skin shiny with sweat, materialized as she was climbing down.

'It's all right,' Laurie said. Her voice was colourless and her face had a bruised, defeated look. 'It won't start. Someone will have to walk to Madingley. Or hitch a lift. Or something. But it won't be me. I've had enough.'

She pushed her brother aside and ran away. Away from the house and its jawing hateful crowd of senseless sleuths. Away from poor, dead Derek about whom no one cared enough to even set the proper forces of the law upon his murderer's trail. But most of all away from Simon whose greed was responsible, it seemed to Laurie, for the whole sordid catastrophic mess.

2

Gordon and Ben, galvanized by the mention of the word POLICE, were packing. Galvanically they hurled clothes, toothbrushes, slippers and night attire into their two canvas suitcases. Frantically rammed-in any old how, lumps, bumps and sharp protuberances were the order of the day. Naturally neither of the cases would shut.

'I'll sit on yours if you'll sit on mine.'

'That's all I need. Kinky sex.'

'Get on with it. We'll have the Old Bill here any minute.'

'Who's to tell them? The phone's kaput and we've got the rotor arm from the bus.'

'For all you know one of those toffee-nosed sods has got a mobile with him.'

'Christ!' said Gordon. 'I never thought of that.' He threw himself with renewed vigour on to Ben's case. There was a splintering sound.

'You've broken the hinge.'

'But did it fasten?'

'No. Can you bounce a bit?'

'Not with one of your coathangers up my arse.'

'We'll have to find some string.'

They blundered around the overstuffed sitting room opening and closing drawers, and peering into boxes watched by dozens of lifeless beady eyes. Both men were wearing the clothes in which they had arrived, speedy dressing having lent the outfits a certain goofy charm. Ben's wig was definitely slipping and his German helmet hat tilted over one ear. Gordon's coat was buttoned skew-whiff all the way up, the leftover wodge of material pushing his chin into fat purple folds. A shoelace was undone and he kept tripping over it, once cracking his head against the case holding the stately, reproving owl.

They threw yellowing tray cloths, ancient seed packets, old knitting patterns, assorted balls of wool and unravelling raffia place mats all over the floor. Finally, in a cupboard full of damaged china, they found a length of orange nylon twine. Ben secured the cases. Gordon opened the window, saying: 'Good job we're on the ground floor.'

'Too right. I wouldn't fancy creeping down that staircase and through the hall surrounded by a load of frigging Pooroes.'

'Fancy that one getting knocked off.'

'No wonder. I'd 've knocked him off just to stop him playing his bloody violin. Go on then – get your leg over.'

'As the camel said to the Arab.'

Ben stared at his brother. 'You can't get anything right, can you?'

'I thought that was pretty good.'

'Go and see if the coast's clear.'

Gordon climbed out of the window, climbing back five minutes later. 'The young laird went belting down to the garage. Laurel must've been there already. She came running out into the garden. He went back to the house.'

'Let's go now, then.' Ben dropped the cases out of the window then perched on the sill looking back into the room. 'Seems criminal, don't it? Taking off from a gaff like this empty handed.'

'Specially since we've been bowing and scraping without a penny piece to show for it since five o'clock yesterday.'

Gordon's tone was nicely judged. Part resentment, part resignation and a little thread of hope. He was very proud of that cunning little thread. Ben would have been most suspicious had his brother not at least attempted to make him change his mind. He might start asking questions and discover that the butler's jacket and trouser pockets were well and truly lined already.

For Gordon had taken the remarks made by his younger brother the previous evening deeply and woundingly to heart. Perhaps it was true, he worried, whilst mournfully coddling his damaged leg, that if it were not for him the whole family (except Dad of course) would even now be tucking into enchiladas on the sun-soaked Spanish equivalent of Easy Street. With Gordon, to think was to vacillate. But after the discovery of the body, when it became plain that a quick scarper was on the cards, he acted.

While Ben was in the garage disabling the bus Gordon had dragged himself up to the Greuze room only to find his quarry, the jewel-stuffed casket, had disappeared, presumably into the drawer of the bedside table, which he discovered to be locked. Reflecting bitterly that the higher up the social scale you went the harder it was to find anyone practising the virtue of simple trust, he was hobbling back along the landing when the jade intaglios and gold-framed miniatures on the half moon tables caught his eye.

Now he said: 'We're due something,' thinking, even at this late stage, to get clearance for his illicit haul.

'You lift as much as a teaspoon and I'll chop your fingers off. This place is going to be swarming with rozzers before too long. If our luck turns bad and we get picked up all they can get us on is borrowing the bus. We can say we were shit scared after the murder and desperate to get away.'

'But . . . we got the future to think of, Ben.'

'If I sit on this sill much longer I shan't have a future. Got your keys?' Gordon produced a huge bunch from his overcoat pocket. 'We'll dump the bus in Oxford and pick up a family job. Be careful how you drive with that leg.'

'I'll be OK.' Gordon forced confidence into his voice. Actually his mind could get but small purchase on his calf muscles, which seemed to be made of cotton wool.

Ben dropped to the ground. Gordon prepared to follow, then paused, looked around, his gaze halting at the prie-dieu where the owl sat, unblinking, under its dome. Carefully he lifted the glass and placed it on the carpet. Then he poked the owl forcefully in the stomach. The bird wobbled, fell off its rock and collapsed into a heap of sawdust and feathers. Gordon turned to his brother and smirked.

'For God's sake,' said Ben. 'Don't be so bloody childish.'

On leaving Simon, Laurie had run blindly away across the lawn and into the trees before her feet, being turned by memory back on to the comfort circuit, blundered once more into the vegetable garden.

But such was her distress and apprehension that, for the first time since she could remember, the high walls seemed to offer neither solace nor protection. She still felt intensely vulnerable standing there alone under the brazen sky. She must retreat further. Find peace and quiet; become immune from the raucous and fearful pantomime unfolding back at the Grange. She made her way to the large Dutch greenhouse and closed the door. Sanctuary. The humid warmth enveloped her like a cloak. Half the panes were whitewashed against the heat. Behind them she felt sheltered and secure. She sat down on an old kitchen chair with no back and closed her eyes. She became aware that her hands were balled tight and that she was gritting her teeth. Slowly she unclenched her fingers, parted her lips and opened her mouth slightly, feeling the muscles of her jaw become pliant and relaxed. She became aware of a mixture of exotic and homely fragrances. Heady Chinese jasmine and *Lilium longiflorum* and the unmistakable earthy warmth of tomatoes. In this case Saint Pierre.

A bee, punch drunk on pollen, was stumbling from

one exquisite arabesque of lily petals to the next, its buzz vibrant and ecstatic. Laurie envied it. How marvellous to enjoy such a simple and ordered existence. No problems for him when he finally staggered back, dusty legged, to the hive. Nobody jumping on him wanting to know where he was at fourteen hundred hours when a drone on the eighth cornice got his.

Laurie groaned, recognizing how foolish she had been to believe that she could shed terrible things simply by retreating into a childhood haven. Instead, riven with disquiet, she had brought all the chaos with her, staining the wholesome serenity that lay around.

She wandered up and down the strip of narrow flagstones that made the greenhouse path, worrying about the unpicked tomatoes, stroking the silvery-green fleece of alpines packed closely in their trays. But plants had lost the power to heal. Sick and shuddery, she sat down again.

She thought, as she had already done over and over again, of the people back at the house, one of whom must be a killer. Yet how could that be? What earthly reason would anyone have for getting rid of Derek? The only obvious suspect (Sheila) had been out of the house all morning and cleared of last-minute murder by the maid's statement. And why should Bennet lie? Unless both she and Gaunt were Sheila's accomplices. This all seemed so frankly incredible that Laurie, even at the moment of being strongly tempted at the comforting neatness of such a solution, felt compelled to abandon it.

Part of the trouble was that the intense theatricality of the weekend helped to muddy up all the sightlines. A houseful of strangers is introduced. Next morning they all don false personas and prepare to take up the threads of false relationships purely in the interests of producing a false death by a false murderer.

Except that it hadn't worked out like that. Which made it all so . . . extraordinary. Yes – that was the word.

Extraordinary. The more Laurie thought of it the more grotesque and unreal the whole affair appeared. In her mind she watched the cast of characters passing back and forth through the penumbra dividing truth from fiction. They all wore different faces. Or perhaps different masks. But what were they truly like?

Was Rosemary just a pretty little flirt? And Sheila her svelte, high-cheekboned counterpoint? Surely there must be more to Gilly than the braying monocled twittishness he chose to display? And were not the emphases given by Mother and Mrs Saville to the antique nuances of class, tribe and status so resourcefully – even picturesquely – dreadful as to beggar belief and turn both ladies into parodies?

And what of Fred? Laurie had regarded his crass and ebullient chauvinism as at the worst charmless and mildly offensive. Now she wondered if it could not be indicative of a much darker macho aggression, seeking a handy outlet. Finally there was Violet. Laurie had watched more than one film where the foolish-faced middle-aged woman had, in the last reel, been revealed as a super spy and, casting aside glossy wig and simper, savagely delivered the *coup de grâce*. Only Martin (there it was! That dear remembered face) was plainly completely innocent.

Then it struck Laurie that every single one of these people had an alibi. No wonder the idea of an outsider had taken such a firm and popular hold. It was the only thing that made the whole terrible business explicable, for Laurie agreed with Sheila that Derek seemed to be the last person to take his own life.

Then, her thoughts having completed their wretchedly fruitless spiral, she was recalled to the present by the angry *zzz* of the heavy-laden bee who had mistaken the flightpath to freedom and was hurling itself against one of the clear glass panes. With a pang of fellow feeling Laurie opened the door, got a flower pot and

Mackintosh's *Practical Gardening*, trapped the bee and let it go. It flew off into a clump of ragged robin.

She was just turning back into her refuge when she heard a rustle. Strange, she thought, on such a hot, windless day. It was not the shy whisper of disturbed grasses that a small creature might make but much louder, as if a large animal was blundering about. She was not sure from which direction it emanated, only that it was coming from somewhere behind the garden wall. She strained her ears and was sure she heard whatever it was moving away. It was only then that she realized from her held breath and parched throat and the tocsin beat of her heart that she had been afraid.

For the first time it struck Laurie that she might have been very foolish to thus isolate herself so completely from the rest of the group. The sanctuary of the greenhouse, secret and enclosed inside a high brick wall, could, by a terrible turn of the wheel, just as easily become a trap. There had never been any need for a lock on the rusty garden gate. Anyone could walk in. The murderer could walk in.

When the gate creaked Laurie told herself she had imagined the sound. Then it creaked again and the latch clicked as it was closed. Footsteps – soft, secretive on the beaten earth – approached, stopped, came on. Surely, *surely*, prayed Laurie, whoever it is will see that the garden is empty and go away. Standing stock still behind the whitewashed panes she knew herself to be invisible unless the intruder actually came up to the open greenhouse door. And why should he do this? No reason. *Unless he was looking for her.*

Motionless she waited, her heart pounding in such a frenzy it seemed to be trying to escape from her breast and force its way into her throat. There was a thundering, such a thundering in her ears that he would surely hear it. Drenched in sweat, choking on perfumed air, she stared at the opaque glass until her eyes burned, longing for supernatural energy that she might penetrate the milky film.

Dare she look out? Risk her head appearing for a split second plainly visible through an unpainted pane? Why not? If she was very, very quick. Just a glance. Then she would know. And she *must* know. Reminding herself that the odds against him (Laurie did not for a moment think that it could be a her) actually facing the greenhouse when she peered out were three to one against, she gripped the edge of the slatted shelving and, her nerves stretched into quivering tensile wires, moved. Inch by inch by inch. And dodged back. Nothing. He must be in the right-hand section of the garden. That meant creeping along to the other end of the block of whitened glass and going through the whole agonizing process again. This time Laurie decided she wouldn't accentuate the misery by extending the process. Just a quick bob out and back. Less chance of being noticed.

She moved, but too quickly. Careless of her immediate surroundings, every atom and molecule trained on to the great outdoors, Laurie knocked over a flowerpot. It fell and smashed, a very loud smash, on the flagstones. She stifled a low moaning cry. A terrible silence ensued.

And then the footsteps started up again. They abandoned the earthen path for one of gravel. The one that led directly to the greenhouse door. Laurie waited, melting with panic. Images, poignant and ridiculous, surged through her mind. She and Derek, linked dramatically on the *Six O'Clock News*. Scotland Yard investigating. Tearful friends and relatives ringed around her grave watching the shiny box slip away. Everyone liked her, people would affirm, as they always did when it was too late. Simon, drinking too much at the reception, would say: 'She was too young to die.'

And my God, so I am, thought Laurie. So I am. Anger stroked her then, like a bear's paw. Scratching her painfully, hopefully back to life. What am I doing, she asked herself, standing here, just standing, waiting? Tamely, like some sacrificial goat. Is this the spirit with which I led Bedales against Alton Convent at hockey, winning seven nil? Adrenaline tumbled into her blood, firing her resolve. It was too late to run. (The footsteps were nearer now. Very near.) But it was not too late to fight. It was not too late to yell and scream and kick. Or shout *Geronimo!* and crown him with a flowerpot. Or squirt him in the eye with Tumblebug.

So Laurie picked up the kitchen chair with no back, and the second the unknown loiterer stepped through the greenhouse doorway screwed her eyes up tight and brought it crashing down upon his head.

3

Martin had been roaming the grounds for nearly an hour looking for Laurie. He alone – perhaps because he was so consistently aware of her presence – had noticed her slip away. And when Simon had missed her and run off to the garage Martin had left too.

So far he had circled the lake, retracing his morning steps over the Willow Pattern bridge and through the shrubbery, and was now checking the charming and eccentric topiary. Huge cups and saucers, a snake poised waveringly on the tip of its tail and a lion with an austere neatly barbered mane and wild flowering bushy legs. But no Laurie.

Martin felt his general anxiety quicken into a definite stab of apprehension. Where on earth could she be? A picture of her presented itself and his apprehension deepened. She was such a little thing. So vulnerable. He recalled her staggering under the weight of his breakfast tray, her slim wrist as she wielded the big silver tea pot, her tender sloping shoulders. And she was out here on her own. With that bloody man on the loose . . .

At least steps had been taken to inform the proper authorities. Martin had noticed the van going down the drive whilst searching a clump of bamboo on the far side of the lake. Now, negotiating a giant turtle of mixed parentage (box, yew and golden privet) Martin, consumed with worry as he was, yet found himself able to reflect with a small part of his mind on the extreme peculiarity of his position.

He had never thought himself a fickle person. Off with the old and on with the new was a concept quite alien to his nature. If asked his opinion on such a way of going on he would have described it as tawdry in the extreme. Yet here he was, only twenty-four hours ago engaged to one girl, now, thanks to Rosemary's apostasy, disengaged and with his thoughts already warmly turning towards another.

Martin's relationships with the opposite sex had been modest both in number and in the degree of their intensity. He had meandered into one or two rather static relationships which had petered out in an atmosphere of mild goodwill on both sides and then he had met Rosemary. Like most people Martin admired or envied in others qualities that were plainly absent in himself. So he was attracted by Rosemary's forthright bounciness, not seeing how close it was to bossiness, itself a mere scold away from bullying.

But in none of these previous relationships had he felt that sweet protective urge or easy warmth of heart he experienced now when thinking of Laurie. It seemed to Martin hardly possible that he had exchanged no more than a few sentences with the girl, and half of those whilst under the impression that she was someone else. He attempted to consider these emotions coolly but failed. He felt excited but aware that the excitement had a still calm centre. He sat down on a stone, tongue-extending griffin and pondered.

Was this then, this tranquil disturbance and extraordinary *tendresse*, love? The experience of which peerless poets and lesser lyricists alike had sung? 'Some enchanted evening . . . It is the moon and Juliet is the sun . . . Unforgettable, that's what you are . . . Whoever loved that loved not at first sight. . . ?'

Martin sprang up and walked on, overwhelmed and astonished by this marvellous new perception. That it was true he had no doubt. His heart tightened, his blood fizzed, his stomach swooped and his bones were all bendy. But when had it happened? As they had first spoken when he got off the bus? When she had brought up his tray so imaginatively decorated by that lovely marigold? Or just now when he had longed to offer comfort as she sat, white-faced and wretched, in the sitting room? The time was unimportant. The fact, shining with a sock-in-the-eye, klieg-light brilliance, was all. 'I am in love,' murmured Martin and held the realization, like a glowing jewel, in the forefront of his mind as he strolled on.

Strangely enough now that he had put a name to his condition (so common, so unique) the urgent need to clap eyes on his treasure lessened. It seemed enough for now that he could re-create her in his imagination. Picture her elegant in patterned silk, stunning in lamé, shy and pretty in her old blue frock. Each vision seemed to Martin to approach the very pinnacle of perfection. And, with the unclouded percipience of lovers everywhere, he knew that she was as good and kind and clever as she was beautiful.

She would not make the drearily predictable remark if he told her that he travelled in glass houses that he must be careful not to throw any stones. Or scoff at his ambition to one day design and stock his own conservatories for individual clients right down to the last flower and fern. Or laugh (as Rosemary had) if he confessed that occasionally, when the day had been especially dark, he still took Teddy to bed.

Mooning thus Martin almost didn't notice the entrance that led to the kitchen garden. Not wishing to leave any part of the grounds unchecked he went in, closing the gate with great care behind him. Pausing only to reflect that, no doubt due to love's benign intervention, his headache had entirely disappeared he started to look round.

Plainly the garden was uninhabited but Martin, his horticulturalist's soul charmed by the neatness of the vegetable beds, could not resist it. The herb wheel he found especially appealing. He admired the greenhouse, very sensibly semi-whitewashed against the heat (the staff here obviously knew their stuff), and, with the zealous curiosity of the expert, was driven to have a peep inside.

He realized it was occupied as he went up the path and heard something fall. This realization was compounded by the fact that, as he stooped to enter, someone hit him a terrific blow across the head.

Martin's last two conscious thoughts as he plummeted into darkness were: I am being murdered and I shall never see her again.

Both of these perceptions were rapidly confounded. In no time at all he became aware that his name was being urgently spoken. Also that a little light rain was falling on his face. As he struggled to sit up his headache returned with a vengeance. The rain appeared to come from a watering can held by his beloved girl, as did the anguished name-calling.

Now she put the can aside and fell to her knees, crying: 'Darling, darling, *darling*. Oh darling – are you all right? Speak to me, darling.'

Martin, not a whit bored by all this repetition, gave her a woozy smile. 'My darling . . .' he began (who was he to improve upon such dialogue?) 'I think I'm all right. Darling.'

'Oh!' Scarlet-faced, Laurie scrambled to her feet and, rather more slowly and hanging on to the shelving, Martin did the same. 'You must sit down,' she continued, taking his arm and leading him to a sort of stool which she set upright and on to which he gratefully sank. Then she stood, rather as she had that morning in his room, looking at him with that same strange mixture of ingenuousness, excitement and alarm.

Martin on the other hand, although in great pain, felt uncomplicatedly happy. He knew himself to be loved. Laurie had lavished endearments upon him and held

him in her arms. True, this was only after she had
knocked him half senseless with some sort of blunt
instrument but no doubt all would be explained in the
fullness of time. Lack of doubt must be the order of the
day if their courtship were to blossom as Martin was
determined that it should. Meanwhile as she was now
looking quite shattered and appeared to be tongue-tied
to boot, it was up to him to make some soothing remark
and help reduce all the emotion that was charging so
impetuously about. Something light, down to earth but
unromantic (there would be plenty of time for all that
later). Strictly non-inflammatory. Perhaps a joke? (I've
heard of the greenhouse effect but this is ridiculous.) On
second thoughts better not. Such facetiae might only
upset her more. Martin looked around for inspiration
and spotted the perfect opener. Safe, innocuous,
uncontroversial to the point of boredom.

'I say,' he said. 'Those tomatoes could do with
pinching out.'

His honeysuckle burst into tears. 'I've been trying to
do them,' she sobbed, 'ever since Simon suggested this
d. . .dreadful weekend. And there's so man. . .man. . .
man . . .'

'There certainly are,' agreed Martin, looking down
the long aisle at the prodigality of Saint Pierres. 'What
on earth do you do with all the proceeds?'

'My aunt sells them. At the WI market.'

'Why don't we pinch them out now?'

'*Could* we?'

'I don't see why not. I'm in no hurry to get back – are
you?'

'Oh no,' said Laurie quickly. She smiled at him, then
took an old pouched hessian apron from behind the
door, wrapped it around herself and started to take out
the side shoots from the first plant, dropping the green
fronds into the pocket. Martin started on the second.
They worked down one side together and gradually the

emotional tension lessened until it was nothing more than a quietly interesting simmer.

'Don't your aunt's gardeners do this sort of thing?'

'They just come in one day a week while she's away, to do the rough. I offered to look after everything else.'

'A hell of a lot to do.'

'I don't mind. I simply love it.' Martin remembered the off colour fingernails. 'Simon says I was born on my knees with a trowel in my hand.'

'Me too.'

'Really?' She stopped picking and gazed at him with the warmest interest but without surprise. It seemed to Laurie, now that this great benefaction had fallen from the skies (for had Martin not called her his darling?) that all manner of things would inevitably be well. It would be quite unthinkable that he would not share her grand passion. Soul mates came equipped with all the necessary accoutrements for perfect domestic harmony. She waited happily for more of this captivating inquisition.

'Actually I travel in glass houses . . .' Martin paused. Laurie gave him an encouraging smile and he continued, laying his hopes and dreams at her feet.

'I've always thought,' she said when he had finished, 'that there must be all sorts of marvellous plants in China and India which we don't know about yet. Things perfect for your conservatory. George Forrest couldn't have found them all. Then there's the warm parts of Russia . . . Georgia, you know. Or even Turkistan.'

'We must go and see.'

Laurie dropped some shoots and stumbled picking them up. She had not been prepared for that first usage of the sweetest of all the personal pronouns, or the quick piercing shaft of joy.

'I'm going to Pershore College in September,' she said, when she felt able to speak. 'I want eventually to do landscape gardening.'

Martin listened, rapt and amazed. He had not

assumed, he had not *trusted* that their ambitions and interests would, such is the precision of blind Cupid's aim, so marvellously coincide. To Martin the whole revelatory conversation was like being handed the gift of a ravishingly painted box and, on opening it, finding inside another of greater perfection and inside that, one more lovely still.

His heart brimming with gratitude he reached out and took her hand. She didn't look at him but he felt her tremble. Across her brown forearm lay a bar of brilliant orange pollen. He bent his head and blew the powdery dust away. She turned then and he saw that she was crying.

'Dearest . . .' He put his arms around her. 'What is it? Don't cry. I can't bear it.'

'Oh Martin.' Tears sprang from her eyes and streamed down her cheeks. She buried her face in his shirt front. 'I thought I'd . . . killed you . . .'

'Well, I must say you pack quite a punch.' Then, as she continued to weep, 'There, sweet . . .' He touched the silver glaze of warm tears with his lips and they stood for a moment still and close, locked in a daze of luminous reciprocity. And then he kissed her. It was wonderful. Cool and fresh and sweet, like burying your face in a newly opened rose. So he did it again.

Blissfully Laurie, eyes closed, kissed him back. And then, as the comets wheeled in planetary splendour and meteors fell and clouds of stardust settled on their closed lids, it happened. Beneath her feet the powerful shift and glide and click of the earth's great plates.

'Ohhh . . .' cried Laurie, releasing herself and stepping back, wide-eyed. 'Then it's true. It does move. It *really* moves.'

'What's that, sweetheart?'

'The ground. Simon said it was all due to mass bombardment.'

'Ridiculous.'

Dazzled, uncomprehending, Martin smiled at Laurie; loving her skin, warm and freckled like a ripe apricot, her spice-brown hair and endearingly grubby little paws. More mouth to mouth resuscitation. Fifty tomato plants awaited pinching out in vain. This state of supernatural bliss, transcending lust and almost, even, transcending love was savagely shattered by the sound of a gunshot. Very loud. Crack! Shocked into wakefulness Laurie and Martin turned startled faces towards the garden wall.

The swans, alarmed, had risen from the moat and now appeared with a great whooshing of wings passing over the greenhouse on their way to the lake. Then, as Laurie and Martin began to run, there was a second shot followed immediately by a terrible harsh scream.

4

This is how the shooting came about. Simon had returned from the garage with the news that the mini-bus was out of commission, and was now fielding a salvo of anxious and furious questions.

'But what's the matter with it?'

'Why won't it start?'

'Have you run out of petrol?'

'You can't run out of petrol, Violet, standing in a garage.'

'I say – what a snorter!' Neigh whicker neigh, neigh. Neigh neigh.

'Perhaps it needs a push.'

'If anyone expects me to push they're in for a grave disappointment.'

'I'm sure it's not poor Simon's fault, Mummy.'

'What on earth are we going to do now?'

'One cock-up after another, as the warden said on visiting day.'

'Rosemary – cover your ears!'

'It's to stop us getting away. We're trapped . . . *with a killer*.'

'Now, Violet – don't take on.'

'If we could please discuss this quietly – '

'The grounds never lie.'

'Please . . .' repeated Simon. He spread his arms and moved his hands up and down like a conductor demanding a shade more *andante*. People quietened, but briefly.

'Point is, Simon,' said Gilly, 'that if we leave things much longer, then it really is going to look peculiar as far as the bobbies are concerned. One of us is going to have to leg it to the nearest phone. I'd be happy to oblige.'

'No doubt you would,' said Fred. 'But nobody's going to leg it anywhere until we get the truth about this intruder sorted out.'

'What difference does that make?'

'I'll tell you what difference. Simon says he was just an actor – '

'I didn't actually say that.' Simon hesitated. 'And if I misled you I'm sorry. It was only because I felt that one or two people were genuinely frightened. The fact is I didn't hire anyone.'

'In that case, and assuming Sheila's imagination carried her away, that only leaves us lot. So you can see,' Fred answered Gilly, 'why nobody can bugger off. That person might well be the murderer.'

'Let two people go then.'

'And who do you think's going to be daft enough to go out there – ' Fred waved at the distant trees – 'with somebody who might wring his neck the minute they're away? If he's done one murder he won't hang about when it comes to another.'

'Why don't you and Violet go then?' asked Rosemary.

'Oh I couldn't, duck. My feet aren't up to it.'

'Why not send the servants?'

'The servants are useless,' explained Simon patiently. 'One's lame, the other's half blind.'

'We seem,' said Mrs Saville, 'to have given up on the transport question rather easily. Perhaps the fault is not serious but one that a person with some knowledge of engines could rectify. Perhaps Mr Gibbs . . .' Her voice, which had enjoyed a slightly wincing note throughout, as if being lightly brushed by an oily rag, tailed delicately off.

'No I couldn't,' said Fred, well aware of why he had come out top in the possible car mechanic stakes. 'I'm about as likely to be able to start that heap of old junk as

I am to start fanning me tea with me cap. I got a Testarossa. And two blokes to look after it.'

'They're so wearing, aren't they,' mused Mrs Saville aside to Rosemary, 'the nouveau riche?'

'I'm getting sick to death of you, missus. Looking down that great hooter at me and my family. We're as good as you any day of the week. And I'll tell you summat else – '

'Sssh.' Simon jumped to his feet. 'Listen . . .'

Ears were strained. The cough of an engine could be clearly heard. The sound opened up and spread when the vehicle moved from the garage, travelled, got fainter and disappeared. This all happened so quickly that people had hardly registered what the noise was before it had faded completely.

'I say!' gasped Gilly. 'He's legged it. The murderer's got away.'

'But . . .' Simon was astonished. 'I don't understand . . . who could – '

'We're all here,' said Sheila. 'That lets us out.'

'We're not, you know,' Fred contradicted her. 'We're missing young Martin.'

'Martin?' Rosemary laughed unkindly. 'He couldn't murder a poached egg.'

'Where is he then? And come to that – ' Fred winked lewdly across the room at Simon – 'where's your sister?'

'I assume she's helping in the – ' Simon broke off. His expression became deeply apprehensive. He hurried from the room and returned looking even more disturbed. A competent well-organized man who has had his rug of carefully woven strategem whipped from under his feet. His face showed a mixture of panic and disbelief. 'They've gone.'

'Who?'

'The servants. All their clothes, everything.'

'Perhaps you could tell us,' said Mrs Saville, 'how they managed to start the bus when you failed.'

'You must have the number,' said Fred. 'On the hire papers. The police will pick them up.'

'When?' cried Simon. 'We have no phone. And it will take at least an hour to walk to Madingley.'

'They'll dump it if they've got any sense,' said Violet. 'Soon as they get to Oxford.'

'So the mystery's solved.'

'What?' Simon looked blank.

'The butler did it after all,' continued Rosemary with a snide glance at Sheila. 'Or the maid.'

'I never did trust that woman. Her tits were too close together.'

'Fred!'

'No need to get aerated, my duck,' said Fred. 'You know me. I speak as I find. You couldn't have slid a cat's whisker between them. And did you see those feet? Big as herring boxes.'

'What are you getting at?' asked Simon.

'Elementary, squire. I reckon it were a man in drag.'

'*In* . . .'

'I say . . . dash it. . . ' Gilly's round gooseberry eyes swivelled excitedly about.

'You got two professionals there, Simon. Pose as servants. Forged references. Clean up and move on. Better start counting your knick-knacks.'

'I can't believe it . . .' Simon looked around help-lessly.

'Derek must've caught them at it so they rubbed him out.'

'At least the police'll be jolly pleased.' Rosemary smiled at Simon encouragingly. 'Us doing all this detecting for them.'

'You haven't had much to do with the Old Bill, have you, Rosie?' asked Fred.

'Well it's not our fault they got away.'

There was a long pause then. A strange hiatus. The flare of excitement having shrivelled, a stale, flat atmosphere came to prevail. So it's all over? people seemed silently to say.

'Perhaps – ' Mrs Saville eventually turned to the elder Mrs Gibbs – 'as neither of us will be walking to Madingley we might continue our game?' She tried to keep her tone even, but failed. Voracity shone through.

Mrs Gibbs returned a curious smile and said: 'Let's have a leg up then.' Violet looked at Fred, who shrugged, then helped her mother-in-law to her feet.

Mrs Saville suggested that the cards be placed not in their hands but on the terrace table, 'To confirm that the game will continue in a spirit of absolute integrity,' and this was done once both ladies were seated. Mrs Gibbs seemed in no hurry to start playing and Mrs Saville, after looking once at her cards to check that their miraculous consequentiality remained inviolate, held her horses as patiently as she was able. Her heart fluttered and she felt slightly dizzy but infinitely more alive than when she had been sitting in the house. Things were getting definitely sluggish back there now the mystery had been solved.

Although of course in a way the mystery out here was solved too. For the result of the forthcoming game was known, at least to Mrs Saville. Yet she could still feel an agitated tremor of anticipation and was startled to see her hand shake. She looked across at her opponent, so soon to be bested. How ugly Mrs Gibbs was. She sat so still, gazing out over the parkland. Her profile with its hooked witchy nose cleanly etched. Mrs Saville wondered how old she really was. Hard to tell from that crackle-glazed skin the colour of dark caramel toffee and ivory-yellow snaggle tooth.

After five minutes or so Mrs Saville leaned forward but the overture was received with a fierce shake of the head. She sat back again, saying, 'What is it?' Then, anguished, 'You *are* going to play?'

'I'll play when it's all over.'

'When what's all over?' Mrs Saville recognized the pose. The old woman had sat just so, head cocked, at lunch time the second before Sheila Gregory had screamed. Was this to be another such coincidence?

A hoarse whisper came across. 'The murder.'

'But . . . we've had the murder. It's solved . . .'

Mrs Gibbs shook her greasy grey poll. 'You're barking up the wrong banana.'

'You mean there's going to be *another* murder? Heavens!' She sprang up. 'Rosemary!'

'Rose Marie?' Mrs Gibbs cackled. 'A long life. Too long.'

'Then who?' Relieved, Mrs Saville had sunk down again. 'If you know you must do something. Go back in there and tell them.'

'Me?' Mrs Gibbs winked slyly. 'I can't go anywhere. I got a bone in me leg.'

In the library Simon, having announced that as this mess was all his fault, it was only fair that he should be the one to walk to the village, hesitated at the door.

Solemn and encouraging faces urged him to his task. Only Sheila did not look up. She sat head bent, gripping her knees, knuckles shining white. Her body, a hoop of tension, was poised on the edge of her seat like a sprinter on the mark.

Simon opened the door and, at the sound, Sheila sprang to her feet, crying: 'Yes – yes – go! You were right – this farce has gone on long enough . . . Oh *poor* Derek . . .' and burst into hysterical sobs.

Everyone perked up at the onset of fresh histrionics, consoling and soothing. All but Rosemary who rolled back her eyes with irritation while she considered leaving the lot of them to it and hurrying to catch Simon up. She had appreciated the delicacy of his position earlier when he had announced that he must travel alone. It would have looked very peculiar if he had rejected Gilly's offer of company and then agreed to let someone else tag along. But Rosemary, emboldened by the sweet nothings exchanged behind the *Lonicera americana*, was sure Simon would be only too delighted were she to slip away and catch him up.

No sooner thought than done. She tiptoed towards the hall. But hardly had she got there when she heard someone cry out. A violent shout. Either: 'No!' or 'Don't!' Then running footsteps. Slightly alarmed, Rosemary hesitated then found herself propelled forwards by Violet and Fred, the latter crying, 'What's that row?'

Simon raced into view. A voice in pursuit called: 'Stop or I fire!' Simon did not stop. There was a shot. A large vase, high on a marble pedestal, exploded. Yellow and turquoise fragments flew through the air. Rosemary screamed. The front door stood open. Simon sped through. And in fierce pursuit, eyes wild, hair flying and brandishing Gilly's revolver, ran Derek Gregory.

A second shot followed by a squawk. Rosemary turned to Fred in horror. 'He's killed him! Oh Simon . . .'

After a moment's stunned surprise at the corpse's reappearance they all stampeded off over the terrace and on to the green, Rosemary uttering a little trill of relief as they passed a peacock, lying on its back with its legs in the air.

Laurie and Martin, hand in hand, gawped at the riotous assembly. Apart from the gun blasts they could have been watching the frantic final reel of a silent movie. Simon, zigzagging madly across the grass; Derek, zigging where Simon zagged and vice versa, unable to get a bead on his quarry but firing anyway. Once he turned and fired in the opposite direction and the rear column fell on its collective face.

Simon, having covered the distance, disappeared into the shrubbery. Derek stopped then, holding the gun with both hands and bending slightly at the knees in true professional manner. He pointed it directly at Simon's vanishing point and pulled the trigger. Nothing happened. He stood upright, shook the weapon, lifted it and peered down the barrel.

Fred, yelling: 'Don't do that, you silly sod!' ran up and wrenched the revolver out of Derek's hand. By the time Laurie and Martin reached the pair they had been joined by all the others. Derek, Gilly gripping him firmly by the arm, stood in the group's centre, white-faced and shaking with rage, and muttering: 'I'll kill him . . . I'll kill him . . .' Then: 'And I'll kill *you* . . .' He glared savagely at his wife.

'Derek,' she cried. 'What's the matter? What's come over you? Are you mad?'

'Yes, mad. Mad to trust you . . . You fiend in human form. Evil scheming black-hearted trollop!'

Simon stepped out hesitantly from behind a rhododendron. 'It's all right,' Gilly called. 'We've got a firm hold.'

He spoke too soon. Derek wrenched himself free with an enraged yell and Simon disappeared again. Fred and Gilly, furiously in pursuit, tackled Derek and brought him crashing down on a group of daphne seedlings. Laurie ran after her brother.

'Simon! What on earth is going on? Heavens, you look dreadful.'

'Wouldn't you?' Simon's shirt was wet through. His fair hair dark with sweat. His mouth worked with terror and relief. 'You lunatic!' he screamed, in the general direction of the mangled *thymelaeaceae*. 'You homicidal maniac. You want bloody locking up. Oh my God –' Simon's legs buckled and he collapsed. Laurie crouched beside him. Martin joined her and between them they got the quaking figure to its feet.

'Help me get him inside, Martin. Come on, Simon,' she coaxed her brother gently. 'You look as if you could do with a drink.'

'Yes . . . get him a drink. Get him some hemlock. That's the stuff for traitors, isn't it? That's the coward's weapon – poison!' More yells and general vilification followed the trio as they stumbled across the lawn, Laurie murmuring distressedly as they passed the dead bird.

The two matriarchs on the terrace watched their approach with interest tinged, in the case of Mrs Gibbs, with cynical amusement. When they had passed Mrs Saville raised her brows inquiringly but her companion merely lowered one lizard-like eyelid and shook her head.

In the library they eased Simon into an armchair. Laurie poured a large brandy and, finding her brother's fingers apparently boneless, held it to his lips. He downed it in three gulps then his body gave one final violent shake and was still. He breathed more quietly, his mouth stopped trembling.

'Better?'

'A bit.'

'Right.' Laurie put the glass down, looked across at Derek and back to her brother. 'Now, Simon. Will you please explain what the hell is going on?'

Five minutes later several other people having also opted for what Gilly called 'a snorter', the smell of spirits pervaded the room. This added to the headiness already generated by a maelstrom of excited voices, most prominent of which by far was Derek's. He strode up and down, fulminating. 'Let's get the buttons off the foils' was one of his fulminates, interlarded with 'deep waters, deep waters'.

During one of his brief breathing spaces Violet cried: 'But you *still* haven't told us why you're not dead.'

'Ask Jezebel,' shouted Derek, pointing dramatically at his wife. 'Or better still her fancy man.' The finger swung in the direction of his host.

Simon, who had been sitting in an attitude of alarm and dejection, his elegantly barbered cranium resting in his hands, lifted it at these words and gazed around in absolute bewilderment.

'You can look,' cried Derek, whose brush with death had obvious done little to dim his eye for detail. 'I expect there's been a lot of looks behind my back one way or another. And not stopping at looks either.'

Simon opened his mouth and seemed about to speak. Then, apparently overwhelmed at being the target of such a flood of irrationality, closed it again. He frowned. 'I could do with a drink.'

Laurie said: 'You've already had three.'

'I don't care if I've had thirty-three.' His voice sounded raw. 'Desperate measures call for desperate times . . . or something . . .'

'I'll get it.' Fred, ostentatiously holding his hand over his breast pocket wherein reposed the Major Fontaine, poured another large snorter and gave it to Simon. 'Hair of the dog, lad.'

'You shouldn't come out with aspertions, Derek,' said Violet. 'Especially without any proof. Folks get upset.'

'Proof! If it's proof you want take a look at this!' And Derek whipped a paperback from the inside of his jacket and waved it at them all. 'This book has saved my life as surely as if it had stopped an assassin's bullet.'

'I shouldn't think you're in much of a position to talk about assassin's bullets,' said Simon who, now that the *eau de vie* was taking effect, sounded a fraction on the stroppy side.

'Pot calling the kettle – what?' put in Gilly. 'Cut up rather rough yourself.'

'You've got something to do with what's been going on though, haven't you, Simon?' put in Fred. ''Cause it were you that told us he were dead. Fooled me good and proper.'

'Oh – he's great at fooling people, Simon.' Derek's tone was richly sarcastic. 'Well – go on then. Tell them all about it.'

'It's hardly anything to do with me.' Simon sounded defensive now as well as stroppy. 'I was approached – '

'By your mistress!'

'I was approached,' continued Simon, giving the impression of gritted teeth and syllables strained through a fine-meshed sieve, 'by Sheila – Mrs Gregory – who suggested that to placate her husband, who was so upset at being cast in the role of victim he was quite capable of spoiling the entire weekend for all the others, we enact a little play . . . a murder game if you like . . . of our own. It seemed to me a not unreasonable plan. I saw it could inject a note of real drama into our proceedings which, as host, it seemed my duty to do. After all what could be more exciting than to go away on a mystery break only to find yourself in the throes of a real murder?

250

The plan was that Derek should dispose himself in the conservatory covered with tomato sauce to be discovered by his wife and pronounced dead, which verdict to be confirmed by me. Then after an interval, fairly brief – we knew it wouldn't be long before someone insisted the police were called – I would go and tip him the wink and he would appear like Banquo's Ghost to astonish and thrill you all – '

'Simon, how could you agree to such a thing?' Laurie sounded appalled. 'Frightening people like that.'

'And if it were not for the fact,' continued Simon, 'that the wires had been cut – '

'*You* cut the wires!' cried Derek. 'After disabling the bus. No one had brought a car of course. You made sure of that by including rail fares in the price of the weekend.'

'I included rail fares,' said Simon with enforced patience, 'because the cost was rather high and I thought that in one or two cases it might tip the balance. I didn't expect –' a cold glance at Gilly – 'that people would be travelling from the North Pole.'

'Rubbish. All of these things were done to isolate us and make sure the police could not be called. Thus giving you plenty of time.'

'Time? Time for what?'

'To do the real murder. Do you think when you came back and picked up that knife and bent over me I didn't know what you were going to do?'

'I was going to tell you it was time to come out – '

'Hang on a sec,' said Fred. 'There's one or two things don't hang together here.'

'Only one or two? My God.' Simon's laugh sounded a bit on a manic side.

'For a start – how could you be sure,' Fred was addressing Derek, 'that the wife would find you? If it'd been one of us your plan would never have got off the ground.'

'We arranged that the discovery should be made at lunch-time,' said Sheila, who had stopped crying and now spoke with an almost feverish conviction, looking from her husband to the rest of the gathering and back again as if trying to spread assurances between the two. 'Everyone else would be at the table eating. I would naturally be the person to go and see where Derek was.'

'It took you long enough to think about it.'

'And we agreed,' Sheila ignored Rosemary's interjection, 'that Derek would spend most of the morning in hiding. He was worried that whoever had drawn the murderer's card might spring a mock attack and spoil the whole plan.'

'But you told us – ' Violet to Sheila – 'that he was hiding to test the murderer's ingenuity.'

'Well I could hardly tell you the truth, could I? It would have spoiled the whole thing.'

'No . . .' Violet still sounded puzzled. 'I suppose not.'

'An unnecessary concern in any case – ' Derek snatched back the conversational reins – 'because the murderer's card was held only metaphorically. And then by – ' he turned, pointed at Simon and fixed him with his glittering eye – '*the murderer!*'

'What bally nonsense,' chimed in Gilly. 'We don't know who's got the card.'

'There was no actual card,' cried Derek. 'My wife's lover saw to that.'

'Will you please get this into your thick head.' Simon rose shakily to his feet, glaring at Derek. 'Now watch my lips carefully. I met both you and your wife for the first time yesterday afternoon. I had never clapped eyes on either of you before. And at the risk of appearing rude I would like to say that if I never clap eyes on either of you again it'll be light years too soon.'

'Might I say something?' Laurie spoke urgently, addressing Derek as he opened his mouth to reply. 'I intended to take your place as victim. Just before I went

252

to bed I told Simon this. He made no attempt to argue or dissuade me. Which he surely would have done if your suspicions are correct.'

'Oh no.' Smugly Derek shook his head. 'He knew, you see, that by the morning I would be so intrigued by my wife's vile and cunning plot that I would not wish to change.'

'I don't know, love,' Violet demurred. 'It all seems a bit elaborate to me. All this journeying about. Coming away for a – '

'But don't you see?' exclaimed Derek. 'If I was killed at home she would be immediately suspect. Here, surrounded by witnesses, she arranges a cast-iron alibi. Simple.'

'*Simple*?' groaned Simon, and leaned back in his chair.

'You're still not making yourself all that clear, Derek,' said Fred. 'Are you trying to say that all this was set up before we even got here?'

'From the day my wife drew *The Times* advertisement to my attention.'

'But . . . it was a joke, Derek. A laugh. I never thought you'd take it seriously.'

'Nonsense. Whodunits are my overriding passion. You knew I wouldn't be able to resist.'

'But that's precisely why I thought you *would* resist. Because you're so . . . well . . . puritanical about them. I never dreamed a group of people playing about . . . making fun . . . would appeal to you at all.'

'Liar.'

'Here, I say.' Gilly sprang up. 'There's no need for that sort of language.'

'Are you sure, Derek,' said Fred, gently as if soothing a fractious child, 'that you haven't got it all wrong? I mean . . . it's a bit . . . far fetched.'

'I think it's the reading,' suggested Violet. 'You read too much of one sort of book it's like eating too much of one sort of food. You get indigestion. Only in your mind. Fantasies, like.'

'If we're back on books,' said Gilly, 'perhaps you could explain what that one is you've been waving at us and how it's supposed to have saved your life.'

'Ahhh yes.' Once more Derek held up the book so that the title was clearly visible. 'A grave mistake of yours, Sheila – making such a lengthy lunch. It gave me an extra half hour, you see. By one o'clock I'd shaken the sauce – '

'By the way,' interrupted Laurie, 'when did you take that? And the knife? I was in the kitchen all morning and I didn't see you.'

'Not quite all morning,' replied Derek. 'After I had interviewed Gaunt, Bennet went into the washing-up room to scrub the potatoes and you left to take a tray upstairs.'

'So I did,' said Laurie and, reminded, locked glances with Martin. Rosemary, who had not failed to notice the haze of mutual content in which the couple sat, sniffed loudly.

'But to return,' said Derek, knee-bending his nut-cracker legs and lurching into the summing up, 'having distributed the sauce and with nothing to do but wait I noticed half a dozen paperbacks on the little iron table by the door. Imagine my delight when I realized they were all written by the great dame herself, Agatha Christie. An ominous discovery, to say the least.'

'Nothing ominous about it,' said Simon. 'I needed some sort of scenario for the weekend so I drove into Oxford and picked up half a dozen paperbacks. I chose "the great dame" as you are pleased to call her simply because she was the only writer on the whodunit shelf whose name rang a bell. I'd never heard of any of the others. After all, it's hardly a genre on which any intelligent person is going to waste their time.'

Derek stopped his pacing. Thunderstruck, his face

suddenly grey, he turned on Simon. Clutching at his chest, he gave a broken cry followed by a long feverish moan. He swayed, his knees folded, his eyes crossed.

'Ay up!' Fred leapt to the rescue. 'He's going.'

Sheila also rushed to her husband's side. Together she and Fred lowered Derek into a chair and watched, dismayed, as he seemed to fight for breath.

'Put a key down his back.'

'That's for nosebleed, silly.'

'Put his head between his knees.'

'Put a ferret down his trousers.'

'Ssh . . . he's saying something.' Sheila stopped fanning her husband and put an ear to his lips. 'What is it, dearest? Tell Sheila.' She listened, frowning, then relayed the vital information. 'Water . . . he wants some water.' Laurie fetched the syphon and a glass. 'Honestly, Simon,' Sheila continued crossly. 'What did you have to say something like that for?'

'Well, how was I to know?' Simon looked put out. 'He didn't react like this when he thought I was trying to kill him. Where's his sense of perspective?' he added, forgetting that a prerequisite for a sense of perspective is a sense of humour.

Derek absorbed several swallows of water and slowly returned from his near-death experience. He got triumphantly, if shakily, to his feet and curled his lip at Simon, no doubt to push home the intelligence that this further attempt at permanent dispatch had been no more successful than the first, before launching once more into his imaginative reconstruction of the crime.

'*Death*,' he cried dramatically, repositioning his paperback, '*on the Nile*. I'm sure you are all familiar with the plot.'

'I saw the film,' said Violet. 'That Maggie Smith. She can't half wear clothes.'

'She don't wear clothes,' corrected Fred. 'That were Diana Rigg.'

'He's right,' agreed Rosemary. 'Maggie Smith wears those awful cardigans.'

'I didn't reckon much to Albert Finney.'

'It weren't Albert Finney on the Nile – ' Violet neatly evened the score – 'it were Peter Ustinov. Albert Finney were on the Orient – '

'Could you *please* pay attention,' glowered Derek, 'otherwise I shall lose my thread. Hardly had I started to peruse the book before the whole thing came rushing back to me. Simon – note the similarity of nomenclature – Simon Doyle having been "attacked" – ' Derek hooked quotation marks out of the air with his index finger – 'was seemingly incapacitated by a gunshot wound when the murder of his wife took place. He was, of course, faking, using red ink for blood. A clever alibi brilliantly conceived. Now – ' he gazed at them fiercely in turn, imprinting his conviction – 'for red ink read tomato sauce. And for the other vital property – a clean white shirt hidden in the wardrobe – read . . . this!'

They all stared at the garment that Derek, with a stagy gesture, whipped from beneath his jacket and waved aloft like a banner. 'Rolled up and hidden behind a cushion on the settee.'

Laurie said: 'But that's my gardening smock.'

'What?'

'I leave it in the conservatory between visits. Sometimes when I prune things they're full of sap. And then there's the spraying. It can make quite a mess so I like to wear a cover-up. It's usually hanging behind the door but it was so grotty I decided, as we were having guests, to tuck it away somewhere.'

'Oh.' Derek looked down at the smock. 'I thought it was a shirt.'

'If you'd unrolled it and had a good look,' said Simon, 'you would have seen that not only is it not a shirt but that it is far too small for any man to get into. Or be put into.'

'You say that now – ' Derek was already bouncing back – 'but by your own admission you have no interest in horticulture. How would you know that it was merely a gardening smock?'

'I've never heard such a load of old claptrap,' returned Simon. 'First I plan it all so brilliantly that I leave you shut up with precisely the book that gives the whole game away. Secondly the shirt, so crucial – although God knows why – to the success of this farcical enterprise is found, on close examination, to be fit only for a midget.'

'Take that back!' Martin leapt to his feet and Laurie pulled him down again.

'Yes, what is the point of the shirt?' cut in Violet. 'It's so long since I saw the film.'

'The one stained with tomato sauce, in other words the one that gives my wife and her lover their alibi, must obviously be removed once the real stabbing is perpetrated. It wouldn't do for the police to see it, after all. A clean one then has to be put on the body. Elementary.'

'The only thing elementary about that tortuous bit of deduction,' said Simon, 'is the level of intellect that could dream it up in the first place. You haven't got the brains of a wombat.'

'Now,' said Derek, still mountebanking about, vain and unperturbed by insults, 'we come to your third mistake.'

'I have only made one mistake, Derek, and that was accepting your cheque in the first place. Three weeks ago when Sheila told me – '

'A-ha!' Derek stopped dead in his tracks. White faced, nostrils fluting at the sweet smell of success, he almost snorted in triumph. Then he recommenced his perambulations, walking in a slow, stately manner to the fireplace where he leaned his arm across the mantle.

'I think you all heard that, ladies and gentlemen. "Sheila told me." Yet ten minutes ago, in this very room, you heard that man say he had met neither of us before yesterday in his life. A fatal slip, Hannaford – ' Here Derek's elbow came off the mantelpiece and he re-positioned it before concluding. 'I rest my case.'

'She rang up.'

This was the second time Laurie had cut the ground from under Derek's feet. He frowned at her then transferred this expression of displeasure to Simon and Sheila as if suspecting a mass conspiracy. 'Quick thinking, I must say.'

'I took the call myself,' continued Laurie. 'She asked a bit about the house and grounds, and about the menus. As it was so expensive I think she needed reassurance that it would be money well spent. Then she wanted to know about the murder game, how it would be set up and all that, so I put her on to Simon.'

'I in my turn,' said Simon, 'explained that everything would be done to create an atmosphere of sinister intrigue and chilling authenticity. It seemed plain to me that she had got in touch solely to establish that the whole experience would be the sort of thing that you – ' he looked unpleasantly at Derek – 'would really enjoy. And look at the thanks she got. I wouldn't like to have your conscience.'

'It's *your* conscience we're discussing here,' shouted Derek. 'If we can find it.'

'Look – supposing,' said Gilly, 'potty of course, but just supposing you're right and all this elaborate set-up was to give Simon and your wife a watertight alibi, who was supposed eventually to have committed the murder? After all with a real body the police are going to investigate pretty thoroughly. They're not going to give up and go away just because we all say we have alibis.'

'Precisely. And here is my third point. This is where the mythical intruder comes in – '

'Hark who's talking about mythical,' cried Fred. 'You were the one who said you'd actually seen him.'

258

'Ah yes.' Derek rosied up a bit at this admission. 'I was deceived by shadows – it was quite dark because of the storm – and by my wife's conviction. It wasn't until the following morning checking the terrace and finding no disturbance in the earth that I realized this man did not exist. In other words *my wife was lying*. Now – if this were not part of some prearranged plan why on earth should she do such a thing?'

'But that's my character.' Sheila fumbled in the pocket of her linen dress, produced a card and read: ' "Lorelei is a neurotic and hysterical woman in pursuit of Kit." I thought screaming and carrying on was the right thing to do.'

'It was that,' agreed Violet. 'Got us off to a flying start.'

'Then why – ' Derek keenly closing in – 'if it was merely part of the game, did you keep it up when we were alone?'

'Because you were so happy, darling. You loved it – you know you did. You couldn't wait to get out there with your little magnifying glass and look for clues and footprints. How could I tell you I was just pretending? The whole weekend was for you.' Sheila wrung her hands and said, running the words together into one long wail, 'I wish I'd never come . . .'

'Jolly handy,' chipped in Gilly, 'her drawing just the right sort of character – '

'*Nom d'un nom!*' exclaimed Derek, disconcertingly switching role models in mid-dénouement. 'D'you think such a crucial detail could be left to chance? Sheila scrapped the card she drew then wrote out the necessary alternative.'

'I didn't!' Sheila thrust out the card. 'Look if you don't believe me – that's not my writing.'

'In that case – ' Derek roamed, thinking on his feet – 'your lover . . . wrote the card . . . and . . . and slipped it to you after dinner. Of course! That's it. Probably in the library when my back was turned.' Satisfied, Derek beamed proudly round the room. 'I now approach my conclusion.'

'Thank God for that,' said Simon.

'*The Murder in the Locked Room.*'

'Of course. The murder in the locked room.' Simon's voice had a gentle lunatic-harbouring tinge. 'Why didn't we all see that? It's so obvious. I think I'm going to cry. Or get drunk.' His eye homed in on the decanter. 'Probably both.'

'And its inevitable corollary, the secret passage.'

'Definitely both.' Simon reached for a glass and prepared to further soothe his shattered nerves.

'There isn't one, Derek,' said Laurie. 'Really there isn't.'

'It leads,' said Derek, swanking splendidly, 'from the Degas room to the conservatory. Hence their decision that I should be murdered there. My body would be spirited away up the staircase.'

Simon groaned, drank deep and groaned again. Rosemary, defensive on his behalf, said: 'That's absolutely mad. If Simon knew about the secret passage why did he keep going in and out through the conservatory door?'

'That was a red herring –' Derek almost hugged himself with satisfaction – 'to put you all off the scent.'

'Excuse me,' said Martin quietly, 'but I think you're making a terrible mistake.'

'Oh?' Derek, having handled the warp and woof of the summing up to his entire satisfaction, frowned at this attempt to introduce a knot in the cloth.

'Your theory's very ingenious but it can't possibly be true.'

'What?' Derek did not look at all pleased at this suggestion that perhaps his wife was not, after all, trying to coax him into an early grave. 'And why not, pray?'

'Because if you remember, at your own suggestion,

Simon shuffled the cards in the bowler hat – a perfectly ordinary hat as I'm sure you will agree, having examined it most carefully afterwards – before he passed it round. We all saw him do it. And he didn't touch the hat with his other hand. Indeed if I remember correctly he held his hand in the air as he went round, actually making a joke about it. "Nothing up my sleeve," I think he said. So how could he or anyone else be sure that you would draw the victim? And without this assurance the whole elaborate plan which you have just, I may say quite brilliantly, described – ' here Martin paused for breath whereupon a spattering of admiring applause on Derek's behalf broke out – 'could simply not get off the ground.'

There was a long pause while the ripples from Martin's quiet, reasonable, authoritative speech spread and spread, touching and impressing them all. Sheila spoke first. She cried out: 'Of course,' and clapped her hands like a child and her tears, like a child's tears, dried immediately on her cheeks. She sounded quite giddy with relief and ran over to her husband, blinking her puffy eyes, grabbing his arm. 'You do see Martin's right?'

'Of course he's right.' Simon put down his glass and smiled widely. An expansive smile with, it seemed to Derek, an infuriating hint of forgiveness lurking round the edges. 'In fact I was about to mention that very thing myself.'

'Oh Simon.' Laurie sounded cross at this attempt to muscle in on her loved one's sharp perceptions.

Derek stood in the centre of the room, his face a tormented mask. Rage, disbelief and bitter disappointment fought for supremacy. So might a drowning man look finding a perfectly strange life flashing before him. His shoulders drooped, his mouth gathered into a sour twisty pucker. How could they (his whole mien put the question) do this to him? How could they, with one tweak of a single loose end, so casually unravel the wonderful construction of tortuous deceit he had so zestfully compiled? He had offered them complex corruption of the deepest dye; they had shown him sunny lack of complicity and guile. What ingrates. Resentment springing from hurt vanity welled up in Derek's heart and he hated them all.

'You're not the first person,' said Simon kindly, 'to have mistaken theatrical simulacrum for the real thing.'

'How dare you patronize me!'

'That wasn't my intention, I assure you.'

'There we are then,' cosied Violet. 'All's well that ends well.'

Fred said it had been a lark and no mistake. Gilly that it was all just too Sunnybrooke Farm. Laurie and Martin held hands and Rosemary gave Simon a smile so full of Western promise it was all he could do not to leap across the room and carry her off upon the instant. An end of term, jamboree-like atmosphere prevailed.

'We can start all over again now,' said Simon. 'We've still got our scenario. All we need is a volunteer to be the victim and Derek – ' he beamed even more forgivingly across the room – 'can set to and solve it.'

'I think not.' Derek sounded terse. 'Come, Sheila.' He moved towards the door. 'We must go and pack.'

'What . . . what do you mean?'

'I'd have thought it obvious. We are leaving.'

'*Leaving*? But Derek . . . we've got a whole day yet . . . And I do so love it here . . . Oh – please . . .'

Derek's response to this intemperate pleading was to hold the door even more pointedly ajar. Sheila drooped and dragged across the carpet, made a little moue of resigned disappointment back at the others and preceded her husband from the room. Derek followed and the door was firmly closed.

'That's that then,' said Fred. 'Exit the great detective.'

6

Meanwhile on the terrace Mrs Gibbs and Mrs Saville, apparently indifferent to the drama being enacted behind the library windows a bare five yards away, were locked into a highly combustible drama of their own.

Not that the casual observer would have noticed many signs of lively combat. Mrs Saville still sat elegantly upright, Mrs Gibbs appeared to have dozed off under the green hat. But there looped between the two ladies a strong, contractual energy. They waited quietly, aware of their obligations. Then (it was the moment that Derek and Sheila left the library) Mrs Gibbs suddenly sat up. She shoved the wad of notes to the centre of the table, tapped it and said: 'Whaddya bet then, cheeky?'

A variety of expressions flitted across Mrs Saville's gorgonlike features. Annoyance at this familiar mode of address. Alarm and incredulity at the munificence of the gesture. Disgust at such posturing aggrandizement. And, finally, irritation with herself for appearing even momentarily impressed.

For plainly Mrs Gibbs did not intend, could not possibly intend, to wager the entire bankroll. And if she did Mrs Saville would not dream of reciprocating on such a vulgar scale. For she could safely bet every penny she had, knowing her hand to be the highest. At the very thought her ethical sense, dormant for many a long year, twitched sluggishly and shook itself.

Quickly she scanned the figure opposite, registering the spotted knobby hands in their ridiculous mittens so tightly clutching the useless fan of cards. Wasn't it a fact, mused Mrs Saville, that gypsies hated and distrusted banks? And that their worldly wealth was usually tied up

263

in caravans and bloodstock or hidden in some secret niche to bewilder and diddle the taxman? This being the case, that solid wodge might well be Mrs Gibbs' entire life's savings. How shamefully dishonourable then for Mrs Saville, from her impregnable position, to even think of betting heavily.

On the other hand (the pendulum needed the bearest touch) it had been Mrs Gibbs' suggestion that poker should be played so she had only herself to blame if it proved to be a game at which she found herself unable to excel. So reasoned Mrs Saville, closing her ears against her conscience, that gauzy moral whisper that is the voice of the angels. She leaned forward and her eyes glowed with greed as she said: 'We can bet as much as you like. My dear.'

'This – ' Mrs Gibbs poked at the notes – 'against your shiners.'

'My. . . ?'

The old lady pinched her withered-walnut lobes and Mrs Saville slowly mirrored the movement, touching the star sapphires that winked and twinkled in her own. They had been a gift from Theophilus on the twenty-fifth anniversary of their nuptials, silver being considered far too base a metal to strike the appropriately festive note. They had set him back a hundred and fifty thousand pounds.

Naturally Mrs Saville hesitated. Fatally she caught Mrs Gibbs' black-pupilled eye, sparking with malign intensity, and saw there a return of that earlier contempt. She felt angry until the actuality of the situation reasserted itself. There was no need to be angry. Or to fear. She was not a weak creature cliff-hanging from a bluff but an empress rising, holding in her hand the keys of the kingdom. She removed her earrings and placed them on the table.

'Sunny side up then,' said Mrs Gibbs.

Smiling an ineffably condescending smile Mrs Saville

spread out her cards. The nine and ten of hearts. Jack, Queen, King. Mrs Gibbs' face was a picture. Her yellow snaggle tooth worried at her lower lip, a frown puzzled her brows. She seemed to shrink in her chair with disbelief, taking on a patient, doomstruck air. Mrs Saville, with a sorrowful lift of the shoulders, reached out her hand.

'Hang on, hang on.'

Mrs Saville stopped in mid reach. Hang on for what? The old lady placed her cards with slow deliberation on the table. The ten of spades. The Jack, the Queen, the King. Mrs Saville stared, confounded and amazed. Of all the extraordinary coincidences. Here was a hand only a heart-stopping beat behind her own. Mrs Gibbs' final card was no doubt a second king. Mrs Saville tried, as she waited, to make her breathing quietly even but the air was flannelly and seemed to choke her.

Mrs Gibbs reached out and put her final card down, covering it with her hand. She looked across at her companion. A tranquil look. Easy, searching and pitiless; like that of an eagle riding the wind. And then she smiled.

It was on receipt of this smile that Mrs Saville became aware that she had made an awesome mistake. This comprehension came upon her not gradually but instantly, with a sudden terrible assurance. She did not understand how it could be so. Her hand had been magnificent. The cards were from her own pack. She had shuffled them herself and they had been dealt in a straightforward manner barely an inch from her nose. Once dealt they had been kept safe by two disinterested parties and the deck had not been touched again. Yet somehow, between the first opening gambit and the turning upwards of the last card a *volte face* had occurred.

Mrs Saville, her fate accomplished, reflected bitterly on her previous solid, overweening confidence now revealed for the hubristic posturing that it was. Perhaps the very brightness and aggression of this belief had instigated her downfall, activating in the gaudy figure opposite some unnatural goblin spirit of revenge.

For surely she had been bested by no ordinary adversary. As she waited, head bowed (the regulars of the Hawthorndon Bridge Club would not have recognized their proud dominatrix) it seemed to Mrs Saville that this final game was being played out not, as she had presupposed, on the sunny terrace of a country house with a commonplace old gypsy woman but on a dark cold primeval plain with a figure alien to humankind. A casual dealer in chaos and revenge.

And yet, when Mrs Gibbs (having removed her black pearl studs) turned over the fifth card, how artless and unmagical was the winning stroke. A question of simple forgetfulness on Mrs Saville's part. She looked down at the grinning red and yellow figure in cap and bells.

'Jokers wild, we reckoned?' said Mrs Gibbs. 'I claim ace high. My dear.'

Back in the library things had rather ground to a halt. There was an air of indecision about the gathering as if no one was quite sure what came next. Although Derek had been regarded mainly as a figure of fun the withdrawal of his melodramatic vigour and enthusiasm left quite a gap.

Lunch, perhaps because of the post-repast theatricals, seemed to have taken place ages ago yet it was still nowhere near time for what Gilly called drinky poos. Or even tea-ey poos. He tried to jolly things along by giving them a ukelele medley but it was indifferently received. Even 'My Little Girl from Idaho' had but small effect, except on Simon who groaned and put his head back in his hands. Rosemary rushed to his side.

'How are you feeling now?' she asked with an abundance of tender concern, laying cool fingers on what little of his fevered brow was visible.

'I'll be all right.' Simon looked wanly up. He was being very brave as well as very wan but Rosemary could see at what a cost. 'You're so sweet,' he continued, 'to be concerned.'

'I thought you coped quite wonderfully.'

'I don't know about that.' Simon lifted his shoulders. The shrug was all insouciance. It implied that being accused of murder and dodging bullets were, if not actually all in a day's work, nothing to get all steamed up about. 'I'm only sorry other people were frightened.'

'I wasn't frightened,' cried Rosemary stoutly.

'I'm sure you weren't.'

Simon, like Martin, had noted that Rosemary was a chip off the old block. Unlike Martin he did not see this as any cause for alarm, being sure the woman was not born (and that included Mrs Saville) that he could not wrap around his empty bank account. 'If ever I were in real danger,' he went on, implying that Derek's homicidal pursuit had been no more than a frivol, 'you are precisely the sort of girl I would hope to have by my side.'

'Ohhh Simon,' breathed his companion, 'and I would think it just too divine to be there.'

Rosemary responded a hundred per cent (or, as she would have put it, with every fibre of her being) when Simon squeezed her hand. Her smile reflected his own. Both purest tungsten. And although nothing so vulgar as the maxim 'It takes one to know one' would ever pass her lips this comprehension, smothered by clouds of high romanticism, nestled, a nugget of comfortable re-assurance, in her breast. Rosemary acknowledged that at long last she had met her match. And found her man.

She looked across to where Martin was sitting trying pathetically to make her jealous by holding the hand of Simon's sister. Earlier Rosemary had determined to take Laurie aside and put her firmly in the picture. Discovering that her new admirer had been engaged to another only twenty-four hours ago should make a dent in that tomboyish bounce and shine. Then Rosemary changed her mind. Let them have their little fling. She could afford to be generous. And it was hardly sensible to alienate someone who looked fair to becoming her future sister-in-law.

And so the timelag stretched with the two couples billing and cooing and Gilly wondering what kind of cake there would be for tea and if, to make things absolutely perfect, there might also be cucumber sandwiches with the crusts cut off. Fred was pondering on how soon he might decently raise the question of a noggin and Violet, realizing it must be either five to or five past, opened her mouth to enlighten the others. But this inaccurate little cliché was never uttered. For just then from the direction of the terrace came the most appalling sounds. Great rhythmical moos of pain and grief and loss. The call of the female hippo unexpectedly finding itself a calf short. Or a pair of sapphire earrings.

'Mummy!' Rosemary ran from the room followed by Simon and Gilly. The Gibbses looked at each other, nodding sagely.

'She wouldn't be told. The daft gabby.'

'You did your best, Fred. No good blaming yourself.'

Outside Mrs Saville, now surrounded by curious and sympathetic faces, rocked back and forth on her white iron chair, covering her naked ears with her hands. Her eyes were tightly shut and two tears of shame and fury glistened on the enraged scarlet cushions of her cheeks. The tears looked angry too; clear and hard like tiny glass chippings.

Rosemary knelt and tugged at her mother's arm, asking what the matter was. Mrs Saville shook her head. She rocked for a few moments more, gave a deep judder which set her chair vibrating against the stone flags, blew her nose on a large silk handkerchief and rose slowly to her feet. She took her daughter's arm, saying:

'Come, Rosemary,' and walked with a rigid and dignified slowness into the house. The others watched her go. There was about her progress something extra heedful. She picked her way gingerly and appeared to be holding herself together by a great act of will. Five minutes later Rosemary came rushing back.

'Simon – oh Simon!'

'What is it?' She took his arm and led him a little way from the interested group. 'Don't tell me,' continued Simon. 'Mummy's packing.'

'I came to give you this.' She handed him a card. *Miss Rosemary Saville. The Paddocks. Norton Bellings. Surrey.* And a telephone number. 'You will keep in touch?'

'Do you doubt it?' murmured Simon, placing a kiss in the palm of her hand and trapping it by folding over her fingers.

'Ring me next week.' A faint boom came from an upstairs window. 'Must dash. She's lost her smelling salts.'

Simon rejoined the others. He regarded Mother with some sourness. She beamed back radiantly, prodigously adorned. The sapphires did not look at all incongruous in spite of being set off by the emerald felt. Rather did the hat and Mrs Gibbs' dark batrachian features obtain a bloom of reflected grandeur.

Her son came and stood behind his mother, his expression a mixture of rueful pride and disapproval. He shook his head at his host.

'She wouldn't be told – Mrs S. I tried to warn her.'

'Yes, yes. I'm sure,' Simon replied testily. He could see Rosemary's mother for ever linking him in memory with her tragic loss, thus making his entry into the banking fraternity a tad more difficult. In this he did the lady an injustice. Mrs Saville was prepared to forgive anyone almost anything who had firm connections to a moated mansion and a hundred and fifty acres of rolling real estate.

Now, with his plans for the weekend all awry and the guests departing in droves, Simon could see himself being lumbered with nothing but hoi polloi for the next twenty-four hours. He briefly considered offering Gilly and the Gibbses a fifty per cent refund and inviting them also to shove off, then realized he was talking about five hundred pounds and thought again. And, after all, if they became too obnoxious he could always fake a migraine. Laurie could cope. Indeed faking might not be necessary. At the very thought of one more chorus of 'Idaho' Simon felt a definite premonitory stab behind his left eyebrow.

But what was he saying? The dramas of the last two hours had played havoc with his memory. No one could go anywhere. The phone was still out of order, the mini-bus had gone and the nearest taxi (Alf Figgins) was at Madingley. Of course if Derek was really determined to shake the dust he might hoof it down there. But Sheila wouldn't. Rosemary wouldn't. And Mrs Saville certainly wouldn't. This brisk winnowing of names left only one plainly in the sieve.

Simon sighed deeply. He didn't know what appealed to him least. The thought of a four-mile slog in the baking heat or being exposed to the deeply unpleasant atmosphere that would no doubt prevail if he refused to go. He was musing thus when Derek appeared, caped and deerstalkered, followed by Sheila, mopingly hanging on to a white leather hatbox.

But before Simon could open his dissertation comparing the wish for an early departure with the sorry lack of equipment to accomplish same, all necessity for such a comparison disappeared. For the outside world came tootling along in the form of a wire-wheeled roadster going: 'Parp, parp.'

Everyone crossed to the parapet and watched the long scarlet bonnet appearing and disappearing as the drive wove through the trees before unfolding into the straight. The MG slowed up, eased over the rattling drawbridge and, with a final 'Parp, parp' came to a halt in front of the steps. The driver, a young very tall fair-haired man with a reddish complexion and a bluff jolly smile, waved and clambered out.

Laurie, fist against her lips just in time to trap a cry of shocked recall, gazed at the jodhpured figure in dismay. Even in the perfect confidence of her newfound love she had been aware of a tiny niggle tugging away at its blissful centre. And here was that niggle enlarged, clarified and made flesh. Laurie stepped forward, smiled weakly, swallowed and said: 'Hullo, Hugh.'

7

The driver of the red MG was not alone. A girl was in the passenger seat. She wore battered khaki shorts held up by a snake belt and a flowered halter top. She was very pretty and had dark hair tied with bits of gingham in two glossy bunches. She climbed over the door and came towards Laurie, smiling. Laurie felt perplexed. The girl in the shorts looked vaguely familiar and certainly her welcoming cry of 'Laurie!' implied some previous acquaintance.

Hugh said: 'Laurie – are you all right? Simon?' He looked round. 'What's going on? I've been trying to get you on the blower. And then when we saw the bus we thought something frightful must have happened.'

'We were *terribly* worried.'

'Just a minute,' said Laurie. 'I'm not sure . . . This is awful, I know, but . . .' She broke off, embarrassed, staring at the girl. Could impeccably straightened teeth wreak such a transformation? Could awkwardness be so ironed out and plainness so disguised? Laurie recalled her own image in the bathroom mirror the previous evening and knew that they could. Then she noticed that the girl was holding Hugh's hand and her suspicions were confirmed. She said, with no sense of incredulity: 'Pacey.'

'Poppy actually. Younger sister. You remember – I used to put toads in your bed.'

'Little minx.' Hugh beamed as if he had personally put her up to it, but quickly reverted to solemnity. 'The fact is, Laurie old girl . . .'

My god, though Laurie. *Old girl*. How did I ever bear it?

'Just simply can't go on . . . not honourable. Been putting it off – '

'He's been *terribly* worried.'

'The truth is . . . must be said . . . me and Pops . . . well . . .'

'Oh Hugh!' Laurie rushed at her erstwhile fiancé as much to halt continuing exposure as in felicitation. 'How absolutely wonderful – I'm so happy for you both.'

'Oh.' Hugh shuffled a bit, looking like a large shambly dog who has had his bone whipped away and just as inexplicably returned: alarmed, bewildered, hopeful and, finally, delighted. 'If only I'd known you'd take it li – '

'Hugh, Poppy – this is Martin. Darling, Hugh is a . . . um . . . childhood friend and I went to school with Poppy's sister. They're engaged.'

Catching the 'darling', Hugh and Poppy exchanged oopsadaisy glances before rushing into a vocal cover-up.

'So we thought – ' began Poppy.

'Naturally, being childhood friends – '

'That we'd rush over – '

'And tell Laurie – '

'Only to find . . .'

'Yes,' smiled Laurie, entwining fingers with her beloved and feeling a surge of joy.

'How super,' cried Poppy, and Hugh agreed it jolly was. All four stood around looking quite silly with happiness, then Simon spoke.

'I hate to inject a sour note into such an idyllic gathering but did I hear some vague reference to a bus?'

'That's right. It was in a ditch the far side of Toot Balden. It had Madingley Grange on the front so naturally we stopped – '

'We were *terribly* worried.'

'The police were there.'

'We thought it might be you or Laurie.'

'Then we talked to a constable and discovered it wasn't.'

273

'Was anyone hurt?' asked Simon hopefully.

'Just shaken up, apparently,' Hugh replied. 'The officer we spoke to said the people in the coach were at the station – '

'Helping with their inquiries.'

'He didn't actually say that, Pootles.'

'No, but I bet they are. I hope they're charged with dangerous driving. Wrecking your dear little bus.'

'Didn't realize you had one actually, Laurie,' said Hugh. 'It's a bit big isn't it? For two?'

'It's a long story.'

'Was in a hell of a mess. Wings crumpled, lights smashed. Bonnet every which way, wasn't it, Popples? Bit of a write-off, I'm afraid.'

'You must be *terribly* worried.'

'Not at all.' Simon airily waved away the very idea. 'A mere bagatelle in the great artificer's scheme of things. Believe me.'

'Was the van stolen?'

'Oh yes.'

'The police'll be along then.'

'Let them all come,' cried Simon. 'It's Liberty Hall here.'

Hugh, lowering his voice, moved closer to Laurie. 'That chap . . .' He jerked his head in the direction of the car. 'Is he all right?'

Four heads turned. Gilly was draped orgasmically over the MG's bonnet, his cheek nestling against the warm shiny red paint. As they watched he slid off, then, crouching down, started to stroke the wire spokes, making happy little crooning sounds.

'He's fine,' said Laurie. 'He's a thirties buff. Absolutely adores anything and everything from the period.'

'Perhaps he'd like to meet Nanny,' said Poppy.

'Little juggins.'

Derek, who had been circling round the quartet and

274

almost jumping up and down in his efforts to attract Hugh's attention, finally managed it. Hugh said: 'Hullo,' whilst giving the caped crusader what used to be called an old-fashioned look. 'Bit hot for that rigout, isn't it?'

While speaking Laurie saw Hugh's glance stray over to the family Gibbs and back to the MG. He raised his eyebrows at Poppy, who lifted her own delicate arches in response.

'The fact of the matter is,' said Derek loudly, 'we're cut off.'

'Not at all,' replied Hugh. He spoke kindly from his great height (six foot two) as if patting Derek on the head. 'We drove straight here – no problem.'

'It's the phone, Hugh,' interrupted Laurie. 'If you remember – it's out of order and Mr and Mrs Gregory want to leave.'

'Isn't old Figgins still about? Ah – ' Hugh paused. 'With you now, old girl. No phone – no taxi.'

'Precisely.'

'Problem solved. Pops and I'll shoot over. Won't we, little giddykins?' Taking his fiancée's hand Hugh led her towards the car. 'Back in the shake of a lamb's tail.'

'*Please* . . .' Gilly had plonked himself in their path, Adam's apple frantically working, pale with the intensity of his desire, his eyes almost squinting in their determination. 'Couldn't I go? I'd give anything to drive it. I've got a clean licence. Fifteen years and never a scratch. I'll be so careful. You won't know it's been out of your sight . . . – *please* say I can.'

'Well . . . I'm not really insured for – '

'Oh Daddy Bear – do say yes. I'm so happy – ' Poppy clasped her hands prettily in entreaty – 'and I want everyone in the whole world to be happy too.'

Hugh looked proudly down at his little juggins. Gilly, overwhelmed by her graceful intervention on his behalf, seemed all set to swoon on the spot. Laurie thought she preferred Pacey's little sister when she was putting toads in people's beds.

Permission being granted Gilly climbed into the car of his dreams, listened closely to instructions on how to find the Figgins residence and tooled off, crossing the drawbridge with the greatest care and precision. 'Toodle pip,' he cried, adding, 'all I need now is a leather helmet and some goggles.'

'I think all he needs now,' said Hugh, thoughtfully watching the car gather speed, 'is a couple of men in white suits with a straitjacket.'

Mrs Saville and Rosemary appeared, hatted, coated and laden with luggage. Laurie explained the transport situation. Mrs Saville, who seemed already to have regained some of her former *chutzpah*, said: 'Excellent. I hope it's big enough to take us both and all the cases.'

'I beg your pardon,' said Derek coldly. 'We have ordered the taxi.'

'Nonsense. He can come back for you. Oxford isn't far.'

Before Derek, pale with anger, could formulate a suitable reply, Laurie said: 'I'm sure you'll all get in. It's a huge Ford estate.' Then she watched with some amusement as Mrs Saville positioned herself where she reckoned the taxi might arrive only to find Derek stepping directly in front of her. These manoeuvres were repeated several times until both parties found themselves in the middle of the drawbridge whereupon they both started to backtrack.

Poppy and Hugh also watched these shenanigans, politely trying to conceal their amusement. Laurie started to introduce the newcomers. Mother took one look at Hugh's jodhpurs and had hysterics, banging the flat of her hand on her knee and giving loud whoops before disappearing under the table.

Poppy giggled and Hugh, determinedly unpatronizing, shook hands with the Gibbses using a manly grip and a direct glance to establish social parity. Then, these comely formalities accomplished, he sat down, sure he had put the family at its ease. The family, already so much at its ease it was practically running the place, started to chat. Mother climbed back on her chair.

'Something tells me – ' Violet swung her ample bosom cosily at Poppy – 'there's a romance or two in the offing.'

Romance. Laurie looked at Martin. What a pathetically wrongheaded choice of word. So pallid. So ordinary. So inglorious. They reached out to each other.

'And I think,' added Violet, 'it calls for a little celebration.'

'We've got some Krug in the cellar.'

'That ain't all you got.'

'*Mother.*'

'Got a ghost down there.'

'And whose fault's that?' asked Violet sternly. 'All them gyrations in the small hours. Not to worry, Laurie – you won't actually see anything. And he'll fade away once she's gone.'

'Ooohh,' squeaked Poppy. 'Does he have clanky chains and smell all spooky?'

'Ghosts don't smell, potty boots.'

'This one does,' said Violet. 'I couldn't make it out at first. All sorts of fruit, oak leaves, real pungent it was. Then – when he actually manifested – '

'*Mani-* . . . You wicked old bat!' Fred turned on his mother. 'I thought I told you to behave yourself.'

'It's all right – really,' said Laurie. 'I'm not frightened. Just intrigued.'

'What did he look like, Mrs Gibbs?' asked Martin.

'Desperate.'

'I mean physically. If that's not too odd a word.'

'Short. Ginger. With one o' them squared-off weskits. Brown and yeller.'

'Tattersall check,' said Hugh, and Laurie let out an excited exclamation.

'Did he . . . have a moustache?'

'Like a little toothbrush. He were weaving in and out o' them cages grabbing at the bottles but slipping right through. Couldn't get a hold, y'see. Crying, he was, outa frustration . . .'

'It's Uncle George,' said Laurie.

'Of course it is,' agreed Hugh, remembering. 'Poor old fellow.'

Simon said: 'I bet he only comes back when Aunt's away.'

'I think we ought to leave him in peace.'

'Absolutely.' Laurie smiled at Martin, agreeing. 'There's plenty of wine in the kitchen if we want to celebrate.'

'Or we could go out,' said Hugh. 'To dinner. What about the Casablanca?'

'Ooo . . . scrummy.'

'Not taking you, little bunny tummy.' Hugh poked his intended playfully just under her snake belt. 'Little piggy wiggy.'

Laurie caught Martin's disbelieving eye and said, 'I'd love that, Hugh. But the fact is that Mr and Mrs Gibbs and their mother and Gilly are guests here. I can't just run off and leave them.'

'If the wine tonight's anything like it was yesterday,' said Fred, 'you can leave me till the cows come home.'

'Course you can go, dear,' said Violet. 'It's only for an hour or two. What you got lined up for supper?'

'Boeuf en croute.'

'I know how to cook that. We often have a nice fillet for Sunday lunch. All sealed up, is it? Mushrooms in?'

'Mm. It just needs glazing. And there's a toffee pudding to warm through. Butterscotch sauce in the double boiler and I've elderflower sorbet for an alternative.'

As Laurie spoke enthusiasm started to colour her voice. She suddenly realized how very, very nice it would be to get away. She felt she had been shut in at Madingley Grange baking, cleaning and washing up for ever and, although it was not in her nature to be self-pitying, she could not help but compare her contribution to the weekend with Simon's (who had sloped off yet again). Serve him right, she thought, if he was left to entertain Gilly and *los trios* Gibbs for the evening. About time he earned his crust.

'It's really very kind of you, Violet. If you're quite sure. My brother will be here of course.'

'That's settled then.' Hugh, expansive, tilted his chair back. Taking charge. 'After we've booked a table we can walk round Saint John's gardens and have some tea.'

'Lovely,' said Laurie. Martin agreed, Poppy squealed with pleasure then pointed out that she could see Betsy through the trees. As the little red car bumped over the drawbridge Sheila, peering into her bag, cried out: 'Derek – I've lost my comb . . .'

'Good heavens – you can soon buy another.'

'But it was the jade one you got for my birthday. I must have left it on the dressing table . . .' She started to move off. Derek called her back.

'The taxi will be here any minute.'

'Shan't be a sec.'

'But I need you to – ' He tailed off, not wishing to say aloud that what he needed his wife for was to establish a solid pincer movement on the left flank so that both rear doors of the taxi were simultaneously breached. 'Don't be long.'

Gilly, with a great final full-throated roaring rev, parked the MG and climbed out, his face alight with rapture.

'Heaven . . .' he carolled, to the tune of 'Cheek to Cheek', 'I'm in heaven . . .'

'Enjoyed it then?' said Hugh, determinedly un-emotional. 'Super.'

'Oh Laurie – ' Gilly rushed over to their table – 'that one single little jaunt was worth the cost of the whole weekend to me. I've never *ever* been so – '

'What about the taxi?' shouted Derek.

'Coming along behind. Never been so utterly – '

'And speaking of money.' Mrs Saville, after instructing Rosemary not to move from her sprinter's mark, crossed to Laurie's side. 'I trust I shall be receiving your cheque for a refund of the complete amount in both our cases?'

'A complete – ' Laurie was rather taken aback. Mrs Saville and Rosemary had after all been at the Grange for almost twenty-four hours, eating heartily and knocking back the claret as if the grape were about to become extinct. To ask for a hundred per cent refund seemed a bit thick. On the other hand she had lost her earrings . . .

As if picking up the thought Mrs Saville continued: 'My jewels are, of course, insured. I shall be reimbursed to their full value. I shall state on my claim that they were stolen.' She gave Mother a freezing stare. 'Not all that far from the truth.'

'Oy!' said Mrs Gibbs, ears winking like fireflies. 'I'll have you up for scandal – '

'Simon handles the financial side,' Laurie interrupted hastily. 'I'm sure he'll be getting in touch with you.'

Further acrimony was averted by the sight of Figgins' buff Cortina. No sooner had it halted than the three combatants hurled themselves upon it like Sumo wrestlers. Alf, who had the look of a man who'd seen it all before and hadn't rated it the first time, lifted the hatch and started chucking in the bags. Derek, installed in the front seat, wound the window down and stared crossly back at the house. He called: 'Sheila!' then tooted the horn.

Hugh reversed Betsy carefully past the estate car and called: 'Boarding here for the fodder trail.'

As the others prepared to join him Laurie turned to their resident musician. 'Gilly – you'll keep everyone entertained, I know.'

'Just you try and stop me. Plinkerty plonk.' He mimed a vigorous twanging.

'You won't forget "My Little Girl from Idaho", will you? I know it's Simon's favourite. He'd be too shy to tell you so himself.'

'Opening and closing number, Laurie. And at least one encore.'

'Oh at least. It would mean so much.'

'You'll have to perch on the back, you two.'

Martin did so, tucking in his legs. He stretched out a hand to help Laurie. 'Up you come, little fluffy bottom.' She hit him. 'Ow! That hurt.'

'Serves you right.' And kissed him. 'I love you.'

They all waved and called: 'Goodbye, goodbye . . .' Hugh negotiated the bridge and started down the drive. 'I say . . . isn't that a dead peacock?'

'I'm afraid so,' said Laurie. 'It got shot.'

'Gosh and golly,' cried little giddykins. 'And there's not even an R in the month.'

Hugh put his foot down and Betsy gathered speed. The periwinkle dress fluttered and Poppy's bunches of hair streamed in the wind. One of Laurie's curls was blown across her cheek and Martin lifted it and smoothed it back behind her ear. What a lot of fuss, he thought, looking into the deep dark blue eyes of his heart's darling, over a couple of mouldy sapphires.

And so, to the bright shout of trumpets, they drove away. Through the avenue of pleached limes, past the silver birches rising from clouds of pale green ferns and out into the glorious pretty ringtime of an English summer afternoon.

Five minutes later a cream and ebony Phantom Continental rolled in through the wrought-iron gates.

Meanwhile, back in the Vuillard room, Simon Hannaford held his mistress in his arms. Hers were wound tightly round his neck; his, rather more loosely, circled her waist.

'Angel,' she breathed, 'I thought we'd never be alone.' They kissed. And kissed again. Sheila groaned with desire. 'It seems for ever since last Wednesday.'

'Oh it does. It does.'

'I'm sorry everything went so wrong.'

'Force of circumstances.'

'Who'd have thought in a million years that he'd have worked it all out?'

'He's an aficionado.'

'He even twigged about the rail fare.'

'Mm. Got it wrong about the secret passage, though. I really didn't know about that.'

'I thought he was going to kill you.'

'So did I. I searched him for that bloody gun as well when I was pronouncing him dead. He must've hidden it somewhere.'

'We'd have been all right if he hadn't found the book.'

'Bad cess to Dame Agatha.'

'What on earth was it doing there?'

'My sister – being helpful. She said she'd taken in a stack of paperbacks. I just didn't make the connection. We mustn't be too hard on her, though – that smock got us out of a tight corner.'

'Where was the real shirt?'

'Rolled up behind that great pot he smashed. Still there, I suppose, under all the dirt. I wish you'd mentioned he was accident prone. I could at least have boarded out the livestock.'

Sheila interrupted guiltily, quickly. 'Tell me how you worked it so he got the victim's card.'

But Simon would not be deflected. 'I shall be paying for this weekend to the end of my days. Do you realize that blue and yellow vase spread all over the hall is Chinese?'

'Oh.'

'Twelfth century.'

'I'm sorry.'

'He has also put his foot through a Hepplewhite lyre-back. It'll cost practically every penny I've made from this deal to get it repaired.'

'Darling. . . ?'

'You want to see a real murder? Come back in September when my aunt comes home.'

'. . . the hat trick?'

'Oh – that. Well, I started with Laurie to make sure your husband came last. Held the card with the red cross against the side of the hat with my thumb, then let it go. Simple.'

'You're so clever.' Sheila pressed closely to her lover. 'And we were so near . . .'

'We'd have been a whole lot nearer if you'd gone to look for him at one o'clock as you were supposed to do. He wouldn't have had time then for book browsing. I kept giving you pointed looks all through lunch.'

'You were certainly giving someone pointed looks.'

'What's that supposed to mean?'

'Little Miss Rosebud.'

'Honestly, darling. You of all people should know the importance of red herrings.'

'Ohh . . . I see . . .'

'I thought I played that particular fish rather well.'

'You're sure that's all it was?'

'As sure as I'm standing here.'

'Kiss me then . . . not like that – a real kiss.'

'We're a tiny bit pushed for time.'

'Sweetest.' Sheila urged one last embrace in vain. She

sighed deeply. 'I guess I'll just have to wait then . . . till Wednesday.'

'Wednesday might be a bit iffy. There's going to be masses to clear up here.'

'Simon . . . you do still love me?'

'Cross my heart . . .' And Simon, removing one arm from Sheila's waist, laid his fingers upon his breast almost directly over the little square of cardboard on which was written the address and telephone number of Rosemary, that sweet, attractive, unencumbered legatee. 'And hope to die rich.'

'We'll have better luck next time. You'll see.'

'Angel,' murmured Simon, silkily slipping away. 'I have a confession. When I picked up the knife – the moment before he jumped me – I knew that I'd never be able to do it. I'm simply not the metal of which murderers are made.'

'But darling . . .' Sheila's mouth trembled with disappointment. She looked hurt and betrayed. 'You promised.'

'I know. And I'm sorry.'

'What shall we do now then?'

'It looks as if the ball's rather back in your court, my love. In any case I'm sure you'd be much better at this sort of thing than I. Men are so clumsy. All fingers and thumbs. Just keep your eyes open for a suitable opportunity.'

'Trouble is,' sighed Sheila, 'I'm not really an ideas person. I'm better at carrying out instructions.' Toot! Toot! 'Oh – that must be the taxi.'

'If I were you I'd suggest a holiday. Perhaps a second honeymoon. Take him away somewhere. Right away. Abroad. Accidents are always happening abroad. And what with the language barrier and foreign medics no one can ever quite work out what really took place. Take him . . .' Simon's eyes gleamed. 'Take him to Switzerland.'

'Switzerland?'

'Take him to Switzerland,' repeated Simon. 'And send him over the Reichenbach Falls in a barrel.'

The Royal Georgian Hotel, Bath, was breathing a sigh of relief. Not metaphorically but in actual, literal fact. The strength of the exhalation set the copper Trade Winds weathervane spinning, disturbed the spine-leaved palms in the Palm Court Lounge and made the windows creak.

But the relief felt by the bricks and mortar was as naught compared to that experienced by the staff. All had heard the rumour and, though not all believed, a repressed fizz of disciplined hysteria began to prevail.

The second chambermaid, crying quietly in a broom cupboard as she had been for the past thirty-six hours, crept out wondering if such a miracle could possibly be true. The Boots, who had been keeping her supplied with Kleenex and cups of strong Irish Breakfast Tea, gave assurance that it really was. He had got it from a commis chef who had got it from a waiter who had been crossing the foyer when the telephone had barked into the receptionist's face instructions to make up the account for the Queen Charlotte suite.

Trembling with excitement and disbelief the receptionist had run into the manager's office where Harold Peasmarsh sat, his greying hair (rich russet brown a mere two weeks before) veering upright in a mad tangle.

'You will stand by me, won't you, Mr Peasmarsh? When I present the bill?'

'Can it be true?' Echoing the second chambermaid, the light of hope transforming his wretched countenance, Mr Peasmarsh tottered to his feet.

'Gospel. I've been instructed to ring the chauffeur's lodgings. He's to bring the car round in fifteen minutes.'

'I can't believe it. I daren't.'

The manager made his way to the door, stumbling several times in the process, having already had recourse

285

to a little something leading to a much larger something round about eleven o'clock. He thought Carole's question about standing by a bit unjust. It was leading from the front and thus taking all the flak from the enemy's redoubt that had reduced him to his present state of spineless sycophancy.

'Oh God – ' A thought struck him, dreadfully. 'It's not April the first is it?'

'No, no, Mr Peasmarsh,' soothed Carole. 'June the sixteenth.'

'I wouldn't put it past her to jinx the calendar. If ever a woman was in league with the devil she is. And I bet he's scared stiff to open his mouth.'

Positioning himself squarely behind Carole, nerves resolutely uncalmed either by the tapping of her computer or the saccharine strings of the Palm Court Trio, Mr Peasmarsh was yet cheered to see several members of staff he was convinced had either deserted or been eaten alive creeping out of the woodwork and going timidly about their business.

Only the groundsmen had remained relatively un-scathed by the wrathful outpourings of hyperbolic invective which had emanated from the third floor front. Even so young Gary, apprentice bedder-out, had, whilst working beneath an open window, been caught in the slipstream and had to go home and lie down.

Angelo, the head chef, also remained unbrutified. He greeted the trembly waiters bearing rejected dishes from his renowned kitchen with a sneer, taking his revenge in various subtle ways, none of which seemed to make the slightest dent in his complainant's digestive system.

Carole had just totalled the bill when the lift doors opened. Two tiers of luggage emerged and approached the desk. She redirected them outside. As the sweating bell boys staggered off a Phantom Continental drew up at the steps and a second lift descended. Carole gripped Mr Peasmarsh's hand. The string trio, happily afloat on

'The Blue Danube', quietly sank. Miss Curd – lead cello – dropped her bow.

The sole occupant of the lift stalked, glowering, across the carpet, alternately banging her stick on the floor and thrusting it fiercely before her. Carole presented the bill. The departing guest unscrewed a fountain pen and held it poised, like a dagger, over the print-out.

'Have made no telephone calls.' Slash.

'Drunk no afternoon tea.' Slash.

'Dinner on the fourth was inedible. As it was on the fifth, the seventh and the thirteenth.' Slash, slash, slash. 'Last night in sheer self preservation I ate out.

'My laundry was ironed in such a manner I would not have dressed a mangy monkey in it. I would die rather than enter Prinny's Astrological Jacuzzi. And the same applies to the Fitzherbert Carvery, side saddles in a basket.' More savage lunges and swipes.

'Room service Mr Peasmarsh? I have had better room service clinging to the north face of the Eiger in a raging avalanche.' One final deletion, a crisp retotalling and the result was handed back. 'Quite honestly if I couldn't run a hotel better than this I'd join the Foreign Legion. Or shoot myself.' The jaws of her alligator handbag opened wide. 'You will take a cheque.'

It was not a question. Mr Peasmarsh nodded. He would have taken Persil coupons or Green Shield stamps. He would have paid the bill himself. The cheque was passed over, then, pausing merely to point out that tears were never meant to be a man's weapon, she banged and lunged with her stick again and was gone.

The chauffeur, green-liveried in polished high boots, removed his cap and opened the back door of the Rolls Royce. His employer climbed in. As she did so an extraordinary explosion of sound and movement took place in the foyer of the Royal Georgian. Ragged cheers and applause; hoots and cries. All underscored by an Offenbach polka. (One, two, three, *four*.)

287

As the two people in the car watched through the plate glass doors a grand chain formed. Waiters and kitchen staff, chambermaids and page boys, even the arthritic lift attendant all dynamically linked in joyous celebration. They frolicked to and fro. In and out of the furniture, up and down the stairs, circling Carole and Mr Peasmarsh who danced (one, two, three, *hop*) and whirled in a transport of delight.

'I see the lunatics have taken over the asylum.'

'Yes Mrs Maberley.'

'Well – they can't do any worse than the previous incumbents. Drive on.'

Aunt Maude (for it is she who is speaking as our story closes) leaned back against soft, cream leather and wondered if, after the unspeakable fortnight she had just endured, she could really bring herself to start all over again in a few days' time in Torquay. After all, simply shifting a few degrees further south did not automatically guarantee one the holiday of a lifetime. Aunt Maude tightened her lips with irritation. No doubt about it, she infinitely preferred to take her vacations aboard ship where menials who deserved to be castigated either had to stand their ground and take it on the chin or jump over the side. None of this shuffling off or giving notice. Reluctantly she came to the conclusion that she might have to abandon her Devonian trip and thus her master plan.

This had been formed one weekend in April when Laurel and Simon had been visiting. A few days earlier Mrs Maberley had sat, foot tapping with irritation, whilst her solicitor delivered the last of what, in a less softly spoken man, might have been called a series of lectures. Even while smartly shutting him up Aunt Maude appreciated that what he had to say made sense. Although believing (quite rightly) that she was good for another thirty years it was only prudent that her affairs should be put in some sort of order and a will made.

Once this single intimation of mortality was dealt with it could be swept firmly back into the future where it belonged.

She was fully aware of the reasons behind her reluctance to name an heir, or heirs. Her strongest inclination emotionally (to be resisted for that very reason) was to leave the whole estate to her great niece and nephew. To Laurel because she was the daughter of Minette, Mrs Maberley's favourite sister's child, had always seemed genuinely happy to be at Madingley Grange and was the only dependant ever to do a hand's turn about the place. And to Simon because Aunt Maude admired, if reservedly, his brazenly manipulative technique. Also he made her laugh and loved money and things with an uncomplicated guilt-free relish not unlike her own. A final plus – it was Simon's father who had made the last ten years of Minette's tragically short life so happy.

On the other hand (Aunt Maude was very old-fashioned when it came to matters of duty) it could not be denied that Alan Handsom-Norty had some sort of claim. He was her only brother's only child and had visited the Grange four times a year for the past two decades, frequently being sent off with a flea in his ear the minute his foot touched the gravel but still gamely returning next quarter day. Of course on the debit side there had been that scrap of trouble in the City but none of it had made the Top Papers (Aunt Maude's litmus test of authenticity) and seemed now to have quite blown over.

Then there was Hazel's Mervyn. Now nearly eighteen, still looking like a squirrel with nut-packed cheeks yet still unarguably one of the less attractive globules in the Maberley blood line. Add a second cousin in Lanarkshire and Jocelyn, George's pet nephew, and the options really started to open up. At least, Aunt Maude reflected, she would not have to consider Hetty, who used to croon herself to sleep on a Lilo in a fish tank wearing a homemade latex mermaid's tail. She had migrated to the Antipodes. And the best place for her, too.

It was when toiling and moiling over this clutch of assorted claimants for the umpteenth time that Mrs Maberley hit on her brilliant idea. It came to her that the best way to discover who really deserved to inherit the house and gardens at Madingley was to leave them in charge of the place when she departed, ostensibly on her three-month cruise, then to return after a fortnight to see exactly what sort of dog's dinner they were making of it. They could all take it in turn. She saw no problem regarding secrecy as naturally those who had already been tested would not, in their own interests, reveal the sting to those who had not.

When this strategem occurred Laurel was carefully tending the pots along the terrace and her aunt silently admitted that, effective though the winnowing device might prove to be, she would not have entertained it for a moment had it not been strongly biased in the child's favour.

Now, her spirits lifting at the thought of seeing them both again so soon and recalling the extremely unpleasant fourteen days she had just, in the name of duty, endured Aunt Maude wondered if she could not perhaps come to a decision then and there. For what was duty after all? A dry old thing at the best of times. No one ever warmed their hands in the eventide of their life on duty's cold display. Better surely to trust her natural inclinations. (After all, when was she ever wrong?)

And so, her mind made up, Mrs Maberley unhooked her speaking tube and blew down it with some force. A shrill whistle assailed the chauffeur's ears.

'Put your foot down, Fitterbee,' instructed Aunt Maude. 'And we'll be home in time for tea.'

More Crime Fiction from Headline

CAROLINE GRAHAM

'An exemplary crime novel' *The Literary Review*

DEATH OF A HOLLOW MAN

For Detective Chief Inspector Tom Barnaby a visit to the Causton Amateur Dramatic Society's production of *Amadeus* is not an ideal evening's entertainment. But loyalty to his wife Joyce (noises-off), means that attending the first night is a must, and Barnaby knows that an immense amount of hard work has gone into the show.

Backstage, nerves are fraying. Director of the play, Harold Winstanley, has introduced a strict pecking order among the cast but the leading man is taking his role far too much to heart. For Salieri (alias Esslyn Carmichael), suspecting that his wife is having an affair, has decided that the stage is as good a place as any to wring the truth out of the guilty party. It is his final act, though, that proves to be a *pièce de résistance* and when the scene takes a particularly gruesome turn, Barnaby finds that his professional skills are called to the fore.

Superbly plotted and sparkling with vivid characters, *Death of a Hollow Man* is a first-class whodunnit that brings the author to the very front of her field.

'Excellent character sketches of the suspects, and the dialogue is lively and convincing' *Independent*

'Tension builds, bitchery flares, resentment seethes . . . Lots of atmosphere, colourful characters and fair clues' *Mail on Sunday*

FICTION / CRIME 0 7472 3350 0

GLORIA

THE STORY OF AN UNFORGETTABLE WOMAN — AND THE CITY SHE MADE HER OWN

Philip Boast

"A girl's got to get on in the world,
and Gloria's just the girl to do it!"

Gloria Simmonds is a girl who's going places. At seventeen, the life and soul of Marylebone's Wharncliffe Gardens Railway Settlement, up until now she's been happy to stay there, apparently liked, certainly loved and, though she doesn't know it, sheltered from the realities of turn-of-the-century London. Then, in a matter of hours, her world falls apart and Gloria senses she will never be able to piece it together in Wharncliffe Gardens. She must find another life . . .

That night she fetches up in a part of London she never knew existed, a warren of Regent Street's thieves and whores where pimp Willy Glizzard rules supreme. And for the first time in his loveless life, Willy Glizzard falls in love, a love that is Gloria Simmonds' first real taste of the treacherous, turbulent city she will one day make her own . . .

FICTION / SAGA 0 7472 4555 X

More Crime Fiction from Headline

CAROLINE GRAHAM

THE KILLINGS AT BADGER'S DRIFT

AN ENGLISH VILLAGE WHODUNNIT

'Characterisation first-rate, plotting likewise ... Written with enormous relish. A very superior whodunnit ...'
The Literary Review

Badger's Drift – a tranquil English village, home to Miss Emily Simpson, a kindly, well-liked spinster. But a gentle stroll in the woods near her home one day brings an abrupt end to her peaceful existence, for Miss Simpson sees something among the trees that she was never meant to see, and someone makes sure she will never reveal what it was ...

To the village doctor, Miss Simpson's death looks natural enough, but her old friend Miss Lucy Bellringer is unconvinced and eventually drags the unwilling Detective Chief Inspector Barnaby into the case. His investigations reveal an unexpectedly seamy side to Badger's Drift – old rivalries, old loves, new scandals all come to light. And a second, horrifically gruesome killing shocks Barnaby into running the murderer to ground ...

'An uncommonly appealing mystery ... Graham makes her characters humanly believable in her witty and tragic novel, a real winner.' *Publishers Weekly*

'Caroline Graham writes pungently, planting information with artful indirection, bringing baroque characters to life and death with equal aplomb, stretching the readers' wits and finally rewarding them.' *The Sunday Times*

FICTION / CRIME 0 7472 3233 4

Flowers For His Funeral

A Mitchell and Markby Cotswold whodunnit
'A pair of delightful sleuths' Margaret Yorke

Ann Granger

When Meredith Mitchell bumps into her old
schoolfriend Rachel Hunter at the Chelsea Flower
Show it doesn't take Meredith long to realise that she
and the effortlessly self-confident blonde have even
less in common now than they had as teenagers. Apart
from one thing – Meredith's companion, Chief
Inspector Markby. For to the embarrassment of all
concerned, except of course the self-possessed Rachel,
Meredith's old schoolfriend turns out to have been
Markby's former wife, from whom he was divorced
years before in less than friendly circumstances.

The meeting with Rachel is not the only surprise the
Flower Show has in store for Markby – before the
afternoon is out he has a death on his hands. All too
quickly he and Meredith find themselves drawn into
the plush, apparently well-run world Rachel and her
second husband created for themselves in their
Cotswold home, Malefis Abbey, a world which
Markby becomes increasingly convinced harbours a
highly skilled murderer . . .

FICTION / CRIME 0 7472 4770 6